HAZEL

by

BRIAN STUART PENTLAND

Order this book online at www.trafford.com
or email orders@trafford.com

Most Trafford titles are also available at major online book retailers.

Printed in the United States of America.

ISBN: 978-1-4907-1145-4 (sc)
ISBN: 978-1-4907-1147-8 (hc)
ISBN: 978-1-4907-1146-1 (e)

Library of Congress Control Number: 2013914217

Trafford rev. 08/23/2013

 www.trafford.com

North America & international
toll-free: 1 888 232 4444 (USA & Canada)
fax: 812 355 4082

I should like to dedicate this book
to Maurice Reeve

Part of the inspiration for this book
came from
Giacomo & Santi

CHAPTER ONE

Hazel O'hara

CHAPTER ONE

Hazel O'hara

'Are the staff on paralysis training tonight?' came a sharp, sarcastic cry, and Hazel waved his serviette as if the boat was just leaving the dock. 'Darling, over here we happen to be this strange race called 'clients'.'

A waiter moved across the room. 'I heard you the first time,' he spat.

'Darling, how could that be? Do you think the battery has gone in your hearing aid?' and Hazel smiled falsely. 'Another two bottles, darling, because we don't want to interrupt your night off.'

'Arsehole!' The waiter retorted.

'I knew it,' cried Hazel. 'He must be going to win an award for literature. You can tell by his grasp of words that he is going to be a greater writer. Eat your heart out, Barbra.' The other three at the table fell about laughing. Hazel was at it again, never to be put down, a word or generally more than a word, to put people where they belonged—according to Hazel.

He was almost six feet tall, thin as a rake, with green eyes, reddish blonde hair, a very pale complexion, a good nose and strong jaw-line, which sometimes made drag nights even funnier. He had no real patience and no real staying power: when he saw a task ahead, he went for it. The moment it was mastered he became bored and found it repetitious and moved on. He was always the one to have at a dinner party; he was the star in every sense, the entertainer, the clever boy. Boy Hazel was now 35 years-old and had never bothered, except for a teaching job, ever to stay at one job for a period of time after mastering it. He had first trained as a teacher of youngsters from five to eleven and that had worked for a while but then the predictability of it all swept over him and he was off on another avenue. He was, to say the least, a very difficult personality, one minute quiet and considerate, and in a flash, if someone annoyed him, his viper tongue took over. He could slaughter any character within a dining room's length. Even at the hotel where Hazel drank and drank regularly, no-one really thought it worth while to enter into a fray with him, and as a result his friendships were very few—a million acquaintances but real friends only two or three at the most. He was so difficult and far too unpredictable for anyone to get close to him and getting close to him he hated. He found it extremely claustrophobic and demanding.

Yet despite all this he was strangely methodical. His tiny rented apartment was always immaculate. Saturday morning it was always cleaned from top to bottom: no great task given how small it was—a kitchen, a bathroom and a bed-sitting room; nothing of importance in the decoration, in fact it was rather minimalist, a complete contrast to his personality. The only extravagant thing he possessed was an extremely large European painting he had purchased at a smart auction in a very important home, more the result of waving to an acquaintance than bidding seriously. The painting was knocked down "to the tall man with red hair". 'Charming,' said Hazel later. 'The cretin could have said "to the elegant gentleman on my right"—what a limited piece of work!'

And so, over his two-seater settee, hung in a large ornate gilt frame, a European landscape which completely over-powered the whole space. And with time Hazel had become remarkably attached to it, which was odd as everything else he owned when it didn't function or he was simply tired of it he disposed of without any compunction: but the painting always remained.

4

His love life was extremely difficult to know. As Hazel gossiped about everything but never about what he did in his private life, no-one was sure but the stories were many. His tongue, or better still, his repartee, was such that it tended to negate his ever having a fixed relationship or in fact any relationship at all.

He was the supreme entertainer. If he did a drag show, he always used something clever—no Barbara Striesand for him. He used a World War Two nurse's outfit and mimed Gracie Fields's "Wish me luck as you wave me goodbye", which had the queens cheering and screaming for more. He was calculating. He knew very well that to do serious drag meant that there were always going to be bitter send-up comments, so he always got in first. He sent himself up before the others could do so and as such was always a great success. For example, dressing as Doris Day and singing "Younger than springtime", he had everyone in hysterics, especially as he was so tall and in stilettos. Hazel became a vertical image of entertainment. But with the microphone in his hands, it was death to anyone who thought to make a smart comment from the crowd and get away with it. His replies were super-sharp and delivered without a single shred of charity. Hazel was, indeed, someone to be careful of. Even in ordinary situations, for example. Meeting him at the supermarket or at the greengrocer's one could be absolutely sure that the comment he passed was generally not going to be in your favour. Altogether, he was generally summed up as 'a very bitchy queen'.

But he had another side to him that he kept completely secret from people, or perhaps it should be said from all but the two or three people he really liked. He was completely faithful and would do anything to help them and at any cost.

One of these persons was Keven O'Malley. Hazel had carried a torch ever since he had seen him, which must be almost ten years ago. He was extremely handsome, of average height, and with a great body, as a result of a lot of body-building, thick black bushy hair and electric blue eyes. He was the ideal for Hazel and woe betide anyone who passed a comment that was not favourable about him in Hazel's earshot. He was like an Araphoe Indian on heat.

Some years before, after a party in the late hours of the morning, Hazel was obviously one of the last to leave and from inside the party house he heard a scream and much yelling on the street. He dashed to see what the noise was and to his horror he saw two hoodlums attacking Keven, who had also been at the party—and everyone just stood around watching. No-one, not a single person, moved in to help him. Hazel raced forward but not before ripping off a loose picket from the front fence and just attacked. The length of timber swung in all directions and every strike hit the target. The two hoodlums scampered quickly away, using sharp expletives to describe him. He helped Keven to his feet and then turned on the crowd of partygoers. 'Cowards!' he screamed loudly. 'You would let a person you know be beaten up and look at you there—there must be fucking thirty of you and there were only two shits. Don't any of you ever think that if you were in the same situation that I would ever, ever come to your aid. You could all be beaten to a fucking pulp for all I care. Go home, little boys,' he shouted sarcastically, 'it's where you belong.'

Hazel helped Keven to his car, but because he was in pain Hazel drove him home and put him to bed after cleaning him up. Keven never forgot the sacrifice that Hazel had made for him, while the others just stood back and watched; and in any social situation he always welcomed Hazel, which was more than many of his acquaintances would have done.

It was after that evening that Hazel began lessons in kick-boxing and, being tall, with long, strong legs, he began to master this art of self-defence, except that, sometimes, when really angry and fighting in the gym with an opponent, he would have to be physically restrained as he set out to attack his foe rather than use the exercise as a learning process.

Keven O'Malley was a good-looking, successful architect, in great demand from his clients as his work was very thorough and inventive. He lived in a large terraced house in South Yarra and as he became financially secure he purchased it when it became available. He also bought the derelict terrace next door and converted it into his office/ showroom. He had four staff and he streamlined his business so every cent ended up in the right place, namely his bank account. If he saw Hazel in Toorak Road, he always invited him back for a drink and occasionally took him out to dinner. But the Hazel he knew was a completely different character from the Hazel everyone else was obliged to suffer. Hazel was quiet, polite and chattered on to Keven in a sophisticated manner about architecture or interior decoration, world affairs—quite the person to be with, a few sharp funny comments but not the raw humour he usually used.

The other friend he had was Mary Warren. She lived not far from him and often they would go to the supermarket or a film or he would just arrive with a whole meal, everything, wine included, in a large supermarket bag, just take over Mary's kitchen and produce a splendid meal but only for the two of them.

Mary was very overweight, "ten tons of fun", as Hazel jokingly called her but she had a very beautiful face, excellent skin, fine features, blue crystal clear eyes, a full mouth and a mane of auburn-coloured hair. She was good for Hazel; she was the only person he would tolerate giving him a talking-to, and at times a sharp one, without his becoming vicious and retaliating. Mary was Hazel's oldest friend. They had been at school together, the two most outlandish figures at the school in both personality and physical appearance, and it was Mary alone who held the secret as to what Hazel's real name was. He had become "Hazel" at a young age and the name stuck. He used it as a badge; he flaunted it just to make people uncomfortable originally, but with time everyone just accepted that this tall, blonde-haired queen was called Hazel.

They were remarkably similar. Mary and Hazel neither really wanted a relationship as in the past their experience in this field had been rather disastrous or awkward. They both needed their privacy but both swore they would change their ways if Antonio Banderas asked either one of them to marry him. He was their ideal of the perfect man and they never got tired of watching at Mary's house DVD after DVD of him. Mary had in fact framed several photos of the star and had them on a table in the sitting room and any time Hazel found a new photo he would immediately have it framed and it would join the others on the table including the photos of Banderas naked. Even Hazel had a copy of that. So the two of them lived in an odd fantasy world, with Banderas strangely holding it all together.

Mary worked as a child psychologist: she was very good at her work and very dedicated. She had gone to university, completed her studies in record time and started work at once and unlike Hazel remained in the one job all her life.

Hazel at this time had thrown up working as an interior decorator and was working as a waiter in a smart restaurant. The only problem was that his retorts to some of the patrons could never be described as smart. Then, only six weeks before, an emergency occurred in the kitchen of the restaurant, and, as the chef fainted and had to be sent home, Hazel as ever came to the rescue. He donned the chef's hat, put on an apron and off he went. The owner was so surprised at Hazel's ability to change from waiter to super-chef, but all the clients that evening remarked to him that the taste and the presentation were splendid. From then on, Hazel was fitted out in a chef's outfit and was trying his culinary skills on the patrons and with great success. In his inimitable style he did away with the chic printed menus and put up a blackboard, admittedly on a gold easel, and limited the choice to four entrees, four main courses and four deserts. The owner, Godfrey Simms, was in great doubt as to the change, but with a full restaurant every evening when Hazel was working, he changed his mind at once. Hazel insisted that he do something with the interior. 'Darling,' he said to Godfrey, 'it's so old hat—a bare brick wall! So 70s! Get it plastered and put a fabulous chandelier in. Come on—get moving!'

It was at this time that Hazel's bank account started to climb. He had always been careful with money, as two or three times in his life he had been without work, his fault, of course, but he realised the importance of a healthy bank account as it secured him the thing he valued above all, privacy, and that could only be assured if he had his own apartment and did not have to share in order to pay the bills.

*   *   *   *   *

'Darling, I have a night off. I'm on my way over. Open the wine,' and having hung up he collected a bag of semi-prepared food from the restaurant and a couple of complementary bottles of wine and made for Mary's in his pale lilac Volkswagon. He had had it sprayed this colour, his excuse being that even if he got completely drunk he could always recognise it. He beatled up the street where Mary lived and to his joy located a car leaving and so took the space only two doors from his destination.

Mary opened the door to a very excited Hazel. 'Darling, I hope you like lobster,' and went on noisily to describe the contents of the bag which he set down on Mary's kitchen top. 'Well, what do I have for you?' Hazel smiled wickedly.

'Oh, don't tell me.'

'Yes,' cried Hazel, 'but you can't see it until I have a drink.'

They danced about like school children, completely at one with one another, in their own very private fantasy.

'Well, where is he?' demanded Mary. 'I'm waiting,' and Hazel withdrew a neatly packaged frame and handed it to her.

'Happy Birthday, darling.'

'Thanks, sweetie,' was the reply, and she withdrew an antique frame made up at Mirror and the occupant of this frame was a smiling Antonio Banderas.

'Oh, it's heaven,' she screamed, 'and the frame—oh, Hazel, you shouldn't have, but I'm so glad you did.' And she leaned over and gave him a kiss.

'Darling, I have managed to organise a diet food evening.'

'Oh, how boring,' laughed Mary.

'I was just joking, sweetie. You will gain at least twenty kilos this evening.'

'Sounds divine! Bring on the kilos!'

There were lots of "ohs" and "ahs" as Hazel produced yet another treat from the bag.

'Oh, he is so gorgeous,' said Mary, smiling back at the new picture. 'Now, pick up your glass.' Hazel never had any problem with that. 'Have a drink. I have something to show you. Come on,' and Mary led the way down the hallway of this large house which had been left to her by her godmother many years ago. It was a double-fronted Victorian house in Hawthorn, with a large bay window on either side of the front door. All the rooms were large, which was perhaps just as well as Mary, in Hazel's apartment, was always terrified of knocking something over, the space being so very limited.

She directed Hazel to the main sitting room and to his surprise he noted on one wall a beautiful antique gilt frame hung in a vertical position but with a blank white canvas in it.

'Darling,' said Hazel, 'don't you think it's just a bit too minimalist?'

'Oh, Hazel, you are a dill! What do you think of the frame?'

Hazel moved closer and had a good look. 'It's fantastic. Where did you get it?'

'Well, you won't believe this, but a woman I work with said that her mother was being placed in an elderly care centre and invited me over to have a look at the furniture she had to sell. I thought of you, Hazel, but as your apartment is'—and here she stopped, had another sip and looked over the top of her glass—'well, so compact—'

'I think you mean small, don't you? Oh, how could your be so cruel?' feigned Hazel.

'Hazel, why don't you rent a bigger house. You would be much happier.'

'What's happy, Mary, about having a big house! I have so many problems just with my mouse-hole now—imagine if I moved into a space like yours, I would get lost,' and they laughed. 'Well, finish the story, as I've finished my drink.'

'Well, I bought the frame. It was on top of a wardrobe. And also this little table with the marble top. What do you think for? $200. I thought it wasn't too bad.'

'Too bad, sweetheart—you got a steal. A frame nowhere near as ornate or with real new gilding is going to cost you $600 or $700 but the blank canvas?' asked Hazel, frowning.

'Well,' smiled Mary, 'you study it for a moment and just think about it and I'll return with the bottle,' which she did.

'Well?'

'I'm stumped, sweetie, you'll have to let me into the mystery.'

'I've found a fabulous artist who can paint a portrait from a photo. Now do you get it?'

'The answer is no, unless you are going to be immortalised for posterity.'

'Oh, Hazel, sometimes you are so dumb.'

'Really, sweetie,' said Hazel, sharply.

'I am going to have a portrait of Antonio Banderas painted for the frame. Won't that be exciting!'

'If it's done well, yes. If it's not, it will be simply kitch,' replied Hazel.

'Oh well, if it doesn't work, I guess I can use another mirror,' and Mary laughed. 'Come on, Hazel, I am starving for this diet food.'

'To the kitchen!' cried Hazel and they went back to the large kitchen/dining area overlooking a lush back garden. Mary refilled the glasses and was surprised when Hazel put his arms around her ample chest.

'Happy Birthday, and I'm sure the portrait will be just divine.'

'Thanks, Hazel. Later, after dinner, you can help me choose the best—or should I say,' she went on, in a very superior manner, 'the most suitable photo for the frame.'

'What about the nude photo. I'm all for that!'

'Hazel, you're impossible,' she laughed.

After dinner, they watched yet another re-run of an Antonio Banderas movie and chattered on.

'Hazel, isn't he beautiful,' she cooed.

'Yes,' sighed Hazel, 'if only . . .'

'Hazel, what was the big love in your life? I don't mean falling for our Keven O'Malley, but did you ever really feel that it was going to happen, you know what I mean? Oh, Hazel, you're the closest,' and she lifted an empty glass which was refilled at once.

They sat in large, comfortable chairs, it being Mary's home, totally relaxed with their idol in front of them scampering from one brave adventure to another. 'I have had only one love affair that I genuinely cared about.'

'I take it that's leaving out Antonio Banderas and Keven O'Malley,' she laughed.

'Yes,' he said, seriously, and Mary pulled herself up from her lounging position. It was most unlike Hazel to give anything away about the past.

'He was beautiful and so dark—olive skin, black eyes—I suppose a Spanish look. Don't tell me you're surprised.'

'Well, sweetie, things follow certain patterns. But go on, do tell.'

'It was my last year of teacher training. What a fucking waste of time! You learned nothing and no one had anything to tell you.'

'Oh, forget that shit, darling. We all go through it. People who are incompetent in the field always end up instructing others—a sort of lemming culture, isn't it?'

'Sure is,' was the off-hand reply. 'Well, Ashley!'

'Ashley,' said Mary with a twinkle in her eye. 'Miss O'Hara.'

'Forget it. It should have been great. He was just stunning. I can now remember,' said Hazel, being very dramatic with one hand lifted over the brow. 'Ashley, Ashley, don't look back,' he repeated from Gone with the Wind".

'What happened with the relationship?' asked Mary.

'Well,' he said, averting his eyes for a moment from Antonio Banderas, 'we actually had a relationship. Don't laugh, but I did and if the truth be told I loved it. I thought it would last forever. Every time, everything was perfect. Oh, he was stunning, so dark, my dear, so dramatic.'

'Hazel, if this is all true where the hell is he?'

'You ask me,' and he fell silent, watching the film.

'Hazel,' asked a curious Mary, 'finish the story.'

'Hm,' sighed Hazel. 'Oh God, is that the time? I must be off.'

'Forget it, Hazel. Finish the story! Besides, I have another favour to ask you.'

'What is it?' asked a curious Hazel.

'Finish your story first.'

'Well, what can a girl say? Everything was divine, everything was perfect.'

'Well,' interrupted Mary, 'get on with it.'

'We never really lived together, Ashley and I. He had his apartment and a very nice one it was in Domain Road, and so I either stayed with him or he stayed in my mouse-hole somewhere. Oh, at the time it was a mini apartment, which meant one room and you were lucky to get the rest.'

Mary laughed. 'Sounds like mine. Do you remember? Every time I moved, something crashed to the floor,' and they both began to laugh together.

'Well, Ashley and I made all these plans. We really were going to make it happen and then after almost six or seven months he disappeared.'

'What do you mean, 'disappeared'? Was he a student?'

'Yes, he was doing something out at Melbourne University but I don't know what now. It seems a million years ago. He just stopped calling: every time I called him no one replied,' and there Hazel's voice trailed off.

Marry gave a deep sigh. 'Had he met someone else?' she asked boldly.

'I didn't find out for months. I was totally destroyed and had this conviction that everybody was laughing behind my back. The love of my life gone. It wasn't until months later and of all places at the hairdresser's that I picked up one of those society gossip magazines and there he was, my Ashley, photographed on his wedding day at St. Peter's in Toorack. He photographed so well!' said Hazel, sarcastically, 'and the bride, well she seemed, if I can remember, to be some form of wren, smiling at everything and looking like the cat that got the cream.'

'Oh, Hazel, I am so sorry,' said Mary, genuinely. 'Men really are the pits. Have you ever heard from him again?'

'Not a word, sweetie, and I promise you if I ever see him again a nice cup of bunny bait is the order of the day,' and Mary burst out laughing. 'Bunny bait!' and continued laughing.

'And your great love?' asked Hazel, even though he knew what the reply would be.

'Ho, ho!' said Mary. 'Who didn't love Ray Kemp at school?'

'Yes,' sighed Hazel. 'He was divine. I remember once at the school swimming sports—'

'Oh, so do I,' Mary interrupted. 'In speedos with blue and white stripes and so little of them. Those strong thick legs, the fabulous torso with the black hair rising on his stomach from the bathers—and the eyes—' She was interrupted. 'The eyes and thick black wavy hair,' and the two of them looked at one another and burst into uncontrollable laughter and chorused together 'and the dick he was enormous' and they fell about laughing.

'God, he was divine,' said Hazel. 'If I close my eyes and think of shoulders and muscular arms, it's him.'

'I can go one better than that,' cried Mary. 'I only have to think sex and there he is, Ray Kemp, the most beautiful specimen of mankind in the world.'

'What do you think has happened to him?' asked a curious Hazel. 'He was our age, so he must be 35 or 36 now. Do you think he is just as sexy?'

'No idea,' said Mary. 'He probably married that blonde bitch who sat in the front row and he has five kids.'

'What a waste,' said Hazel, 'what a waste. He was so divine and the swimming outfit—' and again they broke into hysterical laughter.

'Now, before I go, what's the favour you want to ask me,' said a surprised Hazel.

'Well,' said Mary, nodding her head. 'Will you come with me to see the artist who is going to paint our boy? You're much more objective about what a painter can do or can see in the subject.'

'OK. When?'

'Thursday morning, 10.30. I have taken time out from the clinic, so can you come to the clinic and we will go from there? Oh, by the way, I think the photo you gave me today will be just fine. What do you think?'

'Yes, I agree. Our Antonio looks so relaxed and how can we put it? 'Sexy!' was the chorused response. That two adults could behave in this way was surprising, seeing that if someone had tried to "send them up" for this passion for Antonio Banderas they would have been totally shocked, not to mention cross.

*   *   *   *   *

The only other friend, or rather a splendid acquaintance, Hazel knew was Jeffery Tyne. He had met Jeffery at the local Post Office, where he worked behind a protective shield of glass to keep customers at bay. They had met again at a party and formed a good relationship, the difference between them being that sex was fine for Hazel but Jeffery wouldn't have a bit of it. He went to gay bars with Hazel and had the time of his life. He was a very handsome man, about six years younger than Hazel and occasionally joined him and Mary for dinner. He found the repartee hysterically funny and joined in, but he could not grasp the passion they both had for the Spanish actor. He thought that a certain part of their development had stopped at about 13 or 14, when school children have crushes on pop stars and collect pictures or cut them from magazines and paste them all over their bedroom walls, much to the exasperation of their parents. It seemed to Jeffery that Mary and Hazel were doing the same thing, only he had to confess on a slightly more sophisticated level. All the photos in Mary's living room were in beautiful and very expensive new or antique frames, which strangely, after a while, seemed quite normal, but for someone who entered Mary's home it must have been quite odd, not a family snap to be seen, just Antonio.

He assumed that Hazel's apartment must be the same, as he had never seen it nor had he ever been invited there. He was never a regular friend as such. He drifted in and out of Hazel's and Mary's social lives.

Sometimes they would see him twice a week and then a gap would occur and they wouldn't see him for a month or so. The only thing they knew for sure about Jeffery was he worked at the local post office and lived at home, or so he said, with aging parents. The rest of his private life was a total mystery and, although Hazel was curious about it, he never pursued the subject with Jeffrey.

* * * * *

'Come in, come in. I have been expecting you,' and a woman of a most uncertain age ushered Mary and Hazel carrying a blank canvas into her studio. She had long hair, pepper-and-salt colour and a very lined face, but electric cobalt blue eyes, a long beaky nose and thinnish lips plastered with bright scarlet lipstick. She was wearing a floor-length Indian-type frock with an embroidered top. In all, she looked, as Hazel said later, like the last of the flower-power people. Her only redeeming feature was her beautiful eyes, outlined heavily in black.

'Well, let's have a look,' she said, in a business-like way, which sounded odd, as she did not seem very business-oriented at all. The large studio was a confusion of things and the strong smell of Indian incense was quite overpowering. There was a mezzanine level along one side and it was up there that there were literally hundreds of canvases, a testimony to artistic endeavour, but obviously not to good merchandising. She took the canvas from Hazel and put it up on a stand and asked for the photo which, sheepishly, Mary handed over. She placed it on an enoscope and switched it on and projected it onto the canvas. She adjusted the direction of the canvas and then the focus of the enoscope. No one said a word. It was the artist who broke the silence. 'Mr Banderas, I see. How do you want him painted?' she asked briskly. Hazel had managed to regain his senses after the environment and the total confusion of everything had overwhelmed him.

'Can you show us an example of your work?' he asked.

'It won't help,' she replied in an off-hand way. 'I'll paint it the way you want.'

Well,' said Hazel, realising this conversation was going nowhere, 'what if I say we should like the subject as such but painted in an eighteenth century way.'

'You mean like Elizabeth Lebrun,' she replied, instantly.

'Yes,' smiled Hazel, 'that would be fine,' wracking his brains to remember who on earth Elizabeth Lebrun was and what exactly her painting style was like.

She must have gauged their lack of knowledge concerning the French painter and said, 'Stay here and I'll get some reference for you.' She disappeared through an Indian-type curtain at the side of the studio. The two of them looked at one another. Never in their lives had they seen such confusion: old geraniums dead in their pots for lack of water, and paint everywhere. This old warehouse-cum-garage had obviously been her studio for many, many years and the passing of time had left it a relic of the past. It was then that Mary noticed, sitting near the edge of the mezzanine section, an enormous ginger cat, surveying them with great curiosity. Mary began to feel a little uncomfortable and the very strong smell of the incense didn't help at all.

'Here it is,' and the woman worked her way across the crowded floor, stepping over piles of old newspapers and magazines, and handed Mary the book she had returned with.

Mary looked for a place to rest the book but couldn't find one surface that was not crowded with objects. In the end she rested it on top of a stack of books which, every time she turned the pages, threatened to tumble to the floor. It was Hazel who took over. He selected a beautiful portrait of a man and told her that that was what they wanted.

'Hm,' she said, looking at it and then at the illuminated photo of Antonio Banderas. 'Yes, I can do it but to get this exact effect it will take time as I shall have to use glazes to get this effect. Is that a problem?'

'No,' said Mary hurriedly. 'Time isn't important.'

'But the quality is,' stated Hazel.

The woman spun on Hazel and her cobalt-blue eyes narrowed. 'Look here, you have asked me for a special effect and I will give it to you. You want an antique-type portrait and not a photo-realistic one. Most of the clients prefer that. Personally, I hate them but it keeps the wolf from the door. I only do what the client wants but I do it well. Do you understand me?'

'Certainly,' said Hazel in a haughty manner.

'The deal is this. $200 now and $500 when it's finished. OK?' she asked, looking at Mary.

'Fine,' said Mary. 'Will you take a cheque?'

'For the $200, yes, but I want the $500 in cash. Leave me your name and telephone number and I will call you when I have finished it. It should take about two months.'

As Mary searched in her copious handbag for her cheque book and pen, Hazel asked if he could see some of her personal work.

'When you pick up the finished canvas, sure, but not now,' she said. Mary wrote the cheque and they said their goodbyes and shook hands. Hazel was very surprised at the strong grasp of her tiny hands, and all the while the fat ginger cat surveyed the parting scene from above.

'Hazel, I thought I was going to die. That blessed incense! I could hardly breathe.'

As they drove back, they recounted to one another the odd woman and her studio.

'You don't think I have thrown away $200, do you?' Mary asked.

'No,' said Hazel. 'I think she is quite honest but I am dead curious to see her own work.'

'It's probably all the stuff left over from the hippy period. Do you think that the place has ever been cleaned?'

'Doubt it, darling. It is such a mess I am surprised she found the book.'

'Oh, Hazel, I had never heard of Elizabeth what's-her-name! I felt an utter dill. Thank goodness you knew.'

'But I didn't, until I saw the pictures,' and they both began to laugh.

'Good heavens, what if this Elizabeth woman had painted like Van Gogh! Oh, poor Antonio.'

'It would more likely be poor you as you would have had to have another portrait painted.'

'Hazel, you are a darling. I could never have done this on my own. I was so scared of moving and knocking something over. There was stuff everywhere.'

'Yes, and you are not exactly sylph-like, sweetie!'

'You bitch, Hazel! Oh, by the way,' said Mary, 'have you heard from Jeffery? I noted in my diary that we are supposed to be having dinner on Thursday night at my place but you are working at the restaurant and I can't seem to contact him. Perhaps you could call in at the post office on your way home and tell him to give me a ring. I haven't seen him for months, have you?'

'Come to think of it, no. Listen, I'll tell him to call you, you can both have dinner and I will join you later for a drink. How does that sound?'

'Dicey,' was the reply.

'Why?'

'Hazel, you know my culinary skills are zero.'

'OK, well, I can call in an hour before work and organise it for you.'

'Hazel, you are an angel.' She pulled up in front of her clinic and said goodbye to him while he swung out into the busy traffic in his lilac Volkswagon.

*   *   *   *   *

Mary entered her clinic. Unlike Hazel she had remained in the one field of study and she had been brilliant. The result of her innate understanding of child psychology had made her quite famous and she certainly did not lack patients. The clinic was elegant and very modern; everything about it was soft, with no hard edges anywhere, all cleverly designed to be soothing and relaxing. Heavy carpet underfoot reduced to nothing the sound of people moving from one place to another.

She had picked her staff and was fair but tough; anyone who overstepped what Mary considered to be the mark she fired without any hesitation, so over the years she had built up a faithful but efficient team of workers. She wasn't comfortable with straight men and being overweight she was aware of the comments passed behind her back and the patronising ones made to her face. She liked gay men: they were not interested in her sexually, obviously, and liked her for what she was, not what straight men thought she should be. Like Hazel, she had a razor tongue and woe betide the man who passed a snide comment about her weight and linked it to a sexual innuendo. So among many of her colleagues she was thought to be a man-hater, and if they were straight and smart they were correct. But she tolerated quite a lot of flack from the friends of Hazel, yet always balanced it with her own comments and always everyone kissed everyone else good night. Whereas her private home was filled with antique furniture, paintings and silver, as she was a great collector and a selective one, her clinic was sparsely furnished with gentle designer prints in large frames, larger tubs of palms, thick beige carpet, soft brown leather settees with pale coloured cushions. This theme followed even through to her office. Here the only exception was a large, framed autographed black and white photograph of Antonio Banderas, who looked out with that mischievous smile at Mary everyday at work and somehow it made her day easier if she just looked up now and again and there he was, a steady image that filled every fantasy.

She checked her diary. She had only one patient today, in forty minutes time, as another colleague had taken some of the hectic schedule off her shoulders. She sat down heavily and began to write up a report on her computer concerning a very distressed and abused nine-year-old girl. She felt a sadness while adding this case to her files. The telephone rang shrilly and she answered. The girl at the reception immediately switched Hazel through.

'Hi, what's the problem?' Mary asked.

'It's Jeffery,' was the reply. 'He's in hospital.'

'What?' exclaimed Mary. 'Was he in an accident? Oh, how awful! How is he?'

'I haven't a clue. I managed to get on to his old mother and she finally gave me the hospital telephone number and the extension to the ward where he is.' He duly passed this on to Mary. 'I'll call you back in ten minutes.'

But it was much sooner than that.

'Hazel, Jeffery's dieing. He has pneumonia and, well, a dreadful complication.'

'What the hell are you talking about/'

'Hazel, Jeffery is dying of AIDS. I spoke to the doctor, who said when he came to the hospital only three days ago he was so debilitated that there wasn't much they could do. The old parents, it seems, thought he had the flu but he has had this HIV for a long time, the doctor thinks. And he has taken no treatment at all. They say it's just a matter of days. Do you want to go and see him?'

'Will he recognise us?' asked Hazel.

'Not now, the doctor said. He is in a sort of coma where he just doesn't recognise anything.'

'Then I am not going,' said Hazel firmly. 'I want to remember him as he was, not as he is now.'

'Fine, said Mary, softly. 'Why don't you call over after work tonight for a drink.'

'Thanks, but I'll take a rain check on that,' and he hung up.

Mary stared at the photo of Antonio Banderas as if waiting for him to say something, but no message was forthcoming.

*　　*　　*　　*　　*

A week later, in blustery spring weather, the funeral was held for Jeffery at the Church of the Sacred Heart and then they followed the cortege to the cemetery, where the priest said the last parting words and the coffin of a young, beautiful man was lowered into a narrow space where he would be protected from or forgotten by the human race.

Mary drove Hazel back to her home, opened a bottle of wine and poured herself and Hazel very full glasses. They just stared at one another, neither of them with anything to add to the morning's event, nothing at all. It had all been said.

'I haven't been to Mass for years,' said Hazel, sitting down in the kitchen area as did Mary. 'I actually felt like an interloper. I didn't even remember the responses, did you?' He was looking straight through the glass doors into the lush back garden and not at Mary.

'Not really. The lady beside me shared her missal with me. I suppose we shall all go just like Jeffery,' she said flatly, hardly having the strength to look about the room. 'Hazel, I don't understand one thing.'

He swung around on his chair and focussed on her. 'Nor do I,' he said slowly. 'If what he told us was true, then how the hell did he catch this fucking virus if he never slept with guys?'

'I know,' said Mary, supporting her head on an upright arm. 'Perhaps he had a private life, which for me is fine, but why lie about it? I don't know one guy who has ever slept with him. He always said he wasn't interested in sex.'

'Well, we buried him today so it goes to show you don't really know your friends at all.'

'Hazel, do you think he had a blood transfusion and caught it from that? It's possible.'

'Perhaps, but I have a nasty feeling Jeffery was sort of telling the truth.'

'What do you mean,' asked Mary, curious.

'Well, if up to some time ago he hadn't had any experience with men and just one night tried it, he probably wouldn't have used or even thought it necessary to use any protection. No experience. Do you see what I mean?'

'Yes. Sadly enough, a colleague of mine told me not a week ago about a young boy some years ago who, the first and only time he had sex, caught this fucking virus and subsequently died, so perhaps you're right about Jeffery. When he felt ill he just refused to face facts and literally just faded away with two ancient parents who thought he had a mild dose of the flu. It doesn't seem possible in this day and age. It's such a waste. He was so sweet.'

'Yes, he was.'

*   *   *   *   *

Hazel was someone not used to making pleasant comments about anyone. Jeffery's death had a numbing effect on him and if he seemed a bitter person before, he moved up a rung to pure acid. His tolerance level was nil and he became, in public, someone to be careful of, as a client in the restaurant where he worked found out. The client was a middle-aged businessman who had taken a young man out to dinner. It should have been as simple as that, two men enjoying themselves, the food and the wine, but it so happened that the young man was particularly pretentious and was out to make a scene to prove to his friend just what a connoisseur of food he was. And it was most unfortunate that the chef that evening was Hazel. The first course was served without any trouble. Then the waiter brought the bottle of wine back to the kitchen. 'That fucking blond bitch claims the wine is corked.' The waiter exclaimed.

'It fucking well isn't.' Hazel moved over and sampled the wine. 'It's fine. What the hell is he going on about?' Here, the owner stepped in and quietened them down.

When the boy sent back the main course, claiming the meat was not cooked properly, Hazel took things into his own hands. He slammed the utensils down he was using and, despite the owner's attempts to persuade him to return to the kitchen, he marched out into the dining area. At six foot plus, in a chef's hat, Hazel was quite a towering sight and the look on his face meant he was out for blood.

'Well, so you are the expert on food and wine, are you?' he asked, in a most sarcastic manner. 'I am surprised you eat at the table; a saucer of milk and a bowl of Kitty Kat is it, every night?' Hazel was loud and the whole restaurant stopped and watched the performance—or 'massacre', depending on the point of view. The young blond realised at once he was in trouble.

'What precisely is wrong with the meat, dearie?' asked Hazel. 'Don't tell me you left your dentures at home again. Trouble with the gums?'

The businessman began to apologise for the boy. 'Take him back to the nursery. Children should be in bed at this hour of the night.'

'How dare you speak to me like that?' exclaimed the boy, in a moment of false courage.

'Oh, sweetie, you have a tongue, do you? But of course you do. Sending everything back, so smart!' Hazel seized him by the back of the collar. 'Get out now! The management does not wish to be sued for serving an under-age delinquent.'

The businessman stood up.

'Oh, you don't have to go, luvvy, just ditch the cheap blond.'

There was a titter of laughter from the tables around the room and Hazel realised that he had an audience and a white-faced proprietor who knew at this stage it was impossible to contain Hazel's fury.

'Go on, dearie,' he taunted the boy. 'Pick up your school bag and off you go to where you usually go—any toilet where you can pick up trade, isn't it?'

The boy turned scarlet and stood up and made for the door but it was not ever for him yet. As he stormed past Hazel, he stupidly spat at him, 'You old bitch!' and did not see that Hazel had slid one of his long legs out and over went the boy, face down on the floor. He staggered to his feet and rushed out of the door.

'Darlings, the next show will be in half an hour, with half a dozen naked dancing boys. Look forward to seeing you divine clients again.' He gave a theatrical bow, sweeping his tall chef's hat in all directions to the applause of the restaurant. As he swept past the waiter, he said, 'Take the old guy a glass of brandy on the house. He looks as if he could use it.'

The owner of the restaurant hated these public scenes but in private had to confess that they were extremely good for business. When clients called for a booking now they nearly always asked what night Hazel was on and when that was determined the restaurant was booked out. It must be said, however, that the owner was now on prescription blood pressure pills.

It took Hazel very little to hit the rage button and one night he hit it with a vengeance. There was a table of men, eight of them, having been at a conference at the large conference centre in Flinders Street. And how they got the address of the restaurant remains to this day a mystery. They settled into a fully booked restaurant, so Hazel and his assistant were flat out in the kitchen. The two waiters were dashing in all directions and the owner himself was helping as drinks waiter.

All was fine until one of the party in the group, obviously having had a few drinks earlier, became quite loud and the waiter asked him politely to respect the other clients and wished him a pleasant evening. For some people it is just not enough. The particular man ordered wine and continued to drink heavily. The food arrived and just as Hazel popped his head round the corner to see the full restaurant, he heard the now drunken man pass a comment about the waiter. 'They're all poofs,' he shouted loudly and Hazel saw red. He swept into the room and up to the table and began. The owner rushed to his bag for another blood pressure pill, absolutely sure it was going to be required. 'So you like the waiter, do you?' began Hazel. 'I think you will have more success with a bottle of champagne and chocolates.'

'I wouldn't give him a bottle of piss,' said the aggressive drunk.

'How nice to have a real cretin in our midst tonight. Have a look, everyone, a real cretin.'

The man was enraged. 'You're all fucking poofs,' he spat at Hazel.

'Darling, at least we are all stars, not a forgotten has-been like you,' and Hazel was beginning to enjoy himself as was the entire restaurant.

'I'll knock your teeth out,' the man threatened.'

'Really, fatty, we could just lift yours out and drop them into a glass.'

The whole restaurant burst into laughter. Hazel had begun. The banter continued but for every line the drunkard had Hazel had two, much to the enjoyment of the customers but not to the pleasure of the owner who was seen in an corner of the restaurant, wiping his brow with a serviette.

'You fucking bastard,' yelled the drunk.

'Ladies, ladies,' cried Hazel, in a very melodramatic voice, 'cover your ears. We have a very low man here this evening with no style at all.' Again, gales of laughter. One client was heard speaking to another: he had never had such entertainment since he had seen Danny Le

Rue twenty years before. The drunk, now really agitated, stood up, pushing his chair over with a crash.

'Oh, we can see he is a real gentleman,' cried Hazel. With that, the man took a swing at Hazel. Now, if the comments were silly, a swing at Hazel (who had now mastered kick boxing) was basically suicide and this he was about to find out. Hazel taunted him until he had drawn him into the open section of the restaurant floor and in a drunken swing he almost connected with Hazel's broad jaw and it was then the alarm button was touched. Hazel swung immediately on one long leg and in a flash the other caught the man on the side of the face and he spun about in complete surprise.

'We are taking bets,' called an elated Hazel. 'Me to win, Fatty to lose.' The man staggered and stupidly, instead of calling it a night, rushed at a waiting Hazel who this time hit home with his foot first on the other side of his face and as he began to fall down stopped him with the full force of the foot yet again in a split second timing, deep into the abdomen. The drunk dropped in a heap on the floor.

'Next!' cried Hazel.

The other seven men looked very nervously at one another.

'Call a cab and get rid of this heap and for the rest of you I wish you a pleasant evening, and to our gorgeous, wonderful, precious darlings, thanks for watching the show,' and with many theatrical bows and great applause Hazel retired to the kitchen to complete the evening meals but made a quick return. 'Darlings, give me an extra ten minutes. We are stoking up the stoves with straw again.' The applause was deafening. The owner was ashen.

And this was the pattern on Hazel's nights at the restaurant. When there was a fool to upset the evening, Hazel was ready. He moved about laughing and gently sending up the clients, who loved it. He once struck on a table one evening: an older man who was part of the group who sat on the end of the table seemed to be ignored by all for some reason and Hazel felt sorry for him. He drew up a spare chair and began a brisk conversation, chatting about all sorts of things.

28

The old man smiled but didn't say much. It was a woman at the table who admonished Hazel for being so informal with someone he did not know. Hazel was in a playful mood, which was always dangerous. 'Darling,' he said, to the heavily made-up woman, 'you don't have a clue about this fabulous man. Anyone can tell he has style and look at you, sweetie. If when I did drag I ended up looking like you, they would throw furniture at me.'

'You bitch,' she spat.

Hazel linked arms with the older distinguished man. 'I told you, handsome, never waste your time on women. Men never want jewels. We just want love.' He said this in an exaggerated way. This continued until Hazel realised he had to return to the kitchen. He stood up but not before giving the older gentleman a kiss on the cheek. 'Let's go and live in the Canary Islands, darling. We will just dance, drink and have sex all day.' He laughed, and disappeared into the kitchen to find the owner fanning himself with a menu cover.

'Hazel, you fool, do you know who those people are?' the owner blustered.

'Clients, darling. They are all the same.'

'Hazel, the man you kissed is a High Court judge and that woman you insulted happens, in case you're interested, to be his wife. We will be sued; just you wait and see. I just can't take this stress,' the owner wailed.

'I know, darling, but you can certainly take the cash, and I will lay a bet they are going to be regular clients, not necessarily with the ghastly wife but I bet our judge is going to eat lunch here very often.'

And Hazel was correct. The judge always booked the same table, but only on condition Hazel was in the kitchen, and although he was always formal, he always insisted to the manager that he would like to have a word with "Our Hazel", as he called him, and an odd but firm friendship developed, Hazel making most of the conversation but the judge having no problems in accepting a kiss on the cheek each time and probably considering it risqué living. Needless to say, the wife never returned to the restaurant after that first fatal evening.

Another funny evening occurred at the restaurant. Hazel had come to an arrangement with the owner, who went by the name of Godfrey, that as he attracted a full restaurant, when he had a friend in it was for free. This was accepted by Godfrey, who was finding that many restaurants he knew about town that were very well known were not filled every evening, yet his was filled to the maximum as a result of his excellent if unpredictable cook.

Quite often Kevin O'Malley ate there by courtesy of Hazel, but this particular night it happened that Keven and Mary were at a table together, because later the three of them were to go to a drag show. The evening started peacefully, with Godfrey, although grateful for the revenue that Hazel generated for him, beginning to suffer a certain nervousness every time Hazel moved into the kitchen. This evening, as the drag show was much later, Hazel brought in from his lilac Volkswagon his drag costume and hung it in what was generally known as the cloak room, but was in fact no more than a small cupboard. The evening was basically quiet until close to closing time when a group of four, two men and two women, insisted they be seated.

'Oh, fuck!' exclaimed Hazel. 'I'll do the first two courses and someone else can do the desserts. You know the arrangements. I have a drag show tonight.'

'But, Hazel,' wailed Godfrey, 'who can do desserts like you?'

'No one, darling, that's why you pay me so well,' and he smiled in a devilish way and moved out to see the clientele.

'Hi, darling.' He moved effortlessly among the diners, making smart cracks, some genuinely kind comments and making sure he had time to speak for at least five minutes with Mary and Keven.

Oh, Keven, he thought, sitting down, how divine, how beautiful! He hadn't said a word but both Mary and Keven read the face easily.

It was then that one of the men in the last group of four began to make a noise. He was very beautiful, but he began to be difficult, complaining about everything. Ordinarily, Hazel would have had a go at him, but because he was so handsome another part of his being decided on a different tack, and he disappeared. In no time, the soft background music faded out. Godfrey began searching for a blood-pressure pill from his bag. New music took over and it was "If you don't happen to like me, pass me by". Suddenly Hazel appeared in drag from the kitchen. To say it was a surprising sight was an understatement. He was in red leather hot pants, a red gingham shirt, an enormous blonde wig and a pair of red patent leather stilettos. The face make-up was exaggerated, to say the least. Later Hazel was to say he didn't have much time. And he began the song.

A good many of the clients were used to Hazel, but these four late arrivals were not, and Hazel worked the handsome guy for all he could. "If you don't happen to like me, pass me by".

Godfrey was beside himself. To fire Hazel was easy but an empty restaurant later was another predicament, so he was caught between the devil and the deep blue sea and if Godfrey had one thought that constantly pumped through his limited brain it was the amount of money he could deposit safely in the bank every Tuesday morning.

Hazel, in this amazing outfit, with those exceptionally long stockinged legs, looked and lived the star. The handsome young man who had begun the complaints was instantly silenced as Hazel worked his way up to the table, miming the song. The young man was aware the whole performance was just for him and he lapped it up. When it was finished, he rose to his feet and applauded, at which a very tall drag queen called Hazel returned and swept up to him.

'Darling, no diamonds, just a kiss!' This, to his girlfriend's annoyance, he complied with.

Hazel disappeared to change, finish the night and then with Mary and Keven dash off to the show in St. Kilda. But this was not before the beautiful young man, on the pretext of going to the toilet, moved into the kitchen where Hazel was in chef's attire, but the face still made up. He walked up and handed him his card. He did not say one word, but just smiled and slapped Hazel on the backside. 'That card's for you.' Hazel smiled and they parted.

The show was even more successful at the drag bar than in the restaurant. Hazel was on top of the world and his repartee on the microphone was acid, though everyone loved it, especially Mary and Keven, who were the loudest cheerers in the bar. At one point, Keven drifted off, looking for a partner for bed. Mary waited with some other friends, joking and attempting conversation, which was almost impossible over the loud recorded music. At two o'clock, Hazel collected Mary and they left: Keven, they decided, had found a bed-mate and had probably left earlier.

'Oh, what am I doing with my life?' exclaimed Hazel, as he drove Mary home. 'Why couldn't I meet an Antonio Banderas and live happily ever after?'

'Me, too,' was the dull response

'I am sick of everything. No one loves me,' cried a melodramatic Hazel.

'Well, I wouldn't go that far,' said Mary. 'How about that young guy in the restaurant this evening? He started off being a bit agro, but he finished up eating out of your hand.'

'You know, 'replied Hazel, putting his foot down and going through a red light, 'he gave me his card. What do you think of that?'

'Fabulous—but only if you do something about it—and you never do.'

'How do you know?' Hazel answered sharply.

'Darling, as much as I love you, in all the years I've known you you have only once got involved with somebody, only once. Ashley. You need to be more assertive.'

'Yes, yes! You know, I would kill for Keven O'Malley. He is so divine.'

'Oh, Hazel, get over it! He loves you but not the dashing-to-bed bit. Why not follow up the card the young guy gave you? God knows, if he saw you in drag and is still interested, it must be quite serious.'

'I will leave that unnecessary comment until the morning, sweetie.'

'You know what I mean.'

'And what about you?'

'Oh, that old story? Who needs 'ten tons of fun', as you put it?'

Hazel felt that he had forced Mary into a corner, conversation-wise, and said, 'I'm sorry. I didn't mean it like that and you know it.'

'I know,' was the genuine reply, 'but sometimes you have face facts. Who is ever going to make a pass at me? Come on, Hazel, I am not fat, I am enormous and I guess I am always going to be like this. But I have one consolation and that's you as a friend.'

'It cuts both ways,' said Hazel, as he drove up to Mary's front gate.

'Do you want to stay the night?'

'No, I'll just go home and cut my wrists.'

'Don't make too much mess, darling. Remember, tomorrow night it's dinner at my place, as it's your night off and we have invited the love of your life.'

'Exactly. Antonio and I will sit quietly and talk of love.'

She kissed him and walked up to the front door, waved back to him and went in.

'Yes, tomorrow night,' he thought. 'How nice of Mary to invite to Keven join us for dinner. Well, if you can't have them, you may as well drink and look at them. I'm sure that's been said before.' The lilac Volkswagon headed back towards Richmond.

*　*　*　*　*

The next day was very busy for Mary, with eight appointments and so when the last case left her office she sat back in her chair and just stared at Antonio. It was then that Hazel's comments and her responses last evening filtered back. She knew she was vastly overweight but in a certain sense she saw it as a security wall which prevented her being pestered by anyone wanting a one-night stand, which was totally beyond her comprehension anyway. Really, she thought, would I be any happier? Out with Hazel and the boys at the pub, fun lunches on Saturdays after the market, getting terribly drunk and feeling very satisfied—even if I could get a man, would I trade all this for him? She smiled at Antonio's photo. I would probably make sacrifices but I would never give you up. Her memory raced back to an afternoon many years before with Hazel at school at the swimming sports and a crystal clear image of Ray Kemp appeared before her eyes, that gorgeous body and that tiny blue and white striped speedos. She winked at the portrait, gathered her things and headed out of her office. Life wasn't really so bad, anyway. Everyday so—called normal parents with children with problems: it was one thing to work with them, another to live with them. Hello, happy evening! she thought to herself aloud, said goodbye to the staff and headed to the underground car park with Hazel's shopping list in her copious handbag, and then drove off to the supermarket and home.

*   *   *   *   *

'Come in, sweetie,' cooed Mary, as Keven O'Malley stood on her doormat with an enormous bunch of white St. Joseph lilies as well as two bottles of wine. 'Darling, how kind! They are beautiful.'

'Come through. Hazel is in the kitchen. He's a bit cross with me, it seems. I made a balls-up of the shopping list at the supermarket this afternoon, but the minute he sees you I'm sure I shall be forgiven.'

'Well, how divine to see you,' cried Hazel, the drama of twenty minutes before completely evaporated. Hazel this evening was at his best, soft, not threatening and besotted with Keven.

'Oh, what a pity they couldn't get it together,' thought Mary. 'They really are good with one another.' And she was right. They gently bounced off one another; the conversation was lively; Hazel's acid outlook was totally gone and a much more than pleasant evening progressed with jokes and funny stories from Hazel, which had them in hysterical laughter. They began, at Mary's instigation, stories about when they were at school, which made the conversation more personal.

'Well, said Keven, 'it was OK for you two. You were together at school and I was a bit of a loner.'

'But not for long, I'll lay a bet.' Mary smiled knowingly.

'Well, not for too long, but, you see, at boarding school my brother was always around so I had to be careful.'

'Do you have a brother?' asked a surprised Hazel, serving up the main course. 'By the way, if you can't eat it, it's Mary's fault.'

'Not true,' she laughed. 'A good cook like Hazel can work miracles in any kitchen.'

'Hm!' Hazel was unconvinced. 'Tell us about your brother.'

'Well, physically we are alike, if that's what you want to know, and unfortunately he is straight, dead straight.'

'How sad,' said Hazel. 'It happens to the best of families. But you didn't sit at school in the library for six years all by yourself.'

'No, I didn't,' replied Keven, emptying his glass only to find that the moment it reached the dining table Mary had refilled it.

'Was he as beautiful as Ray Kemp?' she asked.

'Sorry.' Keven looked confused. 'Who was Ray Kemp?'

'The most gorgeous drop-dead boy in the world. Hazel and I were totally in love with him. I guess we still are. It probably has something to do with idealising the past.'

'He was divine,' interrupted Hazel. 'The body—' and the two of them chorused together 'the blue and white striped speedos,' and began to laugh. They were like children, thought Keven, somewhat enviously. They had been together all their lives, at school, after school, at university, never one away from the other and little things like the blue and white speedos, obviously (he thought) stretched over a suitable surprise, had kept the pair of them laughing for years.

'My time at school was basically in the arms of the Head Prefect,' he smiled gently. 'When I started boarding school in Tendale, he was one year ahead, in fact in my brother's class. I was mad for him and I remember that I amazed myself when, one day when he and I were alone in the library of all places, I suddenly summoned up all my courage and told him I thought he was beautiful.'

'Gosh!' said Mary. 'If only Hazel and I had been so brave to tell Ray Kemp the same thing.'

'Ssh!' interrupted Hazel. 'What happened?'

'Well, he directed me over to a part of the library where there wasn't anybody and kissed me.'

'Lucky you,' sighed Hazel. 'I think Mary and I would have had to tie Ray Kemp down before either of us received a kiss.'

'Speak for yourself,' said Mary, laughing. 'He just missed an opportunity with me.'

'Darling, so has the rest of the world!'

'Bitch! Sorry, Keven, do tell what happened next.'

'Well, he wasn't the Head Prefect then, but he came to the dormitory that same evening as many of the boys moved between beds, so to speak, he joined me and it was great. I was always terrified my brother would find out but for the next three years of school we kept a low profile.'

'Have you ever seen him since?' asked Hazel, jealously.

'No. When we left school and I came to university and he disappeared. I was destroyed. It took me ages to get over him.'

'And your brother?'

'Oh, Peter! Well, he wasn't a great academic—great on the field and probably great under the shower but he went to my parents' property in New South Wales. I guess they thought if he wasn't going to join a profession, he could work on the land.'

'How did that go?' Mary was curious, as this was the first time she could remember that Keven had ever mentioned his brother.

'He hated it and was bored stiff. The Saunders family, that did the administration of the property, were probably not what you would think of as intellectually stimulating and as the local town was an hour away the property was isolated. So he was a sitting duck for a local 'gold digger' called Sandra-Jane. I have forgotten the surname. She moved in, both barrels firing He thought she was great but didn't want to marry her. She was a step smarter than him and the usual scenario followed: pregnant girl, society family, a quick fancy marriage and that was it.'

'Are they still together?'

'Strangely, yes. She controls everything and he just signs the cheques, which is now becoming a real problem as money on the property is not what it once was. They are never there. She hates it and so they travel all the time, especially in Asia. She loves it and he hates it.'

'But didn't you say she was pregnant, and, I suppose,' said Mary, 'had a child?'

'Oh yes,' replied Keven, noticing that Hazel had refilled all the glasses yet again. 'But Sandra-Jane was not interested in the little boy and nor was Peter. They left him on the property with a governess of some sort and I doubt he ever saw them.'

'That's sad,' said Hazel. 'What's his name?'

'Sebastian. He must be about seven or eight years old now, I suppose.'

'And he lives there all alone? No wonder people like me have work from morning to night. I really think parents should be tested before they are allowed to produce offspring. Some of these kids really never recover, or they transfer this sense of rejection into a part of their personality and that works hell for someone else in the future.'

'I couldn't agree more, Mary,' said Keven. 'My brother and the lovely Sandra-Jane are completely irresponsible and, by the way, if make-up were banned tomorrow Sandra-Jane would commit suicide.'

'Really? She puts it on with a trowel?'

'Not only that,' smiled Keven, 'it's the colour. I am sure the shade is called Hawaian Sunset or something but the few times I have seen her, her make up has been bright orange brown with this peroxide blonde straw hair,.'

'She sounds a nightmare,' said Mary. 'Don't tell me she tops the make-up off with long black lashes and electric red lipstick?'

'You got it in one! Barbie herself.'

'Sounds like bad drag.'

'Worse,' said Keven, responding to Hazel's comment. 'Sandra-Jane believes she and she alone is the most gorgeous person in the world. Sad, isn't it?'

'Especially if you're eight years old and called Sebastian.'

'What's the property like?' asked Mary.

'Killkenny is enormous. It's 80,000 hectares. A part of it is very low—producing due to the rainfall but one part, where the soil is volcanic, is—or should I say *was*, profitable. My brother and I spent very little time there, as our parents lived here in Melbourne, so it was like an investment property. But my grandparents lived there always, so I guess you would say in a funny way the family has always been at

Killkenny. But honestly, I haven't a clue about the property, now my brother looks after it—if he and Sandra-Jane are ever there, which it seems is rarely. But it's their responsibility to oversee it.'

'I feel sorry for Sebastian,' said Mary. 'Do you know him?'

'No, not at all. I remember him in a pram, but nothing else. My brother and his wife keep separate lives from me. Only once or twice a year do we sit down with an accountant to discuss finances and that's that.'

'How empty,' said Mary, forlornly, and then the conversation moved back to lighter topics, such as the cute Head Prefect, and Ray Kemp and Antonio Banderas, and they drank and laughed into the small hours, each grateful that tomorrow was not an early day for any of them.

*　　*　　*　　*　　*

The next morning, Hazel woke with a slight headache, not bad but enough to annoy him, so as a result and as he had to work in the evening at the restaurant (which was now beginning to bore him), he took the morning very slowly, and at about midday, and feeling much better, he remembered Mary talking to him about the business card and the good-looking young man in the restaurant. So taking his courage in both hands, he telephoned the number. It rang for a while and then he recognised the voice of the gorgeous young man.

'Yes?' was the reply and Hazel explained who he was and where they had met.

'Oh yes. Listen, can you come to the address on my card 10.30 Monday morning?'

'I don't see why not,' was the cheery response.

'Good. See you then,' and he hung up.

'Perhaps this was it,' thought Hazel, 'at last a gorgeous young guy. Oh, I must tell Mary,' and he telephoned at once.

'What? Hazel, how divine, how splendid! I knew you could do it. Call around for a drink after work this evening.'

* * * * *

'Well, how is Mr. Success?' Mary cried as she opened her front door to see an elated Hazel with a large cardboard carton in his arms.

'Supper, darling.'

'Hazel, it's almost midnight.'

'Exactly, a diet supper.'

'Oh God, here we go again,' she laughed and they made their way down the corridor to the kitchen/dining area and Hazel immediately began to unpack a delicious array of assorted food that he had packed up from the restaurant.

'Here,' he said, handing a bottle of champagne to Mary. 'Pop it in the freezer for ten minutes or so. Look, luvvy.'

'Hazel, a lobster! How smashing! All this to celebrate your 10.30 rendezvous. Wow!' She picked up some smoked salmon. 'Oh, Hazel, also oysters. I hope Godfrey isn't missing all this.'

'Oh, forget him. I am really sick of him. I do the cooking now four nights a week. I do the entertainment. I am the bouncer and he gets the cash. I was the one, my dear,' he said in a grand manner,' that took that rundown rathole of a restaurant and in eleven months look at it! New décor and full, my dear. Full, full, full! But he really is a stingy bastard. I should be getting paid much more than I am. Instead, our fat little Godfrey stuffs all the cash in his fat little bank account.'

'Oh, Hazel, open the champagne and shut up!'

'Well, that's gratitude for you. I bring you champagne, all the joys of the ocean and you tell me to shut up.'

'Oh, darling, you know what I mean.' A loud pop was heard and two glasses were at once filled with a sparkling substance that they both adored and they pulled the two bar stools up to the high kitchen bench, divided the food and, as Mary said, had a delicious binge supper.

'Hazel, do you think this young guy—' and here she stopped and looked directly at Hazel. 'What is his name?'

'Well. The card says 'Ivan Besset'. Does the name ring a bell?'

'No, but it does seem familiar for some funny reason. Oh, Hazel, these oysters are heaven. No, no lemon on mine, thanks, sweetie. Besset. Now, how do I know that name?'

'You've probably read it in the society columns somewhere.'

'Yes, I suppose you're right, Hazel,' said Mary, stopping eating for a moment. 'Do you think he wants you for work, or, how shall I put it, for sex?'

'Mary, how could you suggest such a thing!' Hazel feigned shock. 'Personally, Mary, he can do what he wants. He was divine, wasn't he?'

'Super-divine, darling, just the sort of guy you need.'

*   *   *   *   *

10am Monday saw Hazel attempting to find a parking spot somewhere near this office tower in St. Kilda Road. After wasting fifteen minutes, he found a spot and hurried back to the office building, made his way in, checked with the reception desk and took the lift to the appropriate floor.

A smartly dressed Hazel stepped out of the lift, crossed a carpeted area, and pushed open a large glass door which, in large gold letters, announced BESSET & ASSOCIATES. He was motioned to take a seat in this very plush office space and ten minutes later was ushered into Ivan Besset's office. If the reception area was smart at Besset & Associates, Ivan's office screamed super-chic and super-expensive.

'Good morning,' said Hazel and when Ivan motioned him to sit down, 'now what exactly do you want me here for?' He had a sharp inner feeling that sex was out of the question.

'I have several restaurants and one is in a real mess. I want you to pick it up for me. Same sort of slap as you are doing where you work now. I am certain that's what it needs.'

"Slap" repeated Hazel, narrowing his eyes.

'You know what I mean. At that place where you work it's difficult to get a table. You really have a talent out front. Are you interested? I will double your salary and you will, if you can stand this restaurant up again, take a percentage bonus every six months.'

Hazel said nothing but just stared at this beautiful creature on the other side of the antique mahogany desk.

'Listen, I am busy this morning. Phone me when you have thought about it and we will go from there.' He didn't stand up or offer to shake hands.

'I'll give it a thought,' said Hazel. 'Goodbye,' and left. He had the oddest feeling that all was not well or certainly not as it appeared. He went out into the street from the glass tower and walked slowly to his car. 'Well,' he thought, 'The cash is great but our Ivan Besset is a cold fish.' He had just put the car key into the ignition when his telephone sounded.

'Hazel,' came an agitated voice, 'have you signed anything with this Besset yet?' asked Mary.

'No. Why? What's wrong?'

'Darling, I did some checking this morning. This Ivan Besset is involved with drug trafficking and the police are investigating all his assets. He is in really hot water. Also he has a connection, they say, to the mafia. He is trouble with a capital T, darling. He is drop-dead gorgeous but very dangerous. Come over to the clinic now and we'll have a cup of coffee. Oh, thank goodness you didn't sign anything.'

Hazel drove as in a daze. Ten minutes earlier he was looking at the opportunity of a lifetime, money and a position. Now, according to Mary, if he became involved, he might well be looking at serious legal problems.

'Just my luck,' said a forlorn Hazel. 'Fame and fortune snatched away before I could grasp them.'

'Oh, Hazel, I am so sorry but I only found out this morning and I phoned you at once.'

'He is so beautiful and, it appears, oh so dangerous. My life is a complete ruin.'

'Don't be so melodramatic. The last thing you need at this stage of your life is a brush with the law.'

'I suppose you're right,' he said, 'but he is so beautiful and you won't believe the office, so chic and obviously expensive. He looked divine in a collar and tie and that suit. Oh, woe is me, Mary, woe is me!'

CHAPTER TWO

A Disastrous Realisation

CHAPTER TWO

A Disastrous Realisation

There were two telephone calls the following week, one that brought extreme happiness and the other that changed Hazel's life completely.

The first call involved the painting of Antonio Banderas. The woman in the long Indian dress called Mary to say that the painting, after a month and a half, was now completed and they could collect it on Saturday morning. Mary was, to say the least, very anxious to see it, remembering well Hazel's words 'if it's good it will be great, if it's bad it's just kitch'.

First thing on Saturday morning, Hazel arrived at Mary's with, as usual, a large supermarket bag of 'diet food' and wine, which was duly placed in the refrigerator. Mary was very nervously walking backwards and forwards in front of the empty frame.

"Oh Hazel, what if it's awful? I shall just die."

"Don't be silly! Come on, let's go and see."

Mary drove them to the woman's chaotic studio where the same big ginger cat eyed them as intruders from a cushion on the mezzanine level.

"It's over here," the woman said, and they followed her tiny frame draped in another Indian costume that looked as if it had been washed in the Ganges twenty thousand times; a very shabby little number, Hazel was to say later.

"Oh!" was all Mary could say, and she looked at Hazel. "It's fabulous."

"Yes, it is," and the three of them stood in front of the easel, staring at Antonio Banderas as an eighteenth century nobleman.

"It's one of my better canvasses of this type," said the woman. "He was nice to paint. He has good strong features and he fitted into this type of genre."

Mary dug into her bag and handed the woman an envelope containing $500. She immediately opened it and started to count it out.

"It's all there," said Mary, in a superior way.

"Just checking. I've been short-changed two or three times. It never hurts to check."

"May I have a look at your work?" queried Hazel.

"If you like," and Hazel went up the steep stairs to the mezzanine level, watched all the time by the ginger cat. He pulled out a canvas carefully, to find that it was from the sixties or seventies, in psychedelic colours, all in odd patterns, and then another canvas was 'op art'. This vast collection of canvases was a chronological history of painting vogues for the last forty years. It was an extremely odd situation, all these hundreds of canvases just sitting there and obviously, by the dust on them, there for a long time. He came down, and they said their goodbyes, but before leaving he asked the woman if he sent a picture in the future would she paint a similar painting as she had done for Mary.

"Sure. You know the price, but in future I want the $200 deposit also in cash."

"I think we can manage that," he smiled, and left with the Spanish actor carefully wrapped in white paper.

Back at Mary's house, Hazel climbed up on the little kitchen ladder to put the painting in its frame.

"Hazel, it's divine. Oh, I am so happy."

"Oh, it's really great," he said. "She is an odd person but she is really talented. Thank you, darling," he added, accepting a glass of champagne. They both stepped back and had a good look at the painting in its now new home. "You will have to have that divan re-covered now. Really, that tatty old Sanderson linen that's all worn at the arms—something must be done. We can't have our boy looking down on a damaged divan."

"You're right. This divan was here when my godmother left me the house and I just haven't got round to doing anything about it."

"While you're at it, a new paint job and curtains wouldn't go amiss."

"What colour do you think, Hazel?" she asked.

"I would be tempted to wallpaper the room in soft pink and gold. I remember when I worked in the interior decorating world a year ago, there was a book of samples, Spanish, I think, but there was this divine old rose with gold highlights and an enormous damask repeat. It would be marvellous here."

"And the painting would be more suited to that type of background." She was looking at the green-grey walls. "You know, with Antonio in position, everything now looks very sad."

"We can have a look after lunch, if you like. I know the store is open until four, so we can have a look around and if you like the wallpaper we can have the divan re-covered and curtains made by the firm. Don't worry, sweetie. They will give me a very good discount. They owe me a couple of favours." And they headed toward the kitchen, talking about curtains and looking forward to a 'diet' meal.

* * * * *

The following week, Hazel was at home lazily watching television when the phone rang. Who could that be, and just at the good bit! It's always the same, and he leant over to pick up the receiver. "Yes?" he said, sharply.

"Hazel, it's Keven O'Malley. What are you doing at the moment?"

"Why?"

"Hazel, could you come over to my place at once?"

"Sure. See you in twenty minutes." He changed and, glancing at his watch, noticed that it was 8.00 and he hadn't even had anything to eat yet. Oh well, we may just dash out for a little something. How nice of Keven to invite me over, thought an elated Hazel. He is so divine, and he spun out into the traffic in the lilac Volkswagon, heading for South Yarra.

He rang the doorbell and to his surprise he saw a very ravaged-looking Keven.

"What on earth have you been doing?" he asked.

"Come and sit down here. Have you eaten? I'm sorry to have called you at such short notice. Would you like a drink?"

"Slow down, sweetie. What's the problem? Yes, I will have a drink—and I know where everything is." He moved across the ultra-chic designer kitchen, all stainless steel and terracotta-coloured marble.

"Have you eaten?" he asked Keven.

"No," was the dull reply. Hazel opened the refrigerator and began to get out what he needed for an evening meal. With a glass of wine in their hands, Hazel began the interrogation while preparing the food.

"Now, Keven, what is it exactly?"

"Hazel, there's been a most frightful accident. You won't believe it."

"Try me."

"My brother and Sandra-Jane are dead.

"What?" exclaimed Hazel, helping himself to another drink. "Dead? How?"

"It's not really clear but for once they were in the country and were going home late at night from something in town and whether he fell asleep at the wheel or whether she was driving, I don't know. They hit a telegraph pole head on and were killed outright. I just can't believe it. I was only speaking to him on the phone yesterday and to make matters worse we had had a fight over the usual thing, money, or his inability to organise it and Sandra-Jane's capacity to spend it."

"But what about Sebastian?" asked Hazel.

"Oh, he's OK. The Saunders look after him all the time, so there is no problem there, and remember what I told you. His parents were only very rarely with him so he won't miss them yet. I am going up to the funeral on Friday. What the hell am I going to do now? Thank goodness the Saunders have everything in hand."

Hazel let Keven talk on, while he prepared dinner and opened another bottle. It was evident that Keven just wanted someone to listen to him.

"I don't know what is going to happen to Sebastian but I do know what's in the will. My brother's half of Killkenny becomes Sebastian's, so it seems Sebastian and I are now business partners. Oh, what a mess! What a mess!.

Hazel laid the table in the dining part of the kitchen and the meal was served. "When did you find out about all this?" asked Hazel.

"Five minutes before I phoned you. I'm sorry to drag you into all of it but I just wanted someone to talk to and steer me towards sanity. I don't believe it, I just don't. And Sebastian isn't even eight yet. I guess

Jan will tell him. I hope I don't have to. I believe his governess left a week ago, so another one has to be found. Hazel, the pasta's great. Thanks. I guess we could have eaten out. I've not only called you to listen to me but forced you into cooking as well."

"That's what friends are for, sweetie. If you want me to help you with any of this business, don't hesitate to call. I'm always here." And Hazel lent over to hold his arm, something he rarely did with Keven.

The evening continued like this and they made arrangements that Keven would call him after the funeral and then they would see what could be done. Hazel drove home, quite exhausted: Kevin's helplessness had drained him of any energy that he had had. It was a very tired Hazel that flopped into bed, having an odd feeling that in some way he was to become much more involved in this terrible situation.

*   *   *   *   *

The rest of the week continued normally, with an ever-excited Mary accepting all Hazel's advice about decorating her formal living room.

"Oh, darling," she cooed, over the telephone. "Antonio is going to adore the new room. I think you're right, Hazel, that old carpet just has to go."

"Of course I'm right! And that sample you saw at the shop on Saturday afternoon—I've already taken the initiative and told them to order it. All you have to do is to work out if you want the carpet to go right through the house or not. I suggest you do. Remember the decorating skills of your late godmother left a lot to be desired, especially the floor coverings. A different wall-to-wall carpet in every room—yuk!!"

"But, Hazel, that will mean turning the house upside down."

"Of course it will, and while you have the decorators in, that hideous bright blue hallway had better be painted out and the chartreuse walls in the guest bedroom are something again. Remember, sweetie—strike while the iron's hot."

"Let's hope my bank account can stand the stress," she laughed. "Oh, by the way, have you heard from Keven?"

"No. Strange! I thought he would just go to the funeral and return, but I haven't heard a thing from him, and I don't really want to call him. I'm sure he has enough on his plate."

*　*　*　*　*

Eight days after the funeral, one evening when Hazel had a night off, he was dining and working out a complete overhaul of Mary's house. They were joking and making silly suggestions for decorating, as well as serious ideas that Mary took note of.

"Oh, let's have a drink. I can't think any more," said Hazel, and they settled into the kitchen and checked notes on the colours they thought the most suitable for the rooms that had to be re-painted.

"Oh, who can that be?" asked Hazel, as his mobile phone played a brisk disco number. "Hello? When? Yes, well come over to Mary's. We haven't started dinner yet. OK. OK."

"So who have you invited to dinner?"

"Keven, if it's OK with you."

"Of course it's OK with me, you dill! It's good to see you two together. You make a great pair."

"I couldn't agree more. The only problem is to convince him," and Hazel sighed. "Why is it the men I adore are always so handsome and so impossible to have?"

"Welcome to the club, darling," and they both began laughing.

When, a little later, Mary brought a tired-looking Keven through to the sitting room, "You look like you need a drink," she said, bluntly. "Rough time down on the farm?"

"Old Macdonald never had it worse." She laughed as she poured him a drink. A bottle and glasses stood on the table, with the rest of the room taken up by the antique frames enclosing Antonio Banderos. Keven could never understand the genuine passion that Hazel and Mary had for him. Yes, given an opportunity he would also have taken advantage of the beautiful Spanish actor, but this was a world of fantasy. He thought Mary and Hazel had found a union together as well as an escape from day to day problems in the impossible drama of a certain Mr Banderas.

"Well?" she asked, impatiently.

"Oh, it was just an awful, empty experience," he replied.

"Not the funeral," she said, without much charity, "the painting!" and he noted that directly opposite him the empty picture frame was now filled.

"Good heavens!" he exclaimed. "Is it real?"

"Of course it is."

"It looks so much like Antonio Banderas."

"It's him. I got it last Saturday", and she went on to tell him the whole story, but he had the odd feeling that nothing made sense here. He was faced with a dreadful dilemma and suddenly a portrait of Banderas was much more important to Mary. The whole thing suddenly confused him, and he wasn't sure he would not just be self-indulgent recounting his problems when confronted with her enthusiasm for the portrait.

Hazel appeared with a large tray of hors d'oeuvres. "How's our man from the country doing?" he asked.

Keven now was not sure how to answer, so he just said it had been harrowing. After a few more drinks they moved to the table and Keven became aware that both Mary and Hazel were manipulating him. They were, in an odd way, diffusing the distress he was feeling. Mary was not a child psychiatrist for nothing and between she and Hazel they, ever so slowly, allowed him to recount the time at Kilkenny without letting him become too depressed.

It had, in fact, been a very awkward situation, as Keven's brother was Catholic and Sandra-Jane a Protestant, so instead of one funeral there were two to attend. "They were terrible," he said. "Sandra-Jane's parents hated her husband, and so they boycotted his funeral, something very much remarked on in a largish country town, and not making things easier. When I went to Sandra-Jane's funeral, nobody, can you believe it, nobody spoke to me, as if I had the plague or something. It was really very uncomfortable."

"I'd have thought that they would have been quite pleased that you attended," said Hazel. "I hope you wore black?" he added cheekily.

"Of course! Pour me another drink!" And so, little by little, the emotion was pared away from the facts, to reveal the events of the short time Kevin had spent in the country.

"Oh, that's not the only reason I didn't come back at once. It was because an old friend who happens to be my and my brother's accountant asked me to call and see him before I returned to Melbourne.

"Was he attractive," asked Mary.

"No, unless you like men of 68, but a very fine and honest man. I was shocked when he told me that all that had happened at Kilkenny in the past fifteen years had not been above-board. He couldn't prove anything, but Kilkenny was always showing a loss yet should, according to him, be showing a profit, even allowing for Sandra-Jane's extravagant life-style."

"Do you mean someone is embezzling the profits?

"It seems someone is siphoning off money somewhere, but how Mr Lester doesn't know, and he doesn't have enough proof of anything to call in the police or the tax department. Legally, it just looks like bad management, but he is not convinced."

"So what happens now?" asked Mary, reaching over and helping herself to another fried prawn.

"Greedy, greedy!" quipped Hazel.

"But they must be eaten before they get cold," and Keven laughed for the first time in a week and a half. He suddenly felt a tiny piece of weight lifted off his shoulders.

"I have a program that I hope will resolve all the problems," he explained.

"Do tell us," cried Mary.

"Well, not before I've had another drink or two," and Keven looked at Hazel, slightly narrowing his eyes and smiling.

Hazel melted.

"Well, bring on the bottles," added Mary, with a broad grin. "Oh, Hazel, I don't suppose we have any more of these gorgeous prawns, do we, sweetie?"

"I was going to keep the other dozen and a half for tomorrow's lunch."

"Oh, forget it, Hazel, pitch them in. Keven and I are starving, aren't we, darling?"

"Oh yes." He smiled, but the thought crossed Mary's mind that this particular smile was a little like a cobra just before it strikes its prey—and she was not wrong. Hazel was his usual buoyant self, this evening, preparing everything, filling glasses, chatting casually. Here he was with Keven, and life couldn't be more wonderful. Hazel was elated, but, if he had taken the trouble to look more carefully at Keven, he might have seen the trap that Keven was so carefully baiting just for him. But he didn't and so when Keven sprang the lever, Hazel was held firmly in a vice that is generally called 'emotional blackmail'.

"How is Sebastian copying with this terrible situation?" Hazel queried.

"He cried a bit but not much. He seemed quite detached. He is an odd kid. He is in fact almost eleven years old and I thought he was only eight. He is distant, and, for an eleven year-old, determined and a bit arrogant. He has always got what he wants and has used his power somewhat ruthlessly as his parents were rarely at Killkenny. Whatever he says seems to go. I don't know how Jan lets him get away with it."

"He sounds an angel," Hazel commented sarcastically. "Right, here we go. Another dozen and a half fried prawns." He looked at Mary. "I know, 'diet food'," and they all laughed.

"How's the restaurant going, Hazel?" Mary picked it up first: the comment was too glib and unlike Keven, who couldn't care less how Hazel's work went.

"I'm sick to death with it. I do the work, the public relations and am on a shitty wage. I share nights with the other chef and I know they pay him more and when he is on the restaurant is half empty. When my clients know I am Ms Whizz in the kitchen, it's standing room only. Oh, what a bore it all is!"

Now Keven played his trump card. "Hazel," he said in a soft voice. "I need you," and then stopped and had a drink.

'Ouch', thought Mary, this is going to be painful.

Hazel lifted his glass, took a deep breath and smiled at him.

"Hazel, you are the only man I trust, in fact, I would trust you with my life." As much as this was absolutely true, Mary could see that this conversation was going to make whatever Keven wanted inevitable and Hazel's chance of refusing impossible.

They looked at one another. Mary felt as if she were watching a soap opera but from the outside and was not sure if she should make light of the situation to break this bond or just see how it all worked out. She decided on the latter, supported by yet another drink.

"You said you're sick and tired of the restaurant trade. Would you consider coming to work for me?"

Hazel's heart leapt. "Why not?" he replied, cheerfully. "What can I do for you, bwana." The cobra smiled a smile of assurance. Keven leant across the table and put his hand on Hazel's. "I want you to manage Killkenny for me. I will give you power of attorney to do as you wish, but you are the only person I believe in who can at this moment save me," he said, dramatically.

Eat your heart out, Bette Davis, thought Mary and glanced at Hazel, expecting a similar remark, only to her horror seeing the cobra's strike had been fatal.

Hazel smiled and looked into Keven's eyes. "Well, big boy, what do you pay?"

"As I don't have a brother or a Sandra-Jane bleeding the coffers, I will double what you are being paid now or if you want more we will discuss it and I'm sure we can arrive at something satisfactory." Only then did Keven remove his hand from Hazel's

*   *   *   *   *

"'Bye! Goodnight!" Mary and Hazel waved to Keven as he drove off. They returned to the kitchen. "Not a word," said Hazel, anticipating Mary's reaction to the evening's events.

"Would you like a drink, darling? And have you any idea of what Keven has just conned you into? You must be delirious."

"How can you say that?" argued Hazel. "I'm sick of the restaurant and I need a change."

"'A change'," screeched Mary, "'a change'! Good heavens, Hazel, it will probably be me who has to dash to this Killkenny for your funeral. The countryside of outer New South Wales is known for its clever sheep and extremely limited Australian men, who despite what you think most probably fuck amongst themselves but an outsider is completely out. They will not only see you as a threat but as a fucking target. Hazel, you are my dearest friend and in the past you've done some, well, how shall I say it, some silly things but this is insane. Besides, I don't have a large black hat for your funeral."

"Don't exaggerate," he replied, casually.

"Exaggerate!" cried Mary. "Hazel, you are out of your tiny mind. Don't you remember what Jeffery described to us about growing up somewhere near this god-forsaken Killkenny? Darling, these men may at sixteen or seventeen be pleasant and often pretty ratbags, but the moment they become eighteen and can drink publicly at the local hotels, sweetie, they all become insufferable macho morons and everyone of them is injected with a formidable dose of intolerance. It's obligatory and so the nice young man of seventeen in two years time becomes insupportable and their relationship with men always comes first. Men fit into their lives first, second and third, and after that, perhaps, girls. Hazel," and her voice began to rise, "this moronic culture, this limited scenario, doesn't go on for a while—it's for ever for these men. It seems from my reckoning and what Jeffery said that they live only for other male company. What! Go to the pub and spend all night with the girls? Well, only if you have to find a quick cover and lay a girl, get her pregnant so you have to get married. That's the mentality you're working with and if you don't marry, well, that leaves you open to comment and as they not only work with sheep but think like sheep, if you don't live the same, fucking, empty emotional lives as they do they will brand you a poof. Isn't Australian hinter-culture smart?" She stopped and took a drink.

"Are you finished?" demanded Hazel.

"Not quite," was the sharp response. "And the women, dearest Hazel, they are a race by themselves. If you look feminine, the others immediately assume you are after someone's husband. The general dress for women in the zone is strictly bull dyke, and I am not kidding. You have seen the rougher girls at the bars. Well, sweetie, they have nothing on the real things. They are tough and nearly all dress as men and are generally over-weight. Even I would not cause a comment there. But the attitude is tough. I suppose it must be to survive. The men have beer guts, most if not all are lousy lovers and ninety percent don't believe it really possible a woman can have an orgasm. The fact that they are just sober enough on a Saturday night to make a feeble effort at love-making should, according to them, satisfy the misses for the week. What a fucking life-style, and the worst of it is it is self-perpetuating. And God knows what you will find with Sebastian, an eleven year-old who will need to be booked into my clinic for a year's intensive therapy. Crazy! It's just crazy!"

"Are you done now," enquired Hazel, sarcastically.

"Only one more thing and I'll keep silent."

"At last," was the catty reply.

"What about me, Hazel?" she asked softly. "We have been together all our lives. Not to have you near me is unthinkable and yet here you are preparing to leave my life and it seems without too much worry." Here she stopped and looked down into her empty glass.

"Mary," said Hazel, realising that she was clearly very upset. "This may only be for a short time. I love the country."

"Your concept of the country is Berwick rolling hills where we went to the riding school amongst the oaks and poplar trees. Where you are going you'll be very luck to even find a tree on the flat red earth—and as for the dust! Oh hell, Hazel, I shall miss you so much."

"Me, too," was the whispered reply.

"Tell Keven you just can't do it."

"I can't. He means so much to me and I know you're not wrong. He is using me, but it's Keven and look, if Antonio Banderas asked you to swim the English Channel what would you do?"

"Darling, that's easy. I am so fucking fat I could float across without any trouble, so the analogy isn't quite there."

* * * * *

The next morning saw Hazel in Keven's office. They walked up the street to his solicitor and a power of attorney and legal guardianship of Sebastian was drawn up, giving Hazel the power to organise and control the financial affairs at Killkenny. They were told the documents would be rushed through and they could have them in two days.

"I can't give you any advice at all about the running of the place. There are obviously problems but I can only suggest that the first thing you do is sit down with Mr Lester, my accountant, and listen carefully to what he says. He is a very astute man and has an ear to the ground, and, Hazel, for God's sake be careful, especially in the pubs. The locals are not the smartest in the world."

"You sound like Mary. She spent all last night after you left trying to convince me to refuse the offer. But I've accepted because I want to help you. So how long is it going to take to sort all this out?"

"That's entirely up to you, Hazel. You have to decide, you are the expert organiser, so you will instinctively know when you can leave everything working well, and only then. I will, in the meantime, pay to have all your things moved to a flat in East Melbourne. I own three of them in a modern block, not the smartest in the world, but with a view across Powlet Reserve from Grey Street. If everything works out, it's yours, my present. And your wages will be paid into your bank account and you can draw on them from the end of this week. All your expenses at Killkenny will be covered, so don't worry. Your skills and organising ability are going to be stretched to the limit. My brother did nothing and neither did I, I suppose, so now you have to put everything in order for Sebastian and me." He smiled. "After you pick up a copy of the legal documents, you can organise when you leave to suit yourself. I will give you the Saunders' telephone number and they, in turn, will be advised of your arrival. Hazel, this takes the weight of the world off my shoulders."

"Well, don't place it on me, sweetie. I don't want to re-iron my shirt again! Oh, by the way, I have a favour to ask of you."

"Just ask," replied Keven.

"It's Mary. She is not exactly happy about this move, so, well, if you could perhaps take her out to dinner every now and again it would make everything a bit easier for her."

"It's not a problem. I might just arrive with the supermarket bag like you and make dinner for her—'diet food', I think you both said." Here, they both laughed. and Hazel headed for home.

*   *   *   *   *

At the end of the week he thought he would leave on Saturday, stay somewhere along the way and then make for Killkenny on Sunday. Oh, it's very 'Out of Africa!'

That evening, having handed in his notice, he contacted, between gaps in the cooking, most of his favourite clients, to say he was leaving for what seemed like new pastures, and that Friday night was his last, so if they wanted a table and a good bash-up, they should book a table now.

The last night turned out to be just as Hazel predicted, a real bash-up. The owner, Godfrey, was extremely worried about it. "Fully booked," he said, weakly, "we shall really miss you, Hazel. What about raising your salary?"

"Too late. You should have thought of that months ago," replied Hazel as he walked past him into the kitchen to begin preparations, and leaving a large suitcase in the cloak area.

And in they flocked. Mary and Keven had a small table near the kitchen and the rest were squeezed in like sardines. Godfrey, as tight as ever with money, had actually put on extra waiter for the evening, an unthinkable extravagance. The noise was extremely loud, with everyone chatting and moving from table to table, saying hello to friends and all commiserating on Hazel's decision to quit the restaurant world. Mary was a little frosty with Keven to begin with and started with, "I think you have used Hazel shamelessly."

"Listen," he replied, "I don't know anyone I trust more or who has the capacity to take this matter in hand, do you?"

"Why not speak with your so-called Mr Lester? I'm sure he could sort it all out," was the brisk reply.

"Mary, I have spoken to him and he said to me if there wasn't someone in place at Killkenny to keep an honest eye on the situation it was destined to get worse, so what am I to do?"

"Use someone else," was the reply.

At this moment they were interrupted by the drinks waiter who was in a hurry to take their order as the table to the left was beckoning him to take their order as well. They chose the wine and the conversation returned to the same subject.

"I think this emotional blackmail is totally unacceptable," said Mary. "You knew very well Hazel would go for it hook, line and sinker, you know how crazy he is for you and you used him."

"Perhaps I did."

"Perhaps!" cried Mary.

"Hazel is the only person I know that can resolve this mess and I am not going to let him sort it out without a generous financial remuneration. I suppose he told you I am giving him one of the flats in East Melbourne."

"Yes, he told me and I have to agree it's a very generous offer, especially as Hazel hasn't any security, but," she said, a little more calmly," how long is this country escapade going to take? Three months? Six months?"

"I have no idea. As I said to him, it's up to him. If he can right the property in three months, well and good. I honestly have no idea. The place is in a real shambles."

"And the child? What about him?"

"I will leave Sebastian in Hazel's hands to decide what is the best avenue for him and then we shall decide together."

"Sweetie," said Mary, with a sharp mile," Hazel happens to be the founder member of the King Herod Association. He has real difficulties with children and no patience with them, so I think this is going to be a very big problem."

"He's lucky he knows a good child psychologist then." Keven looked her squarely in the face.

"Huh!" was her only response.

The wine waiter broke the tension between them and poured a glass of wine, then disappeared back into the crowded restaurant but not before he and Keven had exchanged glances and smiles.

As it was Hazel's last night, the cooking was over the top. Godfrey was anything but happy about the generous portions and the atmosphere was one of a large party rather than a restaurant crowd. When the last main course had been served, Hazel made his appearance at the entrance to the kitchen. "Darlings, no desserts for a moment or two, but drinks, yes," and disappeared. Keven looked at Mary. "Do you think something's wrong?" he asked.

"No, I think Hazel intends to go out with a bang." She wasn't wrong. In less than ten minutes, the curtains swung apart and Hazel appeared in the most hysterical drag outfit ever. He had taken a full white wig and added white twigs sprouting all over it. He had on a man's long black jacket with heliotrope lapels in satin. He had orange leopard leggings and absolutely huge built-up platform leopard skin boots to the ankles. He was tall to start with but with this extended wig towering up and the amazing built-up boots he was a vertical vision. A CD began, and after the hysterical laughter had died down, he began to mime 'I want an old-fashioned man' as sung by Ertha Kitt. It brought the house down.

Hazel was at his best. He moved effortlessly around the room, leaning against this person or the next, having a great time, and it was to the judge, who generally only made lunch, but tonight was also present but without the painted wife, that Hazel paid great attention. When the number was finished, he tottered back to the exit, turned and opened the jacket to screams of laughter, as underneath he was wearing a bikini in bright orange, both top and skimpy bottom. As the applause grew louder he flipped the jacket fronts open again and again—to the owner's horror.

And so the evening continued, with Hazel slipping from table to table, chatting to all in this amazing outfit. "Encore, encore" was the cry and Hazel, ever willing to please, repeated his number with everyone laughing and joining in. After this, he made an exit, leaving a very excited and happy clientele.

After the dessert had been served, music was again heard and slowly the noise died down with everyone waiting for another spectacular—and they were not to be disappointed. Suddenly Hazel swung out into the crowded room to thunderous applause. This time he was dressed in a long black sequined frock, exceptionally high heels and a black wig that just towered over the tight black sleeves of the low-cut bodice. 'Funny how an empty day can make a person say what good is my life' was the beginning of the song and off he went. Mary and Keven were in tears of laughter, as were most of the diners. After this dramatic number, Hazel, without changing, swung into more jaunty numbers, with everyone joining in. Mary pulled Keven to her side and spoke loudly into his ear, "So you are going to send Hazel to Killkenny and evenings like this will become as extinct as dinosaurs." He looked at her, but did not reply.

After the evening was over, Keven invited Mary and Hazel back to his place for a drink but they both declined for very different reasons, Hazel expected to be leaving for Killkenny the next day and Mary still not forgiving Keven for tricking Hazel into doing his own dirty work and sorting out a situation that would undoubtedly make a great gain for his pocket.

Hazel did not leave the next day, due to what he described as an unnecessary hangover, so he decided to leave it and go on Monday.

He was not tied to a schedule, so it did not much matter; in fact it gave him time to finish packing all this things up properly.

"But the offer of a flat is not bad," said Hazel. "You know I could never have saved the money to buy an apartment."

"Well, that's about the only decent thing in this very shaky deal," replied Mary, organising a light dinner for him that evening. "The rest of the deal just stinks. You've been had and that annoys me."

"Come on! Please don't make it more difficult for me," he begged.

"OK, OK," and changed the subject. "So what have you done with your photos of Antonio?"

"Oh, they're packed. They go with me, of course. And have you heard from the decorating firm?"

"Yes, I forgot to tell you. Friday afternoon they called me at work to say they would start on Wednesday next, so I shall have to shut down the house completely. Oh well, it's something to do. At least the house will be all finished when you get back. I do hope it will not be for too long."

"Darling, I shall slap them into shape and be back in a flash."

"I just hope so," she said, forlornly.

"Mary, don't be too hard on Keven. He's a great guy."

"Really? I'm sure I'll be charm and light to him," which sounded to Hazel not unlike a sneer.

*   *   *   *   *

The next morning, a very full lilac Volkswagon swung onto the freeway and Hazel headed in the direction of the New South Wales border. He was completely without regrets. He knew he was going to miss Mary and Keven, though in his heart he knew it was Mary he would miss more. In the mid-November morning, he surveyed the surrounding suburbs as he headed northwards and after an hour's driving the houses became more and more separated and the beginnings of an early summer began to show in the grass on the side of the road which was turning a light straw colour. The trees seemed to be moving slightly and Hazel thought to himself that if Killkenny was like this it was not going to be so bad, but the further he went the drier it became and, he thought, just a little sadder. There were large empty fields without cattle or sheep, just stubble covering the ground.

He pulled up at about one o'clock, drove off the main road and opened a little picnic pack he had prepared. He found the noise of the passing cars irritating and the constant cawing of the crows boring. He finished rather quickly and again set off to the border where he had booked a motel for the night. He was genuinely surprised that the landscape altered so much: there were large towns but before and after them was just space. The identical landscape went on for kilometre after kilometre.

He stopped and asked the man filling his petrol tank how long it would take him to reach his night stop and was told approximately two hours. With a certain sense of having to get there, he headed off with his CD player screaming music out for all to hear.

At about 6pm he arrived at the motel. He was exhausted, from the long drive and the boring landscape and beginning to wonder why he had accepted the deal without first having a look. The motel was on the outskirts of town and a very seedy place; painted sky blue, with yellow doors with screens in the same happy shade. It did little to perk him up. He checked in and then went for a shower. There was no bar, just a depressing dining area which served a meal between 6.30 and 8.00. After his shower, he stalked through the fly-wire door to this uninspired dining area directly behind the reception desk and took a seat. In one corner sat a middle-aged couple who seemed quite at home. The sloping ceiling had metal supports showing and as the ceiling was cream the supports were painted gloss brown, supposedly, Hazel thought, to make them look like wooden beams. The green walls were covered in the most hideous kitch, photos of the local football teams, large badly-framed Chinese prints that someone had obviously given as gifts, a clock set in a shell case and so it went on, each piece as tasteless as the other, and, after the meal, Hazel was convinced that 'tasteless' was a fitting adjective for the food as well.

The next morning, after settling his account with the bored proprietor, he set off for the last leg of the journey. Now the landscape began to change dramatically. The trees seemed to be fewer and he began to see what Mary had described: a reddish-brown colour began to appear between wizened clumps of dried grass and the sky seemed to be more intense. The blue was so blue it seemed as if someone had put a filter over the whole sky area, and it was becoming very hot. It was, in Hazel's view, basically inhospitable. He couldn't even see a house; nothing, just a long black road with shimmering heat that seemed endless. Out of this shimmering occasionally came a distorted truck, and the closer it came the sharper the details of it were, until it passed and in his rear vision mirror it again distorted into a wandering glare and then disappeared altogether.

This was his repeated experience for more than three hours of driving: nothing, an absolutely empty canvas that seemed to stretch on forever and was completely flat with just a hint at what might be hills or mountains, but which seemed to be light years away.

He stopped for petrol at a lonely service station only to find an equally lonely middle-aged man who refilled his petrol tank and pointed to a sad dwelling that he described as the café where Hazel bought some dried sandwiches and two cans of some type of fizzy liquid. He returned to his air-conditioned car, escaping the searing heat, and headed on down the highway.

About an hour later he passed through an extended untidy town call Bradbury and it was here he stopped and telephoned Killkenny and took final directions to the property. He did as instructed, passed up the main street, out past houses that seemed exhausted by time and heat, with gardens and trees which seemed even more abandoned—and everywhere this bright red earth with tufts of dry grass. 'Continue for about ten kilometres,' were the instructions, 'then you will see a wrecked old church. Turn right and continue for another eleven kilometres and you should be here.' At which the speaker promptly hung up.

'At last,' thought Hazel. In due course he found himself at the crossroads and on the corner he saw the church. He was fascinated, stopped his car and stepped out into the late orange afternoon sun and walked across to it. It was constructed entirely of corrugated iron: the idea had been grand but the materials economical. It was not a large structure and he noted that the local vandals had left their mark. It was severely damaged inside, one of the front doors hung on one hinge, the other half was face down in the red dusty earth.

He went inside and gasped. Not one pane of glass remained intact. Shards of it lay scattered across the floor underneath upturned and broken pews. The whole interior was covered by a blanket of red dust. He made his way over upturned pews and glanced at the graffiti sprayed on the walls, which were smashed in sections and made of masonite attached to the bearers. So Hazel gazed bleakly at the corrugated iron that now was the only cover for the skeleton of the church. The altar rails were broken in several sections, the result of a vandal party, it seemed, and the gate missing. The church had two side altars and the main one. The side altars were damaged but the high altar was almost totally destroyed, with bits of the gradines in splinters on the floor. He stepped over the debris and pushed aside a door that had been partly ripped from its hinges to find a sacristy in an equally distressed state, everything torn or broken and sprayed with graffiti. He noticed beside a side altar as he returned, a spot where someone had defecated. His eyes, as he went to leave, were automatically drawn upward to a rose window above the front door. Tiny shards of vicious primary coloured glass clung to what was left of the putty, which once held all the glass in place. He picked up a blue piece from the floor and it had a tiny piece of acid etching on it: perhaps, he thought, the centre of the rose window held the monogram of Christ once and he glanced upward again at the cast iron form which still remained intact.

He stepped out and looked about. One of the two toilets standing at the back of the block of land had collapsed and the other was at a very quaint angle. He stepped over the broken door, having jumped down as the steps had just rotted away, and saw in a patch of dry grass, a board. He casually turned it over with his foot and on the back saw some writing. It took him some minutes before he worked out what had been painted on it. The top part was completely rotted away: time had taken its toll but the middle part stated ST. ANTHONY: the rest of the letters were missing at the bottom.

He returned to his car and headed off for the last eleven or so kilometres, feeling hot and quite depressed. He tried to puzzle out what satisfaction the people who destroyed the little church could have received. He could find no answer at all. It was quite sad if destroying a church in the middle of the country gave someone an enormous sense of satisfaction. What type of people could they be, he wondered.

If he had had his wits about him, the wrecked church would have prepared him, but he was tired and hot and when he had done the eleven kilometres he saw on his right a conglomerate of buildings that looked like a wrecker's yard, and half hanging off a post, in roughly painted red letters, was the word 'Killkenny'. He braked.

I could just drive on. No one would know, he thought. Damn Keven! This is the pits. It's a bomb site or worse, and he turned his laden car into a pot-holed track that led immediately to a hotch-potch of tin buildings. No wonder the brother and Sandra-Jane were never here, he thought. It's hideous.

He got out of the car and glanced at his watch. Six o'clock. Not bad for two days' driving and I am still sort of in one piece. He heard a loud bang from the fly screen door and an enormous man stepped out in a loose shirt and shorts with old tennis shoes on.

"Hi, I'm Hazel," he said.

"I'm Jan. Yer late, yer know."

Hazel's eyes opened as if his pupils had been dilated.

"Good God, you're a woman," he said in surprise.

"Smart arse," was the snarl.

"Oh, this is going to be just great," he said aloud, shaking his head.

"Come on. Move your arse. Dinner's on the table," and with that, glancing at the shambles which Keven had described as the homestead, Hazel followed Jan inside. The gloom as he entered surprised him and the smell of boiled mutton on a hot day like this made him feel slightly nauseous.

"This is Bob and that's Pat," said Jan abruptly. 'Sit down at the end. Oh, by the way, that's Seb,' and Hazel, having acknowledged the introductions, sat between Jan and Sebastian. All eyes were glued to the television set, so conversation was limited. He was clearly a mild disturbance, but no more. But they were all in for the shock of their lives in the forthcoming weeks.

Sebastian, in between looking at the television set, glanced sideways at Hazel every now and again but conversation for Hazel was strictly between him and Jan.

"You'll be shaking up in the governess's house and Seb can move back there tomorrow."

"I don't want to," was Sebastian's sharp reply.

No one answered him. It was if everyone was completely isolated.

God help us if the TV ever broke down, thought Hazel. Every time he asked a direct question Jan's stock answer was, 'We'll talk about that tomorrow.' Her broad Australian accent was only bettered by Pat, who looked, according to Hazel, like a pig, big, pink and half as intelligent. He was dressed as was Bob in the apparent uniform of Killkenny, runners, shorts and tee-shirts the dirtier the better. It seemed Bob's conversation was nil. A grunt every now and again meant Pat or Jan had to lift their enormous frames and fetch yet another can of beer.

"I'm surprised you have room for food in your fridge," said Hazel sarcastically.

Missing the point, Jan replied, "Oh this fridge here in the living room is for beer. I've got another in the kitchen."

"Silly me," muttered Hazel.

The food was so fatty he ate only a little but downed a can of beer without any trouble. And still the conversation was nil. Sebastian refused to speak, as he was cross that he would have to return to his bedroom in the governess's cottage and not sleep on the divan in Jan's living room.

It wasn't that the room was dirty, it was just untidy, chaotically untidy. The décor was non-existent. Things were brutally nailed to the walls or glued, in the case of a scene from a calendar of two Tasmanian devils feeding. There was a large rug depicting a leaping tiger, a shelf on one side which held half a dozen sporting cups, and the large fridge for beer, taking pride of place on the side of the room nearest the kitchen. The wall nearest it held the TV set, together with the long and very battered laminate table and a mixture of chrome and vinyl chairs, and a sagging divan and two armchairs, one missing an arm. All this on a linoleum floor. The effect was very, very depressing but the things Hazel found most horrendous were the fly strips hanging off the ends of the long fluorescent tube which, when turned on, gave the room an even more terrifying aspect. And no one spoke to one another; it was the TV which dominated everything completely.

Jan, when her favourite quiz programme was over, offered to show Hazel his new digs. He said goodnight and there were a few grunts which he interpreted as replies. He followed Jan's large frame out of the door onto the veranda and across a dusty section in front of the house to a pair of cottages, one larger than the other, made of tin with verandas trimmed in cast iron, but all rusted. Jan swung the door open on the smaller cottage nearest the main house and Hazel entered after her—*with* her would have been impossible given the narrowness of the hall.

"Why two cottages?" asked hazel.

"Years ago one was for the indoor staff and this one for the governess. When there wasn't one, the staff used it. Now we haven't a governess or staff, just you." She said this in a disdainful way.

"Thanks, love you too, Jan," was Hazel's sharp return.

"Don't get too smart and just remember the kid's your responsibility."

"Oh, says who?" said Hazel in surprise. "I'm not here to look after Sebastian."

"Well, nor the hell are we. Sort it out with the brother in Melbourne. We have our work and the kid is not part of it. Have you got that clear?"

"Perfectly, Jan darling. Oh, by the way, you must give me the name of your hairdresser. That look is so fetching."

"Fuck off!" was the response, followed by a loud crash of the screen door as she put considerable strength behind it.

Hazel looked around. If the living room at the house was ghastly, it was at least lived in and showed it, but this cottage was totally denuded of everything. A single bed each in the two tiny front rooms, a dining room with a wooden table and three chairs, a very rudimentary kitchen and a bathroom in the skillion section and the fourth room under the main roof had as its occupants two old wardrobes that stared at one another from opposite sides of the room; no curtain, only dark brown Holland blinds; not a picture. It cut the bleakest of scenarios. No wonder Sebastian didn't want to sleep here.

"Yours is the other room."

Hazel jumped in surprise. He hadn't heard Sebastian enter. Hazel look at him. "Have you always lived here?" he asked.

"Yes, what of it?" he answered defiantly.

"But it's hideous."

73

Sebastian just slammed the door loudly, going into his room.

Hazel went out to his car and brought in the necessities for the evening. 'This is a nightmare you could make a film about. 'Strangers in Hell' would be an apt title,' he thought. 'Oh, Mary was right. I have been well and truly conned.' He settled his things into his small bedroom, ever so conscious that the door across from his was well-closed. He hoped Sebastian had opened the window or he might die of asphyxiation, but having lived here all his life he probably knew how to survive.

Hazel unpacked a few things and then sat on the edge of a very squeaky bed. 'What a depressing hole,' he thought, as he sat on the sagging frame. At this moment he jumped with surprise as his telephone rang. He reached over and picked it up.

"Hazel, are you in one piece?" cried Mary.

"Darling, only just. This place looks like Mars—red soil for miles and miles."

"How are the people?"

"The pits," was his answer.

"Oh, Hazel, I shall not say I told you so."

"You just have, haven't you!"

"How many people are there?"

"People!" exclaimed Hazel. "'Things' would be a better description—plus Sebastian who here revels in the name 'Seb'."

"What he like?

"I haven't a clue. He obviously hates me and refuses to speak, so that's a blunt start and the Saunders, well, I can't begin to tell you. First there seems to be the matriarch of the family, our Jan, darling. She would make a hardened bull dyke shake with fear—enormous and with a big round face which lies in folds, especially around the

74

eyes and neck and the hot climate has roasted her to the shade of a scorched peanut. But the hair! I'm, sure that Bob, that's the hubby, drops a pudding bowl on the scalp and just chops with a pair of shearing shears. It's something again! And those lumpy cellulose legs in men's working shorts are really something more. She is the only one I have had any conversation with. The rest seem totally mute."

"What about the husband?" asked Mary.

"Our Bob, well, he seems a slightly feminine version of Jan, except there are no pendulous breasts, just an enormous stomach that has a navy blue tee-shirt stretched over it, which is a real test of endurance for the cotton. His face is bright red. I imagine he has blood pressure problems, with a bulbous nose and grey-green eyes and orange black hair, or what's left of it. He waddles, not walks. Altogether he's a frightening example of someone who doesn't care about his appearance, but I suppose as the two of them are much the same they probably don't see a problem, day in day out."

"But you said there was another adult."

"I exaggerated. I think Pat the Pig is super-remedial and to give him the title of 'adult' could only refer to his age, nothing else. He is positively revolting. He is just like a pig, except pigs have a certain charm. Pat—no! He has no hair and his fleshy pink skin goes everywhere and in great swags. He really is frightening, dressed just like dad but as far as I can see he makes it from the TV to the fridge. By the way, Mary, the large fridge in the sitting-cum-dining room is filled with cans of beer. He gets out what is necessary for the three of them and then goes back into a battered armchair with a fixed glazed look in the direction of the TV screen."

"Sounds just our man," laughed Mary."

"It seems the principal diet here is based on boiled mutton. The whole house stinks of it."

"Are you living in the house with them?"

"No, thank goodness! I'm sharing the governess's hovel with Sebastian and I am not exaggerating. It's constructed out of tin, a cute façade but nothing inside but a bed, a table and a chair. Very minimalist décor!"

"And Sebastian?"

"Well, I can't tell you much. He refuses to speak to me and sees me as the intruder or the new governess here to scold him again. He's a very pretty boy. He looks a bit like Keven. He has a mop of thick, black, curly hair and blue eyes—quite a stunner, but not very tall and a bit over-weight, but this is due to Jan's culinary skills, I'm sure. He has a vacant look, nothing like Pat-pig, but there doesn't seem to be any youthful energy at all. He seems a young old man just gliding thorough life without bumping into anything. He doesn't appear lonely, just uninterested. It's as if he's tired or something. The result of no stimulus, I suppose."

"I think, Hazel, you have a little problem," commented Mary.

"That's the understatement of the year," he said.

"So what are you going to do about him?

"I don't know. I've only been here one evening. I'll check out the lie of the land tomorrow and then take Keven's advice and make an appointment to see Mr Lester and go from there. Oh, I can't tell you how depressing my room is! Not even curtains, just a slightly ragged dark brown holland blind to keep the world at bay."

They chattered on about the decorating which was to begin the following week in Mary's home and the conversation only made Hazel's bedroom seem even more forlorn.

After Mary's call, he arranged a photo of Antonio Banderas on a rudimentary side table with his telephone and watch, then climbed into bed, exhausted and hot. He drifted off to sleep with a chorus of dogs barking at some night animal.

* * * * *

The next morning, he woke early and made for the bathroom, only to be followed in by Sebastian. Hazel turned around. "Good morning, Sebastian," he said, politely, if not a little formally.

"Hi!" was the dull reply. Hazel turned on the tap only to find that the hot water was non-existent and the cold water flowed without much conviction.

"How the hell do you shave in cold water?" Hazel exclaimed.

"Dunno," was the reply.

Hazel made for the kitchen and discovered a quasi-antique gas stove. "Exactly!" he exclaimed. "No gas. How can you live in these conditions?"

"Dunno," was the reply again.

"Oh, fabulous!" and he offered Sebastian the bathroom first, which the boy said he didn't want anyway and disappeared back to his room to dress while Hazel began shaving in tepid water.

What a start to the day! I can't even boil water to shave with, let alone make a cup of tea. "Sebastian!" he shouted.

"Yeah?"

"Where do you have breakfast?"

"Jan's."

"Great! What do you have, mutton sandwiches?"

"What?" Sebastian replied, not understanding Hazel's sarcasm, and with that and a loud bang of the wire screen door, he headed across to the Saunders' residence and went in search of breakfast with yet another banging of the screen door.

After shaving and attempting a wash, Hazel also dressed and crossed the empty space that seemed littered on both sides with old machinery and drums of all sizes standing vertically and horizontally, all with a coating of red dust, and quietly rusting away. He went into the sitting/dining room to see Sebastian slowly eating cereal while watching the ever-present TV. Hazel made for the kitchen, which he had not seen before, and said good morning to Jan, who was attempting to do something with a joint of meat that confused him no end.

"Tea or coffee with your breakfast?" asked Jan.

"Just a pot of tea, thanks," said Hazel. "Some of us have to watch our waistline."

"Smart arse," came the sharp reply.

"Jan, why isn't there any hot water in the cottage?"

"No one asked for it. The water in the tank heats up in the daytime so when you have a shower at night it's hot enough. Where's the problem?"

"Simple. I don't suppose you shave in lukewarm water, do you?"

"Huh. Speak to Bob and he'll fit a gas cylinder to the cottage. It used to work once."

It was the attitude: Sebastian had the same one. Nothing seemed to be important. It was as if to use any energy in this hot climate, even mental energy, was a waste, and so the least path of resistance was always taken.

The banging of the screen door announced Sebastian's departure and Hazel took his pot of tea and a cup into the dining area, and straightaway switched off the TV. Jan came in to find out why the last banal conversation had ceased.

"Sit down," said Hazel, pouring himself a cup of tea. "Would you like a cup?"

"Don't mind if I do."

My God, conversation—I don't believe it, he thought. "Tell me about Sebastian."

"He's a poor little bugger, that one. No one seems to want him. He's been here all his life. Look at the situation now." Jan filled her mug to the top. "Even his fancy uncle doesn't want him, so he just stays here with these stupid girls who come and go, who claim to be governesses. They're all piss weak. I dunno if Seb can even write, let alone read. I've never seen him read a book.

"Where did he do his lessons?"

"In the cottage. There's a room with a table and chairs."

"God, how depressing! Why on earth wasn't he sent to school, or is to too far away?"

"No, not at all, but Mrs La-de-dah Sandra-Jane said that the locals were too common for her son and he must have a governess. What a fool she was! She didn't have a brain to bless herself with, always in fancy clothes, here for a couple of hours and then back to the hotel at Bradbury, leaving the little guy completely unsure as to who the hell she even was. He grew up in the house here and when he was five went to live with the governesses, one after the other, each as limited as the next. He wouldn't work. They couldn't or wouldn't force him, so that's where his education stops."

"It's a pity that there wasn't a school bus somewhere in this area," Hazel said, wearily.

"But there is. That's the fucking joke."

Hazel lifted his head up and stared at Jan. "What do you mean?"

"It passes the bloody front gate here every day."

"What? he exclaimed in horror. "You mean that Sebastian is illiterate at 11 years old and the bus passes the front gate?"

"Just what I said."

"That's insane, completely insane."

"You got it in one," answered Jan, draining her mug of tea.

Hazel questioned Jan about all manner of things and little by little a pattern was formed and the conclusion of it was 'indifference'.

He left Jan to her culinary skills in the kitchen and headed out into the blinding morning light to look around. From the myriad of sheds, large and small, lean-tos, the two cottages, one large, one small, and Jan and Bob's house, the architectural vista was a disaster. Obviously when a building was required, it was just erected with a minimum of effort and, by look of it, the minimum of finance. The end result was a total complex of desolation. He wondered how on earth a property like Killkenny could possibly have used all the rusted pieces of machinery that lay about and whether Jan and Bob's house was the original homestead.

He wandered around to the other side of the house only to discover that the principal door to the house now in use was the back of the house, not the front. The front looked as if it had never ever been used, just a mass of rubbish and old equipment including an old fridge that stood as a sentinel to past times. Nothing, it appeared to Hazel, had ever been discarded. It had just been laid aside and this vast conglomerate of used things added to the general look of abandonment, with dogs barking in the background and a motley group of hens that scratched the red earth seeking a morsel to eat, and not at all concerned about Hazel as he walked about, trying to understand. But there was no plan at all.

He went to the cottage and telephoned Mr Lester for an appointment but was told this was impossible until Friday as he was in Sydney. He put down the phone and left his room, glancing across the narrow hallway into Sebastian's room. As the door was wide open, he walked in and was horrified by the confusion. Again there was nothing on the walls; above the window was a wooden rod with wooden rings and shreds of cotton dangling from them; a single bed, not made, was pushed up against one wall and an old painted chair doubled as a side table, but there were clothes all over the floor, scattered in twos or in a heap here and there and obviously unwashed. Hazel immediately went back to Jan to find out what the problem was.

"It's not my fault if he doesn't leave his things in the basket in the wash house. It's his bad luck," she said, in a brisk, off-hand manner, "and seeing you are now in charge you can take care of it all. The wash-house is off the end of the veranda. Go to it, Hazel." She laughed, for some reason.

Hazel was infuriated and stormed out, slamming the screen door. He made straight for the wash-house, which was, in fact, a corrugated lean-to. He swung the door open to a furnace-like heat inside, as well as a great mess. He seized the wash basket, returned to the cottage and attempted to sort out which clothes were clean and which were not. He gave up and threw them all into the basket and went back. While the washing machine took the first of many loads, he set about looking for some furniture to stack the clean clothes into.

He opened the next-door cottage and jumped back in fright. There stood two large plaster statues of St. Mary and St. Anthony, and boxes of church artefacts. The church linens and one or two vestments were strewn across the floor in the first room. He let the blind up and with a rush it rolled itself up with a flapping sound. The harsh light entering made the room look even more surreal. Every type of religious artefact seemed present and not necessarily in good condition.

It's just like the rest of the place, thought Hazel, forgotten—but where on earth did all this stuff come from? And then he remembered the abandoned church, half an hour down the road. Perhaps someone had saved all this from the vandals.

He went into the other rooms that were stacked high, almost to the top of the window frames, with furniture. It was impossible to enter. He wondered how on earth someone had managed to get it all in there and packed so tight. And so it was throughout, apart from room full of the church stuff.

He once again went over to the house to ask Jan about the contents of the other cottage. "I need a chest of drawers for Sebastian's room."

"There's one off the veranda, the second door," as she continued what she was doing.

Hazel made his way down the veranda to the second door, gingerly opened it and found it also had furniture stacked everywhere and none of it obviously ever used. He saw a good antique cedar chest of drawers to one side, as well as some other items he thought might serve for the cottage. He took one drawer after another across and waited until lunchtime for Pat to help him move the carcass over into Sebastian's room.

The boy showed no interest at all that he now had a chest of drawers in his room, nor that all his clothes had been washed and ironed by courtesy of Hazel, who, that evening, tried to get some answers to the puzzle of so much furniture stored in the house and cottage but the quiz programme on TV proved to be too important for any of them to take time off to explain what it was all about, so he gave up and worked out that Jan was at least at her most talkative early in the morning over a mug of tea.

*   *   *   *   *

The next morning, early, Hazel rang the Principal of St Mary's Primary school at Bradbury and asked for an interview, which was duly fixed for 12 noon, which suited him perfectly.

"Another mug of tea, Jan,"

"Thanks. Don't mind if I do."

"Well, sweetie, where does the furniture come from?"

"The homestead, of course.

"Of course," he replied, puzzled. "What homestead?"

"Killkenny, you dill!"

"You mean all that furniture was here in this rundown house? This is the homestead?"

"No, stupid! The homestead is half an hour in from the front gate. It hasn't been lived in for fifty years or more. It's too far from the front gate. After the O'Malleys died, the family never lived there. They went to Melbourne and this house was built and the two cottages moved from the old homestead down here and all the furniture was brought down and stacked here for some stupid reason. I would have left it there. Who needs it? It's all that heavy old stuff."

"But what about the religious things?" asked Hazel.

"Oh, so you've been poking around, have you? Well, that stuff all came from the church after the vandals first broke in. Mr O'Malley sent Pat and Bob and they brought everything back here and the arseholes did the rest to the church. Poor old Mr. O'Malley, probably turned in his grave!"

"Who owns the church?" asked Hazel curiously, drinking his tea very slowly, sure that when the cup was empty Jan would cease to give him any more information.

"The church belongs to Killkenny," she replied.

"What do you mean?"

"Well, the O'Malley family built it and looked after it. It served this area for sixty years or so and look at it now. I would personally cut the balls off the kids that have done the damage."

"I might just help you."

"Jan, do you have a sewing machine?"

"What! Need a day dress do we?" and Jan let out a hearty laugh.

"No, I thought we could find an old tent and I could alter it for you for an evening frock," was Hazel's quick retort.

"Smart arse!" was Jan's usual reply when Hazel bettered her conversation-wise. "Of course I have a sewing machine. What do you want it for?"

"I'm going to Bradbury this morning. I plan to buy some curtain fabric for Sebastian's room. It's so depressing with that rod and the shreds hanging off it."

"Use the shop in the Main Street, Cromies. They have the best stuff. There's a discount joint in Church Street. Have a look but it's all shit quality."

Hazel gazed about Jan's living room as she whisked the cups away. How the hell would she know about taste or quality? he thought, looking at a pair of bright orange terylene curtains suspended on cupboard hooks from the architrave of the window, and then at the settee in blue and grey vinyl. He stood up and said to Jan that he wouldn't be in for lunch.

"Suits me," was the reply from the kitchen.

*   *   *   *   *

Half an hour up the road, close to the semi-destroyed Church, he was surprised to see close to the other side of the road a very deep precipice that dropped down almost eight metres. He stopped the car and got out into the blazing sun. It was so strange: the land was dead flat and yet here was a land fault that stretched away like an ancient river bed that had been cut away with time. The depth and width of it were considerable. Let's hope there aren't many drunks on a dark night, he thought, as the deepest part was close to the road, though a stout fence, with a warning sign, was there to protect the lone motorist.

He passed the church, turned left and headed for Bradbury. He had not realised that it took quite so long to arrive there; by his watch it was almost an hour. You wouldn't want anything here in a hurry, he thought.

He pulled up in front of St. Mary's and went into the office, ten minutes early. He was dressed in well-pressed jeans and a pale blue shirt, with smart brown leather shoes. First impressions, he said to himself.

A bird-like figure opened a side door. "Oh, Mr. O'Hara, I believe you have an appointment with me," and Hazel followed a short, red-haired woman into a very modern office.

"Well, what may we do for you?" she asked, and Hazel related the whole tragic story of Sebastian's life.

"Well, we can definitely take him. He is a Catholic?"

"Well, yes, by baptism, but his knowledge is probably very shaky."

She smiled. "Well, as it's mid-November, there's only a month before the Christmas vacation. It would be better, I think, to enrol him for the next year."

"Oh no," he replied quickly. "He has got to get used to the rhythm of schooling before he will make an effort to learn. Couldn't you please take him for this month. I have no problem paying the fees."

"Oh, it isn't that, Mr O'Hara—"

"Oh, do call me Hazel. 'Mr O'Hara' is so formal."

The little red-headed woman frowned and turned her head. "'Hazel'! Well, well. It seems we share the same Christian name," and laughed. Hazel just smiled. "Well, Hazel, as it's only a month, it's the least we can do for you. We will run some tests during the month to determine what year level Sebastian will fit into next year."

She stood up and went to a filing cabinet, coming back with several sheets of paper. "Will he bring his lunch or eat in the dining hall? Parents have a choice."

"He'll eat in the dining hall," replied Hazel, feeling suddenly odd, never having had to make decisions about someone else's life, let alone a non-communicating eleven year-old.

"The uniform you can purchase at Cromies. They carry everything for us, but a white shirt and black shorts in this climate are about all he will need. Will you fill out these forms, please."

"I'm afraid I don't have any idea of his mother's maiden name," he said as he started to fill in the blanks.

"I do," was the sharp reply, and she took the form from him and filled it in.

"Did you know her?"

"Oh yes, unfortunately I have had quite a bit to do with my second cousin—a very self-indulgent woman."

"So I've heard."

"I tried repeatedly to persuade Sandra-Jane to put Sebastian's education in my hands and not with governesses, but she would hear none of it, and as a result I never saw much of her toward the end. You see, my part of the family was Catholic and her part Protestant and she was not exactly pro-Catholic, so Sebastian didn't stand a chance until now. It's sad. I spoke to her husband about the problem and suggested that he attend the state school but she wouldn't have it and as she controlled everything we now have a student who is way behind, from what you said."

"Well, I believe so. Jan Saunders said that he hadn't learned anything at all and does not relate to anyone."

"I can understand that. Sandra-Jane was rarely here. She hated the place. By the way, where are you from, Hazel, if I may ask?"

"Melbourne. Keven O'Malley has given me the job of sorting out Killkenny and its problems."

"That's going to be quite a job, with Bob Saunders behind you all the time."

"What do you mean?"

"Well, he is a slow but very determined man. Don't underestimate him. He controls Pat completely. I have known them for years. They used to attend Mass regularly once upon a time. Now it's Easter and Christmas," and she laughed, as did Hazel.

"Oh, what about the bus?" he asked.

"Don't worry, I will inform the driver. You see, he lives in a town the other side of Killkenny."

"Good heavens, I didn't think there was anything beyond Killkenny—just desert."

"Oh no! There is the Wallace homestead, about 20 minutes further on. I went to a reception there once. Their daughter comes to school at St. Mary's, so it will be company for them both for the first part of the journey and then the rest of the students for St. Mary's and the state school are picked up. If Sebastian is at the gate at 8 o'clock next Monday, he'll have his first day here."

Hazel pulled out a cheque book and wrote a cheque for the following year's fees. "If there are any extras, please let me know, and it's very good of you to take Sebastian straightaway."

"I am so glad you're going to send him here, Hazel. I promise I shall keep an eye on him and if there are any problems I shall call you at once." Hazel stood up. "Don't forget this." She gave him the uniform requirements sheet, shook hands and smiled.

"Goodbye, Hazel." He held his hand in hers.

"Goodbye, Hazel," and they both laughed.

From the school he headed for Main Street. As he pulled up in front of a pompous Victorian building whose sign showed it to be Cromies, he was about to get out of the car when all of a sudden it really sank in how Keven had taken advantage of him and had told him of absolutely nothing. He had washed his hands of any responsibilities. He had found a stooge, namely himself, to scrounge around amongst the rubble of past lives, resurrect an eleven year-old boy, get everything ship-shape while he stood back watching to see what would happen.

He became angry, not so much with Keven but with himself. He was a grown adult and he was mixing with people he did not particularly like, just so Keven could stay put in Melbourne in his smart office with his smart friends.

He was aware of the forceful slamming of the car door as he headed into Cromies with Sebastian's measurements for a school uniform. The dull man who served him was called Rodger, which Hazel worked out from the small staff badge pinned to his short-sleeved open-necked shirt; a more lack-lustre person, he thought, would be difficult to find. He purchased the uniform, plus the extras, but said he would not purchase the jumper yet as the weather was such that it would not be needed.

"Please yourself," was the scintillating reply.

Hazel then went to the drapery department to see what curtain fabric was available for the cottage, only to be dealt with by Betty, an equally tired assistant, with, as he thought, the same hairdresser as Jan. The selection was, to say the least, limited and the colour range frightful. 'The brighter the better' seemed to be the theme in this department. Who on earth would buy electric-purple curtains with large woven holes in terylene, he thought, and then remembered similar ones in orange hanging in Jan's living room! Oh God, how depressing!

He left with the uniform and headed to the shoe shop with a pair of Sebastian's shoes in a plastic bag and was strangely enough served by a young man who was quite helpful, and attractive too. Well, he thought to himself, all is not lost in the sticks. He purchased a pair of black leather shoes on the condition that if they did not fit well he could exchange them for a size larger or smaller. Then he went off to the discount fabric store.

Here he was more in luck and after rummaging about the disorderly racks of fabric he found a cream-coloured one with a tiny celadon-green woven square repeated on it and duly purchased at a very good price enough to do his and Sebastian's bedrooms. Then he chose a cream and pale blue canvas-type fabric for the room with the table. He hoped to convert it into a sitting room long with the room with the two wardrobes. He had not realised how much time he had been spending and grabbed a sandwich at a take-away place, filled up with petrol, stopped at the supermarket and then drove back to Killkenny.

On his way back he ran through his mind again and again that Keven wasn't taking any share at all in this so-called adventure. He had been the bunny, just as Mary had said. If he left tomorrow, nothing would change. This snail's pace of life would continue and perhaps one day a dull Sebastian would begin to talk. Who knows, he thought, and who bloody well cares?

* * * * *

When he got back he called Sebastian away from the ever-present TV set and explained that next Monday he would begin school. He expected fireworks but there were none, the only response being a 'If I have to' and he went back to the TV, as if this monumental piece of news was nothing.

Hazel walked back to the cottage. I can't go on like this—it's insane, he thought. The only conversation is with Jan in the morning over a cup of tea, otherwise there is just an emptiness.

When he walked into the cottage, he noted on the lone table two beer cartons filled with documents and receipts, exactly as he had asked Bob for. Oh fuck, what am I going to do with this mess? But the telephone ringing answered the problem for him.

"Yes? Oh, Mr. Lester, yes, listen, I have two beer cartons of documents here. What shall I do with them? Very well, tomorrow at 10.30. Goodbye."

Oh don't tell me, he thought. Another hour's drive in and out. I don't believe it. Why is everything so far away out here? And he stood on a chair in front of the window with his newly purchased fabric, assessing the task ahead.

* * * * *

Early on Friday, Hazel asked Sebastian if he wanted anything from Bradbury. The answer was 'I dunno'. As the shoes fitted well, with a bit of space in the toe, there was no necessity to return to the good-looking boy in the shoe store. Bugger! thought Hazel. It's the only decent thing I've seen apart from the sheep dogs!

Arrived at Mr. Lester's office, he pressed the buzzer and the door opened at once.

"Come in, Mr. O'Hara. I've been waiting to see you."

"Me, too," was Hazel's dull reply.

"How is Killkenny treating you?"

"Don't start me," warned Hazel. "No one seems to have a tongue in their heads, not even Sebastian."

"What have you decided to do about him?" he asked, as Hazel sat down.

"He starts school at St. Mary's on Monday."

"Very good." Mr Lester stared across the desk at Hazel, a well-preserved 68 year-old, with sharp eyes, a mop of white hair and very well groomed. He had a kind face, in fact it was a little bit feminine and exuded a soft, gentle confidence that Hazel liked at once. He felt sure that what he said to him would remain exactly that, confidential.

"Now," started Hazel, "I need some answers, or I think I may as well just head back to Melbourne. I have been here less than a week and I still don't understand anything except that I've been had."

"You mean by Keven O'Malley," Lester said, turning his head a little.

"Exactly," was the reply.

"Well, if you want my opinion, you are correct. Keven, like his brother, has never taken any responsibility for Killkenny, nor for that matter did their parents, so vultures like Bob Saunders have profited."

"What about all this mismanagement of funds?"

"Well, the problem is this. As long as there was enough to pay everyone, no one complained. I have spoken to Keven and his late brother time and time again but they just let sleeping dogs lie because they couldn't be bothered to do anything. The only one who did was Sandra-Jane, which is why Killkenny is in such a mess. Do you know," he went on, shifting in his chair, "that Killkenny was the finest holding in this zone, followed by the Wallace's properties, and look at it now, a shambles physically and money-wise. All due to indifference. We pay out three wages a month, and for what?"

"Just a moment, don't tell me Jan is paid?"

"Yes, a small amount for looking after Sebastian, and the men get full wages."

"You mean two wages and Jan's?"

"Oh no, I mean three full adult wages, Bob, Pat and Matthew."

"Who the hell is Matthew?" asked Hazel.

"He is the other son."

"You don't mean there is a matching Pat the Pig, do you?"

Mr Lester began to laugh. "'Pat the Pig'" and continued laughing. "Pat's a poor boy who does exactly what his father says. He doesn't even think without Bob's permission. He's very sad."

"Well, what about Matthew?"

"He's very different. He and Bob argue from daybreak to sunset. They seem to hate one another. He has had a sad life, Matthew. His father, always from what I am told, disliked him and he grew up quite rebellious, but a very likeable boy. He doesn't look anything like them."

"Thank the saints for that!" exclaimed Hazel. Lester laughed again.

"He was, I am told, forced into a marriage which failed and I believe at present he is in the next town finalising a divorce and a degree of nullity. Make what you will of that. But if you want my advice, it's this. If I were in your position, I would take Matthew into my confidence and just wait for a while until Bob overplays his hand and begin to give Matthew the running of the property. He's a clever boy—'boy', I say, but he must be almost 36 or so now. He is a few years younger than Pat. Jan's all right, strangely. She can be depended on despite what you think of her, but I would suggest caution with Bob and Pat and don't whatever you do underestimate Bob. He's fat and lazy, but he's as cunning as a rattlesnake. How he has managed to milk the property dry I haven't worked out yet."

"Oh, by the way, I have two beer cartons of documents for you."

"Thank you for that!" said Lester, in a bland voice.

"What caused the decline of the property? Jan told me the other morning that there is another homestead on the property."

"Yes, there is. I haven't seen it for years. It is some way in. It was constructed close to a good well but when Keven's grandparents died, his parents already lived in Melbourne so they just closed it up and every one moved down by the main gate. I presume to save time, as it's a 20 to 30 minute drive in, if I remember. A big, double storey house with a tower and all in tin."

"Really in tin?"

"Yes. You see, there was originally a great deal of rivalry between the O'Malleys and the Wallaces and so, to have a house grander and larger, the O'Malleys used a cheaper material. The Wallaces' homestead, next to Killkenny, is an enormous single storey weatherboard with verandas around it. I haven't seen that for years, either, but I believe it's in very good condition and the Wallace property is flourishing, while Killkenny is almost bankrupt. A very sad state of affairs."

Here Lester stopped and went across to a small bar in and asked if Hazel would like a drink.

""You see, the big division between the O'Malley family and the Wallace family was the church.

"The wrecked church, you mean?" asked Hazel, sipping his drink.

"Exactly. There was to be a church built between the properties and being originally two wealthy Catholic families they were to share the expense of the construction and upkeep of it. I don't entirely remember the story now, but old O'Malley went ahead and built the church as far as possible away from the Wallace property and on his land, so he controlled everything, much to the Wallaces' annoyance, and he dedicated it to St. Anthony as his Christian name was Anthony. This didn't endear him to the Wallaces at all. I'm told that when Mass was said, the Wallaces always sat in the back row and never made conversation with the O'Malleys and vice versa. Really, it seems so silly now but at the time it was quite a feud."

"But who owns what is left of the church now?" asked Hazel.

"Oh, it is the property of Killkenny. It has never been the property of the Church. The priest came once a fortnight, if I remember, many years ago, but the maintenance was the responsibility of the O'Malleys."

"Have you seen the church lately?" enquired Hazel, finishing his glass.

"I haven't been out that way for years. In fact, I saw the young Wallace man the other day in town here, but he had to be pointed out to me. I just didn't recognise him. You see, he, like Keven and his brother, went to boarding school, so I just lost touch with them all and their parents, I confess. I believe he married. Young Wallace must be about your age. It was a society wedding, I'm told. They have a daughter, but rumours around Bradbury are not very favourable about Mrs Wallace. Her name is Cherly. The locals think she is a bit of a snob but who knows? Perhaps she just doesn't wish to mix with the locals and you can hardly blame her, really. Imagine a night with Jan and Bob," and he laughed.

"Don't forget Pat the Pig," and both of them roared with laughter.

Hazel left Mr Lester's office and headed for the hardware store to buy curtain rods, which were missing in the cottage, screws and other small odds and ends. He checked his list and left with everything he required, including paint and paint brushes and two large drums of floor varnish, as the multi-coloured lino was driving him mad.

CHAPTER THREE

Matthew

CHAPTER THREE

Matthew

When Hazel returned, he offloaded his purchases and went into the room with the table and, sitting there on top, was Jan's sewing machine. He dumped all the bits and pieces on the floor and immediately went to see if Bob had connected the gas to the stove and the hot water system. No such luck. 'Oh, fuck!' was his sharp comment. He set about trying the sewing machine as there were two hours before he would eat a ghastly fatty meal with Jan and family. He looked in the fridge at all the things he had bought but was unable to cook any of it, then uncorked a bottle of wine and helped himself to a drink. He had wisely bought glasses at the supermarket, as well as all the rudimentary items for the kitchen and dining room, as there was nothing at all in the cottage. After the first glass, he rolled out the fabric and began the process of curtain making. By dinner-time he had almost finished Sebastian's and felt quite pleased with himself.

The evening meal was, as always, accompanied by the TV blaring out and everyone glued to it, with Bob, Pat and Jan drinking beer from cans and Sebastian downing Coca-Cola. It was the smell of the food that Hazel disliked, always or mostly, lamb it seemed. Mutton but always mutton—boiled! There must be a million ways to serve this meat but why the hell was it always boiled with an ample serving of potatoes? No wonder Sebastian was overweight. He said his goodnights and left them all to it, returning to finish the curtains. At least, he thought, listening to a CD, he didn't have to hear another quiz programme on television.

The following day saw Bob and Pat attempting to connect the gas cylinder to the system in the cottage. Because it had been a long time since the old cylinder had been used, they had to unscrew it, as it had rusted tight, and this brought out a great string of expletives, as Bob brought the heavy spanner down on his thumb. Finally they announced in rather harsh tones that it was all working. They ambled off toward the house to have a beer, with Bob still shaking his thumb. The slamming of the screen door announced that they had made it to their destination.

Hazel, all day Saturday, painted the interior of the cottage with soft clotted cream and pale celadon green shades that finally masked the bright pinks and harsh blue that had been the major colour scheme before. By Saturday night, Hazel was exhausted: to paint was not such a trial but in this never-ending heat every brush stroke had been a real effort.

*　*　*　*　*

Sunday was to be the day that directly changed his life forever. It started out as usual and in the morning he finished the last of the painting. He was very proud of his workmanship and, being tired, accepted lunch at Jan's. They were half way through the main course, which was the only course, of cold lamb and salad, something he thought was a vast improvement on boiled mutton, when a car horn was heard. To Hazel's utter amazement, Sebastian dropped his cutlery and ran to the door screaming for joy, 'Matthew, Matthew!' Hazel looked at the other three, who just carried on eating as if nothing had happened. Sebastian bounded out into the bright glare and ran up to a small jeep-like car and as Matthew got out Sebastian threw his arms around him, chattering ten to the dozen.

'I'm going to school on Monday,' he said, excitedly and hugged him again. 'I missed you,' he said and held on tight. All this Hazel watched from behind the closed screen door.

'I missed you, too,' and they walked toward the house hand in hand.

'I have a uniform to go to school with.'

'Is it nice?' asked Matthew.

'I have a white shirt with a design on the pocket and black shorts and new black shoes. But I want to stay here with you.'

'You will be a good boy at school for me, won't you? I need you to read and write really well so you can help me with the accounts.'

'I will be good,' replied Sebastian, excitedly and pressed his body against Matthew's.

Hazel moved back to his place at the table, the television still blaring, but he noticed that Jan had set another place and a very generous serving of everything was loaded on his plate. Sebastian's chattering heralded Matthew into the dining area.

'How did it all work out?' asked Jan.

'Everything's all right now,' was the response. Hazel saw that Bob and Pat continued to watch the last half of the midday news, completely ignoring Matthew.

'Hi, I'm Hazel.'

'Hazel bought me my uniform for St Mary's and he is painting the cottage,' announced Sebastian. Hazel was surprised at his effervescent behaviour, so that for a moment he wasn't aware of Matthew's presence.

'Hi, I'm Matthew,' and he reached over and shook Hazel's hand. He certainly isn't like Pat the Pig, he thought. He is divine. With that revelation firmly fixed in his mind, he beamed. Matthew was indeed nothing like his brother, exactly the opposite in every way. He was tall, almost Hazel's height, with a very handsome, tanned face and thick black hair. From this attractive face two bright blue eyes shone out; he had a strong face and full lips, so when he smiled it was infectious. Sebastian was all over him. The change was complete, from his previous monosyllabic responses. He couldn't be stopped; he chatted on about the dogs, every tiny detail that had happened in his uneventful life, giving Matthew a day by day coverage of what he had done whilst Matthew had been away/

'Sebastian,' said Matthew, 'why don't you have a look on the back seat of the jeep. There is something for you,' and with a yell of joy, Sebastian leapt up from the table and raced off to retrieve his gift.

'He loves you very much,' said Hazel, to Matthew.

'We have been together all his life.' At this point Bob stood up, belched and then made for the door, with Pat as his shadow, only to have Sebastian collide with them as he bounded in. He raced across the room and flung his arms around Matthew.

'A new game. Thank you,' and he kissed him, which was reciprocated, after which he disappeared into Matthew's bedroom to use the TV and fit his new game into the DVD system. Jan tidied up, leaving Matthew and Hazel to talk. Hazel couldn't believe how handsome Matthew was, muscular tanned arms covered in fine black hair and large developed hands.

'So you are here to save Killkenny, are you?' he smiled.

'Only with your help,' replied Hazel.

'Hurry up, you two,' said Jan. 'I can't stand around all day listening to you two chatter on.'

Matthew finished his meal in silence and when Jan removed his plate, Hazel offered him a drink at the cottage as the air in the dining room was so stifling.

'Wow! Not bad for a week's work,' exclaimed Matthew, as he entered the cottage.

'Two days work, actually and a bit to go.' Hazel retrieved a bottle of wine from the refrigerator and two glasses. They sat in the bleak room with just the table and two chairs. The windows, being opened, as were the doors, and all covered in the necessary fly wire protection, a faint movement of air made the room a trifle more bearable.

'I spoke to Mr. Lester on Friday. I find him a really pleasant and intelligent man.'

'Yes, he is. I don't know him very well but he has always been nice to me. But, tell me, how did you manage to get Sebastian into St. Mary's. It's fantastic. At last he can have someone else to talk to except me.'

'I think Sebastian would much prefer to be with you.'

'That's fine, but he has to learn. Here his schooling has been terrible. That stupid Sandra-Jane was living in the nineteenth century—governesses! I was always worried that she would just send him off to a boarding school and forget about him, but you seem to have saved the day.'

'I'm not so sure of that,' warned Hazel. 'I really have no clear idea of what on earth I am doing in this God-forsaken place.'

'Saving Killkenny,' smiled Matthew, as he helped himself to another drink.

'I'm going to put you in charge of Killkenny.' Hazel gazed into his blue eyes, thinking of every ploy possible to win his heart.

'There'll be fireworks from Dad, you realise.'

'I'm ready for it,' Hazel replied nonchalantly. 'I've spoken to Lester and the figures just don't add up. I'm sorry but it appears your father is somehow emptying the property's coffers.'

Matthew said nothing at first. 'We don't get along, not at all.'

'Well, I'm glad to hear that. We must now organise a proper accounting system to find out exactly what's happening. I suppose you know more or less what the situation is.'

'More or less,' was the soft answer.

'Will you take me tomorrow to see the homestead?' asked Hazel.

'Only if you can ride.'

'Why?'

'Well, the drive in hasn't been used for years and there are sure to be trees down or branches, so a truck couldn't pass, but horses can skirt the problem and we can get in without any trouble.'

'OK, let's make it the day after, as I guess we have to start pretty early and as it's Sebastian's first day at school it would be a good idea if we saw him onto the bus at least.'

'That's fine with me. I have a few things to do tomorrow, anyway.'

'What are you doing for dinner?' asked Hazel, courageously.

'What are you talking about?'

'Well, if you would like to join me—and I guess if we can possibly drag Sebastian away from the TV—I would like to cook a meal here. After all, Bob has finally changed the gas cylinder this morning and has a sore thumb to prove it.' He laughed at the memory.

'Why not? In the house no one speaks at all.'

'Tell me about it,' laughed Hazel. 'It really is so depressing and although Jan's always on hand with the meals, they are so fatty, which is why Sebastian is overweight. He needs to lose at least three or four kilos, so he's going to eat with me here whether he likes it or not, but if you're here every now and again it will make it easier for me.'

'A deal! I'll have the pleasure of dining with you this evening,' was said with a theatrical sweep of the hand, 'and don't worry, Sebastian will be here as well.'

'Fine.'

'So now I must go and do a bit of organising in the shearing shed. A section of the flooring has started to collapse.'

'Don't forget, Matthew, you are responsible to me not your father from now on, so any ideas on improvements or clearance for finances for maintenance—and God knows this place looks as if it could do with some—you come to me.'

'Well, things are looking up.' Matthew left with a smile on his face. Hazel was elated and rushed to the telephone to tell Mary he had just seen and was having dinner with an angel.

He worked in top gear: the old sewing machine of Jan's was heard racing up and down, hemming, over-sewing, lining and then there was silence as he hand-sewed the curtains to their wooden rings, and so up they went. He went to the other cottage and managed to extract four dining chairs and a narrow side table. The room looked transformed, with curtains, decent furniture, a white table cloth that disguised the old oval table, and candles.

'Oh, thank goodness I bought those,' he said to himself. They were a part of his purchases at the supermarket. And there was white china to match the rest. 'Hm, very romantic.'

The stove might have been connected to the gas but it had only two temperatures, furnace or off. 'Oh, fuck it!' he cried aloud and was forced to change his menu to work around this impossible appliance in his newly painted kitchen.

He could not believe the change in Sebastian. When he asked him to do something, he was quite happy to oblige; perhaps Matthew had said something to him, or more likely it was because Matthew was there and he wished to please him. He knew the feeling.

An excellent meal was prepared and served. Matthew was most complimentary and even Sebastian said it was nice. 'I had something else in mind but that furnace in the kitchen is just impossible,' Hazel apologised.

'Hey, if you're interested I could change it for the one in the wash house.'

'Great, though I don't remember seeing one there.'

'It's in the corner with a lot of junk on top. It was in the house until Mum wanted a much larger one and so the old one, which works perfectly, was dumped in the washhouse. But I warn you, you'll be cleaning it for a week.'

'Sounds fine to me,' Hazel shrugged, 'and this one can go to the tip. I suppose there is a tip around here somewhere?'

'Yes, but it's quite a way away. I once wanted to hire a truck and get rid of all this stuff around the house and sheds but Dad wouldn't hear of it.'

'Organise it as soon as possible. This place really is a disgrace. Now, off to bed, Sebastian. Remember it's school tomorrow.'

Sebastian stood up, placed his arms around Matthew and kissed him. 'Goodnight, Matthew. Will you come and see me off to school tomorrow?'

'Sure will,' and he kissed him again.

'Goodnight, Hazel, thanks for dinner,' and he left the room, going first to the bathroom, then to bed.

'That's the first time he's spoken to me,' said Hazel.

'Don't worry, he likes you. It takes him a while to sort people out but he instinctively knows good from bad. He's had a rough time growing up,' and Matthew went on to tell Hazel about how his parents were rarely there and weren't interested in him. He had served his purpose in being born, which was all he was required to do from Sandra-Jane's point of view. The pregnancy secured the marriage and that was it; nothing more was given or needed according to her and so it had been Matthew who had taken Sebastian to his heart and they were inseparable.

'He obviously loves you very much. He's very lucky to have someone like you.'

'Thanks,' was the only response.

Hazel tried to turn the conversation around to his private life but he wasn't interested in talking about it, so they moved back to more mundane things such as the removal of rubbish or whether they should call in a scrap metal man first.

Changing the subject after a while, Hazel asked Matthew if he knew the Wallaces. 'No, I don't. I've seen the owner in the street in Bradbury but I've never spoken to him. Why?'

'I'm curious. Keven never mentioned anything to me about the Wallaces, in fact he never told me anything about anything, it appears.'

'So why did you come here?' asked Matthew, opening another bottle of wine.

'A long story.'

'Do you love him?' Hazel was shocked that Matthew could be so blunt. He had seen Matthew as a beautiful creature but strictly a country boy. To ask him a question like that assumed that Hazel had made an error of judgment. He decided to be frank. 'I've always thought Keven the most beautiful man, but, in case you are wondering, I have never slept with him—oh, not for the want of trying, be we are or were just good friends.'

'Were?' queried Matthew.

'Well, I realise I have been conned into this Killkenny routine and I initially believed that by doing this job—although I haven't done anything yet except enrol Sebastian at school—it would endear Keven to me. But I now know I have been a fool.'

'Well, I'm glad you are off Keven, as I've never liked him much. He seems a loyal fellow but it's always him first, the same as his brother. We didn't have much in common that I can remember. You see, they were rarely here and when they were they stayed in the house, that's why it's so big. The two extra bedrooms and the bathroom were for them but they may have only used them half a dozen times in their lives.'

Hazel realised that Matthew was a much more complex person than he had thought but decided to let it go and just enjoy him, but he stood up and said, 'Thanks for dinner, Hazel. I'll see you tomorrow. Oh, bye the way, if you are going to hand organisational power over to me you had better inform Dad. We don't want any crossed wires, do we?' He smiled, and Hazel saw him to the door, and then, as he was clearing up, thought that Matthew knew much more about male sexuality than he was letting on.

* * * * *

'Come on, Sebastian, you can't be late on your first day at school.' The boy showered quickly and dressed. Hazel had a carefully calculated breakfast on the table, as carbohydrate-free as possible, and as 8am approached there was a knock on the wire screen door.

'Can I come in?' shouted Matthew.

'Any time, big boy,' was the jaunty reply.

'Wow, you look great, Sebastian.' And the boy immediately hugged and kissed Matthew.

'Do you like my uniform?' he asked.

'Yes, you look great,' and he took from his pocket a box. 'This is for you,' and Sebastian took out a watch.

106

'Oh, Matthew, a watch!' and he allowed him to attach it to his wrist.

'Now you will know when it's time to come home,' and he kissed him and the three of them walked to the front gate where they waited only five minutes before a cream bus was seen snaking its way through the early morning heat shimmer, coming into perspective as it approached the gate. A kiss and a hug and Sebastian's face was seen squashed against the window as the two men waved him goodbye.

'I'll miss him,' said Matthew, quietly, as they walked back towards the cottage.

'He'll be back about four o'clock,' replied Hazel, in a lost way.

'I'll get Pat to help me with the stove,' and Matthew disappeared.

Hazel noticed Bob with his hands in his shorts pocket being busy doing nothing. 'Bob!' he called out. 'Can I have a word with you?' and Bob ever so slowly ambled over to Hazel, who decided to strike hard and sharp. 'Bob, I have given Matthew the responsibility for the maintenance of Killkenny and I know you will support him.'

'Do you?' was the sharp reply.

'I'm trying to sort out the finances of Killkenny and Mr. Lester considers we are missing finance somewhere.'

'It's just been a bad year. We have them, you know.'

'Yes, but not for twelve consecutive years. There's something wrong.'

'Don't look at me,' responded Bob and walked much more determinedly toward the house. For Bob, Hazel had been like a tiny moth that flutters near a light bulb, not really annoying and sure to either get sick of the light or burn its wings and die: but now this moth had taken on a new and much larger, not to say, more annoying role. To send Sebastian to school was one thing, but to put Matthew in charge of maintenance of the property—it didn't take a genius to work out that before long Matthew would take over the whole running of Killkenny and that was exactly what he did not want. If before it had been an effort to say 'good morning' or 'good night', these pleasantries were now not on as far as he was concerned. It was all out war, as he said to Jan. 'I'm not having a poofter at my table,' which left Jan in an awkward situation, to say the least. Where there was no Hazel, there was no Sebastian and it seemed now, no Matthew.

Matthew and Pat dumped the stove at the back door of the cottage and for most of the morning, with the help of cleaning fluids, Hazel managed to remove a year or two of mutton fat from the back and sides, not to mention the inside, of the oven. Pat helped Matthew disconnect the old stove and it finished like everything else on a heap to be sorted out one day. In the afternoon the cleaned stove was duly installed and to Hazel's delight functioned perfectly. The rest of the day he continued to make the cottage as minimally institutional as possible. The last of the curtains was in place and he glanced at his watch at ten to four and slowly made his way to the gate, only to find Matthew was already there, sitting under at tree in the shade waiting for the bus to emerge from the shimmer on the roadway.

'You're early,' smiled Hazel.

'Always was,' was the smart reply and they chatted idly for a few minutes.

'Dad is anything but happy.' Matthew smiled.

'Who cares? Do you know, I have been through on my laptop ten times today all the information Lester has given me and I still can't find what's wrong here. There should be much more money in the accounts.'

Matthew said nothing, which gave Hazel the odd feeling that, as beautiful as he was, he knew a great deal more than he was prepared to tell. Finally, and a few minutes after four, the shimmer on the road began to show a colour rather than a form and sure enough, in another few minutes, the form of the bus became apparent and the closer it came the more precise its image.

Sebastian was off the bus in an instant and in Matthew's arms, kissing and hugging him. It was then Hazel realised something he had not seen before or rather had not twigged: they were physically very, very similar—the thick, black hair, the shape of the face, the attitudes they struck, the strong nose and jaw line but particularly the eyes, those cobalt blue eyes, nothing pale or watery, just a perfect colour that, with the tan and black locks, was, in Hazel's mind, 'the tops'.

Sebastian had had a good day at school, it appeared, and he recounted it all, hand in hand with Matthew as Hazel carried his school bag with the emblem on the side. He didn't stop talking. Hazel was amazed that from a week of no conversation it was now this, such a change and he knew quite well it had everything to do with the man whose hand he held.

Matthew didn't come to dinner but said he would come over after he had spoken to his father. The dining table seemed to be the place where everything was decided. Sebastian chatted on with Hazel who drew out the conversation with all sorts of questions to keep it going. The boy had changed, and his fresh clothes were laid out for the following day, a process he was to follow for many years.

'How was the Wallace girl?' asked Hazel.

'I don't know. I didn't speak to her. She's a bit funny but I sat next to a nice boy and he showed me everything—where to get a drink—Hazel, they have these taps and when you turn the handle the water squirts up and you drink it. I liked it a lot. And for lunch we all sat in a big room and some ladies gave us something to eat but first we had to stand and a woman with red hair said something and everyone said something back to her and then we ate. I didn't say anything because I didn't know what to say.'

'Well,' said Hazel,' we'll find out and you can practise here so you can be as good as the others.'

'Yes, I'd like to be like the others.' The conversation continued and eventually Hazel went to the kitchen to prepare dinner.

In the house, it was six o'clock but Hazel, being used to a city time schedule, was going to sit down with Sebastian about 7 o'clock. He was watching the television, which Matthew had sent over from his room and just before 7, as Hazel checked the meal and emptied another glass, a tremendous shouting match was heard from the house. The two of them moved to the front veranda, both very concerned about what was happening. Sebastian went to run across, but Hazel him back. 'Let Matthew have his say, Sebastian,' and he put one arm instinctively around his shoulder and held him. The boy was clearly upset and kept looking up at Hazel. 'Is Matthew all right?' he asked again and again, but he didn't have to wait long. Matthew appeared, obviously furious, as he slammed the screen door behind him. Sebastian rushed across and threw his arms around him. 'Matthew, Matthew,' he cried, 'are you all right?'

'Yes, I'm OK.'

'Come on, handsome, dinner is served,' and Hazel smiled as Matthew came toward him arm in arm with Sebastian. Another setting was laid at the table and Sebastian was instructed to light the candles, something he really enjoyed doing.

They kept the conversation light, listening to the boy recount his first day at school, but Sebastian had heard and sees the scenes of shouting and threatened violence between Bob and Matthew and it upset him. He was afraid that something bad would happen and Matthew would go away: for an abandoned eleven year old this would be the end of the world.

After Matthew had tucked him into bed, which basically meant covering him with a sheet and kissing him goodnight, he moved backed to the dining room and closed the door so as not to disturb the boy.

'I'm sorry. This is my fault,' said Hazel. 'I spoke to Bob this morning.'

'So it seems,' was the reply. 'Apparently you are now forbidden to enter the house.'

'Oh, thank God—saved from viewing lesser than suburban interiors,' and for the first time since he had walked in Matthew broke into laughter.

'I must say you do have a way with words,' as he helped himself to another piece of apple pie Hazel had baked. 'Sebastian's very lucky having his own private chef.'

'Remember, Matthew, if things get tough, you can move in here for a while. We need only a bed in the room across from the dining room—after all, who needs a living room?'

'Thanks, I might just take you up on it. You never know.'

'You're right, you never know.'

Before he left, Matthew said he would be ready for the ride into the property to see the homestead directly after Sebastian was off to school.

'Shall we take something for lunch? Yes, why not?' suggested Hazel, not waiting for a reply. 'I'll prepare a picnic lunch and we can be back before Sebastian's home.' With that Matthew left, but not before holding Hazel's arm tightly. 'Thanks for everything,' he said, and he left, making sure the screen door closed without any sound that could have woken Sebastian.

Hazel cleaned up and began preparations for the picnic lunch. It was so strange. In such a short time he had managed to fit into the rhythm of country time. Ten o'clock was late, the house was generally in darkness and here he was thinking in the same way. 'Gosh, ten o'clock,' and then he laughed. 'Only two weeks ago I never finished work before midnight or later.'

* * * * *

The next morning they saw Sebastian off to school and then, while Matthew brought over the two saddled horses, Hazel scurried inside and returned with two large bags, one with food and the implements, as well as two bottles of white wine in a cooler bag.

'You're too much, Hazel!' laughed Matthew.

'You'd better believe it!' And they mounted and made their way at an easy pace toward the heart of the property. Matthew was not exaggerating. The drive must once, thought Hazel, have had an avenue of these gum trees. Matthew said he was quite correct, and that the avenue went on for miles, but many had died and just collapsed. No one had bothered to clean up or replant any. They continued their ride, protected here and there by the trees, but the roadway was in very poor condition and after only twenty minutes they had to dodge around six long fallen trees.

'You're a man of mystery,' said Hazel at last. 'You keep everything in tidy boxes, don't you?'

'I suppose so,' and Hazel had to accept that he was going to have to wait a long time before this man opened up to him.

As they came closer to their destination, Hazel noticed his companion was much more relaxed and more jovial, although sometimes he thought a little too jovial at his expense, but he was so beautiful Hazel couldn't believe it. No wonder Sebastian loved him, his advantage being that he could hug and kiss him—just his luck, Hazel thought.

The ride was very pleasant: it had been years since Hazel had ridden but he held his saddle well. 'Does Sebastian ride?' he asked, breaking a silence.

'Yes, he does. I taught him when he was about five years old. He is a bit of a cowboy and not very good at dressage because he gets tired of being told what to do all the time.'

'I hope it's not like that at school.'

'No, don't worry. He'll be fine—I know he will.'

The clear blue sky and the blazing sun with the smell of the gum trees and the constant cawing of crows made this morning for Hazel seem special, even though he could remember better places and better temperatures, but today, with Matthew, he wouldn't have traded places with anyone.

Yet another diversion faced them, but, to Hazel's surprise, it was a partly collapsed bridge. 'What on earth is a bridge doing out here?' he asked. Matthew pointed to the slight hill on their right. It appeared that if there was a lot of rain, this particular section became flooded and the water drained down under the bridge into the valley on their left. Hazel looked to the left but couldn't see what Matthew was talking about. All he could see were patches of dry grass and red soil everywhere. They walked the horses down and around the broken bridge and up the other side and continued talking of everything and nothing.

'Only another ten or fifteen minutes. When the house was built and horses were the only means of transport, this homestead was considered very isolated, so it was almost self-sufficient, as you'll see, with buildings that served specific purposes, that were all designed to last.'

'Matthew, I must say your gift of a watch to Sebastian for his first day at school was very thoughtful. I was so concerned about the uniform and his school bag I never thought to give him a gift. Being a guardian is not so easy, is it?'

'Not at all. But you are doing a great job. Sebastian hasn't stopped talking about his bedroom with the curtains and new paint job. He really is quite impressed. And as for the watch, I bought it in a shop that was closing down so the price wasn't bad, and I bought it for Christmas, not for now. But I figured he would get more use out of it now, and so now I have to think of another present for him.'

'Yes, and its only about six week's away, isn't it?'

'Are you staying here, or are you going back to Melbourne?' Matthew asked.

'I haven't really thought of it,' replied Hazel truthfully. 'I've been so busy organising the cottage and trying to work out where the money is going. Lester has sent me another email with a lot more facts and figures. It all seems a jumble to me.' Matthew said nothing, but looked across and smiled. He knows much more about this problem than he is letting on, Hazel thought.

The last part of the ride was uneventful, with both of them getting to know one another. The horses were now used to stepping over branches or being directed off the drive and back again. Hazel noticed again how many trees were missing from what once must have been a formal drive.

'What sort of music do you like?' he asked casually.

'All sorts, but believe it not I really like ballet music. I have quite a few CDs. Do you find that strange for a country boy?'

'Not at all,' was the answer, 'but I will lay a bet it's not Pat's favourite music,' and laughed.

'No, Pat is definitely a country and western fan.'

'And that's the one type of music I loathe. Ghastly stuff!'

Hazel noticed it first, because the textures were so different: two enormous date palms stood sentinels to the entrance of the homestead block—and then he saw the house itself and reined his horse. If he had seen a mature dinosaur grazing nearby he could not have been more surprised. It was enormous! This huge rectangle of tin stood proudly for all to admire. 'Good heavens!' was all he could say, and edged his horse closer to the building. So this was Killkenny, a statement in tin and corrugated iron that had been constructed to show that a certain Anthony O'Malley had left his mark on this planet for eternity, a grand building, with a great deal of architectural detail—but made of tin. Hazel was unable to grasp it all, the surprise, or even shock, was so great. He sat silently trying to understand why he was so confused.

'It's quite a house, isn't it?' commented Matthew.

'It most certainly is.' Hazel stared at the façade. The complex was laid out symmetrically as one entered, between the two huge but very bedraggled palm trees. A large space unfolded that was heavily planted with a different type of eucalyptus tree, not as tall as the ones that lined the drive, but they spread out more with very thick, heavy-looking limbs. The foliage was darker and denser in this large area, to right and left, leaving a huge rectangle with six or seven of these other trees where there were the foundations of previous buildings, which must have formed a courtyard for the main house.

'Where have those buildings gone?' asked a bewildered Hazel.

'Well, the cottages at the gate came from here and perhaps the nucleus of our house also. I'm not sure, you see. The move to the front gate was done long before we came here, so I am only guessing about our house.' Matthew dismounted and tied his horse up. Hazel followed suit. Off the horse, the building seemed even larger.

'When was it built?

'I'm told about 1840 to 1850. You see there was another building here before it and old Mr. O'Malley pulled it down and had this one built and apparently then laid out the surrounding buildings in the same manner but all in tin. As I said before, because it was a cheap building material, he could build bigger and grander without spending a fortune, although it seems to me he did spend quite a considerable amount here, as the building bug bit into him relatively hard.'

Before exploring the main house, Matthew drew Hazel's attention to the reason the homestead had been built here, the water. To the right of this large courtyard but close to the main house was a brick complex of troughs for sheep. Some were badly cracked and the water idly trickled out onto the earth and in that zone green grass thrived. Hazel walked over to investigate and glanced at the grass as one would an exotic orchid. 'So all this water just goes to waste, does it?' he asked and his shoe went down into the soft mud.

'I'm afraid so. This section of the property has virtually been forgotten,' and they walked back to the front.

The impact was overwhelming, due to the fact that there were trees at the front but nothing behind the house, just that flat red earth that seemed to continue into infinity and a heat haze that blurred the image of the empty landscape. The façade was symmetrical with an even number of windows right and left that were repeated again upstairs. The thing that gave the character to this huge form was an impressive porch section two floors high. The top of it was trimmed with ornate cast iron and the balcony on the first level had a decorative balustrade with the same sort of ornamentation. The porch was topped by a sloping two metre tin tower that finished in a square at the top and was barred with a cast iron fence protecting the flag pole which was the pinnacle. The tower and its many fine veranda posts with tiny capitals on the freeze above was the major feature of the house. It was not a practical building for this zone, as the rest of the walls were not protected by verandas and so the sun mercilessly beat in on the tin walls all day long. Some of the sheets had become loose with time but the odd thing was that at the front the tin was flat while on the other three sides it was corrugated, as was the roof and tower. Underneath the spouting were decorative corbels which gave the house a still more pompous look. It appeared that at some stage it had been painted a stone colour but most of it had disappeared with time. The only paintwork that remained was that around the windows, of an ochre colour, and the main door downstairs with a fanlight over the top, painted the same shade. On the upstairs veranda a pair of French windows opened out so one could see anyone coming up the drive from a long way back, as the front porch was on a direct axis with the long, straight drive. The windows were generous, with four large, rectangular panes of glass, two up and two down. Although it gave the appearance of being completely abandoned, the house still had a determined air of grandeur despite the material that it was made of.

'Can we go inside?' asked Hazel.

Matthew laughed. 'You're the administrator, not me! Of course we can go inside,' and he led the way. The front door was not locked, so once up the two stone steps they moved into a dark but very hot interior. Directly ahead was a staircase and a landing that boasted an arched window in coloured glass. The same garish colours they very probably used in the church, thought Hazel. To the right and left were large reception rooms, not furnished but with paintings still hanging on the walls, covered in shreds of old cloth. The light fixtures were draped in the same way and everything was covered in a thick film of red dust. Behind these two rooms were yet two more large rooms, but less decorative and beyond them again a maze of small rooms that functioned once upon a time as scullery, kitchen and service areas.

They started up the stairs with Hazel wondering if they were in fact safe. 'Don't worry,' said Matthew, 'the house looks a wreck but it was built very well,' and they inspected the first floor, with the same plan as below except that the two front rooms were large and gracious, each with an ornate cornice and huge ceiling rose. The space behind was divided up into several smaller rooms, one obviously a type of bathroom with no plumbing, only a tin bath hanging bravely on a peg on the wall. Obviously all the water would have to be brought up in buckets. Hazel looked around and then opened the French doors onto the upper level of the porch.

'Don't step out there!' cried Matthew. 'The timbers out there are probably rotten.' Hazel drew back rapidly and closed the doors. His hands were covered in red dust. 'Well,' he said flippantly, 'I guess it's the maid's day off!'

'Look's like it. I think we could do with a drink. What about you?' and they went downstairs, with Hazel gazing at everything, mentally making a note of all of it.

He spread a cloth on the ground under one of the spreading gum trees and unpacked their lunch, but it was the bottle and glasses that were the first priority. While Hazel opened the first bottle, Matthew took the other and walked to the water system and plunged it into the cold water. 'You know, Hazel, the water from the well is freezing cold. It's odd; you'd expect it to be tepid.'

'In this climate you would, yes,' replied Hazel, handing him a full glass.

Facing the house, on the left, away from this large forecourt area, stood an ornate coach house and stable block, again in tin, and topped with a much smaller tower, similar to the house and also in poor condition.

'If you look past the coach house, the land drops suddenly about two metres and stretches for miles. They built here so that if there was ever a flood this position was safe and they had access to the main road. In fact, the Wallaces' homestead is built on the same position on the other side of the sunken land mass, about two miles away.'

Hazel prepared lunch, swishing away the occasional irritating flies.

'Wow!' exclaimed Matthew. 'This is quite a spread.'

'Made with my own tiny hands!' smiled Hazel. 'But the thing I can't understand is why they took most of the furniture to the gate and left the paintings on the walls and the curtains and pelmets intact. Wouldn't you have thought they would have moved everything?'

'Yes, it is a bit odd. I just don't know.'

'Oh, there's no electricity,' said Hazel.

'That's right. Perhaps that is why they packed up and headed to the gate. It was too expensive or just too difficult to bring the power in here. Remember, it's a long time ago.'

'Yes,' as Hazel helped himself to another drink and filled Matthew's glass as well. 'But all the wallpaper peeling off, and the red dust everywhere inside. I didn't notice a broken window, did you?'

'The dust seeps in everywhere, especially if there's a wind storm.

'Matthew, does it ever rain here?'

'Believe it or not, yes, but not very regularly. But when it comes down it really pours and because the ground is so dry it runs off quickly and this causes erosion, so everything floods if we get a lot of rain.'

'Apart from the trees down the drive and the trees here around the front of the house, there aren't many about the property that you can see.'

'In the back part of Killkenny there are more trees but you're right, there are not many trees in the front of the property. I wanted to begin to plant lines of trees to give shade and also where we have erosion problems to halt the soil moving, but Dad wouldn't have a bar of it.'

'Oh, wouldn't he?' smiled Hazel, mischievously. 'I like this place here. There's something magic about it. Its isolation—it's like having your own little world.'

'Yes, that's true. It's a very special place. The aboriginals believed that this spot had a magic quality, something to do with the water being so cold.'

'Really?' and Hazel surveyed the façade of the house yet again.' Not bad, he thought, not bad at all.

'You like it, don't you? said Matthew. 'I can see you making plans already,' and he smiled at the thought.

'It has the most fabulous possibilities and imagine when it's totally restored it's sure to be grander than the Wallaces.' Hazel swept his hand around, dramatically.

They finished a late lunch and the wine, but Hazel insisted on another tour of the interior. It was the first two grand rooms as one entered that caught his imagination, the pressed tin ceilings in pale green, pink and highlighted with gold; the dust filled curtains which hung in shreds, the covered paintings and central light fixtures—but despite all this it was not an unhappy atmosphere. The house had been forgotten but it had originally been built with a certain pride and that remained totally intact.

They rode back, continuing to dodge tree trunks across the drive and had a good half hour before a very enthusiastic Sebastian leapt off the bus into Matthew's arms and hurriedly began recounting his adventures at school.

* * * * *

That evening, after dinner without Matthew, and with Sebastian in bed, Hazel, as he did every two or three nights, telephoned Mary from the kitchen, with the door closed so as not to disturb the boy.

'I'm so glad you called,' she said. 'I have some interesting news for you. I went yesterday evening to a dinner party with Keven and his friend.'

"Friend', did you say?' Hazel interrupted.

'Yes, can you believe it? After all these years, he has fallen for a young architecture student.'

'How nice for him,' was the sarcastic reply.

Mary paused. 'What's wrong? You knew he slept around.'

'Yes,' came the even more brittle reply. 'I know he slept around, as you put it. How's the renovation of the house going?'

'Oh, everything is going to plan,' she replied, awkwardly, very aware that the news about Keven was not what Hazel wanted to hear.

They continued to talk but it was rather stilted and Hazel didn't even bother to tell Mary about Killkenny. He ended the call on a ploy that Sebastian was calling and he would call back the next evening. He sat staring at the newly-installed stove but not seeing anything. If he had at that moment been looking at a Rembrandt it would have been no different. 'Had', yes that was the correct word. He had been had. Keven had used him and that was it. There had been no sentiment at all, just words used to pursue a fool—yes, a fool—to do what he didn't wish to do himself, and now he was fooling about with a young architecture student and he, Hazel, was sitting in the middle of what seemed to him at this moment to be the end of the world.

He had an overwhelming desire to smash plates or glasses or anything, but thought better of it with Sebastian asleep, so he tiptoed out of the back door into the dark, hot night, accompanied only by the sounds of the dogs barking now and again. He walked to the front gate and sat on the log that Matthew used when he waited for Sebastian to arrive from school. All of a sudden, a great sense of emptiness swept over him and he began to cry quietly, the tears streaming down his face. He held his head in his hands and let this feeling of abandonment sweep over him.

He didn't know how long he had been there but he finally roused himself and went back to the cottage. He entered the kitchen and to his surprise found Matthew sitting there having a drink. He immediately stood up and came over to hold him. 'Are you all right?' he asked in a worried way.

'Yes, I am fine, just a case of self-pity, I'm afraid. Would you pour me a drink?' and he sat down and explained his plight. 'No fool like an old fool,' he said.

'Not at all,' was the reply. 'You had a dream, about someone who used your dream for his own benefit. I'm sorry to tell you it happens all the time.'

'Thanks,' replied Hazel, flatly. 'I may just leave suicide until tomorrow.'

Matthew laughed. 'If anyone can survive in this part of the world it's you. Come on, we have had governesses here for five years and in two or so weeks you have made a home for Sebastian. It's more than any of them did and don't think that Sebastian is not appreciative because he is.'

'Well, it appears that in this world I can make one person happy.'

'Not just one,' was the quiet reply.

'Why do we think that if things were just a little bit different everything would work out well for us? Why are we so stupid?'

'I don't think it's stupidity. It's more the idea of sharing with someone special and that doesn't always fall into place, but the fact that we have these feelings for someone else and we don't look for reward or money, makes us part of the better half of the human race.'

Hazel stared at him. Matthew had never spoken to him like this before. 'I suppose,' he began quietly, 'that your situation is the same, the divorce and everything.'

'No, that's very different. That was a real case of stupidity, of being in a difficult situation and not having the courage to tell everyone to mind their own business.' Here he stopped and Hazel stood up, went to the fridge for another bottle of wine, opened it and poured them both another glass.'

'I shouldn't,' said Matthew.

'Think of it as a nightcap,' and Hazel smiled.

'That's better,' Matthew responded. 'You look much better when you smile.' Hazel said nothing but slowly finished his drink. 'It's the hurt inside that annoys me. Keven was not my lover. I guess I was kidding myself that with time he would be. What an idiot I have been. Oh well,' with a sigh, 'I suppose the world will keep turning.'

'Yes, it always seems to,' and Matthew stood up, heading for the door. 'I'll see you tomorrow. Goodnight, Hazel, and don't kid yourself—you are doing a great job here, despite the rat in Melbourne.'

Hazel laughed. 'Thanks for the lesson in philosophy. I'll see you in the morning.'

As he lay in bed, the overwhelming sadness began to change ever so slowly. Hell has no fury like a queen scorned, he thought, and began to think of revenge. I could just toss it all in and return to Melbourne. Then he remembered that he did not have an apartment and as he'd only been on the new job so short a time and hadn't really done anything Keven would not give him the apartment in East Melbourne. What should he do, what should he do . . . and he drifted off to sleep with a chorus of barking from the sheds behind Jan and Bob's house.

* * * * *

The next morning saw a very different Hazel, determined and out for blood. The two of them saw Sebastian off to school, and this morning, for the first time, Sebastian kissed Hazel after Matthew, before climbing aboard and disappearing into the heat haze.

"Well, it seems you're now part of the family.'

'Well, in that case why don't we have a family reunion in *my*—' and Hazel emphasised the word, 'in *my* dining room in exactly half an hour? Organise it for me, will you, and I'm including Jan.'

He turned back to the cottage, and, immediately inside, dialled Mr Lester and asked exactly how much money remained in the accounts and what was expected. He hung up, worked out a few tidy bits of arithmetic on his laptop and waited like a spider for the prey to enter.

When all were seated, Hazel began, 'We are all moving back to Killkenny.' There was dead silence, as everyone looked at each other. Hazel looked at Pat: 'You and your chainsaw will start today to cut all the fallen trees into moveable sections, find an open space to put them all together and when there is no wind, and with the district fire brigade's permission we shall burn the lot. I don't want one twig left. Do you understand me?'

Pat just nodded, terrified that if he said one word and his father was not happy with him there would be trouble.

Hazel turned to Bob next. 'You will assist him, but while this is going on, the flocks of sheep are to be moved to the back of Killkenny where fodder is much more available and that will probably require a bricklayer to put the troughs in order, as the one near the homestead is badly cracked and the water is escaping.'

'Do it yourself,' was the brittle response.

'Oh no, sweetie! You lift your arse and get going or you're fired. Do you understand—fired?' Hazel was getting angry.

'Matthew, telephone the electricity company and get them to lay an underground cable from the gate to the house. Let's see if we can be ready for the move just after Christmas.'

Bob was black with rage. He knew only too well that Matthew had been speaking to Hazel, otherwise how would he know about the back section of the property being more productive. 'I'll only do what I have to,' he spat at Hazel.

'You will do exactly what I tell you, Bob dear,' replied Hazel sarcastically, 'or, sweetie pie, you will do a stretch in prison for embezzlement. Please yourself. Oh,' he went on, lowering his voice in a theatrical manner,' I do hope you understand.'

Bob pushed his chair back and stormed out of the cottage.

'Just a minute!' called Hazel to Pat, who automatically did the same as Bob. 'I haven't done with you yet, or you,' turning to Jan. 'That drive must be opened up as soon as possible. Do you understand? For the moment, the cut timber can be pushed to the side, and,' raising his voice,' I do mean 'for the moment'. I am not going to have Sebastian's heritage ending up as a scrap heap like this complex at the gate. Is that clear?'

'Yeah. I'll start now.' Pat made a quick exit, to find Bob glowering with rage at being told what to do "by a fucking poof", as he said to Pat.

'Jan, darling,' began Hazel,' you will sort out what you need and what you don't, because in a week or so a large truck will arrive to take all this shit away. Not one piece of unnecessary furnishing or equipment do we keep before the house moves back to the homestead. Do you hear me?'

'If you think I am going to live in that old wreck, you're wrong,' she shouted.

'Oh, sweetie, I am not wrong. You most certainly are *not* going to live in the homestead.'

'I expect you think we will live under canvas, do you?' she replied bitterly.

'No, darling, the greater part of the house you are living in will be transferred back with or without you. I quite frankly couldn't care less.'

'Smart arse! And just who *is* going to live in the homestead, then?'

'Why, don't you know? Come on, Jan, you're so fucking smart. Work it out.'

She said nothing, just looked at Matthew for support, but there was none coming.

'I'll just let you into a little secret, Jan babe. The people taking up residence in the main house will be Sebastian, me, of course,' and here he smiled,' and Matthew.'

Jan spun round on him. 'You, living in the big house!' she said, in amazement.

'So it seems,' was his reply.

She pushed her chair back with a grating sound on polished floor. 'You're fucking mad! You don't have a clue what you're doing,' she shouted, waving her fat finger at Hazel. 'You're wrong, you know.'

Hazel answered softly, 'I know exactly what I am doing and I am going to do it. I'm sorry that you are going to have to put up with Bob yelling and howling insults at me, but that's the way it has to be. Now, sweetie, have a look around your house and everything that doesn't work or you'll never use again, put on the heap near the shed with the tractors and we shall get rid of it.'

She did not say another word but the sharp closing of the screen door meant she was not a happy woman.

'How the hell did you know about the back pastures?' asked Matthew the moment Jan had left.

'Why didn't you tell me?' asked Hazel. 'Anyway, no matter what happens here your job is secure. Sebastian without you would wither away and die, or, even worse, end up Pat's weight.'

'But who told you about the back of the property?' Here Hazel bluffed. It had only been a theory after an off-the-cuff comment Sebastian had passed, and so Hazel now played Matthew out for all he could to get to the truth about the mismanagement of the property. 'Well, Lester and I have been doing a Miss Marple and we stumbled on the answer to the problem here. How long have you known about it?'

A long sigh was Matthew's initial response. 'Always, I suppose, but I could hardly have my own father put in prison, could I?'

'You couldn't, but I could!' was the swift reply. 'Now, what's your version of the story? I don't plan to call the police tomorrow, so you can relax for the moment. Now, sweetie, what about the back of this property? And if my memory serves me right, I think you said Killkenny and the Wallaces' property have a common boundary. Am I right?' He lifted one eyebrow, while Matthew sat quite still, not seeming a hundred per cent sure if Hazel knew what he was talking about or was bluffing. Hazel suddenly realised that he would have to push very hard or lose this moment and be none the wiser. 'Matthew, darling, do you know how many years in prison you get for embezzling other people's money? And I wonder how the law accepts the term 'accomplice'?'

'Are you threatening me?' asked Matthew.

'Not yet,' and there was another silence, until Matthew broke it with, 'Yes, you're correct. Dad and the Wallace guy have come to an arrangement about using the back pastures of Killkenny—'

'And—?'

'Not all the bales of wool are sold with a Killkenny stamp on them.'

'But they have the Wallace stamp?'

'Yes. What do you plan to do?'

'For the moment, it's more what you are going to do. You will immediately contact the electricity commission and say we have an emergency and have the electricity cable laid to the main house. Then, my handsome young man,' Hazel was feeling well in control, 'you will locate a company that transports houses and we shall move the two cottages, Jan and Bob's house or the main part. The skillion parts can be demolished and the church on the corner can all be transported to the homestead.'

"When?'

'Yesterday! And, by the way, you had better move your bed into the room across from the dining room here. I don't want Bob or Pat cutting your throat in the middle of the night?'

'Who told you about the pastures at the back of the property?' Matthew asked again.

Hazel swept up and kissed a surprised Matthew on the forehead. 'No one, sweetie. It was a wild guess and if men don't come in occasionally, a guess will.'

Matthew shook his head. 'I suppose you think I am as guilty as Dad?'

'No, I don't. Your father was in charge, so the responsibility is his and although the fact that he determined policy here doesn't exactly clear you, Pat or Jan from taking Sebastian's money—because that's what you have all been doing—I am prepared to look at the situation from another perspective. With Sebastian's irresponsible parents and Keven's indifference, it doesn't make for a loyal partnership but the thing that saves you is Sebastian's love.'

'I haven't touched the money. I get exactly what Mr Lester sends me in a cheque once a month, the same as Pat and Mum. What has happened to the so-called extra I have no idea at all.'

'I believe you,' said Hazel. 'Now, off you go and make the telephone calls. Oh, and I shall need a carpenter, an electrician and a plumber—now!' He smiled. 'It's all right. The world hasn't fallen on top of you. In fact, you may just find that the opposite has happened. Bob is not going to do anything to upset the applecart now, especially as there is a jail sentence if he is reported, so as from this moment you are totally responsible for the running, and I may say the recovery, of Killkenny.' Matthew stood up, but his knees felt very weak and he had a foreboding that all this change might be good but in the long run it was going to be Hazel pulling the string, not his father, and someone else would be manipulating his life as in the past, but not him.

*　　*　　*　　*　　*

There was exactly six weeks to Christmas. They were frenetic: quotations, rejection of them, new quotations, the organisation of moving the whole living area into the homestead zone. It was enormous. Although Bob had no alternative, he still could not be considered co-operative and Hazel lost no time correcting him and demanding that what he wanted done was done.

One afternoon, Hazel sat with Matthew waiting for the school bus. 'In the future, meeting the bus is going to be a little more difficult,' said Matthew. 'The homestead isn't just a few paces away.'

'No, it isn't, but that's not a problem. We shall organise our time. Oh, and by the way, every day we are here I mean to ask you what are those wooden frames in the grass over there?' he said, pointing to two, large thick decorative wooden carved panels.

'Oh, they were the front gates.'

'Really?' Hazel got up to check them out. 'But the bottom section seems to be missing on one of them.'

'Yes, they've lain there for years and the bottom one, which touched the ground, has just rotted away.'

'Can we have them repaired?'

'I suppose so. It's just a matter of finding a carpenter that can do the work.

'Well, guess what your task is for the next week.' He smiled at Matthew.

'Thanks a million, Hazel! I suppose you want the brick pillars replaced and the curved wall as well?'

'Got it in one,' replied Hazel in an offhand manner, and moved over to survey the broken or rotted gates, and then turned back to Matthew. He was beautiful—no he was deliciously handsome and with the new feeling of control he seemed to be more in Hazel's grasp, except that his private life was completely mysterious. He would not speak of it at all, which kept Hazel at bay. He wasn't keen on Hazel taking over the making of all the great changes at Killkenny, but on the other hand he knew very well that without the knowledge of his father's and Pat's mismanagement, he could not have done it at all. The blackmail was loud and clear: 'Do it, or I will expose you.'

If Bob hated Hazel before, now he loathed him and was genuinely afraid that a wrong gesture or word might just set this hysterical person off. He might receive the worst of it, namely exposure for fraud at Killkenny over many years. Bob, behind Hazel's back, was most critical about moving. The little church he couldn't see the point of, in fact he was all for torching it, but wisely decided that to anger Hazel was not very clever. But all this reorganising of the buildings took time and then logistics had to be taken into consideration. The drive might be clear, with a new bridge, but to move everything at once meant no toilets and no running water for more than a week or so. Yet Hazel was determined to do it.

The plumbers and carpenters began work on the homestead almost at once, but as Christmas loomed, the work was still not completed.

School had broken up for a seven week vacation so Sebastian found himself without his new friends, but he was overjoyed to be spending all his time with Matthew, and now as Matthew was in complete control Hazel thought it a good idea that Sebastian should get to know the running of his own property.

'Well, what are we doing for Christmas? asked Hazel, one evening a week before the big day. Matthew was now resident in the cottage, which pleased both Hazel and Sebastian immensely, with the latter waking very early and bounding into his bedroom, waking him with his arms around him and kissing him. Quite often, now Sebastian was on holiday, Hazel would join them with a cup of tea for Matthew and fruit juice for Sebastian, who to Hazel's great delight was beginning to lose a few kilos. It was at these moments that Hazel yet again was constantly surprised at their physical similarity.

The Christmas celebrations, it appeared, were to fall well before the move to the homestead and as every year Jan spent Christmas Day and the following day with her sister at Bradbury, Bob and Pat were left to their own devices, which consisted of television and beer. Hazel decided to have a Christmas in the cottage for Matthew and Sebastian. They would drive to Midnight Mass at Bradbury and then have a late lunch the next day. Sebastian was very excited. Hazel noted that he never became boring or obsessive or needed special attention: he was simply happy in Matthew's presence and now in Hazel's. He helped Hazel make a Christmas cake. 'We should have done it in October, I'm afraid,' confessed Hazel, 'but we didn't have that much time. Next year, sweetie,' he went on, giving him the bowl to scrape out and digest, 'we shall have a big Christmas party and invite your uncle. What do you think?'

Sebastian put down the plate scraper he was using to extract the last bits from the bowl and looked up seriously. 'Hazel, why do we need Keven?'

'Well, he's your uncle,' and then realised that Sebastian hadn't given him the title 'uncle'.

'I think,' the boy said determinedly, 'you, me and Matthew are quite enough.'

Whether it was the way he said it or perhaps it was the emotion that Hazel received from this message, but he turned around completely and kissed the boy. 'Thank you,' were all the words he could muster, and he turned hurriedly back in case the tears in the corners of his eyes were showing.

Three days before Christmas, Matthew returned from Bradbury with a Christmas tree: actually it was a Norfolk Island pine in a big pot with two boxes of lights and tinsel and coloured balls. It was if it were the first time in his life Sebastian had had a Christmas. His enthusiasm was infectious, the two men joining in the enjoyment with him.

'Later,' said Matthew, 'you can plant the Christmas tree at the homestead and you will have a Christmas tree for life.' He put an arm around Matthew's shoulders as he was on his knees trying to work the light system out. When he was completely bent over, Sebastian hopped on his back like riding a horse, laughed and then fell forward to kiss him on the side of his face.

'I love you, Matthew.'

'I love you too,' and he rolled over onto his back and hugged the boy with his eyes full of tears.

'Darling,' interrupted Hazel, 'would you run over and ask Jan if she has some fine wire.'

The boy jumped up enthusiastically and raced out, the screen door slamming behind him. Hazel took a deep breath and looked directly into two very wet blue eyes. 'One day, Matthew, you are going to tell me everything.'

'One day.' He wiped his eyes and stood up. 'Thanks for what you are doing for Sebastian this year for Christmas. I suppose it's really the first time he has had a Christmas with a tree and presents and

I believe, according to him, the most special Christmas cake in the world.'

'Christmas only works if everyone tries,' replied Hazel, who was generally considered cynical on the subject. Yet here he was setting up with the other two a Christmas tree in the corner of the dining room and planning to go to Midnight Mass an hour away and then back. He had found it difficult to buy a present for Sebastian and it had been Jan who had told him of an antique-cum-gift shop at the back of a very seedy arcade in Bradbury, and it was here he managed to buy gifts for all.

There had been a nineteenth century painting of a dog similar to the dogs Sebastian played with at Killkenny, so gift number one was purchased. As Matthew was so mysterious, and never gave any information about himself it was impossible to know his taste. Then Hazel saw, in a box in a corner, part of an ornate ruby glass kerosene lamp. 'Do you have all the pieces for this?' he asked.

'Certainly,' replied a rather withered, grey-haired woman with snake-like eyes. 'Are you interested?'

'Depends on the price and what it looks like set up.'

'All my prices are reasonable,' the woman snapped,' as is my merchandise. None of this rubbish you find in the local stores. I happen to sell quality goods.'

'And who would doubt you?' smiled Hazel, not exactly sincerely.

The grey-haired woman mounted the ruby lamp and told him the price, at which Hazel narrowed his eyes and said, in an confident voice, 'Listen, I am purchasing the dog painting, a lamp and I may just be interested in that large landscape oleograph in the gilt frame. Will you give me a price for the lot?'

She scratched the side of her mouth, looking at Hazel. 'What do you want, luvvie, blood?'

'No, sweetie, just a fair price,' at which the haggling began.

He then paid a visit to the supermarket and was sorely tempted to return to the shoe shop to see the handsome young man. 'But of course, Sebastian needs a pair of slippers if we move into the homestead,' he persuaded himself and joyfully swept into the store to purchase the said slippers.

'Well,' said the attractive young man, 'I thought we should never see you again.' Instantly, Hazel was ready, being well experienced in the field of dealing with young men who thought they could con older men simply with a few words and a smile.

'I thought I'd just pop in to break your boredom.'

'Thank God you did,' sighed the young man. 'Oh, by the way, my name is Gerald. And yours?'

'Hazel' was the reply.

'Oh, I am sorry. What did you want,' he asked, with a feeling of confusion of which Hazel took full advantage, asking 'Well, what are we doing for Christmas?'

'Oh, the usual family stuff.'

'Dashing off to a capital city for New Year, I suppose?'

'Oh, if only! If life here becomes any more exciting I shall cut my wrists for the first of the year,' smiling at Hazel.

'Don't do that, handsome. You never know what's around the corner.'

'I'll just wait,' was the response and a pair of burgundy slippers with a little coat of arms embroidered on the toe and marked 'Made in China' was placed in a box.

'Gift wrapped?'

"Why not?'

'You're not from around here, are you?' the assistant asked.

'I am now. I'm resident at Killkenny.'

Gerald fumbled with the knot and looked straight at Hazel. 'Killkenny—Matthew!' He gave a sigh and recommenced tying the bow on the shoe box.

'It has its moments,' quipped Hazel, jauntily. 'Happy Christmas, Gerald. I am sure the next year will see us the best of friends.'

'I have an odd feeling you're right. Happy Christmas, Hazel.' He looked much happier.

As Hazel headed back to Killkenny with the lilac Volkswagon filled to bursting, he thought about Gerald, but more so he thought of Matthew. What was it about this man that seemed to captivate everyone? Why was he so damned secretive about his life and the divorce or decree of nullity? What the hell was it all about—and, by the way, he thought, how does the good-looking young man in the shoe store also know and obviously think more of him than just a customer? Hm . . . I wonder!

He recounted all of this to Mary, who was bitterly disappointed that he was not coming back for Christmas. 'Oh, Hazel, you are so selfish! I am here all by myself and you are lonely up there. Come on, have a break, bring Sebastian with you if you want. I have three large bedrooms.'

But to no avail. Hazel, for the first time in his life, felt an aura that was taking him in hand. It was nothing he could actually describe. It was a feeling—was it Matthew? or was it Sebastian? or was it, in fact, power? He tried think it through logically in bed, with Matthew in one room and Sebastian in the other, the three of them confined in this small cottage, and, as Hazel turned over, he knew he wouldn't have had it any other way but, the split second, before he dozed off, it was the vision of Killkenny, the homestead, the tower—and in a state of half-consciousness he knew that Killkenny was claiming another victim, but in this case a willing one.

*   *   *   *   *

'Hazel, it's 10.30, we have to go now,' urged an anxious Sebastian. 'The Mass will be finished before we get there.'

'Coming!' was the cry, as Sebastian dashed in yet again to look at the presents under the tree in the dining room, and then out again. Jan drove alone, as Bob and Pat were to return alone and Hazel, Matthew and Sebastian went together. It was a very warm but comfortable evening and the church was packed. Sebastian stayed between Hazel and Matthew but this was not before Hazel had purchased at the door three mass books, knowing that if they wished to participate these were essential.

It was during Mass that Hazel looked around the congregation and to his pleasant surprise there was Gerald, but with an extraordinarily tall woman who defied description. After the Mass, Hazel remained very close to Matthew, especially when Gerald came over and wished them a happy Christmas, which they all echoed.

'I'd like you to meet Carmel,' smiled Gerald.

'Charmed!' said Hazel, to this extraordinary woman who had long, straight, black hair, very made-up eyes, a long nose and extremely arched eyebrows. Her lips were scarlet and her nails lacquered black, and on top of the black hair was a black mantilla. In fact, all her clothing was black and in a jersey type of fabric that clung to her very thin body.

'We are going to be exceptionally good friends,' she said to Hazel in a theatrical voice.

'Without any doubt,' he replied, equally theatrically, but noticing Gerald's eyes resting on and drinking in the perfect form called Matthew.

'We must be going, darling,' said Carmel to Gerald. 'If I don't get a drink I am sure to pass out.' Matthew laughed as he held a very tired Sebastian in his arms.

'Let's see if we can organise something soon,' said Gerald.

It was then, although Hazel had his back to the person that passed, that he felt a sharp tension in his body. When he turned to see who it had been, he saw only the back of a man moving quickly away, followed by a blonde woman. He had the oddest feeling—or was it a sixth sense—that he knew him. But how?

'Come on, let's get you home,' interrupted Matthew, but this was not before they had wished Jan a happy Christmas. Hazel gave her a kiss: 'You will have to wait till you get home for your present.'

Jan looked quite embarrassed. 'Oh,' she said, stepping from one foot to the other, 'you didn't have to get me a present.'

'I hope you'll like it,' and they all moved off toward the car.

Wishing Bob and Pat a happy Christmas was possibly the correct thing to do, but Hazel thought it came so close to hypocrisy that he would give it a miss.

Sebastian was carried by Matthew to his bed, as it was by then twenty past two in the morning. He undressed him and covered him with a sheet, then went to the bathroom, but on his return saw Hazel with two glasses of champagne.

'I think we should drink to *his* birthday, don't you?' he asked. Matthew smiled a sensual smile, which seemed to say why not. 'And how do you feel after your first month and a half here?

'I'll tell you next Christmas in the homestead,' laughed Hazel. They finished their drink and Matthew for the first time held Hazel in his arms. 'Thanks for everything,' he said, 'and thanks for looking after Sebastian and me so well.'

He kissed Hazel on the cheek and disappeared into his room. Hazel tidied up and went to his own bedroom but even though it was so late his feet had an odd sensation that they could have danced all night, especially with the man who had just kissed him.

*   *   *   *   *

Hazel was woken early the next morning by shouts from Matthew's bedroom. 'Get off!' he yelled, laughing with Sebastian.

'Come on, Matthew, let's open the presents. Can we?'

'You'd better check with Hazel,' was the reply.

'Hazel, Hazel!' was the next shriek, as Sebastian burst into Hazel's room. 'Can we open the presents now, can we please?'

'Go and put the kettle on and then we can open the gifts.' And Sebastian thundered down to the kitchen, whilst a bleary eyed Hazel dressed.

He made it to the dining room just as Matthew did. 'Happy Christmas' they chorused together.

'Let's open them now,' cried a very excited young man.

'OK. You hand the gifts around. They all have names on them,' and Sebastian took a parcel he knew had 'To Sebastian, Happy Christmas' written on the label.

'No, you have to give them all out before you can open yours,' explained Hazel and this being duly done, Sebastian had a great time pulling apart the wrapping paper to discover that Hazel had given him a painting of a dog very similar to his favourite hound that seemed to bark incessantly. And from Matthew he received a new game and a white shirt. 'Wow!' was his only reply and he sped to his bedroom where Matthew's TV sat to try out his new game. But before he started he raced back to the dining room to see Hazel and Matthew's faces as they opened his gifts to them. The small boxes were identical and inside, amongst the shredded paper one to each box, was a Christmas decoration in glass, a copy of nineteenth century ones which Sebastian, when he had had to go to Bradbury to have his hair cut, had seen in the gift shop close to the barber's and thought were beautiful. He had asked Matthew for some money, disappeared, come back with the two boxes, returned the charge to him and told him not to tell anyone as it was a secret.

'They are beautiful,' said Hazel and reached over to give him a kiss. 'Thank you, very much.'

'Mine's great. Thanks, Sebastian.' Sebastian said nothing but it was very obvious he was extremely proud of having selected the correct gift and he sped back to set his new game in motion.

Matthew slowly opened his gift from Hazel and was astounded at the beautiful ruby kerosene lamp with a matching engraved ruby shade. 'Hazel, this is just too extravagant. It's fantastic. It really is' he said, assembling the pieces.

'Well, don't I get a kiss like Sebastian?' teased Hazel and Matthew turned and kissed him. 'Thanks a million, Hazel.'

Hazel felt slightly weak but opened his gift. It was a beautiful designer tee shirt, wrapped around a bottle of French champagne. 'You didn't have to do this,' he said, softly.

'Oh, but I did.'

Hazel stood up and walked over to him and held him. 'I think this is the nicest Christmas I have ever had.'

'Me, too,' was the reply and they stood silently in one another's embrace.

'Matthew, come and have a look. The game is fabulous.' Matthew moved to Sebastian's bedroom, followed a little later by Hazel with a hammer and nail.

'Well, where do you want your painting?' The boy looked around the room. 'On the wall at the end of my bed, so I can see it every night before I go to sleep.'

Hazel found the correct spot and before long the painting of the dog was on the wall.

'You do have a smart bedroom now,' said Matthew, with a smile, while Sebastian sat on top of him.

'I'll leave you to it,' said Hazel, and disappeared in the direction of the kitchen to prepare his special Christmas lunch, in between yells and hoots of laughter coming from the bedroom. He dashed backwards and forwards between the dining room and the kitchen and laid a special Christmas setting just for the three of them. He had even found in Bradbury a shop selling Christmas crackers; he hadn't seen them for years and thought they might just add a bit more to the day as well as all the other trimmings.

At midday he joined the two of them and said the first part of lunch was ready. Sebastian, in his excitement, had forgotten breakfast and was now, in his own words, 'starving'. Hazel had also bought a good bottle of champagne and this began the celebrations—even Sebastian was allowed a little. The food was delicious and they worked their way through course after course, each one complementing the other. Not even Sebastian could eat any more and left the table to play with his new game, while Hazel and Matthew settled back to yet another bottle, laughing and joking about people they had known.

'Do you know Carmel and Gerald well?' asked Hazel.

'No, I don't. I've seen them about but I've never had any opportunity to go out with them. Remember, I have generally been here and as it's an hour in and after a few drinks you have to get back with the police about, it just isn't worth losing your licence, especially when you could end up without a car, stranded here. I know quite a few people, but I just don't see much of them. I generally make contact when I'm in town for the barber or the dentist.'

'I think a night out with Gerald and Carmel could be fun,' smiled Hazel.

'I'm sure it would.'

'Well, perhaps we shall wait until the homestead is liveable and then have them out for a lunch or dinner. What do you think?'

'Great idea! But let's get Killkenny in order first. And I must say, Hazel, your hat is very becoming!'

'As is yours, sweetie,' and the two of them fell about in helpless laughter as they still had the contents of their respected Christmas crackers on. Hazel's was bright yellow crepe paper cut in a zigzag form on the top with a large picture in a circle of a pair of budgerigars. Matthew's was the same design, except it was scarlet red and in the decorative circle contained a large parrot with his head turned sideways as if to wonder at the quantity of alcohol Hazel was consuming. And all the time Tchaikovsky's 'Nutcracker Suite' was playing romantically in the background.

CHAPTER FOUR

Adapting to Country Life

CHAPTER FOUR

Adapting to Country Life

Mary missed Hazel like crazy and even though they conversed every second evening for Mary it was just not enough. This evening she called just as Hazel was lazily thinking about Christmas dinner.

'Oh, I'll just throw some scraps together,' laughed Hazel, they spoke on, until he said that duty called, and, by the way, did she get her Christmas gift? She had, but Hazel had to say that the gift Mary had sent for him was still probably trapped in a post office while its occupants were out celebrating.

'Oh well, darling, look at it this way. I will be the only one receiving a New Year present,' he said, laughing. They wished one another the season's greetings, he hung up, then dashed to the kitchen to retrieve from the top of the fridge a medium-sized container of kerosene. He re-set the table quietly as Matthew and Sebastian were asleep together in Matthew's bed as it was the largest, so he tiptoed about preparing a magic Christmas dinner. The gift he had given Matthew was filled with kerosene and so instead of candles this tall elegant lamp cast a glow of ruby red that filled the whole dining room. From the somewhat miserable central light fixture he fixed wires and hung lots of burgundy streamers with gold and silver threads, all in paper, so when finally roused at 7.30, the two walked into a magic room full of coloured red light. Hazel had closed the blind and the curtain to create the special effect. If Sebastian was overwhelmed, so was Matthew, who had never known anyone who had gone to so much trouble just to create a moment, just as he did with the food. He and Sebastian ate everything. It was perfect, the presentation always the best. Nothing was just ordinary.

Matthew remembered one evening when everyone had been tired and hot. Hazel had gone to the large service yard behind Jan and Bob's house and collected in a bucket thirty or forty stones of all shapes and sizes and called them to the table that was laid out like a Zen garden. Every evening it was the same, some evenings more extravagant than others, but there was always an effort put in to make the two of them feel special. Hazel loved it as, for the first time in life, he had the thing he had always sent up and said he despised, a family, his very own and in a genuine way they were very dependent on him. Emotionally, little by little, he was being drawn in under their soft magic charm and to be without them now was something he could not bear to think about.

Mathew's ideas about Hazel had changed dramatically. His first impression had been that he was a queen with a sharp tongue and lots of one-liners. This initial impression hadn't changed much, but he was discovering that there was much more to him. He knew Hazel put on a front rather than showed any emotional involvement but he remembered well the evening when Hazel had dissolved in tears at the knowledge that Keven now had a young permanent boyfriend. He was about to show Matthew yet another side to his personality and it was one that determined his feelings for Hazel once and for all.

* * * * *

Between Christmas and New Year, it was necessary for Hazel to go to Bradbury to sign a contract concerning the removal of all the buildings to their new location, dependent on the introduction of electricity. Pat was oddly quite proud of having virtually single-handedly cleared the main drive, organised the new bridge planks and begun with a digger to make holes for the planting of about a hundred trees, not to mention the large number Hazel insisted on having behind the homestead, as looking into 'never-never land', as he called it, was bad for a sheep but totally depressing for a queen! Pat also dug a trench for the underground electricity cable.

Hazel found the office of a local draughtsman who organised the work, the contract was signed, a deposit paid by cheque, and the receipt duly handed over. All this was dependent on the electricity company installing the cable from the gate, but the church could be moved at any time, as could the shearers' quarters, which were to be taken from right of the road way back behind the shearing shed, into a zone where there was a small group of old gum trees. Hazel had said to Matthew he didn't believe it was possible for twenty or more men to shower behind the building with one shower head on a block of cement. 'Don't worry, Hazel, I can promise you you would never fall in love with any of them, dressed or naked,' laughed Matthew.

After dealing with the draughtsman, Hazel decided on a quick drink at the pub, then a dash to the supermarket and home but it didn't work out quite as smoothly as that. He chose to drink at the Railway Hotel, which was, needless to say, close to the railway station. The other two hotels were at the other end of Main Street. The Railway Hotel was a long single-storey red brick structure with a veranda along two sides: the entrance to the bar was at the junction of the two verandas.

Hazel parked his car and walked into the dim interior, that had large ceiling fans swishing around. There was a feeling of time having stood still, Hazel was sure, sixty years ago. The interior was the same. The long polished wooden bar was panelled, there were tiny tables along the other side near the large, stained glass windows in shades of green and red, mirrors behind the bar, which held a myriad of shelves supported by long, thin turned columns which displayed all manner of alcohol. He had the odd feeling that these many bottles were just ornament; the fluid consumed in this establishment would be almost exclusively beer.

A lilac Volkswagon parked outside was, for the locals, considered odd, if not downright foolish, but Hazel, having caught the ambience of this establishment, was ready. He asked for a large glass of dry white wine and the not-unattractive barman served him with a smile that was returned, but a group drinking at the other end of the bar thought that to ask for wine was tantamount to asking for trouble and an overweight, particularly unattractive, number called Brendan pushed his way down toward Hazel. The rest of the bar waited to see what would happen. Brendan was a bully and used his weight to force his way and his limited ideas on his peer group, rather sad considering he was forty four years old. He staggered up to Hazel and shouted, 'Fuck off out of here. No poofs allowed!'

'What's your name then, sweetie?' asked Hazel flippantly, but the effect of this remark had everyone on their toes, waiting to see the result of this suicidal phrase.

'Mine's Brendan. What's yours?

'Oh, Brenda!' whined Hazel, and Brendan knew he was being sent up and knew instantly also on this level he could only lose face, especially as there had been a titter when Hazel spoke. It was about this stage that Gerald and a work companion entered at the other end of the bar and were to witness something they would never have thought possible. Hazel baited Brendan and stupidly he did not notice that Hazel was not standing flat-footed on the floor but on the balls of his feet, ready to move. Brendan swung the first punch, missed but upset Hazel's drink and another at the bar. Immediately, the bar cleared, leaving Hazel to confront this aggressive drunk. 'You shouldn't have done that, Brenda. You are a fat, clumsy old fart.'

Brendan was furious, especially as there was hysterical laughter behind his back. He took another swing at Hazel, who deftly moved out of the way. 'Now, Brenda, if you do that again, I could get cross,' murmured Hazel in a very theatrical way, and stupidly Brendan took a third swing, catching Hazel on the very edge of his broad chin. Hazel spun into action like a top whipped to its maximum and, on one leg, he spun around and caught his opponent on the side of the face with his foot. The man stood for a moment confused, then a fist straight on to the nose and yet another swing of the leg resulted in a mighty crash, as he fell headlong into a small table and dropped unceremoniously into a large motionless heap on the floor.

'Next!' called Hazel, casually. The bar fell into silence then clapping was heard. It was Gerald and his workmate. Strangely, the clapping was infectious and Hazel was deemed the hero of the day. Two friends of Brendan delivered him to the local hospital with two broken ribs and a broken nose, which, covered in plaster, became his signature for some time, and a great deal of laughter was the extra pain he had to bear for his foolish encounter. But it was Hazel who was the star. The management, which had constantly had trouble with Brendan, were elated, Hazel's glass was instantly refilled and Gerald joined him at the bar.

'Well done.'

'I could have done it better in stilettoes and fishnet stockings but it's a bit early in the evening, don't you think?'

'Oh, but of course,' and Gerald burst into laughter, as did the rest of the drinkers in earshot.

So, by the time Hazel had been to the supermarket and returned home, Gerald had already called Matthew. What an excuse, he thought and graphically relayed every detail. 'Kick boxing, I believe it's called. Brendan was flattened like a tack,' and burst into laughter. 'You should have been there. Hazel was as cool as a cucumber and 'our dear Brenda' as Hazel called him, was awash with blood. Oh, you should have been there! The Railway Hotel has never had such a show.'

'Hazel, are you all right?' came a voice, as he dragged the supermarket bags from his car.

'Of course I am all right, Matthew, what's wrong?'

'I've just heard about the fight at the Railway.'

'Oh, it was nothing that can't be resolved with an hour or two of mouth-to-mouth resuscitation.'

'You are just impossible, Hazel,' and instinctively put his arms around him.

'If only I didn't have these bags in my hands, we could be married tomorrow,' and laughed. 'Here, take some of them,' thrusting two bags into Matthew's waiting hands.' He looked into Matthew's deep blue eyes. 'Don't worry, Matthew, I can look after myself, and, if and when it's necessary, both you and Sebastian,' and moved indoors, followed by Matthew, now completely unsure as to exactly who and what this person was that he was following, a supermarket bag in each hand.

The next morning, Bradbury was spilling over with the incident at the hotel, with much mirth from all, as at one time or another Brendan had made things difficult for everyone, the trademark of a bully, but now the boot, so to speak was on the other foot and cries of 'Brendan, careful—I see a lilac Volkswagon' followed him about for some time. The nose in plaster, like a defeated dinosaur, only made the visuals more apparent.

Matthew and Sebastian were out early the next morning, as were Bob and Pat. The whole of this eighty thousand hectare property was to be returned to the use of Killkenny. The access gates had been removed between the Wallace property, the openings wired up and once again the flocks of merinos moved about on the better pastures at the rear of the property. Hazel hadn't fired Bob; he had thought about it but realised he had a hold on him now, and, he being Bob, would be forced, whether he liked it or not, to do exactly that Hazel wanted. One other reason he hadn't fired him was because he was an expert in animal husbandry and the merino rams from Killkenny fetched very high prices. From this manoeuvring position, Hazel felt relatively secure that Sebastian as a mature young man would be able to take over a financially buoyant property.

But the day after Christmas, before Jan had returned, Hazel put the sword deep into Bob's ribs and twisted it. The conversation was short and to the point. Hazel saw Bob late afternoon, having returned from overseeing the repair of some leaking troughs. 'Bob, I need to speak to you,' he said, in a business-like tone.

Bob moved over and lowered his eyes. 'Wader ye want?' he said aggressively.

'You have bled this property for ten or so years, so your bank account must be very healthy.'

Bob said nothing but withdrew a packet of cigarettes from his hip pocket and lit up. 'So, sweetie, you will deposit into my hands A$150,000 within seven days.' Bob inhaled at just the wrong moment and began to cough. 'Go fuck yourself!' he choked.

'Oh, I'm all right, thanks,' was the reply, 'I haven't arrived at that desperate stage yet.'

'Smart arse!' came the response.

'Well, Bobby, in seven days. Oh, by the way, then, I believe, we shall be all square, so to speak. I do hope you understand me clearly.'

'Very,' was the sharp retort and he waddled away, using an amazing array of expletives under his breath.

Three or four times Hazel had decided to have this fraud issue out with the Wallaces and each time Matthew had talked him out of it. 'Not yet, Hazel. We have everything organised now. Let's get Killkenny in good working order before we begin another feud.'

It annoyed Hazel that at certain times Matthew seemed to lack the courage to tackle this Wallace problem. 'Who the hell is he, anyway?' he asked. 'He is a thief and an opportunist who has manipulated your father into doing exactly what he wants to benefit his pocket. I think I should just go over and sort matters out myself. Don't worry, I shan't use your name.'

'Hazel,' pleaded Matthew, 'this situation is much more complicated than you realise. Please don't make things more difficult than they are.'

Hazel was almost convinced to let sleeping dogs lie but not completely. He was still very concerned about many things, especially Matthew's private life. Why was he so secretive? A divorce nowadays is not the end of the world, yet no-one would speak of it. Who on earth had he been married to? Why the secrecy? And if one spoke to anyone in Bradbury and mentioned Matthew, they all fell about spilling in all directions with compliments, even Lester, who sang Matthew's praises from morning to night. In fact, it was the result of his quiet insistence that Matthew was now the manager of Killkenny. Who on earth was Matthew, he wondered? The only person who disliked him was his father: everyone else, it seemed, adored this beautiful man, especially Sebastian, and, if the truth be known, Hazel as well fitted into the group who thought him the most special person in the world.

*   *   *   *   *

Jan returned, having spent an extra day with her sister whom Bob hated (it seemed Bob excelled in hating) to find the house in a slovenly disorder—not that she was surprised. Hazel walked over later with a large rectangular package wrapped in bright blue paper. He knocked on the screen door but entered without anyone bidding him in. 'Hi, troops!' he called.

'They're not here,' came a cry from the kitchen. 'It seems there's a fair bit of work to do in the back pastures. Bob and Pat will be back about seven,' and she rounded the corner of the kitchen. 'Oh,' she said, as she saw the gift. 'You shouldn't have.'

'It's from Sebastian, Matthew and me, and you can have the gift on one condition.'

'Really?' as she looked over her glasses at him. 'What's the condition?'

'That that fucking terrible tiger rug on the wall goes.'

Jan laughed. 'I don't remember who nailed it up there. It's been there for years.' Hazel handed her the gift and she tore the wrapping paper away to expose an oleograph of Landseer's painting, a large 19th century landscape with the 'Monarch of the Glen'. She looked at it in its ornate gold frame. 'Hey, it's a bit smart for me,' she said, honestly.

'Not at all,' was the reply as he put down a small plastic bag, went to the wall and with both hands ripped the printed rug with the leaping tiger down. Jan said nothing. She just glanced at the large empty space as Hazel set about with a tape measure, nail and small hammer, and in a few seconds, loud bangs were heard as he firmly drove a nail into the stud wall. With Jan's aid, he threaded the wire behind the painting over the nail, with Jan saying, 'No, more left—no, no a bit right—OK, OK, that's fine.' They stood back to admire the addition to the house.

'It's really beautiful. Thanks, Hazel, I really like it.'

'Great. Now, let's put this mutton-soaked tiger in the rubbish bin and the next thing to get rid of will be these ghastly orange terylene curtains.'

'You don't think I have any taste at all, do you?' she said quietly.

'Well, let's put it this way, you'd never make an interior decorator.'

'Would you like a drink? she asked, and disappeared, coming back with a bottle of champagne.

'Wow!' cried Hazel. 'Things *are* looking up!'

Jan lifted her head and turned it slightly toward the newly hung picture. 'It's fine for you guys. As always, everything is easy if you're a man—and you don't even have to be smart.'

'Well, we try,' he responded, flippantly, and then realised that she was speaking seriously.

'Look at me,' she said. 'I've spent two days with my sister. She's a painter, you know, really talented. No one cares, and that because she's a woman,' and she solemnly filled two ample water glasses with champagne. 'It's always the same. Thank the saints Sebastian is a boy.'

Hazel had never heard her speak like this. They had always passed sharp comments, one to the other, but with the exchange of the painting it seemed to have opened up a floodgate of thoughts and regrets. Or had it been, thought Hazel, two days away from Killkenny, not to mention Bob, and the influence of another woman, that had given her the impetus to vocalise another viewpoint? 'Come on, Jan, you have two grown up boys in good health and they *are* good boys, so you have obviously instilled into them certain standards and qualities. That's very much to your credit.'

Jan took a deep breath and moved her hefty frame to the more ample armchair. 'You don't understanding anything.'

'Try me,' urged Hazel, realising she was drinking the champagne like water.

'I may have two good boys, but you have the better one with you,' which was a sharp reference to where Matthew was sleeping. Hazel began to feel very uncomfortable and tried to think of an excuse to leave, but Jan wouldn't hear of it. 'There's another in the fridge,' she said. 'The others won't touch it, but I quite like it.' She smiled. 'I wouldn't have had kids if I had had a choice but as I said, men fuck the world for women.'

'Not all of them,' was his weak reply.

'When I was fifteen or perhaps it was before then, I don't remember now, I felt I had a vocation and I knew the only thing in the world I wanted to be was a nun. I wanted to join the Carmelites.' She looked at Hazel. 'Oh, you can laugh your tits off,' she said, aggressively. 'But you see my father, a man, refused to allow me to, and I needed his signature on the form. Can you believe it?' as she raised her voice. 'I was eighteen years old and my father wouldn't let me join the order, so, in a rush, I was married to Bob. Don't tell me, Hazel, that men can't fuck the lives of women, because I won't have it. Every day I think of the opportunity I lost because my father wouldn't sign a document or pay a dowry. You know,' she went on, becoming ever more animated,' my uncle Samuel offered to pay the dowry and my father stopped him,' and she sank even further back into the vinyl armchair. 'It's all gone—my whole life is all gone.'

'Come on, Jan,' urged Hazel, feeling very awkward. 'When we have you moved back to the homestead everything will be great.'

'Says who?' was the blunt retort.

'Jan, listen. You have Matthew. He is so wonderful. He is a real example of your upbringing.'

'Wake up, Hazel. The only thing in Matthew's life is Sebastian and if you're bright, which I'll give you credit for, you will have worked all that out a long time ago.'

'Talking of Sebastian, I must get over to the cottage and start dinner.' He stood up as did Jan, with a great deal of effort. 'Just a tick,' as she disappeared, returning with her copious handbag and she fumbled into the depths of it and produced a tiny, dark blue box, not wrapped at all, and handed it to Hazel. 'Happy Christmas,' she said. 'It's a bit late but the thought is there.' Hazel opened it to expose a pair of old-fashioned cufflinks in gold, in the form of engraved shields with a chain and bar attached behind them. Hazel never said a word; he just moved across and embraced Jan. 'Happy Christmas,' he said, 'and it's never too late.'

Just before he left, he turned and said, 'When we move to the homestead, those orange curtains are not coming.' Jan smiled and laughed. 'Any way you want it, Hazel.'

He walked back to the cottage with Jan's words ringing in his ears: 'if you're smart, Hazel, you have worked it all out' and this was in reference to Matthew and Sebastian. Work what out? What the hell was she implying, he wondered? Work what out?

Dinner was a quiet affair, with Sebastian exhausted and hungry. After a quick shower and an equally quick meal, Matthew almost carried him off to bed.

Work what out? It was running through Hazel's mind without stop. Work what out?

Matthew returned. 'A day in the saddle is a bit much for him but he did insist.'

'He'll obviously sleep well this evening,' said Hazel.

'What's wrong? You're looking very serious.'

'Oh, nothing. It was just something your mother said.'

'Don't worry, she sometimes has strange ideas. She hasn't had the best of lives.'

'So it seems,' was Hazel's quiet reply, 'but then have any of us?'

'Some more than others,' came back the offhand comment.

'Really?'

'Now, everything's fine, just fine. In a certain sense it's all thanks to you. I must be going to bed. I am dead! Thanks, Hazel. Dinner was as great as always.' He gave Hazel a kiss on the cheek and disappeared into his room. The only noise was the door closing. Hazel cleared the dining room and while washing the dishes the phrase returned again and again: 'and if you're bright, which I give you credit for, you will have worked all that out a long time ago'. He stood with both hands in a soapy sink, looking out into the black night, shaking his head. Work what out?

* * * * *

With delays here and problems there finally the move began. First it was the church, transported to its new and much safer haven. The main homestead, after almost six solid weeks of work, was now functional; the electricity had been connected, but only to the main house, where there were still many rooms not wired to a functional standard and still waiting to be finished. The easiest move was the cottage where Matthew, Sebastian and Hazel lived, as they had gone ahead to the main house. When the cottage was installed in its original place, all the furniture in the larger second cottage had to be transported on the back of trailers or trucks and part was deposited immediately in the homestead and the rest in Hazel's original cottage, leaving the second, larger one, empty and ready to be moved to its new position. There was a great deal of bad language and protest: Jan, Bob and Pat were installed in it in anticipation of part of their original home being transported to the new site. It should have been easy, but it was not. The plumbers had not connected the water correctly and so the main house had water but not Jan and Bob's cottage. 'He did it deliberately, the poof!' exclaimed Bob. 'He's a real arsehole.' It took two days to sort the situation out, which saw tensions high. Hazel also had to cope with Sebastian, who defied him openly, insisting he was sleeping with Matthew and that was that. This was a problem Hazel decided it was wiser to leave in Matthew's hands rather than his own and as a result, in an antiquated double bed, Matthew and Sebastian slept in harmony and for Hazel, in this period of complete readjustment, that was just fine. Personally he thought that of all the re-organised sleeping arrangements and new bedrooms, Sebastian had the best deal.

Moving Jan and Bob's house up to the large forecourt area to the side of the main house was one serious disaster after another. Windows were broken, a large beam in the roofing system, obviously in poor condition, collapsed under the strain of moving and a large section of the roof collapsed, falling sideways like a large tin handkerchief. It was a nightmare, with Bob complaining constantly that this whole move was insane. There were genuine moments when Hazel thought much the same.

He was telephoned by the Principal of St. Mary's to say that she was holding Sebastian back one year as she honestly felt he would have such a problem keeping up with his peers. He was bright, she explained, but the problem was he had no knowledge that was logically organised and so, in the six weeks of school, he had often become confused by the tasks and just sat as if he was on a train but had no idea of the destination. She explained carefully that this was not a sanction on him, but an essential part of his grounding for the future. Hazel agreed and the following evening explained this to Matthew when they had some time together. He agreed with Hazel and the Principal that it was essential to gain a sound foundation if he was to take over the administration of Killkenny. Hazel smiled to himself. Matthew had planned Sebastian's whole life for him; he hoped for both their sakes that everything would work out as planned, and both of them be happy.

Sebastian was not told of this move at school. They took the Principal's advice and just let him work it out for himself. The first day back saw everyone up bright and early. It wasn't just a walk hand in hand to the gate, followed by two or three dogs: the car had to be ready and, a good half hour before the bus was due at 8am, Hazel or Matthew, depending on their daily work schedules, transported an enthusiastic Sebastian to the front gate. He caught the bus, looking neat and tidy, as Hazel would not have it any other way.

Hazel looked around what had only a month or so ago been a working homestead. Tin lay everywhere, with junk, old tractors, equipment that had not been used for years, cement steps sticking up out of the ground, now serving no purpose, rusty tanks on their sides: it looked like an African refugee site, only more forlorn, as there was not a human being or a building complete. 'World War Three' murmured Hazel aloud, and walked amongst the rubble. The shearers' quarters had been moved back closer to the shearing shed, amongst the trees, but the debris of sixty odd years lay scattered about everywhere. He walked up to one of the sheds that was to be demolished and entered through the open door. It was a very large expanse with no windows and at eight in the morning it was hot and airless. The only thing that was interesting about it was the clerestory in the roof which let in a little light, but even those panes of glass had been over-painted to cut out the harsh glare that must have once entered.

As he walked back to his car, a truck came down the road and swung into the gateway. He hurried over to move his car that was blocking access. 'Morning!' shouted a jovial young man, as he alighted from the truck, the back of it filled with bricks and on top two enormous wooden gates.

'Wanna give us a hand with these monsters?' asked the younger of the two men and the three of them, with considerable effort, managed to offload the gates and stand them against a tree.

'The bricking should be finished this week, we hope, and then we'll mount the gates next Monday or Tuesday. I'll give you a ring because we're going to need others to help us put them in place.'

'Fine,' replied Hazel and went to go back to his car. What if it's raining, he thought, and he turned round.

'Anything wrong?' asked the young man.

'Yes, I forgot about the rain.'

'What rain?' He laughed. 'We haven't had bloody rain for ages.'

'No, not now, but in the future.'

'Missed the plot, man, what's it all about?'

So Hazel explained that if Sebastian returned home from school and for one reason or another had to wait for them and it was raining he would be soaked.

'Poor little bugger. I suppose he would. Hey, what about that little building over there?' He pointed to a small tin building that stood parallel to the now empty site and had once been part of Bob and Jan's house. Bob had originally used it for all types of medication for the sheep. It had a lock on the door and no windows. It was about two metres square with a gable roof.

'Perfect.' replied Hazel, 'but how do we get it over here?'

'No probs, mate. It's so small, with rollers under it, we could move it in no time. Mind you, a certain remuneration wouldn't go astray.'

'Done! Transport it parallel to the new gates but back under the first tree, so it looks like a gateman's cottage. A bit of paint and some cast iron trim, not to mention a window—and if it doesn't have a timber floor and it's just earth, brick me in a floor, please.'

'Great! No probs, mate.'

'Oh,' said the younger man, as his assistant seemed to be totally mute, 'I believe you had some fun at the Railway Hotel a while ago,' and smiled.

'So it seems,' and Hazel turned his car back, and headed up the drive.

At lunchtime, he prepared a meal for Matthew. 'I've decided to have a garden.'

Matthew smiled. 'You can't. It's too hot here and the winds are not exactly conducive to herbaceous borders.' He laughed.

'I telephoned the removal firm this morning. They are still in the area and they are going to bring the last big shed up here, the one with the clerestory in the roof.'

'What on earth for?

'For a garden, of course,' and left the room as one of the electricians had called out for him. There was a problem with the location of a switch. When he returned and saw a most perplexed Matthew he said, 'Don't worry, sweetie, all will be revealed in good time.'

'Of that, I am sure.'

'Matthew, we must get the site cleaned up near the gate and where the church once was. It makes the property look terrible.'

'Yes, I know, but the rubbish truck is out this week with radiator problems. They promise me next Monday for sure, and there are four men, so they will completely clear the site. Nothing will be left at all, not even the old hen houses.'

'When all this is done, there will have to be a whole new section of wire fencing put up. I see that when they moved the shearers' quarters, the idiots demolished a section of the fence.'

'OK. Pat and I will see to it after Monday. It's probably easier for the rubbish removers to bring the big truck in through the broken fence rather than risk demolishing the new gate pillars.'

'Right.'

Matthew had taken his position of manager very seriously and now twenty thousand head of fine merinos were on the much better tract of land at the back of the property and he, Pat and Bob had their hands full with long overdue maintenance and looking after the stock. It turned out to be more than full time work for his father and brother. If the front of the property near the gate looked like a bomb site, the homestead was unbelievable. A shattered church was the first thing one saw on entering between the palm trees, which had old dead fronds hanging in all direction. Then, on that side, was the old governess's cottage that Hazel had lived in. It held all the furniture and was partly re-packed with it. On the other side of the square, symmetrically opposite, was Jan and Bob's reduced house and in front was the Killkenny homestead itself, set well back. The initial impact of this cluster was of a little but very rundown village. To the far left of this and quite some distance away were all the original service buildings, one by one being repaired by the three carpenters who came five days a week and enjoyed a beer with Bob and Pat after work each day. The very last building was to be set in place on Friday morning, and Sebastian watched from the bus window as the huge truck and trailer system swung around and entered through the dismantled fencing system.

It had been decided that it was easier to take the shed apart and then reconstruct it, as apparently that was how it had arrived at Killkenny. Bob vaguely remembered the story but as Hazel wanted to know the history Bob feigned complete forgetfulness: that was one word Hazel hadn't. He said to Bob that on Friday morning he wished to see him, so, under sufferance, Bob arrived at the house. To say he was surprised at the work being done was an understatement.

'I believe we have a little cash transaction to sort out,' began Hazel remorselessly.

'Wait! I'll be back.' Bob returned with a shoe box and handed it across. 'It's all there.' And then turned on his heel and left, to join Pat on the truck, as they headed out to check the stock and to do yet more maintenance on the run-down fencing system. Hazel closed the door and moved into the dining room. He opened the box and found it all in A\$100 notes, packed in tightly, A\$150,000. So this was how our Mr. Wallace paid, in cash, nothing going through the banks, no way the income tax department could trace the money but how much more was there, wondered Hazel. He tied the box up with the string that had originally bound it, went to his bedroom, hid it and then went downstairs to the sound of 'Where does he want the bloody thing?' He stepped into the blazing light and raised his hand to cover his eyes and replied, 'I want the bloody thing here. Fit it on to the side of the house so that the dining room window is central to the narrowest part.'

'Sure, mate,' and the team of men scurried about, measuring and talking amongst themselves in hushed voices.

'I can't believe this streak of pump water flattened the hell out of Brendan.'

'Well, he did.'

'God, we'd better be careful. Did you see Brendan's nose?' and they began laughing.

'A guy the other day yelled out to Brendan as he was in Main Street 'Look out, Brendan, a lilac Volkswagon!' Brendan almost shit himself.' And the four men broke into more gales of laughter.

*　*　*　*　*

When Matthew collected Sebastian after school, and having finished his first week, Sebastian seemed very content, chatting on about his adventures at school and said he had met a nice boy and they had shared the same desk table. And he had been to see the principal.

'What for? Were you in trouble?' asked Matthew, concerned.

'Oh, no. Hazel told me if I couldn't work something out or I had a problem I was to go and see her.'

'What was wrong?'

Well,' began Sebastian, as they sped along the dusty drive. 'All the students had a red book for English lessons and I didn't have one. The boy beside me—he's called Eric—shared his with me.'

'He sounds a great friend/'

'Yes, he is. Anyway, the Principal was very nice, too. She said she had met Hazel and she went to a big bookcase and gave me a red book, and these sheets are for Hazel.'

But that was not all that had happened in the Principal's office. After she had given him the book, he thanked her and was about to leave, then turned and looked at her.

'Can I help you with something else?' she asked, kindly.

'Yes, you can. Hazel said if I don't understand, I am to ask you.'

'And Hazel was right,' she replied, supressing a smile.

'When we have lunch, everyone says grace. I don't know the strange words and this morning in church I didn't know the words to the prayers. Everyone else does, but I don't.' He looked directly at her with his electric blue eyes.

She stood up and went to her filing cabinet, but couldn't find what she was looking for. She returned to her desk and immediately found the information. The printer had delivered into its tray a copy of the grace on one sheet and a copy of the Lord's Prayer, Hail Mary and Gloria on the second. 'Take these home to Hazel and he will teach you to say them. You can bring the sheet with you when you come to Mass on Fridays. Here!' and she pressed a key, and a second copy appeared. 'This one you keep for Friday mornings.'

'Thank you,' he answered, very formally. 'You are a very nice lady,' and left, closing the door quietly behind him. The Principal just sat looking at the back of the door. 'He is a really sweet boy,' she sighed, 'and a very beautiful one.'

*   *   *   *   *

When they drove into the large space in front of the homestead, Sebastian was amazed at the big shed that had once been at the front gate and was now attached to the side of the mansion. He looked at Matthew.

'What's it for?'

'Hazel tells me he is creating a garden for us.'

Sebastian turned his head and two sets of blue eyes met and then swung back to this large structure with a clerestory, attached to the house.

'Oh,' was the boy's reply, 'a garden for us!' and dashed towards the house to show Hazel the sheets of paper that he had to learn the contents of.

The dining room, when he entered it, was pitch black. The building had been attached to it, so the room was hot and dark. He went on a tour of inspection, with everyone saying hello to him, and he enjoyed the attention. He finally found Hazel explaining what he wanted to the electrician. The urgent problem was that the carpenters could not start any finishing work until the electricians were finished, and there was a similar problem with the plumbers, so it was a bit here and a bit there, and, in Hazel's opinion, oh so slow.

'Hazel, look!' and Sebastian proudly pulled out the sheets he had to learn.

'Well, aren't we lucky we have an expert to teach you these prayers.'

'Who's that,' asked a curious Sebastian.

'Why, Jan! She's an expert at this.'

'Is she really?' the boy was rather unsure.

'Absolutely. The first prayer is 'The Grace'.'

'Yes, I know and it's in Latin,' he said with a knowing smile, 'and the rest on the other sheet are in English.'

'Very good. Come on. Off we go and we'll see your instructress,' and off they went to Jan's house. This was also in disarray, but nothing like the main house, as, apart from closing off the end section, which was demolished, thus leaving the façade symmetrical, Jan's of all the repositioned houses was the most liveable.

'Can we come in?' shouted Hazel.

'Sure. What's wrong?'

'Nothing. You are going to teach Sebastian his prayers for school.'

She said nothing. Perhaps it was the association of the words 'prayers' and 'school' and a little boy in front of her that made it very difficult for her to swallow. She looked at the first sheet Sebastian handed her and she read it out aloud, hardly glancing at the sheet. 'Benedictus Benedicat per Christum Dominum Nostrum,' and she took a deep breath and looked at the following sheet.

'The Principal says I can take this sheet to Mass but I would like to be able to say the grace in Latin. All the other kids know it by heart. Do you think it will be hard?'

Hazel saw a mist forming over Jan's eyes; it seemed like a perfume of the past, an old scent that revives part of one's memory in waves but only the warm, secure parts.

'Sure. I'll help you,' she said, softly, 'and don't worry. I'll teach you here, and every time you have a meal at the house with Hazel and Matthew you can say grace for them.'

'Oh yes,' he said excitedly. 'Matthew will be very surprised.'

'I'm sure he will,' she replied drily, and so that became the pattern. Sebastian at every meal looked at the card Hazel had prepared and was always in front of his place setting, while Matthew and Hazel always pronounced 'Amen' to his satisfaction.

* * * * *

The following week for Hazel finally saw the great change. The men arrived not on Monday, as promised, but Wednesday, and first cleaned the church site completely, then began the real work near the gate, which took them until late on Friday evening, with eight truck loads of discarded rubbish to return the area clean and free of the heavy coating of rubbish.

Hazel also received a call from Mr Lester, asking if he had a moment and could call in to see him on Thursday. Thursday was Jan's day once a week for shopping and she always left early in the morning in order to have lunch with her sister and then return with the weekly supplies.

Hazel and Jan left independently on Thursday, but decided to meet up in Bradbury for at least a cup of tea. Hazel had a list as long as his arm of things that had to be done, but at the arranged time he met Jan and they wheeled their shopping trolleys around the supermarket, chatting about what was right and what was wrong with the world, not to mention Jan complaining bitterly about the prices being always higher. In one aisle, she most unceremoniously poked Hazel in the ribs. 'It's her,' and looked the other way. Hazel turned to see a woman in perhaps her late thirties, well dressed, with almost white blonde hair carefully managed, stalking about without any concern for anyone else. After she had disappeared down another aisle, Hazel asked, 'Who is she?'

'It's the Wallace woman, Cherly,' she virtually spat out, 'a ghastly person,' and they continued their shopping spree.

At the entrance to this large supermarket was a coffee lounge where one could just drop the bags and have a respite from the pressures of keeping the family fed. It was here that, according to Hazel, they encountered the most extraordinary woman he had ever met.

'Jan, how nice to meet you after so long. Do sit down.' Hazel seemed for the moment to have been forgotten, then, 'Oh, how do you do. My name is Doris Wallace.'

'Mine's Hazel.'

'Well, do sit down. I have heard all about you. How charming to encounter you here.' The woman must have been a bit older than Jan, but it was hard to tell. She was dressed to kill, as Hazel related later, in a smart dress with lots of heavy gold chains and grey hair that was firmly lacquered. The lines on her face were few but it was the eagle eyes that were the problem, and under them a set of determined lips, painted scarlet. To begin with, she ignored Hazel and chattered on to Jan aimlessly but little by little drew Hazel into the conversation, though only on her terms. Hazel took her for a woman of means and assumed she was resident on the property next to Killkenny.

'Oh no, dear,' she said to him, 'that's another part of the family.'

'Do you know them?'

'No, he doesn't,' said Jan, answering for him as the waitress arrived at their table.

'Wadda yer like?'

The orders were taken and Doris settled back for a chat with a captive audience. 'You're lucky you don't know them, well, her, I mean; Cherly is a pain in the arse.'

Hazel was surprised at Doris's conversation. It went from very formal to quite common without any problem but she obviously saw herself as a great lady. 'Only married him for the position and had to toss in a great sum of money to kick the property on again. What a waste!' Here Doris picked up her cup of tea with the little finger extended, making the action seem ridiculous. 'And you're Hazel. Well, I was very curious,' here she paused, 'to meet, how shall we say—politically correctly, of course—an openly gay man. How pleasant!'

'Thanks.'

'It's fine with me. I think all men are—how shall we say politically correctly—gay, don't you, Jan?'

'Probably,' was Jan's retort.

'You see, Mr. Hazel, we live lives dominated by men who have this bizarre attitude that they must be with women and you know neither the women or the men find this a satisfactory situation, all a bit of a waste from my point of view,' and then changed the conversation. 'I say, Mr. Hazel, did you notice at the bar if they had any scones with jam or cream?'

'I'll have a look,' replied Hazel, rising and wondering if Doris ate men with sauce or not. He returned with a large plate of the requested produce.

'Oh, how nice!' and Doris immediately helped herself to one. 'Oh, not as nice as mine, but acceptable,' she went on in a superior manner. 'I believe you are the toast of the Railway Hotel?'

'I have enjoyed a drink there.'

'I believe Brendan got quite a surprise, thought he would flatten a poof—oh, I am sorry, politically correctly a gay man—and make himself the hero of the moment. I know all about it. My son was with him, and took him to the hospital.' She carried on in an offhand way, 'He's disproportionate, Brendan, you know. My son Ted, well he says as big as Brendan is his cock is small, smaller than one's little finger. Oh, it's all the same isn't it?' She smiled as she helped herself to another scone. Hazel was fascinated by this sharp, emancipated woman. 'Men are basically all the same,' she went on, looking at Jan and then at Hazel. 'They make a mess of everyone's life. Mind you, I said to Fred when I married him, one bit of funny stuff and I will ram a poker up your arse.'

'I imagine it had the desired effect.'

'Worked perfectly! I never had any trouble with him. You have to let them know where you stand, these men.'

'How many children do you have?' asked Hazel.

'Three moronic men! Can you believe it? When I was at school, a few classes in front of Jan, Reverend Mother always told us to be careful of the consequences of men and did we listen? No! And look where I am. My eldest, married to a, to say the least, very limited woman, with a brain like a budgie, though if it wasn't so she wouldn't have married him. Even Father Ryan was doubtful about the marriage. He came and saw me, you know. I told him: one was as stupid as the other, so neither of the two homes was ruined.'

Hazel broke into laughter, which was obviously what Doris was waiting for. 'Do you like the name 'Doris'?' she asked, moving her chair so she was looking directly at him.

'I think it's fine.'

'It's awful. It's the name you give the house cow. I've always hated it,' and she gulped her tea down. 'Well, Mr. Hazel, what are you going to do except build castles?'

'Castles?' he asked.

'Come on, the re-building of Killkenny. The other Wallaces are furious. Personally I am ecstatic. I can't bear that bitch Cherly. How about you, Jan?'

'Not a bar,' was her clipped retort, and Doris took over yet again. 'My other sons are, to say the least, not brilliant, but it's my fault. If I had listened to Reverend Mother I would have married an intelligent man, not a bandicoot like Fred, but, you see, Mr. Hazel, in our day we didn't have a choice. You married or you just didn't and if you did marry, the family generally organised it. Oh, how sad the life of a woman is! One son married to a bird brain and as plain as a pikestaff, the second Brendan's offsider, who seems to know the dimension

167

of every penis in Bradbury, and simple Simon at home, who likes cooking and cleaning. Mind you, I am not complaining in this day and age. Home help is hard to come by. I believe you do the cooking now at the homestead, Mr Hazel?'

'Yes, I do. I worked as a chef in a restaurant.'

'Well, I suppose that helps,' Doris said, in a patronising manner. 'It's men! They are just the scourge of woman-kind. We end up with big properties and our parents have this obscene idea we should be dynastic. How stupid! What do you think, Jan?'

'I couldn't agree more,' and she excused herself to look for the toilet.

'Look at her,' said Doris, 'can you believe she was once a vaguely attractive girl? And look now! She's like a rhinoceros going for a drink from behind. I can't understand how some women let themselves go. But I must be fair.'

Hazel was in grave doubt that the word 'fair' had ever crept into Doris's vocabulary. She moved her chair a little closer to Hazel's and then looked about, while taking her third jam and cream scone. 'She's had a rough time, Jan, you know. First she wanted to become a nun. She would have been a good nun, to be sure. Even Reverend Mother pleaded with her father. He was a real shit, a woman hater, probably,' as she smiled at him. 'If we are being politically correct a repressed homosexual idiot, not that it follows, my dear.'

'Thanks,' replied Hazel through slightly gritted teeth.

'So, you see, it all happened at once for Jan. She couldn't become a nun. The uncle, I believe, was going to pay the dowry but her father forbad it. Her father made a shocking investment and lost everything. Can you believe it? Everything! They were virtually on the street. You see the madness of men, Mr. Hazel—no woman would have done that because they know they have to look after a family. It's just men, stupid, oh so stupid!' and she waved her skinny arm about in the air, 'and then this old shit married her to Bob. Well, really, I know we are Catholics, but I am sure Father Ryan would have given absolution to

Jan for committing suicide. Imagine waking up in the morning and Bob moving across—oh no, it's just too horrible to think of! Jan really is a saint. And then there was the problem of the Spaniard.'

'What Spaniard?' Hazel was very curious.

'Well, Mr Hazel, when Matthew was born, Bob didn't believe that he was his son. With Pat that could never be disputed but Bob, knowing all about animal husbandry, I mean wouldn't you think he would have used his brain instead of giving Jan hell for years. Father Ryan spoke to him very firmly several times. Oh, if we had all listened to Reverend Mother!' she lamented.

'I don't understand. What do the Spaniard and Matthew and Jan have in common?'

'Oh, you are slow to catch on, 'she smiled. 'You see, Mr Hazel, Jan's great great grandmother was, I think, Spanish.' Hazel looked at here, waiting for the magic explanation. 'Well,' she said, 'I thought a practising homosexual would be more intelligent,' and poured herself another cup of tea. Hazel signalled the waitress to bring as many scones and cream as were left. He had the feeling that Doris, as unnecessary as she was, was the first person giving him the information he sought, namely about Matthew.

'Well, you see, it's genetic,' and she stared at him.

'You mean his appearance?'

'Of course! Look at the locals here. If there was a Mr. Slug contest you would have the judge out for months.'

Here Hazel broke out into laughter. Doris narrowed her eyes and quickly glanced towards the ladies' toilet, only to see Jan returning. 'Mr Hazel, one Spaniard is understandable—but Sebastian?'

Hazel knew instantly what she was implying and chose to show an indifferent expression. 'And the other Wallaces?'

'Oh, them!' she said, with a wave of her bony arm once more. 'Can you imagine? They really aren't Wallaces at all.'

'What do you mean?' he asked.

'Well, the family only had a girl and what a pain! Do you remember Angela?' she asked Jan.

'How could I forget her? She was in the same class as me—a real bitch, then.'

'Seems to run in the family,' and Doris glared at Hazel. 'Oh no, Doris, I mean Cherly.'

'Yes, of course,' she replied, not one hundred per cent sure that he wasn't having a go at her. 'Well, Angela was the only girl and so she married, or was to marry, a very rich man called Edwards, I think, but her father would only let them marry if he changed his name by deed poll to Wallace, to keep the family name alive. I believe there was a kerfuffle with Father Ryan, who thought it was very pretentious, which it was, of course,' she shrugged, straightening the front of her cardigan and then dissolved into helpless hysterical laugher.

'What's so funny?' asked Hazel.

'Listen to the story,' interrupted Jan, who had obviously heard it many times before. Doris felt for her handkerchief and dabbed her eyes, but it was obvious that this story was dear to her heart.

'Angela was a big woman,' she began, 'and was always heavily corseted in public—you know the type. All in one, bra and corset. She had legs like a billiard table but she for some reason only the saints know saw herself as Vivien Leigh—you know, 'Gone with the Wind' matriarch and all that sort of thing. She always wore suits made of silk—she had the cash—and blouses with prissy Peter Pan collars. On a woman at that age it was ridiculous, though there were sensible shoes, since she was very tall. She looked a bit like a moving wardrobe.

'Get on with the story!' interrupted Jan again, 'or we shall be here till sunset.'

'Very well,' came the brisk reply. 'Anyway, every time they arrived at Mass with Ashley, of course,' here Doris put on a very funny false Southern American accent, 'she always had this stiff corseted figure and with the same suits—I've no idea where she got them—no store carried fittings that large here in Bradbury—and with matching Bretton-type hats which she must have had a hundred of for Mass, to show us how elegant she was. And she always wore a large corsage pinned to her lapel.' Here Doris collapsed into laughter again. 'I'm getting there,' she snapped at Jan, while wiping her eyes. 'Those Wallaces always had the pew in front of ours. All the Wallaces sat one side, the O'Malley's the other. Anyway, the Mass was almost finished—we'd got to the Agnus Dei—and Angela let out a scream. Everyone turned to look and out of the corsage had come some sort of insect, a beetle thing, and headed for her ample bosom and because she was so corseted she couldn't get the thing out. Poor bloody insect! She had probably shoved the pin up his arse, anyway!' and she began to laugh again. 'Anyway, Ashley, like the O'Malley boys, went to boarding school, I think at Tendale, the Mauris Brothers or the Christian Brothers, I don't remember. And now Angela is so big she can't do anything. She sits or lies in bed all day and our charming insincere Cherly rules the roost. He's weak, Ashley, you know, but I haven't seen him for a while. Every time there was a family reunion I always used to telephone two or three days ahead to announce I shall have a headache. They don't even call now, thank goodness. They have a girl, I think, Ashley and Cherly. How that happened can only be called a miracle and I'm not kidding.'

Here they all began laughing. Doris suddenly stood up. 'I must go. You know, when I was at school, Reverend Mother said gossip was a venal sin. How the church has changed. Nowadays it's considered an essential part of survival,' and she disappeared into the crowd with her supermarket bags leaving Hazel to pay the bill.

'She always does that,' commented Jan, annoyed.

'It was worth every cent,' and they said their goodbyes. Jan went to finish her chores and then as usual every Thursday went to lunch with her sister.

Hazel rushed about, first of all to Mr. Lester. 'Come in, come in, Hazel. Would you like a drink?'

'No thanks. I'm in a bit of a rush. I have spent more time than I had expected with Doris Wallace.'

'Oh, good heavens, what a waste of time!' and he went to his desk and pulled out a sheet of paper. 'I have tried to contact Keven, but it appears he is in Asia with a companion, according to his office.' He noticed Hazel's body tense a little and his eyes narrow. 'So that leaves you according to the legal side completely responsible for Killkenny. There must be quite an expense in the refurbishing of the place.' He spoke slowly. 'I have to hand it to you, Hazel, you seem to make a penny do a pound's work.

'I'm afraid we must,' Hazel replied. 'There is still a lot more work to do.

'And no real problems with Bob?'

'None now,' smiled Hazel. 'I took your advice and it's Matthew who is now in charge but basically it's all of us working for Killkenny or for Sebastian, however you look at it.'

'Great! Do you realise that Killkenny comes with certain properties in Bradbury?' Hazel relaxed in is chair, saying he didn't know. 'Well, it has eight properties which render not a great deal but it's not a weight on the property. I phoned you the other day because the two shops beside the supermarket and the large space behind are part of the Killkenny estate. The supermarket has offered 1.8 million for the lot. What do you say?' He looked at Hazel as he stood up and smiled.

'We,' and he emphasised it, '*we* will not take less than 2.5 million and the offer is open for only five working days.'

Lester was, to say the least, surprised at Hazel's sharp business acumen—or, he thought, was it arrogance? 'I'll put your offer to the buyers this afternoon and let you know the moment we hear something.'

'Mr. Lester,' went on Hazel, 'email me with every holding that is Killkenny's but only when you have a free moment.'

They shook hands and Hazel exited the office. All he wanted to do was tell Matthew. 'No, no!' he said to himself, 'Later, later!' He was now rushing to the demolition yard, the glazier and then to lunch with Gerald and Carmel.

'Oh God, I'm going to be late,' as his car screeched to a halt in front of a demolition yard just across from the railway yards. He walked up the black metal drive, littered with every form of demolished house fitting possible, all neatly stacked. 'Wadda yer want?' came a sound like a dog about to bite.

'I'm looking for windows.'

'Oh yeah, what sort?' and then the boy—he must have been thirty five to forty—glanced into the drive and saw Hazel's lilac Volkswagon. 'Come in, mate! I believe our Brendan has a plaster nose!' and went into gales of laughter. 'Whatever you want, you can have.'

'It's a pity he doesn't look like Antonio Banderas,' thought Hazel. 'I might move here for life.' But unfortunately the similarities between the demolition salesman and Antonio Banderas were nil.

'Windows, yeah, we got heaps. They've just demolished the old part of the hospital and we got the job. How many do you want?'

'May I have a look at them?'

'Sure, over here. I believe our Brendan went down for the count,' at which he started laughing. 'He's a real arsehole, that guy. He loves picking on someone who is smaller and that's not hard, he's so fucking fat. And his two offsiders haven't got a brain between the three of them. The Wallace guy is always sucking someone off. What an arsehole he is! And then they think it's smart to come on heavy and beat the guy up. You know, Hazel,' he said with a grin, 'if you stick around these parts for a while you could end up a hero.'

'It's not really my scene, the hero.'

'You never know, mate. You just never know. Now, what about these?' and Hazel found himself looking at a group of thirty or so windows, long Victorian type, with all the architraves intact but many of the panes cracked.

'How tall are they?' he asked, taking out of his hip pocket a sheet with the measurements he required. 'Great! Perfect! And do you have any French windows?'

'Ya mean type doors? I have two pairs but one is a bit damaged, and I have a deluxe pair.' He gave a superior smile.

'Let's have a look, then.'

The two pairs were ordinary, but unusually tall, which was exactly what Hazel was looking for though the bottoms of both would have to be substituted as they had stood in water or something and were very rotten, but he was absolutely correct, they were deluxe. This other pair of French doors had come from the old Commercial Bank in Bradbury. They were French polished and the glass was one large pane in each door. They were completely acid-etched, of the finest quality and also came with all the architraves.

'Will you give me a price for twelve windows, the two pairs of French doors and these as well,' said Hazel, and the haggling began.

Finally, a price was agreed. Hazel moved closer to him: 'If I pay in cash with no receipt?' The man looked about him, as if expecting someone to leap out from under a stack of old doors or from behind the wall of broken windows. The negotiations began again, but this time the bartering was in a much quieter tone.

'I'll also take that decorative piece there,' said Hazel; it happened to be a square section that fitted across a hipped roof with its own little roof and a weather vane on top.

'Wadda yer want that for?' the man asked.

'Oh, for Sebastian's bus shelter,' said with a straight face.

'Oh yeah.'

'These prices are delivered, of course. Cash on delivery, whenever you're ready,' and he disappeared down the black stone drive and off to the glazier.

'He's a skinny bloke to have flattened Brendan,' thought the demolition man, as he added up what they had agreed on. 'And he's also a fucking skinflint when it comes to cash,' he decided.

One more call! 'Oh, what time is it? I have only fifteen minutes and then lunch at the Railway Hotel. Oh, why can't I find a fucking car park?'

Finally, he rushed into the glazier's. The empty-looking store was exactly that—empty. He saw the proprietor sitting at a desk, black strands of greasy hair pulled across his scalp, a full face accentuated by glasses with very thick black frames.

'Yes?' was the slow reply from behind the desk.

'I'm in a dreadful hurry,' cried Hazel. 'I need to know two things. Do you supply glass that blocks out forty or fifty per cent of light?'

'Yes, we do.'

Oh god, I don't believe it! An automaton, thought Hazel. 'And do you stock coloured glass? I mean glass that's flashed but has been etched or sandblasted?'

'We don't carry it but we can arrange it.'

'Great. Get yourself out to Killkenny and you'll have a lot of business.'

'I'll take your name,' said the man, slowly and to Hazel's surprise disappeared from sight. Hazel looked from right to left, only to discover that the man behind the desk when on the floor stood barely a metre tall. He moved over to a blank wall with Hazel suddenly feeling odd.

'Is this what you are after?' he asked, very slowly, and Hazel glanced at a sample of glass that had a pattern incised into it.

'The colour is too harsh,' he replied. 'Don't you have something a little more subtle?'

'We may have,' was the slow, flat retort and this tiny man fumbled around in a box of glass samples searching for what Hazel was seeking. 'I once had a lilac and pale blue but I will have to contact the supplier. There is a lady here in Bradbury who does sandblasting, but not acid etching. Is it a problem?'

'No,' replied Hazel, extremely anxious to get out of this awful store with mirrors everywhere and a red cement floor. It was one of the most inhospitable shops he had ever been in. But the man had been most helpful in his slow-motion way and the agreement was he would send out Otto to see what had to be done, as Otto understood everything.

'Great!' said Hazel, and left this tiny chap his telephone number and fled.

He was now late, something he hated to be. All his life he had been punctual; if there was one thing he disliked intensely it was being kept waiting so he tried never to put himself in the reverse situation. He sped down Main Street and around a corner to where the Railway Station was. Lo and behold there was a parking space right in front! Before he leapt out of the car, something struck him: 2.5 million dollars! 'Oh God! What have I done? Oh, well,' he thought, 'at least Sebastian will reap the rewards, not to mention an easy finish to Killkenny.' He made for the Railway Hotel on the other side of the street as fast as possible.

He walked into the dim interior, glancing in all directions for Gerald and Carmel. He noticed an arm in the air, wavering about and squinted his eyes. He moved across, with the barman smiling, 'Welcome back, Hazel!'

He turned to say thanks as he scurried over to the able where Gerald and Carmel were. 'I'm so sorry, 'he began, 'but I got held up between the demolition man, Mr Lester and a quaint man at the glaziers'.'

'Forgiven,' said Carmel, with a rare smile. 'I believe you also met my aunt this morning?' Hazel looked puzzled. 'Yes. Doris.'

'Oh, she's a bundle of laughs,' he said, sitting down.

'Well, that's one word for her. She is basically a bitch but I don't really mind her, except that she tends to repeat the same stories over and over.'

'I'm so sorry, really, I am never late,' Hazel repeated.

'Have a drink' and Gerald filled up the empty glass obviously waiting for him.

'What did Aunt Doris have to tell you?'

'Well, a bit of everything.'

'I'll bet you heard the phrase 'politically correct' a hundred times.'

'Well, not exactly a hundred but she has a way of using it. I am now not to be described as a poof but as a gay man.'

'Wow! And all of that in the first encounter with her!' laughed Gerald. 'She's also a relative of mine. She loves to drive a tack in with a sledgehammer, a bit tiresome but sometimes very funny, especially when she attacks the straight men. She won't say anything aggressive towards gays but straight men are her target.'

'Also straight women,' added Carmel in a deadpan way. 'She is a real bitch.'

'She spoke of the Spaniards,' said Hazel and then had the strangest feeling he had offended someone as there was silence. He looked either side of him and there was no response at all.

'Let's see,' said Gerald as Carmel bent down to a very expensive Hermes handbag in black crocodile. She moved it to one side and opened an imaginary pocket on the left side of the bag and withdrew an invisible pack of cards. Gerald at once cleared a place in front of him and Hazel obediently did the same. She had no expression at all. She shuffled this invisible pack and first placed a part of it in front of her. She then placed one invisible card in front of Gerald and then of Hazel. As the dealer, he turned her cards first. 'Lovers' was her response. 'Father and son' was Gerald's as they turned the cards over. Hazel complied with 'Chums'. No one said a word. She collected the invisible cards and with a certain nonchalance returned them to the non-existent pocket in her bag.

But for Hazel, if this was very odd, the fact was that directly afterwards the subject was taboo; neither of them referred to this exercise for the rest of the afternoon. They ordered lunch and chattered on basically about the shortage of beautiful men, with lots of anecdotes of the 'if only' type, until they were surprised at the sound of an ambulance siren, which pulled up at the hotel and from a side door retrieved someone and drove off at high speed. 'Who was it?' 'What's happened?' was the general conversation of the thirty or forty people in the main bar area.

'Mr Hazel, here you are! What a happy coincidence—not, of course, that I believe in coincidences. I am well above all that superstition,' announced Doris, as she swept in and plonked herself down on an empty chair at their table. 'You know, Mr. Hazel, years ago we women were forbidden to enter this hallowed space. It was left only for drunken men, who went outside to vomit in the gutter if they could make it there or piss on the walls just outside. How times have changed,' she smiled, not acknowledging either Carmel or Gerald. 'Mr Hazel and I have been discussing the world this morning. And I must thank you for your generosity in paying for my morning tea, very gracious of you.'

'A great pleasure,' he replied theatrically.

'Get a glass, Doris,' said Carmel without any affection; Doris stood up and returned with a glass which she soon filled from the bottle in the cooler.

'I hope you're looking after Mr. Hazel,' she added, glancing at both Carmel and Gerald.

'Yes, Auntie,' was the chorused response.

'Have I told you about Darwin?' asked Doris, in a very concerned tone.

'No, have you been there?'

'Oh, Mr Hazel, you are silly. Darwin was a person. I think he must have been Australian.'

'No, Auntie, he was English.'

'Can't have been, otherwise why on earth would we have called a city after him? He was a strange man, you know.' She looked straight at Hazel, whilst the others just refilled their glasses and stared into the middle distance. 'He had this idea that men came from monkeys or apes—same thing.' She brushed back her well lacquered hair, and then carried on, 'Reverend Mother wouldn't have a bar of it, but you know Brendan?'

'We have met,' answered Hazel.'

'Oh, so you have. Well, Brendan's father and Darwin must have been friends or at least they met.'

'Really?' said a surprised Hazel.

'Oh yes. You see, Brendan's father was probably why Darwin thought men came from monkeys.' Here, Hazel became confused and his frowning showed it. 'Oh, Mr. Hazel, when Brendan's father had a lot to drink he would take off his clothes—well, he left on his underpants.'

'Thank God for that!' exclaimed Carmel.

'And, you know, he would bound around on all fours in the bar here. He was very hairy. I once peeped in through the little Snug opening. Oh, quite a sight, I can tell in only his underpants!'

'I can only think of one thing worse,' commented a straight-faced Carmel, which had Gerald and Hazel in hysterics.

'By the way, Auntie,' asked Gerald, 'what was the ambulance here for?'

'Oh, it was for Heather O'Riley. She had a turn.'

'Really? What happened?'

'Oh, I'm not sure,' replied Doris in an offhand manner, 'but it may have had something to do with our conversation.'

'What conversation?' demanded Carmel.

'Well, she was going on about her daughter Sandy—you know, her netball champion. You know, Mr. Hazel, when we went to school it was called basketball, now they have to call everything by another name. So pretentious, I have always thought.'

'Well, what happened?' asked Gerald.

'Oh well, Heather was going on about Sandy not having a boyfriend and having no prospects of marriage and I told her that she was an irresponsible mother. The politically correct word for her daughter was 'lesbian' not 'dyke'. Really, she pretended she didn't know what I was talking about, and when I explained about the sexual thing . . .'. She smiled wickedly and downed yet another glass as Carmel signalled the not-unattractive barman for another bottle.

'What on earth did you say to her?' asked Gerald.

'Oh, I explained about dildos.'

'What!!' exclaimed Carmel loudly. 'Then what happened?'

'Well, she went all funny, so I got her a tumbler of brandy and she drank it like water, stood up, but only for a moment, and then fell across some chairs. She was quite peculiar, was our Heather.'

'You've probably poisoned her with alcohol.'

'Don't be silly!' retorted Doris. 'A little drink goes a long way.'

'I'm sure,' stated Carmel, deadpan.

'You know, Carmel, Mr. Hazel and Matthew are restoring Killkenny.' This was the first time she had thrown Matthew's name into the conversation, which may have been an accident, but both Carmel and Gerald picked it up at once.

'Where are the ram sales this year, at Killkenny or at my nephew's place? asked Doris.

Hazel was completely out of his depth. 'What ram sales?' he wondered. 'Oh, obviously at Killkenny,' was his saving reply.

'How nice,' replied Doris. 'It will be like old times.'

'Do you still have the podium with the green umbrella and the gold sheep?' asked Carmel. At this point Hazel thought it was going to be easier if he confessed he didn't understand anything about the conversation, but it was Gerald who lent over and placed a hand on his, an action not missed by either Doris or Carmel.

'You see, Hazel, the ram sales at Killkenny were very important. The merino studs brought very high prices and old Mr. O'Malley built a type of podium for the auctioneers—very theatrical—and it had a big umbrella, tin I think, to shade the auctioneer but on the supporting vertical rod was a metal sheep in gold and on top a little umbrella in miniature for the gilded sheep. It was quite famous. Is it still there?'

'I'll have to check with Matthew. We have so much work going on at the moment that gilded sheep may just have to wait a little'

'I'm surprised *he* has the nerve to come here,' interrupted Doris, looking at the bar where a tall but solid man had just walked in, in collar and tie but without a jacket, since it was so hot. He had short black hair and very black eyes, with an elastic smile surrounded by a fairly heavy beardline. He chatted at the bar and then ambled over to their table.

'Hello, Doris, how are you?' he beamed.

'Mrs Wallace to you,' she spat back at him. He moved a little away and then returned to the bar.'

'He's despicable,' she stated, 'despicable,' and as he ignored their table Doris became more and more agitated.

'Settle down, Auntie, he's not worth the trouble,' urged Gerald. Perhaps that was the red rag to the bull or could it possibly be the last two or three glasses of white wine? Doris hauled herself up into the attack position.

'O God!' sighed Carmel, looking up at the ceiling fan circulating the air. 'This is all we need.'

'You,' shouted Doris in a more determined voice than usual. 'Dare to drink in this hotel!'

'It's a free world,' was the reply.

'Really? And what's your definition of "free"? Wife? Mistress? Is what it is?'

'I knew this was going to happen,' sighed Carmel again. 'She isn't going to stop.'

'Well, isn't life great if you are a man!'

He did not over-react to Doris for one very good reason. David Osborne was the solicitor for most of the Wallace families; he held most of the business for most of the Catholics in the town and from the large properties surrounding Bradbury, so to antagonise Doris was tantamount to bad business.

'Come on, Doris, let me buy you a drink.'

'Mrs Wallace, to you,' she repeated. By this stage everyone in the bar was all ears. 'You,' she screamed. 'Only the O'Malley's were smart enough to move their legal business to Mr Lester and what have you done for us? Nothing! And your charges are astronomical. All for nothing! But that's not all. You haven't even been to Mass, not once for him.' She was yelling, spreading herself like an aged Marlene Dietrich, with both scrawny arms stretched out along the bar. 'He hasn't even been dead three months, you know. He is much luckier being with the saints than with a father like you,' she spat. At this stage, Doris held the floor and the side bar spilled in to catch the drama. David Osborne was smart enough to work out that this woman was going to cause him trouble but every time he attempted to placate her he did exactly the opposite.

'You see this animal?' she yelled, spinning on Hazel, with Carmel burying her head in her hands. 'His little son died as a result of him cavorting with his secretary cum mistress. What should we call her, Mr. Osborne?' she went on, sarcastically. 'He drowned while they were fucking—isn't it the truth?' She shook a bony hand in his direction.

'You're drunk,' he said, and made for the door.

'You will pay in hell,' she screamed. The air was electric. 'The little boy drowned because they weren't interested in him. He got lost, tried to cross the stream, fell in, hit his head and drowned. But his father hated him, and why? Oh, we all know! Because he was a little eleven year-old who didn't like football, who wasn't like the other little boys. He liked to dress up. He was marvellous and his father thought he was embarrassing. The very learned Mr. David Osborne had a prospective homosexual son. They were fucking,' she repeated, now directing it all at Hazel. 'The little boy got lost. They were supposed to be on a picnic. They sent him off so they were alone for half an hour so he could raise his three centimetre cock and they just forgot about him. The father and the secretary, her!' And here Doris went into full flight. 'Bev, our Bev, dripping in tennis bracelets and diamond rings, necklaces, spending her days sucking three centimetres to ejaculation—or is it five centimetres? His wife did tell me.' Here, even Gerald looked down at the table. He knew, like Carmel, there was no stopping Doris. 'I, for one, like Mr. Hazel, will move all my business on Monday morning, to Mr. Lester's office and so will all of you,' she ended up, narrowing her eyes, 'unless,' and this a little more quietly,' you wish to pay for another diamond bracelet for our Bev.' And she smiled viciously.

CHAPTER FIVE

A Resurrection

CHAPTER FIVE

A Resurrection

The work progressed well at Killkenny, but for Hazel it was all too slow. After the conversation with Lester he had spoken only to Matthew about the sum of money he hoped to raise by the sale of the two shops and the large block of land behind. 'I think we should keep the information quiet for now,' he said.

'Hazel,' laughed Matthew, 'how long have you been here? You can't keep a secret like this. The whole town and everyone else will know the minute you've signed the contract.'

'Oh well, I don't suppose it matters,' he replied, offhandedly, 'but the money will come in handy.'

'It certainly will. The fencing is costing a fortune, not to mention here,' and he looked around the large living room with a table in the centre where they were eating. The builders were still having trouble adapting to what Hazel wanted with the shed, that, as he announced to Matthew and Sebastian, was to become a winter garden.

'A winter garden?' queried Matthew.

Hazel nodded. 'If we can't have a garden outside because of this ghastly climate, we shall have a garden indoors.'

Sebastian looked first at Hazel, expecting a further description of what on earth a winter garden was, and then to Matthew, who was also a little confused.

'O, ye men of little faith,' quoted Hazel, as he cleared the plates away, 'you'll see, you'll see,' and he returned with a sweet he had made, much to Sebastian's pleasure. 'By the way, Matthew, what happened to the auctioneer's umbrella?'

'Good heaven, who told you about that?'

'Carmel Wallace, a few days ago. Where is it now?'

'Well, it's all rusted, but parts of it, I think, are in the little room over the coach house. I'll have a look tomorrow for you, why?'

'Well, this year the ram sales are here, not at the Wallaces.'

'Really,' said Matthew, with a smile, 'I guess that means all the rotted timbers at the sale yards have to be replaced.'

'Sure do—oh, by the way, where are the sale yards?'

Here Matthew broke into laughter. 'Hazel,' he went on, in a falsely exasperated way, 'it's the mess of tangled wooden fences behind the stable block.'

'What?'

'Those are the sale yards, but it's all fallen down. They haven't been used for years. What do you expect?'

'Hm, well, at least we have the umbrella—or bits of it,' and Hazel sat down heavily, reaching for his glass. 'I think we should make it in copper.'

'We? Oh no, Hazel. If you want someone to remake the thing you had better speak to Pat, not me. He is the expert solderer, not me.'

'Do you think it will take a lot of copper?' Hazel queried.

'No idea,' was the reply.

Sebastian excused himself and made for the other large living room, half filled with furniture, with a television set sitting majestically on an upturned crate. Hazel and Matthew continued to discuss the building progress and the slowness of it.

'I received a telephone call today. All the windows and doors should be delivered tomorrow morning, and we're to be blessed with Otto at 11.30.'

When Matthew asked who on earth Otto was, Hazel went on to describe the adventure with the tiny man in the glazier store and his sidekick. Otto was to begin the measuring for all the broken glass in this homestead complex. Jan, for one, had not stopped complaining about several panes that had been broken in the re-siting of her house.

Hazel had decided not to tell Matthew about the money Bob had handed over in the shoe box. He wasn't sure why, but he wasn't telling him—his sixth sense told him to just wait.

Matthew disappeared to watch television with Sebastian, who immediately sat on him, laughing and playing. Matthew took the telecommando and changed channels; from the makeshift kitchen Hazel could hear music he vaguely recognised. After clearing everything away and just before he headed to the living room, his telephone rang. 'Hello, Hazel here. No, not tomorrow, but Thursday, yes, the morning is better for me. Very well. Goodnight,' and he hung up. 'I wonder what she wants,' he thought, and went into the hallway with the large arched window which still, at eight in the evening, had strong light pouring in through those ghastly red and yellow border panes.

Matthew and Sebastian were watching a performance of Prokofiev's 'Peter and the Wolf', Matthew with his arm around Sebastian, telling him the story as the ballet unfolded. Hazel refilled the glasses and they watched in silence. Sebastian's head became heavier and heavier until it lay against Matthew's strong chest and he began to doze. 'I think we'd better put you to bed, Sebastian,' said Matthew, who picked him up and carried him off upstairs. He returned in a quarter of an hour to regain his seat on the leather Chesterfield, one of the few pieces of furniture from Killkenny that didn't need restoration.

'He's quite tired,' he said.

'Who isn't in this terrible heat?'

'It gets hotter next month.'

'Impossible,' replied Hazel, not looking at him, but concentrating on the dancing.

'February can be the worst month of the year.'

'Oh, what joy!' was Hazel's sarcastic reply. 'Oh, by the way, I had a call from the other Hazel.'

'Oh yes? Is there a problem at school?' Matthew looked concerned.

'No idea. I'll find out Thursday morning, but she didn't seem too concerned.'

*   *   *   *   *

The next morning saw a large truck with twelve windows, two pairs of French doors and a separate set of French windows sweep up the drive.

'Fuck! What a mess!'

'Thanks,' said Hazel. 'We're in a transitional stage.'

'Transitional? You're kidding! Looks as if a bomb went off,' and the demolition man and his young sidekick carefully unloaded all the windows and doors plus the decorative window and the little fleche with the weather vane that was destined to sit proudly on top of Sebastian's all-weather structure at the front gate. Hazel called the man aside and discreetly handed him a manila envelope with the agreed sum inside.

'Thanks,' he smiled. 'You should bulldoze the fucking lot and start again,' he said as he surveyed the homestead and then the out-buildings, 'and that!' pointing to the little church.

'It happens to be the O'Malley family chapel,' Hazel said very pretentiously.

'Give us a break, mate. You couldn't even keep pigs in it! Well, you know where to find me if you want anything else. See you!' and the truck disappeared down the drive, with clouds of red dust following it.

Hazel sat down on some of the builders' packaging and just stared about him. In this reflective mood he saw for the first time exactly what the demolition man saw, five tin buildings, all in a very sad state of repair, building materials and equipment everywhere. He slowly raised himself to his feet. What had he done? He had taken an enormous liberty in moving everyone back here. Not one building, residential or otherwise, was in good condition. Everything needed to be remade and the money—oh yes, he thought, the money! The shoe box account would soon be drained. If only Lester had called to say the sale of the shops and land had gone through. 'It's all going to have to be sold to pay for this,' he thought. 'If this shop deal falls through—oh God, what have I done?' And for the first time, a certain realisation overcame him. He had done this because he was angry with Keven who was now galavanting about Asia with his young boyfriend. He had done it out of spite and now all of Sebastian's inheritance was starting not to look quite so bright. 'Perhaps I should have come to some arrangement with the Wallaces and we should all have stayed at the front gate.'

He moved across towards the little church, with all its shattered windows and the two broken doors leaning against the front. He went to walk past and then realised there was someone inside: he could just see a silhouette against the harsh light that was coming in from where once must have stood the main altar. It was Jan and he was taken aback. He had the feeling he was trespassing and moved quietly away, back to the main house.

He was stopped by Pat, who asked him what he wanted done, as he had been speaking to Matthew. Hazel was preoccupied: he still felt that by having watched Jan in the broken down church, sitting in a pew in an area of total disarray, he had done something wrong. It was as if he had trespassed into her private life without permission and he felt badly about it.

'Oh, yes,' he said, shaking his head. Where was Matthew, he wondered? She had oddly unnerved him, but he still couldn't work out why—a lone woman praying in a derelict church. Yet she wasn't alone, he thought. She was to have been a nun, and obviously knew a great deal more than he did.

Then he explained to Pat about the metal umbrella and silently followed him to the little room upstairs in the coach house.

'There's not much of it, is there?' he commented, glancing at the pieces of rusted tin. 'Matthew says you want me to make another. I can, you know. The only subject I liked at school was geometry. I was a bit of a dill at school.' He spoke quietly. 'Matthew was the clever one, not me.'

'Not true,' replied Hazel. 'Matthew says he can't make a copy of this and as you can, tell me how much copper we need and I'll get it for you this morning, as I've got an appointment in Bradbury.'

'I'll try and work it out now.'

'More or less,' said Hazel, not wanting to put Pat in a position where he made a mistake and felt bad about it. 'We can always get more later.'

Pat thanked him, well aware of the opening Hazel had offered him. 'Oh, where's the sheep? Ah, he's here, with the cross.'

'What cross?' asked Hazel as Pat pulled out from underneath a rusty piece of tin a very well modelled sheep in cast iron with a hole right through his stomach.

'It's for the pole that holds up the umbrella and the cross went up on top of the miniature umbrella that's above the sheep.'

'Well, give me some measurements in an hour and I'll get some copper for you to start on the project.'

'I'll need some big pieces of paper and some pencils, as well.

'Absolutely,' was Hazel's response and he left Pat to survey and calculate the quantity of materials he required for his masterpiece. Hazel then walked back across the yard in the blazing heat but steered clear of the church lest he disturb Jan.

Matthew came towards him. He looked at the beautiful man, walked up to him and embraced him tightly. 'Hey, are you OK?' asked Matthew.

'I think so,' replied Hazel as they moved apart. 'Do you really think we shall ever finish?' He sounded dispirited again.

'Of course! We have to finish it all for Sebastian's sake.'

'Of course. For Sebastian,' Hazel agreed.

Suddenly, up the drive came a little van sending dust up in all directions.

'Expecting someone?' asked Matthew.

'This is sure to be Otto.'

The van swept into the forecourt and out stepped the most quaint little man. He could hardly have been five feet tall, balding and with a very round, pleasant face that suggested grand things. He had a way of moving his arms as if he were a prince from some faraway kingdom. He had the most enormous stomach which was balanced by the largest buttocks Hazel had ever seen, so he was perfectly balanced it seemed.

'Well, well, we do have a problem,' said the little man, grandly. 'Where do we start?'

Hazel took him indoors to look at the stair window and then all the other broken windows to be replaced. 'These,' he began. 'Most are cracked anyway,' pointing to the twelve new windows to be fitted into the winter garden and the clerestory glass, which also had to be replaced with the glass that would cut out forty to fifty per cent of the direct light.

'Can be done, but not until the windows are in position. Are there any other decorative windows to reglaze?' he asked in a haughty manner.

'Yes, the church.'

'Oh, a family chapel. How charming!'

'Charming' was probably not the word he would have used if he had seen the interior full of graffiti and not a piece of glass in the frames. 'Oh, we do have a problem,' he said.

Hazel was feeling very edgy this morning and Otto was not helping at all.

'I suggest,' the glazier said, with a grand sweep of his stumpy arm, 'that we begin with the stair window and then the church, but that graffiti will have to go. I really can't have my employees looking at that sort of thing.'

'I didn't exactly do it myself,' snapped Hazel, briskly. 'I believe it's the work of your local illiterate louts, as you can see by the spelling.'

'Oh, but of course. What colour are you thinking of?'

'Pale blue or pale lilac, cool colours, and the large centre panes in fifty per cent block-out grey, I think, 'replied Hazel, being just as pretentious. 'The coloured surrounds must all be sandblasted in a suitable and tasteful design.'

'Oh, I couldn't agree more, Mr. O'Hara. Thank goodness you have managed to take this—how should I say—forgotten property over and are so devotedly resurrecting it.'

Hazel responded with a dull 'Thank you.'

'Well, the moment I have the samples of the flashed glass I will bring them out to you immediately.'

'How kind you are,' cooed Hazel, thinking that if Otto continued in this vein he would personally strangle him.

'As for the designs for the sand-blasting, we have a stock of them and they can all be adapted to any environment. I shall bring them along as well and then we can start work. So very pleasant to have the pleasure of meeting you.'

'Likewise, I'm sure,' and the little white van swept grandly around the courtyard and disappeared like the truck before it in a cloud of fine-red dust. Hazel ran his hand through his hair, or mop of hair, the result of his not having been to the hairdresser. 'Oh fuck! This Otto is going to kill me,' then, realising what time it was, he walked quickly over to the builders to give them a design with measurements he had drawn up and told them to begin on the winter garden. He went back around the front of the house now, being only too aware of the state of everything. Then his phone rang. Yes, he would be in town today if he could get away. Yes, he would call in at Mr. Lester's office and was it good news? The reply was so vague that he felt like screaming. To cover all these costs, now, not to mention three adult wages, they were going to have to sell what they had. 'Oh, why, why did I come here,' he thought,' as Pat came across the yard.

'I have written it all down,' he announced, with a satisfied smile, 'but of course it depends on the width of the copper.'

'Yes, I suppose it does,' agreed Hazel. Today, everything was getting to him.

'Oh, Mum says she wants to see you before you go to town.'

Hazel pushed Pat's measurements into his pocket and headed to Jan's house. 'Jan!' he called out at the door, and she came to open it and step down, as the veranda floor was still not installed.

'Would you get some coarse sandpaper for me,' she asked. He knew before she explained what she wanted it for. 'I'm sorry, but the graffiti in the church is shocking.'

'Yes, I know,' he said softly. 'I'll most certainly get a supply of it.'

He turned and began to walk back to where his car was parked under a tree.

'Oh, Hazel!' Jan called out, walking over to him. 'Thanks, but you don't still have to pay me a salary. Sebastian lives with you, so now I don't do anything.'

Perhaps it was the forlorn sight of her in the destroyed church or the complete honesty of rejecting a salary she thought she was not entitled to, or everything put together, but he just held her in his arms very tightly, not the easiest task, considering her size! 'Your salary will continue as you are teaching Sebastian his prayers.'

'I don't have to be paid for that,' she said softly, looking directly into Hazel's eyes. 'That's more than a pleasure.'

'When the church is finished,' Hazel continued, smiling, 'you will have to take on the responsibilities of sacristan, you know.'

'Thanks,' was all she said as her ample frame moved back to her verandaless house and the flyscreen door slammed closed.

* * * * *

He was late and he hated being late, but what could he do? He had had to wait for Otto—what a character and what a shape!

He thought he would do things logically, first Lester. He was shown in by a very efficient-looking secretary of about forty. 'Come in, Hazel,' was the welcoming cry. He walked in and sat down.

'Well, I must say you look a bit tired this morning.'

'It's probably afternoon now,' he said.

'In fact it is. Well, shall we get straight to the point. The supermarket chain will not accept 2.5 million.'

'Great,' muttered Hazel. 'This is all I need today—Otto and a business disaster.'

'Oh, you've met Otto? He's quite a character but very, very efficient.'

'I'm sure he is,' agreed Hazel without enthusiasm. Then he jerked his head up as he heard Lester say, 'The contract is here for you to sign.'

'Sign what? I thought you said they wouldn't agree to buy?'

'Oh, I didn't say anything of the kind. You can sign here. The price they are going to pay is 2.3. I took the liberty of saying you would accept.'

'Mr. Lester, you're a saint!'

'I'm afraid not, but this should help finances at Killkenny. The other properties in town I would suggest you hang on to. One of them has a vacant block of land beside it for sale. I am suggesting that from the sale money from the others we purchase this vacant block of land as it's going for very little indeed. The family are settling a death, so they are out to liquidate everything and the house on Elm Drive with a vacant block as an attached asset could only double the price of the original block.'

'Go ahead and purchase it,' urged Hazel.

'On the condition that there are no problems with the titles—and there are none, I can assure you—the supermarket chain wishes to settle in thirty days. Not bad, I think. You know we have been so busy this week. Can you believe it? Do you know Mrs Doris Wallace?'

'Yes, I have had the pleasure.'

'Well, it seems she is not happy with the Osbourne practice and has transferred everything here, as have quite a few of Mr. Osbourne's clients. I can't think what he has done to upset them.'

Hazel smiled. 'Mrs Wallace may end up being your best public relations officer.'

'Really? Are you sure? I drink at the Commercial Hotel.'

'Perhaps a glass at the Railway Hotel may net you even more clients.'

'I see your point,' and he nodded his head. 'Perhaps in thirty days we may just do that—a little celebration together.'

'Why not? Hazel agreed, and he fled for his second appointment at St. Mary's.

*   *   *   *   *

'I am so sorry I am late. It's been one thing after another today. Is something wrong with Sebastian?' he asked.

'We have a little problem. I see him every week. You know, he always comes to me on Thursday afternoons, because he dislikes competitive sport and he refuses to join in. So he comes and has a chat with me and then he takes himself to the library. I wouldn't force him to play— I don't believe in it. You see we had another little boy like Sebastian, well not exactly the same, but his name was Timothy Osbourne.'

'Good heavens,' exclaimed Hazel. 'Doris Wallace went crazy in the hotel about this little boy.'

'I'm not surprised. He was just so special. He was a very slight boy with a mop of blonde curls and big light green eyes. He was like an exotic tropical butterfly. He was admirable, moving quickly and softly. He was with us at St. Mary's until half-way through last year, when his father withdrew him and placed him in the state system. You know,' she went on, staring at Hazel, 'his father moved him because he thought we were sheltering him too much and he had to get out and be the same as the other boys. He couldn't, though. He was just so beautiful and the one person in this world he loved, can you believe it, was Doris Wallace.'

'So that's why she was so angry with the father.'

'She hates him like poison and now the little boy is dead.' Here she stopped and reached for a tissue, but didn't use it. She leaned down and from a lower drawer in her desk took out a large manila envelope and opened it. Out came ten figures cut in paper and all the hands joined to make a human chain. Each one had different coloured trousers and bright shirts, all very well fitted and glued.

'It's beautiful, isn't it?' she said and carefully folded it up again, replacing it her drawer. 'He never did sport, either. Every Thursday afternoon Doris would come and they would sit in the corner of the dining room, cutting out things in coloured paper. Doris always ordered the paper from a supplier in Melbourne.'

'Were they related?'

'Yes. Timothy's mother was of the Wallace line, but she has been in very poor health for years and now the cancer has spread through her whole body. She doesn't even know that Timothy is dead—she's on so much morphine she just doesn't grasp anything now. So, you see, Doris and Timothy would, every Thursday afternoon, work with beautiful coloured papers. They used to cover little boxes, which were done ever so well, so precisely. Timothy had the skill and Doris encouraged it. The local hardware shop kept all the little boxes, so Doris collected them and then they went to work creating these little masterpieces. He saw Doris every Sunday at Mass and always sat with her. I don't think Mr. Osbourne was happy about it at all. Everyone knew he attended Mass as a public relations exercise for his business. He has most of the Catholic business in his hands.'

'Or did have,' interrupted Hazel.

'What do you mean?'

'Doris Wallace has moved all her accountancy and investments to Mr. Lester.'

'Good for her. I am thinking of transferring the school's business into his hands, also. Osbourne should be shot to let a little boy like that wander in the bush all alone.' Here she stopped and this time did use the crumpled tissue to blot the corners of her eyes. 'I'm sorry,' she went on, quietly.

'Don't be,' said Hazel.

'I'm drifting off the track. I don't mind Sebastian going to the library to read while the others play sport, but he doesn't read—he flicks through the pages and looks at his watch, waiting for the bell so he can go home. He's very proud of his watch.'

'Yes, he is. Matthew gave it to him the first day he came to St. Mary's.'

'Yes, he told me his whole world is Matthew and you.'

'I think it's very much Matthew. He loves him very much.'

'Encourage that love, Hazel,' she said firmly. 'There's enough hate around for everyone, but never enough love.' She sighed. 'In our little talks each week I get a running newsletter of everything that happens at Killkenny and I can tell you Sebastian is so excited about the winter garden.'

Hazel laughed: 'If it ever gets finished.'

'Oh, it will,' she smiled. 'Sebastian's waiting for it. Now, I have an idea, but it depends on you,' and here there was a pause, 'and Matthew. Freda Carstairs was once a music teacher here and retired but misses the school terribly. She is not old and I was thinking that as she now takes private students I wonder if I could convince her to come here every Thursday afternoon to teach Sebastian the piano. What do you think?'

'It sounds a great idea.'

'I don't know how much it would cost you.' Here Hazel interrupted. 'As from this morning, money is not a major problem.'

'Good. Do you have a piano at Killkenny, because I am afraid without one Sebastian may see the lessons as empty. He will obviously be out to show Matthew his skills. Oh, by the way, your teaching of his prayers is very good. He likes to be able to recite them with the others.'

'Oh, not me,' shrugged Hazel. 'Jan is teaching him.'

'Congratulate her for me, then. Jan hasn't had an easy life. She is a good person. Now I have forgotten: did I ask you if you have a piano?'

'Yes, you did, and the answer is yes, but I am sure it's filled with red dust inside.' They both laughed.

'In this district, everything is filled with red dust. If you like—and if Sebastian is happy with this idea—I can send our piano tuner out to Killkenny. He comes to the school once a term. We have four pianos here and don't ask me why but they always seem out of tune.'

Hazel stood up and thanked her, suggesting that he had taken up too much of her time.

'Not at all,' she replied, as she followed him to her door. Then she seized his arm. 'Hazel, please be careful of Sebastian. He is just like Timothy Osbourne, not physically but mentally. Very bright and very particular—like tropical butterflies.'

'I promise Matthew and I will be very careful with him.'

'Never let him go away without being able to be contacted, will you?'

'No, we won't,' at which Hazel bent down and kissed her on the cheek. As he went down the path and towards his car he saw a chain of brightly coloured people made by a little boy who, of all the people in the world, had loved and been loved by Doris Wallace. He sat in his car looking straight ahead. So that's why Doris had reacted violently the other day. Why in this place do you have to learn these things so slowly? Why the hell won't people just tell you?

* * * * *

201

He then made for the hardware shop and they rolled up a length of copper for him, put lots of paper around it, big sheets and a dozen sheets of coarse and another dozen of medium sandpaper and with great difficulty inserted it all into his car.

'OK. I've done that. The supermarket and then home.' But it was not to be quite so simple. After the copper had filled most of the back and part of the front of his car, he had ordered a bit more than Pat had asked for, but it was the width of the damned stuff, not the length that was the problem. A quick dash to the supermarket and then home. It was now 3.30. He had grabbed a sandwich at the bakery along with the bread and a few little bits and pieces but was still very aware of keeping Sebastian's carbohydrate level down. He was beginning to lose weight and in the face was starting to look like a little man, not the same overweight youngster, and his shorts for school had come in one notch at the sides. He then made a quick dash to the supermarket, always aware that more than an hour away means you have to do without things. He glanced at his list and then his watch and telephoned Matthew. 'Can you collect Sebastian?' he asked. 'I'm still in the supermarket and by the way we are 2.3 million richer, so I'm looking for champagne.'

'Sure. I'll collect him on the way—and good work, Hazel.'

Hazel said thanks and hung up. Looking at his list, he went from one aisle to another very systematically. This had been a lesson he had learned well from Jan: write down what you are missing all the time and so he had a large pad in the kitchen. He had finished one aisle and then he heard a voice he knew only too well. As he turned the corner there was Doris Wallace holding court just short of the freezer section. 'Oh, Mr. Hazel, how are you?' she exclaimed.

'Very well,' was the reply, and, pushing his shopping trolley to one side, he swept up and automatically gave her a kiss on the cheek.

'Oh, Mr. Hazel, you are a one! We've just been talking about Heather having a funny turn at the Railway the other day. How peculiar!' She turned to a very butch woman in tee shirt and shorts. 'You know,

Anne,' she began,' I don't understand why our Hether was so confused about netball playing and dildos.'

Anne turned bright purple and stepped back to apologise to the shelf she had backed into.

'I have to be going. See you!' She quickly disappeared.

'Oh!' exclaimed Doris, with a knowing look at Hazel. 'Silly me! I forgot she was the coach of the netball team. How could I have forgotten!'

After that comment, everything was bland in comparison until a trolley whizzed around the corner, blocked in its passage by this little group.

'Oh, Cheryl, I haven't seen you for ages,' cooed Doris, obviously, to Hazel's mind, ready for fun. 'How is everything on the property?' She said this in the most deadpan way.

'Fine, Doris, just fine. Look, I'm in a bit of a hurry, so if you women would just let me through.'

'Oh, Cheryl, you're always in a hurry—but probably not to get home.' Doris was pretending she was looking at some produce in small bottles on the shelf.

'What's that supposed to mean?' snapped the platinum-dyed Cheryl.

'Oh dear, what did I say,' Doris was all innocent smiles.

'You know exactly what you said,' spat Cheryl.

'Do you dye your hair yourself, dear?' asked Doris, baiting her.

Cheryl loathed Doris, and family reunions which occurred once a year were sheer torture for her. She hated the Wallaces: if the men were stupid, the women all came equipped with crocodile teeth.

'Cheryl, do you know our Mr. Hazel?' she asked.

'I'm not interested in this type of man,' came the superior reply.

'Oh, Cheryl, the politically correct way to say that is a gay man.' Here Doris paused to see if her audience was attentive. She need have had no fear—all ears were open. 'But how forgetful of me,' and here Doris feigned a laugh, 'you're an expert in this field. We all have something to learn from someone.'

Cheryl was furious that Doris, in front of a group of people she would never have deigned even to speak to, was being brought into a conversation that she found, to say the least, awkward.

'Dearest Cheryl, how is Ashley?'

'Fine,' came the clipped reply.

'Oh, how nice! No more boarding school reunions?'

Cheryl now realised that Doris was out for her blood, not Ashley's. She attempted to push roughly through the crowded aisle of shopping trolleys.

'You only have to ask, Cheryl. It's just like being with Ashley's friends, isn't it? Who is where?' And at this point Cheryl hit the attack button and spat at Doris, who was close to her: 'Keep your evil mouth shut! If I had a lighted stick of dynamite I would plunge it into your mouth.'

'Oh,' Doris came back, quick as a whiplash, 'but I should remove it at once, dear, and place it in an orifice of yours that is obviously rarely used.'

Cheryl drew her hand back and with maximum force swung it across in the direction of Doris's face, only to have Hazel block the stroke and grasp Cheryl by the wrist just, and only just, missing Doris's face. She probably deserved it, thought Hazel, but not here.

One of the women, holding a jar of gherkins, was so overwhelmed at the performance that she raised her hand to her mouth, forgetting she had the gherkins in her hand and down they crashed, little gherkins swimming amongst broken glass and vinegar. 'Oh, Doris, I am so sorry,' gasped the confused woman, for some reason assuming she had dropped the jar in Doris's own home.

Hazel noted that Doris had not moved an inch, even when she must have seen the slap coming. She stood defiant. 'You bitch!' snapped Cheryl, leaving her shopping trolley and dashing up the aisle with her handbag tightly clutched to her side.

'She is a very silly girl,' was Doris's only comment. 'Now, do come with me, Mr. Hazel. There is a special this week on soups. Do you like them in this weather? I like them chilled, ever so tasty,' and off they went, heading in the other direction.

'Well, sweetie,' asked Hazel in a very familiar way, 'what is Ashley all about?'

'Well, I thought you would know.'

'Listen, Doris, I knew many years ago a man in Melbourne called Ashley Wallace, but I will lay a bet it's not the same one.'

'Can't be, Mr. Hazel. You see, he went to school with the O'Malley brothers, at Tendale. Well one doesn't want to repeat hearsay—'

'Try,' interrupted Hazel.

'Well, it seems that as we are being politically correct of course, that Ashley and Keven were, how can I put it?'

'Lovers!' was his sharp reply.

'Oh, Mr. Hazel, I forgot you knew Keven—well, very well!' She raised her eyebrows.

'No,' he said bluntly, 'but it wasn't for the want of trying.'

'Oh, you're lucky. The O'Malley men lose their looks quickly. One wouldn't have you with a faded O'Malley man, Mr. Hazel,' and she gave him a wicked smile. 'I think Ashley thinks he is still head prefect. Why is it, Mr. Hazel, men really never grow up?'

'If only you could tell me,' he grinned.

'Depending on the man, I may just be able to help you—you never know. I didn't want to say anything in front of the other women. They do talk so!'

Hazel raised his eyebrows.

'Oh yes, Mr. Hazel, people are such chatterboxes around here. You must be careful.'

'Oh, I will. Thanks for the advice.'

'I hear that you sold the properties for 2.3 million,' she murmured while looking at soup labels. 'I presume the ram sales are at Killkenny this year, especially now the illegal, or should I saw the casual, gateways have been closed at the back section of Killkenny?' She spoke in a tone that was exactly the same as if she had been recommending one brand of soup against another.

'You don't miss a thing, do you?' remarked Hazel.'

'At my age, you can't afford to. Well, I must be off.' She took three or four paces and then returned, and in a manner that was completely different she held Hazel's arm with a grasp that surprised him. 'Promise me you will look after your little Spaniard.'

'I promise' and he gave her a kiss. She turned and smiled. 'And the other one as well.'

'Given half the chance.'

'That's the spirit,' she laughed and disappeared down another aisle amongst late afternoon shoppers.

Hazel stopped at the bottle department and took two bottles of champagne, with some frozen items in his freezer bag (another tip from Jan). As he headed back towards the car he heard in the back of his mind a comment that repeated and repeated: 'Never let him go away without being able to be contacted'. He spun around and walked back up Main Street, past six shops and into a store that sold electrical goods. He bought the simplest portable telephone available and put A$40 on it. As he headed out, he passed a sale basket filled with CDs. He put his parcels on the ground and quickly flicked through them and at the bottom of this jumble was a copy of Prokofiev's 'Peter and the Wolf'. He returned to the girl and asked if she had any more ballet music and she quizzically looked at the CD. 'I didn't realise it was ballet music,' she commented in a nonchalant way. 'No call for it here, but there's a box of old stock in the storeroom. The next time you're passing, stop in and you can have a look. See ya.' Laden with supermarket bags and the purchase from the electrical store, he headed off to Killkenny in the exhausting pitiless heat of late February.

*   *   *   *   *

When he arrived, the first thing he did was put the champagne in the freezer and before he unpacked the rest he went directly to the dining room to see the carpenters' progress.

'Finally,' he exclaimed. The two beautiful French doors stood fitted into the space that had once been the window, and when they were swung open one entered directly into the large shed with the clerestory that had six fitted windows either side, symmetrically placed, and the other two French windows in the corners of the end wall, leaving a large solid wall directly ahead when you entered.

'A fountain. We need a fountain near the end of the garden room, that's what we need.'

'What do we need?' Hazel spun around to see Mathew behind him. 'Well, it's all coming together,' he smiled, 'but I must confess I can't imagine it finished.'

'Patience, patience,' said Hazel. 'Come on, let's have a drink. Where's Sebastian?'

'He's with Mum. She helps him with all his homework now. She seems a different person.'

Hazel completed stacking all the groceries away. 'Oh, I forgot I'd got this for you,' and he handed Matthew the CD of 'Peter and Wolf'.

'Thanks, Hazel, it's very kind of you.' He squeezed his arm.

'A kiss would be better,' teased Hazel and to his pleasant surprise Matthew kissed him.

Hazel stared at him. 'Well, it's certainly been worth waiting for. Open the bottle, beautiful, it's time to celebrate 2.3 million dollars and Mr. Lester's good health.'

So when Sebastian returned, the music of 'Peter and the Wolf' was playing, with Matthew and Hazel chatting and laughing.

'How was school today?' asked Matthew, as the boy slid into his arms.

'It was OK,' he said very quietly.

'I have a telephone for you,' Hazel said, at which Sebastian extracted himself from Matthew's arms and crossed to Hazel's chair. 'Listen to me very carefully,' he went on, in a serious tone. 'This is not a toy. I will program four telephone numbers into it, mine, Matthew's, Jan's and the Principal of St. Mary's. If you are ever in trouble, you just switch it on here and then press one of these buttons and you will contact one of us. Do you understand?'

'Yes,' he replied, very surprised at Hazel being so stern about a telephone. 'Hazel, why don't I have any money like the kids on the bus?'

'What do you mean?' asked Hazel.

'Well, when we get on the bus and at the edge of Bradbury, the bus stops and they all get off and buy an ice-cream.' Here he stopped and looked at the floor. 'But I can't have one because I haven't got any money.'

Hazel felt a lump rising in his throat and he instinctively drew the youngster toward him and embraced him. 'Sebastian,' he said in a whisper,' you can have money whenever you want it. Why didn't you ask me?'

'I didn't know how to. I haven't had money before.'

'I'll tell you what, we shall find a box and you can put it on the dressing table and I will always leave money in it for you. If you need more, tell me and you can have it at once. Never ever be afraid to ask me for anything.'

The boy moved back to Matthew and leant up against the side of his chair, smiling. 'I'll just go over to Jan. She has a box I know she doesn't want.' There was a banging of the screen door as Sebastian fled over to Jan to tell her he was going to have money. She was also surprised, as it had never crossed her mind, like the others, that he needed money, as everything was paid in advance for him.

Hazel took a large gulp of champagne. 'I feel a real heel. Here we are drinking champagne and he couldn't even buy an ice-cream.'

'I never thought of it, either,' replied Matthew.

Hazel repeated to him the interview he had had with the Principal, firstly about the little Osbourne boy and then about the piano lessons.

'Sounds fantastic to me,' said Matthew,' but I tell you the grand piano in the other room there, under canvas, will need a lot of work.'

'Like everything here,' sighed Hazel. 'How's the work amongst the sheep?' He grinned.

'They're just as nervous as ever,' answered Matthew, laughing. 'Finally the fencing contractors have completed the most damaged sections and now we are starting some boundary work. The two windmills are in working order, the troughs have been re-bricked and now hold water, as does the one near the house here. But I see one of the tanks on the side is leaking. It's been soldered before, but I think we need a new one.'

'Order it,' said Hazel. 'With this sort of capital let's get as much finished as we can.'

'The guttering here needs totally replacing, as it does on most of the buildings. It's just rusted away.'

'But do you think we shall ever use them?'

'It does rain, believe it or not,' insisted Matthew.

'I'll wait until I see it. Oh God, is that the time? I haven't even started dinner. Sebastian will be starving.'

'He's not the only one!' laughed Matthew.

'OK, you lay the table. I'm off to the kitchen,' but before he reached the entrance hall and started for the kitchen Sebastian made a noisy entrance.

'Here, Hazel, look, I have a box. Look!' He showed Hazel an old shoe box with a lid.

'It'll do for now.' He smiled as he ran his hands through the boy's black bushy hair. 'Here.'

Hazel pulled from his pocket a ten dollar note. 'Open the lid.' Sebastian did so very rapidly and closed it again sharply after the note had been dropped in. He fled upstairs to place the box on the chest of drawers in the room he still insisted on sharing with Matthew.

After he had said grace, they chatted together, with Sebastian obviously elated that he could also buy an ice cream the next day, the same as the others. 'I might just buy two,' he said, with a wicked look in his eyes.

* * * * *

Pat was more than pleased with the copper and used the large sheets of brown wrapping paper as patterns for the umbrella. At every moment when he was not helping the others, he was to be found in the old coach house cutting and soldering his great work of art.

With the weekend in front of them and the workmen not there, Hazel began a systematic plan for organising the work. The interior of the main house was almost finished in the sense that the electrical wiring and plumbing were now complete and the carpenters had made good progress but the greater part of the house had to be re-plastered as the old lath and plaster, even though it was papered over, was in a shocking condition. It was badly cracked and in sections it had crashed to the floor. So, thought Hazel, the plasterers can start on Monday, and if they work half a week on each room—Oh God!—it will be next Christmas before it's finished! He sat on a packing crate in despair, glancing about at the beautiful pressed metal ceilings and then letting his eyes slowly move down the crumbling walls with the shredded wallpaper. The carpenters were also, on Monday, to start lining the garden room in cement sheeting, as it had to be a lining material that, if it got wet, would not be a problem, and the flooring then had to be brick paved. Oh, it will never get done, he sighed, but boldly picked up his telephone and called the interior decorating store he had worked with to ask as a favour if they would send him a particular sample book of wallpaper and another one of fabrics, offering to offset any costs.

'Only for you, Hazel,' was the reply. 'You are not going back into decorating, are you?

'No, this is a private house.'

'You had better let the Post Office know. They tend to get excited about large packets.'

'Will do,' he confirmed.

Sebastian spent most of the weekend helping Matthew and as they were working not so far from the homestead they were home for lunch each day, laughing and joking all the time, but as soon as dinner was over Sebastian was asleep in Matthew's arms.

*   *   *   *   *

The next week began with a change of plans yet again. Hazel finally agreed to Jan's house, as it was now called, having the veranda put on, so the workmen, instead of starting work in the garden room, began on it. The plasterers arrived, so the furniture, such as there was, was moved to the other large reception room, including the dining table. In less than half a day, the workmen demolished the lath and plaster walls in the reception room and by the late afternoon had one newly plastered wall complete. The four men worked very rapidly, which surprised Hazel. All the old lath and plaster was taken out and loaded into a skip but the dust! It was everywhere and Hazel thought it was better if they all moved back to the governess's cottage as they were likely to die of asphyxiation. So move back they did: this time Sebastian returned to his old bedroom alone without any problem but on his chest of drawers stood a shoe box that he constantly lifted the lid off to check the contents. He was sometimes genuinely surprised, as Matthew, as well as Hazel, contributed to the shoe box funds.

*   *   *   *   *

Thursday spun around yet again and this was the day that was most exhausting for Hazel. It meant shopping in Bradbury, still an hour and twenty minutes away. First, the drive in, in the glare of the early morning, after setting all the workmen to their tasks, and then working through the famous shopping list, as he had discovered to forget something was fatal: one and a half hours in and one and a half hours back was a long way to go for 2lb of potatoes. So he now, like Jan, bought in bulk, and as Thursday was also Jan's shopping day they quite often met up and Hazel would deposit in the ample space of Jan's four-wheel drive the purchases that just wouldn't fit into a lilac Volkswagon. He was beginning to think that the Volkswagon might be smart for the city but way out here not quite so convenient.

He stopped off at the Post Office to advise them that he was expecting two large or one very large parcel and would the delivery person please deposit them in Sebastian's rain shelter.

'Oh, Mr. O'Hara, how do you do. We've heard so much about you.'

'Have you?' he replied.

'Oh yes,' said the matron behind the counter. 'I believe you are putting in a winter garden. Sounds strange for out here, but it must be wonderful.'

'If it ever gets finished,' he muttered.

'Oh, are you lacking materials?' she asked, as the two women in the queue behind him listened intently.

'As a matter of fact, yes. It's difficult to locate what I want in Bradbury.'

'Oh, you won't find anything here, Mr. O'Hara. You will have to go to Mortlake. I have a nephew who has a large nursery with lots of ornaments and pots and things. He's the best in this district. Such an arty person, very talented, if I do say so. Just a moment,' as she reached into her handbag beside her to draw out an address book. 'Here we are.' On a piece of paper she wrote down 'Robert Patterson' and the telephone number. 'I'm not sure of the address exactly, but call first and he will tell you exactly where he is located.' When Hazel started to thank her, she continued. 'A pleasure—and don't worry about the packages. I will personally have a word with the delivery girl.' As he left, he had a feeling of two pairs of matrons' eyes drilling into his spine, as they moved up to the counter to cross-examine the lady behind as to who he was and what exactly was a winter garden.

On Thursdays he always now met Carmel and Gerald for lunch at the Railway Hotel about 1 o'clock, as most of his rushing about was completed and he liked to collapse and catch up with the weekly gossip with a glass in his hand. He was always at the same table with Carmel and Gerald, having started not to eat but definitely to drink.

'Hi Hazel,' was the greeting from the good-looking barman.

'Hi! Another bottle, I think.'

'Coming up,' he said breezily, as Hazel flopped down into a chair.

'Does this heat ever finish?'

'Sort of,' Gerald replied. 'How are you, anyway?'

'Exhausted. We have had to move out of the main house and the plasterers are demolishing everything and there are literally clouds of that fine white dust that gets up your nose and down your throat.'

'I can imagine,' agreed Carmel, drily. 'What did you do with the furniture?'

'We've tried to put it back into the big cottage but no go, so it's all standing on planks in the garden room. Oh, so attractive!'

Gerald laughed. 'This place sounds as if it's going to be a palace when it's finished.'

'If it's finished,' groaned Hazel, as the attractive barman brought to the table another bottle and removed the empty one.

'Gerald,' said Carmel,' why is it that when the barman comes near you take on the distinct look of a Labrador dog that has just run two miles?'

'Ha, ha, such humour, Carmel!' retorted Gerald sharply.

'Listen,' said Hazel, trying to change the subject, but before he could start the barman announced that the last orders for lunch would be taken in less than ten minutes.

'Oh, what are you having?' asked Gerald, glancing carefully at the menu written on a blackboard.

'Hm, I'll have the roast turkey—oh, no I won't,' said Carmel, looking further down the list, 'I'm having the salad with assorted cold cuts.'

'Sounds good to me also,' agreed Hazel.

'I had thought of asking for some hot meat,' said Gerald, still surveying the board.

'Darling, the search for hot meat has always been your problem!'

'Bitch!' was the casual retort. 'OK, I'll have the same.'

'You don't have to, Gerald. There is such a thing as choice on the menu.' At which point the waitress arrived. 'We'll have two salads and assorted cold cuts, and he,' she went on,' wants some hot meat.'

At this the waitress giggled. 'He's on late shift this afternoon, if that's what you want to know.'

'I'll have a steak and salad,' said Gerald, narrowing his eyes and then smiling falsely at the waitress.

'Well done or rare?'

'Medium.' So the waitress left, grinning from ear to ear.

'How far is Mortlake from here,' asked Hazel.

'From here or from Killkenny?'

'From Killkenny,' he said.

'About an hour and a half. I don't think I've been there for years. Why?'

'Well, I'm told, via the lady in the Post Office, that there is a big nursery with pots and things. I thought I might pay a visit.'

'When?' asked Carmel, sharply.

'Well,' replied Hazel, rather surprised, 'early next week. Why?'

'If you would like some company, I wouldn't mind going and having a look myself.'

'That would be great,' Hazel replied. 'You coming, Gerald?'

'I can't all next week. I'm confined to barracks selling footware to cretins. I can't tell you what a strain it all is.'

'It shows,' said Carmel, drily. Gerald chose to ignore the comment.

'I can be at the front gate and we can go in my car,' offered Hazel.

'Not on your life, Hazel. You just wait at the homestead. I shall arrive and then transport you to Mortlake. You don't think that I'm going to miss an opportunity to see Killkenny in the making, do you?'

Hazel laughed. 'You're in for a disappointment, I think. It's still a bit of a wreck.'

'Date fixed.' She smiled, which was rare.

* * * * *

The meal was finished and Carmel began to frown. 'Are you all right?' said Gerald. and reached over to hold her hand that lay on the table. She slowly withdrew it and reached down to unzip an imaginary pocket in her handbag and to withdraw the invisible pack of cards. She did not deal them to anybody but seemed, according to Hazel, to lay out six or seven in a row, then move them from one place to another. Then she gathered them all together and turned them over. She jerked her head up and stared straight at him with an intensity that made him feel uncomfortable.

'What's your legal position with Sebastian?' she asked.

'I have power of attorney for Killkenny.'

'I didn't ask you that.' Her voice was hard.

'I have shared legal guardianship over him, as it was necessary for the legal side of things here.'

'Who do you share it with?'

'Kevin O'Malley. Why?'

'Before you go home this afternoon, call and check with Mr. Lester. It's very important to know exactly where you stand with regard to Sebastian.' She collected the cards and returned them to the invisible pocket, then continued as if nothing had happened. Both she and Gerald passed funny remarks about people they knew, but Hazel felt a chill, even on a day like this, run right up his spine. What the hell was wrong, he wondered, and then realised he didn't exactly know the whole legal situation with Sebastian.

'Oh, well, what a pleasant surprise. Not in the shop, Gerald?

'No, Auntie. How are you?

'As well as maybe,' was Doris Wallace's reply. 'And how is Killkenny, Mr. Hazel?' totally ignoring Carmel, who signalled that, as Doris had arrived, another bottle and glass were required, but as the attractive barman was very busy he put the opened bottle and glass on the bar and a jaunty young man brought them over instead.

'Oh, thank you, Trick,' said Doris. 'Do you know Mr. Hazel? He's rebuilding Killkenny.'

'Hi, I'm Trick. Glad to meet you,' and they exchanged a hand shake.

'I have known Tricky Thompson since he was born,' began Doris. 'Always the joker, is our Trick.'

He was about five feet four tall—or short—depending on the point of view. He had a very good looking face with enormous pale brown eyes that just screeched the devil, was always laughing, always happy, and extremely popular at the Railway. He was the one who always accepted a dare and ended up doing the most stupid things to everyone's entertainment. He was kind and very considerate but he had this streak in him that made him get up to the most ridiculous high jinks.

'He's never changed, has our Trick,' Doris continued. 'I remember when—'

'Careful, Doris, I don't want you giving away my secrets'.

'Tricky, your secrets are so public as to not be secrets at all. Anyway,' she went on, not giving up, 'as I was saying, Mr. Hazel, our Trick went to the Agricultural Show we have each year. Now it's pretty poor, but once it was quite the thing. Everyone went, you know. I came second one year with my blackberry jam. I was beaten by Caroline Timms, fairly, of course, but I for one know she never sterilised her bottles very well. I personally would never touch the stuff she made when they had streets stalls for the church. Anyway,' she repeated, 'our Trick was bit silly—'

'It's years ago,' he protested.

'Don't interrupt,' insisted Doris, draining a glass and letting Carmel refill it, with a look on her face which said that they had all heard the story before. 'Well, Trick decided to attract the attention of one of the girls, so he whipped his penis and I was told he wiggled it about, but he hadn't seen old Mrs. Riley, and as she was very old fashioned, always carried a parasol, when she saw our Trick exposing himself she swiped and hit it.'

'Hit it!' exploded Trick. 'The old girl drew blood!'

'But what I don't understand,' Doris continued with a grin, 'is that old Mrs Riley had glasses that looked like the end of bottles. How could she have seen to hit such a tiny target?'

Doris got what she wanted: everyone laughed, including Trick.

'That bloody parasol had a metal tip and she obviously stamped it on the ground when she wasn't using it as an umbrella. I mean, like a walking stick, so the metal edge was like a knife. I had a bandage on it for weeks and when I went to have a piss, well you can imagine.' He burst into laughter. 'I'll never whip it out again near anyone with a parasol, that's for sure! Nice to meet you, Hazel. See you all around. Bye, Doris.' He gave her a kiss and disappeared back to the bar.

'I have always thought that Trick was descended from a leprechaun,' commented Doris. 'In fact, I am certain. He really is the nicest and funniest man around.'

Carmel added, 'You won't believe it, but he is married to the most beautiful girl in town—rich, everything going for her and she is so jealous of Trick. She absolutely adores him.'

'I've thought of that,' said Gerald, coming back into the conversation. 'It's probably because he's not boring. At home they probably laugh and joke all the time, not like all the other married couples, who don't say anything but just gaze at the television screen.'

'Goodness, I had never thought of that,' Doris said, in a surprised way. 'I never saw you as a deep thinker, Gerald.'

'Oh thanks, Auntie,' came the sarcastic reply.

Hazel suddenly cried, 'Good heavens, it's half past two. I have to pick up Sebastian at four. I must be going.'

'Don't forget we have a date for next week. Let's make it Tuesday, and if something comes up, give me a ring, otherwise I'll be at Killkenny early in the morning.'

Carmel smiled, with Doris none the wiser for once about the arrangements and Carmel definitely not giving any information at all to her as to why she would be at the homestead that day.

Hazel raced straight to the car and, sitting inside, instantly telephone Mr. Lester. 'He's very busy, I'm afraid,' replied his neat secretary. 'I don't give a damn. This is important.'

She switched him through and he apologised at once. 'I'm sorry, I know you're busy but it is essential I know about the guardianship of Sebastian.' His voice was tense.

'Just a moment. I know exactly where that file is.' Lester returned.

'Give me the information in layman's terms, please.'

'Well, it's like this, the legal guardians of Sebastian O'Malley are Keven O'Malley and yourself, shared equally. This was what Mr. Keven O'Malley wanted. He obviously had a great trust in you. If either of you pass on the other takes complete responsibility until Sebastian turns twenty one years old. The other part of the document states, as you put it, in layman's terms, that should Mr. Keven O'Malley pre-decease you, the whole responsibility for Killkenny and

Sebastian is yours. Is that clear enough? I didn't realise you didn't have a copy of this document. I will have it copied at once and sent to you in tomorrow's post.'

'Thank you so much, Mr. Lester.'

'It's a pleasure, Hazel,' he replied and hung up.

Twenty one years old, and he's eleven now, so that's another ten years. Oh, I am going to be ancient before he legally takes control, positively ancient, he sighed, and knowing he had approximately half an hour before setting off home he returned to the supermarket, collected all his frozen items and a dozen bottles of cold wine, as Jan had taken the rest for him. He then sped off toward home.

*　*　*　*　*

He passed the bus, stopped at the service station that sold the ice-creams and smiled as he drove past. He wouldn't stop and collected Sebastian as he was probably enjoying the privilege for once of being the same as all the rest, licking an ice-cream as they travelled home on the long ashfelt road that disappeared into a heat shimmer.

He pulled into the drive and had to draw in to the side as the plasterers waved to him as they departed and headed back to where he had just come from. The bus finally arrived. Hazel couldn't believe it could be so hot and not a single cloud was there in the bright blue sky. He looked about before the bus came completely to a halt and in this split second it came to him again that it would be ten years before Sebastian was twenty one. He sighed. Then another thought entered his head; ten years fixed with Matthew and a smile crept across his face. The passenger door swung open and Sebastian appeared and then nursed the packages that were on the seat on his knee and began to tell him about his first music lesson in a very excited tone.

'She is very nice and she can play the piano very well. She played a little piece for me. She is very clever.'

The very clever woman, namely Freda Carstairs, was a carbon copy of Mrs. Doubtfire from the film, the hair, the glasses, the clothes, the shoes. It had been for Freda an exciting day, as it had been for Sebastian. She had thought that at sixty two, although she looked and dressed much older, she had had enough of teaching children and had decided to retire, but she missed St. Mary's dreadfully and this opportunity to return she had jumped at. The Principal was one hundred per cent sure that Freda and Sebastian would hit it off splendidly and she was correct. After ten minutes with Sebastian, she had fallen under his spell, his big blue eyes watched everything she did and he began to learn under her careful eyes the skills necessary for playing the piano. She had been filled in by the Principal with Sebastian's whole history, so she was prepared for him, but what she wasn't prepared for was his appearance. She thought him to be the most beautiful child in the world, which is quite a claim, but it was Freda's opinion and no one would have dared to attempt to change it.

After her first lesson with Sebastian, she went to speak to the Principal using every exotic adjective to describe him. It was then that the Principal brought up the amount to be paid for the lessons as they were not covered by the school and Killkenny would have to pay for them, but the school would offer the room and piano as part of Sebastian's learning experience. Freda just looked at Hazel. They had known one another for years, both as colleagues and occasionally on social outings, a dinner at the Railway once a month or so. 'I don't need to be paid,' she smiled. 'I know that Sebastian will pay me in another way. I feel lighter and happier than I have felt for years. He is such a wonderful little boy.'

'Come on, Freda, that just won't do. If you have a private student you have a rate and you charge it and it must be the same here or I can't allow you to take him on as a student.'

'Very well,' and Freda gave a price that was ridiculously low seeing that she had to travel to and from the school every Thursday afternoon just for the boy.

'I'll tell you what, Freda, why don't we have dinner if you're free early next week at the Railway and I'll tell you what Sebastian's guardians think.'

'Sounds very pleasant to me. I'll give you a call to confirm it.' She left smiling and then realised that, back at St. Mary's again with her own private student, life wasn't so bad at all and what a private student! Oh, those eyes, she thought, so beautiful!

The Principal telephoned Hazel Thursday evening to discuss the issue. Hazel told her that Sebastian was delighted with Mrs. Carstairs and was now saying he wanted to be a famous piano player with her. The Principal, more than pleased, told Hazel that Freda Carstairs had also sung the praises of Sebastian and then she discussed the matter of the fee. 'We will pay whatever you recommend,' and suddenly realised he had used the term 'we'. It was something that she also picked up. A fair price was agreed on and Hazel had the choice of paying directly or having the school pay, then each term or yearly Hazel would re-imburse St. Mary's. The latter was agreed and they said their goodbyes. Hazel walked back to the dining room where Mathew was sitting as they had no living room at the cottage and explained the deal.

'I said we would accept whatever the principal thought was fair and I think we have received a good deal but there is no piano here until the main house in in order, I'm afraid, so Sebastian will just have to wait.'

'I think we all understand,' said Matthew, emphasising the 'we' again. Hazel smiled and then told him about what Carmel had said and Lester had followed up on.

'Does that mean we—' and here he stopped to emphasise that he was included in the decision making, 'that Sebastian doesn't have to go to boarding school at Tendale?'

It had never crossed Hazel's mind that this was even in the equation. He looked at Matthew's face, seeing instantly something that had never crossed his mind: Matthew was terrified of being separated from

Sebastian and as all the O'Malley boys went to this boarding school he was very concerned that history was to be repeated.

'I know of no good reason to send Sebastian away to school. St. Patrick's at Bradbury has a fine reputation. The Principal told me when I spoke to her some time ago. No, Matthew, we shall not be sending Sebastian away.'

The effect of this was overwhelming. Matthew remained motionless, as if an enormous weight was slowly, ever so slowly, moving from his shoulders and sliding down his back onto the floor, leaving him as light as a feather. He stood up and embraced Hazel. 'Thanks,' he said, simply, and in this firm grip Hazel felt warm tears run down his neck to his tee shirt and they just stood there, both with the realisation that Sebastian's life could and would be decided by 'we'.

*   *   *   *   *

The next day being Friday saw the last rush to finish work before the weekend and now, with the exception of the decorative cast iron which lay in sections on the ground, Jan's front veranda was finally completed. But the winter garden, as a result, lay incomplete, filled with boxes and furniture from the house whilst the plasterers continued their very dusty work. Hazel set down his laptop and yet again began to work out the arithmetic of keeping this property buoyant. It was, he thought, like an old elephant trying to stand up, but at this stage he decided it had only risen as far as its knees. The expenses were building up again and again and even with this large injection of 2.3 million dollars there was not going to be enough to settle back on and drink champagne. Everything had cost much more than he had thought and after the extravagant bill for fencing by a contractor, which was absolutely essential, this 2.3 million was going to start to drain away very quickly. The thought of an overdraft was absolutely the last gasp, he thought. To settle an overdraft on an eleven year old boy was just not on, so this meant re-thinking the expenditure. The house had to be finished, of that there was no question. Some of the out-buildings were being repaired under the direction of Pat and Matthew, but the winter garden and the church

223

were now looking like luxuries. He sat down and calculated yet again and found that if the plasterers, who had been contracted on a fixed quote, kept to it, then they were all right, but they were going to have to be very careful.

The carpenters told him that on Monday they would attach the cast iron on Jan's veranda and begin directly lining the winter garden, as they had already installed the windows. But the church? Hazel thought he would wait until Monday and see what the builders had to say about it. And the timbers were to be delivered for the sale yards during the next week. 'Oh, does it ever finish?' thought Hazel, closing the lid of his computer and stepping outside to the sound of voices and hammers and the heat that never abated.

The weekend passed tranquilly, but Saturday night, because of the heat and the fact that the cottage was made of tin, Matthew and Hazel moved their beds onto the veranda and two large mosquito nets were draped above them. Sebastian slept in Matthew's larger single bed with him while the other bed, end to end on the narrow veranda, held Hazel.

Talking to Mary in Melbourne, as he religiously did every Sunday evening, he said the veranda must have been fifteen degrees cooler than the oven they called the governess's cottage. And as usual, they exchanged all their news and gossip about the people they knew in common. Mary said she had seen Keven, as he was back in town with 'the boy'.

'Really?' answered Hazel, in an offhand way. 'Do you realise he hasn't called me once in three and a bit months. Well, it doesn't matter. It's his loss and I'm sure the piece he is with is just charming.' Mary thought it wise not to reply to his sarcastic comment.

Little did Hazel realise that sleeping on the veranda was to become a permanent thing until the house would be finished. It was always the same, Matthew with one arm over Sebastian and both of their faces looking out across the square through the trees to Jan's house. Every morning, Hazel would collect the bed linen, fold it and take it inside then in the evening, before Sebastian went to bed, he would remake the beds, not difficult as it only meant two pillows were needed and two sheets for each. Will this heat ever finish, he wondered?

*   *   *   *   *

Monday saw a scramble to get ready and Hazel's lilac Volkswagon beetling down the drive to transport Sebastian to the bus. On his return, he sat down with the head carpenter and they discussed the next stage and the ever present problem of estimates, while the other two men began the work of screwing into position the cast iron lace on Jan's veranda.

'How long do you think this is going to take?' asked Hazel, as his arm wearily swept around the large unlined space that was destined to become the Garden Room.'

'Well, if we are not interrupted,' which was a reference to Hazel stopping one project to complete another, Jan's veranda, 'I should say a week should see it done. All the windows and doors are in, and all the cement sheeting for the walls is here, so it's straight ahead.'

'Fine. Now, come with me for a moment,' and he took the carpenter to the church. They had to step up into it, as when all the buildings had been relocated here they were put up on cement stemps fifty centimetres above the ground, to allow for air flow. Elsewhere open base boards surrounded the buildings, giving them a much neater appearance. But the church had not been started. The carpenter looked about and, scratching his head, asked Hazel exactly what he wanted.

'Well, the doors are ruined at the bottom and the hinges have been ripped and broken. I could happily shoot the bastards.'

'After me!' was the reply. On the walls where there had been the graffiti, as a result of Jan's work, there was just a red smudge or a black one, so one had no idea now what had been written before.

'Please yourself. The bottom half is done in masonite and all the sheets the bastards kicked in we can replace. It's not a big job. The big job is to paint it and replace—fuck!' Here he stopped. 'The bastards haven't even left one piece of glass intact.'

'Not one,' muttered Hazel, dully,' and Otto will not install the glass anywhere here until the building is completed, for some reason.'

'He's a particular one,' grinned the builder.

'You can say that again!' responded Hazel.

'Look, Hazel, let's see. We will replace the masonite—it seems nearly every panel at foot height is kicked in. I will take the doors with me tonight and leave them with the joiner, and by the way, what's that?' He pointed to a large box-type construction on its side.'

'That, believe it or not, is all that is left of the main altar. The vandals strangely never destroyed the two side altars, just kicked in three panels here. But the main altar is badly broken up on one end.'

'Do you want me to drop it off to the joiner as well?'

'I suppose so,' replied Hazel, unenthusiastically.

'Listen, Hazel, just a minute.' The carpenter pulled from his hip pocket a measuring tape and measured the panels of the side altars and main altar. 'They are all the same size, except that the main altar has two more panels across the front.'

'So?'

'Look how the panels are fitted in.' He showed Hazel the upturned structure. 'You can take out the panels easily and replace them with whatever you want.'

'Sorry, I've no idea what you're talking about.' Hazel looked puzzled.

'Why not put marble in the panels?'

'What! It would cost a fortune.'

'Just a tick!' The carpenter checked the measurements again and using his telephone spoke to someone, whilst Hazel looked at the shocking state of the building and went into the sacristy to re-discover the broken drawers that once held the vestments and then returned to the carpenter, who had just finished speaking.

'I forgot,' Hazel warned him, 'the shitheads have smashed the drawers in there. He pointed to the sacristy. 'It's just so fucking depressing.'

'Well, this might just cheer you up. I have telephoned the joiner and stonemason. The difference in making ten new panels or replacing them all in stone is A$3 more in stone. What do you think?

'Really?' Hazel looked amazed. 'Are you sure? Isn't marble expensive?' knowing full well that it was, from his days in the decorating trade.

'You see, Hazel, the size you want is 3cm less than what Charlie has.'

'Lost the plot,' said Hazel, smiling and mentally calculating this exercise.

'Look, Charlie is laying the new floor in the council chambers and the flooring, because he has bought it in bulk, is much cheaper. If the marble slabs are a little bit bigger, you'll never be able to see it, because I can just knock up a piece of wood to support it. From the front it will look as if the panels are exactly the right size.'

'Hm, what colour is it?'

'Well, that's the problem. It's not white, it's a terracotta colour.'

'That not a problem at all. OK, and don't forget to take the drawers as well and order the new masonite for the walls. Oh God, I could kill these fucking vandals and I will lay a bet they all come from 'good families'.

'That's generally the pattern,' replied the carpenter, and ambled off to check that the iron lace on Jan's veranda was being put on correctly.

Hazel stood, just looking about the empty shell, trying to imagine it complete, and didn't hear someone enter behind him. He moved aimlessly forward, glancing at the window without the glass, where the heat of the outside swept through from one side to the other.

'I have something to ask you.'

Hazel jumped in fright and spun around. 'Jan, if you are trying to give me a heart attack, that's just the way to do it.'

'Sorry,' was her quiet reply.

'So what do you want?'

'It's this church,' Jan replied.

'I know. I know it's been the last to have work started on it but it appears after the garden room the carpenters are starting here. They will take all the broken pieces to the joiner this evening so if there are any other broken things like this pew, they may as well all go together. This can be your project, Jan, and no sneaking up behind in the future.'

'Have a look at the ceiling,' she said.

Hazel glanced upwards and then shot a glance to a side window where a magpie had landed out of the hot morning sun. 'What about the ceiling? he asked.

'Well, the panels are symmetrical.'

'So?'

'Don't you see?'

'I'm afraid this morning is not my morning. The carpenter has been talking in circles and can you believe it we are to have marble panels in all the altars, and I am trying to do a budget.'

'Don't get too excited,' she warned. 'I was just going to offer an idea and it doesn't have to cost much.'

'Oh, really? What a joke! Have you any idea what this is all costing?'

'Just remember, Hazel,' she replied sternly, 'it was your idea to move everything back here.'

Hazel took a deep breath and spoke dejectedly. 'Yes, you're right.'

'But you did the right thing. In the future Sebastian will have something to be very proud of. If we were still living at the gate he would be off and gone as soon as possible.'

Hazel had not been fully facing her, but he slowly turned and said, 'Sebastian.' His mind began to race: no Sebastian, perhaps no Matthew. 'I'm sorry, Jan. What did you want?' But he wasn't concentrating. No Sebastian. No Matthew. This was the formula that swung from one side of his head to the other.

'What do you think?' asked Jan.

'Say that again.

'Aren't you listening to me, Hazel?'

'Sort of, but try me again.'

'I said my sister's a painter. Well, if the carpenters can get the panels off the ceiling—and it shouldn't be difficult—or cut new ones to go over the top of them, I am sure I could convince her to paint them.'

Hazel was just about to pass a sarcastic comment about local painters but stopped himself and asked Jan to show him some sketches and if they were what was wanted they would give her the go ahead. But she would have to make it snappy as the carpenters would only be at the site for another fortnight or so. Jan, without another word, disappeared and was seen giving, or asking for, measurements of the ceiling panels.

Hazel was still very concerned that no Sebastian would probably mean no Matthew. He walked over to the house where the two main rooms were ready now for the joins between the large sheets of plasterboard.

It was in this partly finished room that it dawned on him: the more spectacular Killkenny was the greater the chance of everyone staying.

But Hazel had the equation back to front and didn't realise it. The correct version was simple: wherever there was Matthew there was going to be, without a shadow of a doubt, Sebastian, and it took him a while to grasp this. As a result, economics now took a back seat to his million and one plans to establish a base so splendid that neither Matthew nor Sebastian would ever think of leaving and then the idea that had been just a hint in his creative mind became a necessity. He had, or Killkenny had, to have a swimming pool. How the hell was he going to do it and stay within a budget and how much does a swimming pool cost, anyway?

He scurried off to his bedroom to count out how much of the money he had got from Bob was still there and then in the heat of the dining room he opened his laptop and began to search for the impossible, a deluxe swimming pool that cost very little. He told no one of his idea but it was beginning to become an obsession. Whenever he was alone he was straight to the laptop tapping out messages, which meant his emails were filled with companies attempting to entice him into purchasing the pool only from them.

But strangely enough the answer to this problem, or dilemma, was to come from another source altogether, and when it did there was no one more surprised than Hazel.

CHAPTER SIX

Revelations

CHAPTER SIX

CHAPTER SIX

Revelations

At a quarter to seven on Tuesday morning, a black BMW passed through the two now well-trimmed palm trees, leaving a trail of red dust behind. Carmel was totally astonished at what she saw in front of her. She hadn't been to Killkenny for years and remembered it as virtually a ruin. The ram sales were held here only because of the sale yard set up, but for the past six, or could it be seven, years, the ram sales had been held at the adjacent property, the Wallaces', due to their stock yards and a layout that was much more conducive to this practice, as the long drive into Killkenny had fallen into such shocking repair. So this was Killkenny. She got out from her car and began to look about. She had forgotten that the homestead was so large and so pretentious and the fact that it was evident that so much work was being done here altered completely the dynamics of it.

'Good morning!' came a cry from the cottage as Matthew stepped down from the veranda to greet her.

My God, she thought, he is just stunning! 'Good morning, Matthew. It's been ages since I have seen you.'

'Likewise,' he said. 'Now, could you move your car to the side, as the workmen are due here at seven, and then you can join us for breakfast.'

She did as requested and went into the cottage, passing the two beds on the veranda under the mosquito nets. One, she noted, was larger than the other.'

'Come in,' greeted Hazel, and she was soon sitting with coffee and toast, with Sebastian smiling.

'I'm going to school today,' he told her, 'but on Thursday I am going to play the piano with Mrs. Carstairs. She is very nice. I like her.' He continued munching on a piece of toast.

Carmel glanced about her but her eyes were constantly drawn back to Matthew and Sebastian. She hadn't seen the boy for many years and so had no great knowledge of him, but to see both Matthew and him together was a genuine shock. They were identical, obviously one older than the other, but identical—not one Spaniard but two. She finished her coffee. 'Would you like a quick look around?' asked Hazel, and when she said yes, he added that Matthew would get Sebastian ready and they would drop him off at the gate when they left. As they went out, Carmel was amazed at the trucks and men who all arrived about seven for the day's work. The noise and laughter was unusual for her; the confusion and moving of materials and loud voices seemed to proclaim that they were about to finish Killkenny.

'Do keep a look out at the time,' urged Hazel. 'We must leave at 7.30.'

In the short time available Carmel glanced around the interior of the homestead, all sheathed in new plasterboard ready for filling and then for paint and wallpaper. Hazel took her through the dining room and swung open the French doors to reveal the huge space that was to become the indoor garden.

'It's enormous, she said. 'The whole complex is much bigger than I ever remembered, but this garden room is immense.'

'It should be pleasant when it's finished—whenever that is.'

'By the look of the number of workers here, it won't be long,' she remarked in a dry tone and was taken on a tour of the rest of the block. She was fascinated that the church was now here and quickly looked inside.

'I knew they had damaged it, but I never realised that it was this bad. Not even window frames left.

'Well, yes, but very broken,' said Hazel. 'The joiner has them and then they will go to Otto and when re-glazed they will return and be fitted in, but it is sad, isn't it?' to which she agreed.

Jan had seen Carmel's car and came out to say hello. 'Well, you haven't been for a while, have you?'

'No, not for years. I can't believe the work you are all doing. Congratulations. It seems Killkenny is about to stand up gain.'

'Yes, it's now time for that,' replied Jan, quietly, and Hazel looked at her. This was the second time she had made any positive comment about the return to the homestead and he felt that she was beginning to see it as her established home, as he did.

'Hazel,' came a cry, 'it's almost half past seven.'

'Coming!' and they left Jan to walk back to the cottage.

'I'll take my car,' said Hazel.

'Forget it. Mortlake is a good hour and a half and my car is just that much more comfortable for a drive like that.' She smiled at him, looking as if she were going to the races, all in black with a large black picture hat on, just to add the final touch.

'OK, just let me get my things.' She stood back and waited, a scene she was remember all her life. Sebastian bounded out with his school bag and neatly pressed uniform.

'Have you got your telephone?' asked Matthew.

'Oh no!' and he dashed back in, colliding with Hazel. 'I forgot the telephone.'

'Don't forget the shoebox.'

'Oh, I never forget that,' he laughed.

Hazel walked over towards Carmel and she watched transfixed as Sebastian threw himself into Matthew's arms and they held one another and kissed. The intensity of the moment, the extreme passion of one person for another, gave Carmel the odd sensation that in her own life, somehow, she had perhaps missed something while waiting for the bus.

Hazel asked her, when they returned, would she have dinner with them and she said she would be delighted.

'Good,' said Hazel. 'Sebastian, when Matthew picks you up this evening, tell him we are four for dinner and I want you to lay the table for us and change the candles.'

'Oh, yes,' the boy replied, 'I'm glad you are coming to dinner,' at which he hopped out of the car as the bus made its appearance through the heat haze. He shook hands with Carmel in a very formal way, kissed Hazel and said, 'I won't forget', as he got on to the bus and waved from the back window. Carmel headed off in the direction the bus had come, the opposite direction to Bradbury and on to Mortlake.

She did not say anything for a moment or two, but Hazel anticipated the conversation by commenting, 'He is beautiful, isn't he?'

'They are both beautiful but . . .' and here she stalled the conversation, 'they are identical.'

'Physically and mentally,' was Hazel's reply. 'I know, but what can one say?'

'Very little, it appears. Matthew looks wonderful. You all sleep in the cottage, you said.'

'Well, on the veranda at present. It's too hot in the night inside but in the main house there is air-conditioning fitted as there has been in Jan's house but at present we three are roughing it.'

'That's not exactly my idea of roughing it,' she smiled. 'I can't believe the work you have done. I hear on the grapevine that with Matthew as manager Killkenny is becoming a show property.'

'Well, I'm not sure what that is, but everything he does seems to work, for the last two months the property has been totally overhauled, from fencing to housing, and believe it or not Bob has been relatively co-operative.'

'That I find had to believe. I would be very wary of him if I were you,' she warned.

'We have sorted out the problem between your cousin and Killkenny, I think.' Carmel turned her head for a moment and glanced at him and then turned her eyes back to the long straight stretch of road ahead. 'He's a shit, Ashley Wallace, a real hypocrite. Doris is right. Stay as far away from him as you can.'

'I don't expect to become bosom buddies with him, if that's what you mean.

'No, that's not what I mean. You have closed off the lowlands to his stock, so he must now be feeling the pinch. It's February, remember, and there's no feed, so my advice is to look out. He is without scruples.'

'If he so much as opens our boundary fences this time, I will have the law on him at once, you see, Carmel,' he assured her, firmly. 'I have sent the message back via Bob and I am a hundred per cent certain the message was passed on and received. No one but no one is going to touch Sebastian's inheritance.'

'You seem very protective?'

'Well, perhaps it has something to do with the advice you gave me the other day at the Railway.' She said nothing, looking ahead, but smiling. He realised that he knew very little about her. He had lunch with her and Gerald every Thursday now, but that was it. He didn't even know where she lived or for that matter whom she lived with.

'Have you heard anything from Keven?' she asked.

'Not a word since I moved here. As I'm completely dependent on him financially I've just been playing a waiting game and it appears I've lost. He has a young boy friend and they seem to love Asia, so that's that, I'm afraid.'

'You don't realise how lucky you are,' she said.

'Really?' Hazel glanced out at the endless stretches of the red flat plains.

'Yes, really,' and her expressionless face meant she wasn't going to continue the subject for now.

'How far do you live from Bradbury,' he tried.

'About the same as you. Where you turn right, where the old church once was, I go straight ahead. You and Matthew must come for lunch or dinner soon. I was thinking of inviting Gerald but now I have seen Matthew I've decided that it's not a wise idea.' She gave a laugh. 'Poor Gerald! He's without hope. He falls in love regularly, has an illicit affair and the moment that everything is working he drops him. He's only after the chase, it seems, not the kill, but he has had only two men to my knowledge that have held him firmly at bay. Matthew, and it seems now he's out of the running, and Ashley.'

'Ashley!' Hazel exclaimed. 'Isn't he his cousin?'

'Second cousin, yes, but our Troy Donahue of Bradbury is only interested in him, the impossible Ashley.'

'How strange. He's good looking, Gerald.'

'God, don't tell him that or you will be pushing him out of bed. Look at the game he is playing with the barman at the Railway. He'll get him eventually and predictably make a mess of it.'

'Does Gerald see Ashley very often?'

'Not that I know of. Once or twice he's made contact with him socially at the opening of a show at the Civic Centre, but to my knowledge that's it. You can imagine how Cherly adores Gerald— roughly the same as Doris!'

'I was with Doris at the supermarket the other day when they had a clash.'

'Doris and Gerald are very similar. They both go looking for trouble, but sometimes Doris oversteps the mark. She told me that you saved her from a slap in the face. Personally, favourite aunt or not, I don't think the slap would have gone astray. You see, both Gerald and Doris bait Cherly and she is stupid enough to return the fire. If she just ignored them, there's nothing they could do. Gerald is crazy for Ashley.'

'What does he look like?'

'Of course, you haven't seen him yet. Well, he is my cousin, but he is very handsome, tall, dark and he screams elegance. But to my way of thinking he is cold and a real calculator. I would never trust him,' she said, 'never. But I think that what you have in hand is a one hundred per cent better deal.'

'Oh, if only he were in my hands!' sighed Hazel.

'Don't give up! If it's a contest between you, Gerald or Ashley, to end up with Matthew, my money is on you.'

'Ashley?' was the sharp retort.

'Oh yes, Ashley also has his eyes on Matthew. Well, who doesn't? But you may as well know.'

'He's a prick!' snapped a jealous Hazel. 'First the use of the property that's not his, the incorrect marking of the wool bales—'

'How did you know about that?' interrupted Carmel in a detached way.

'Matthew told me, and to make matters worse not all the money for the rams that were sold at the Wallace property was returned to Killkenny.'

'I told you, Hazel, he is a real shit.'

'Hmm,' he signed. 'What's his homestead like?'

'Not bad. Of all the Wallace homesteads—and I think there are seven or eight—Doris has the grandest. Then there is mine and Ashley's. They are the three most important Wallace estates. But Doris's is by far the grandest. It was built out of its time when this heavy Italianate architecture was out of vogue. Doris's grandfather built this vast house: it doesn't quite have the theatrical impact of Killkenny and it's single storey with a tower but huge. The rooms are enormous.'

'Just a minute,' Hazel interrupted, 'if this property was built by her grandfather, how come she is Mrs. Wallace?'

'Easy, Hazel. She married her second or third cousin and as he had the same surname, she never had to change, mind you the second??????? son is living proof you should never have anything to do with inter-family marriage. Ted is the most stupid louse I know. The other two boys are just simple, but good workers, the girl or 'budgie brain' as Doris calls her, I don't think is going to lift the intellectual level and outlook of the family. Even if their children inherit all their brains, they are in trouble for life. They have the manager's house on the estate but the other two boys live in the main house with Doris. You know, she was going to disinherit the three boys and leave everything to Timothy Osbourne, but with that very sad situation I don't know what she will do now. She hasn't said much about it. You see, Timmy was related to Doris through his mother.'

'It seems everyone here is a Wallace.'

Carmel laughed. 'Seems so, but once there were a couple of other estates in the hands of the O'Malleys, but they weren't good producers and as a result the lines died out, except the Killkenny one, which is the last and it's shared between Keven and Sebastian, so eventually unless Keven forces a sale it will all be Sebastian's.

'What do you mean, 'forces a sale'? It would have to be blackmail, as I have equal power of attorney for Sebastian. He would need my signature to sell Killkenny and he will never get that,' he said, sharply, 'never.'

'Good for you, Hazel. You don't quite fit the pattern of knight in shining armour, but I feel you will do the trick nicely.' She grinned as if she were also in on a secret that no one else knew about.

'Oh, by the way' Hazel asked, 'what is Trick Thompson's real name?'

'Oh, I haven't a clue. You would have to ask Doris. She knows all these things. She is very attached to Trick and always has been. He's good looking but for someone of my height a bit ridiculous.'

'So who is the love of your life? he probed.

'Oh forget it, Hazel. I worked out a few years ago all that romance thing is a waste of time. I had a fling with someone local and then thought, 'Wake up Australian tall woman with rich pastoral property!" She spoke in a grand manner and laughed. 'So I handed him on to Gerald, who made a complete balls up of it and as there was a wife, Gerald came off second best. He wasn't very pleased at all, but talking of affection you realise that Doris is remarkably fond of you. It's quite odd.'

'Thank you very much, Carmel!'

'No, no, I don't mean it like that. It takes Doris years to accept someone. She always remains aloof or demolishes the person but in a short time she has taken you under her wing. I have never seen her like this before, in fact the Railway crowd seem to have accepted you as one of the group. Good going, Hazel. Most don't manage it in two generations,' at which she began laughing, something quite rare for Carmel. She was relaxed today: she was driving, she was in charge and that was the way she liked it. She also in a short time had accepted Hazel. She was enchanted at his one liners and sometimes bitter repartee and today was more than happy to have him in her company.

'Are your parents still alive?' he asked.

'No, I have been a single spirit for years now. My parents died one after the other six months apart when I was in my final year at school. I decided as I now had a property to administer that university was a waste of time. I was the top academic in school, believe it or not.'

'I don't doubt it at all,' he commented.

'You see, it actually had a lot to do with Doris. You see, when I was young, the girls at school were vile to me because of my nose. They always called me names and I found it very difficult to make friends. It was Doris who saw my situation and pointed out to me that the girls—and there were five or six of them—were all, according to Doris, losers, whereas she said I was to inherit the second largest Wallace property and would live in luxury. They would be sweeping their kitchens for life. They used to call me 'ibis face'. So I worked that much harder and managed, to my surprise, to top my class every year. But Doris is a bitch. You know how she goes on about Darwin and the origin of the species. Well, last Friday night, Doris telephoned me to pick her up as we were going to have dinner at the Railway with the other Hazel and Freda Carstairs, ie Mrs. Doubtfire. God, I must be careful—one day I'm going to call her that without thinking. Anyway, Freda was singing Sebastian's praises, who by the way she considers the most beautiful, most talented etc. etc., and Doris was a bit out of the conversation, so she brought up this blasted subject yet again. She always does it when she is not the centre of attention, and she went on to say that she had seen a programme on TV about man beginning from something that crawled out of the sea. Did she let it go? Not our Doris! She recounted Darwin as being a close friend of Brendan's father, the monkey routine and then the bitch said that if all this could possibly be believed then I was living proof of heredity with my nose descended from a pterodactyl.'

Hazel laughed. 'She is terrible.'

'No, Hazel, she is a real bitch, but she is suffering inside and that not even I find smart. She misses Timmy like crazy. Every Thursday from the age of five until he died at eleven he was her lover and much more important he was her friend and this relationship was reciprocated. She tried every trick in the book when Mary went into hospital to take him and his father wouldn't allow it.'

'Why, if he already had a mistress? What was the problem?'

'David Osbourne is another shit, you see. Here in Bradbury and the surrounding district he holds all the catholic interests as local solicitor and accountant, having married Mary who inherited her father's business. Old Mr. Wallace was as honest as the day is long but David Osbourne isn't, as Doris has now found out. Mr Lester is now trying to work out the tangled web David wove to confuse his clients and obviously syphon off money into his own pocket. You'll be pleased to know, like the O'Malleys, but far too late, I have an appointment with Mr. Lester. Thursday morning. So at lunch I can give you the hopefully reasonable report, but Doris is missing thousands from her investments and if she hated David Osbourne before can you imagine her now?'

'But why did the O'Malley's move all their investments and legal stuff to Mr. Lester?' asked Hazel. 'It seems strange, as you would say, Carmel. You either drink at the Railway or the Commercial, and while we are on this subject, why don't you—I don't mean you personally—but why doesn't everyone just say Catholic or Protestant?'

'I don't know. I suppose it's in-talk in a certain way, but if you say someone drinks at the Commercial or the Railway it seems so much softer I guess.' At this point she finally turned the car right, after what seemed to Hazel to be a trip back and forth across the Nullabour plains.

'Well,' he continued the same topic, 'what about the Crown Hotel?'

'Yes. You see, there are three hotels in Bradbury, the Catholic, the Protestant and the Crown Hotel, which was known as 'the blood house'. It was extremely rough and this is where the most limited Catholics and the most limited Protestants originally congregated, with a vast amount of beer under their belts. They decided to resolve everything with a fight, you know. Brendan types unfortunately flourish here. And then Steven Osler purchased the Crown and totally re-developed it. It was on an enormous block of land and he purchased the paddock behind it, asphalted the lot, ripped the original hotel down (which was a real shame, as it was a fine building) and constructed this monstrosity at the other end of Main Street. So the younger members, be they Commercial or Railway, flock there. No parking problems and they can do as they wish until—I think closing time is two o'clock—with a disco floor, a quiet bar, private dining rooms—but the taste, Hazel, is unbelievably bad.'

'Well,' he commented, grasping a little local history, 'the Railway could never be described as chic.'

'No, but at least it has a certain patina of the past. The Crown is lime green and orange in one part and purple and turquoise in another. It's hideous beyond belief. By the way, now that you have prodded my memory, next Thursday you are going to be speaking to Violet.'

'Who the hell is Violet?

'Violet, darling, is the owner of the Railway. She and her husband—you have seen him, good looking with a mop of grey hair.'

'Yes, I think so,' though Hazel was not quite sure at all.

'I have told them you are a famous interior decorator and they are more than anxious for you to give them a few tips.'

'About what? I have so much on my plate at Killkenny. I couldn't possibly take on a job like that.'

'Just a little sensible advice, darling. It doesn't have to be turned into Maxim's overnight.'

'Thank God for that!' he sighed and the conversation continued in this way, with, for the first time, someone giving him straight answers.

'I've always been curious,' Carmel started again. 'Why do you think Matthew married?'

'The million dollar question. I have no idea and he refuses to speak about it.'

'But he didn't have to marry. He didn't have any problem—he could have had anyone, and I mean anyone, in this whole district, man or woman and they would have given their lives for him. By the way, darling,' Carmel smiled at him, 'had he been interested in me he could have had the estate lock, stock and barrel. He is so divine.'

'Yes, he is. So why the hell did he marry someone no one knew, secretively in a civil ceremony and then suddenly demanded a divorce and decree of nullity?'

'You tell me,' shrugged Carmel. 'No one in this town has any answer to the mystery. He was married just two days before Sebastian's parents died and a day after left this girl or woman. I don't know anyone who knows of her, not even Doris and that's saying something.' They both laughed. So, thought Hazel, Matthew was married for less than three days.

'Hey, let me concentrate!' exclaimed Carmel. 'The first left then right. I got these directions, believe it or not, from my poisonous cousin Ashley, who apparently has purchased 60 box plants to layout an Italian garden. What a fool! He is going to have 60 dead box plants in less than three months. They will not take that climate. I should know. I tried it four or five years ago—all dead, the lot. But my handsome cousin knows more than me! But if you do want hedge-type plants, you can get them here, not quite box but not bad and with water they actually will withstand the heat.'

'Sounds ideal. I must have a look,' replied Hazel. 'Oh, over there, Carmel. That must be it.'

'Yes, that's it. It's on the outskirts of Mortlake, just as you get off the main road. Does the sign say 'Harold'?'

'I can't see a sign up—oh, yes, yes, 'Harold's Nursery and Garden Supplies'. This is it.'

*   *   *   *   *

They got out of the car and stretched their limbs. The heat was atrocious after sitting comfortably in an air-conditioned car. Harold's was a very large complex with shaded areas covered in pergolas with brush laid on top to break the sun and there were glass houses to the left and enormous trees in huge plastic tubs. There was all manner of decorative objects for the garden and flowering plants well arranged everywhere.

'I don't care what you think: do it now.' Carmel and Hazel looked at one another.

'Oh, how do you do?' smiled a good-looking young man. 'Staff are the pits around here. All she has to do is water and check the watering system. I tell you if she didn't have that good-looking boyfriend, she would be out of here in two seconds. May I help you? He changed the sound of his voice completely.

Hazel decided to fight fire with fire. 'Well, sweetie, I should like a large fountain.'

'Wouldn't you just!' The owner narrowed his eyes. 'I have a couple here but they are basically here as decoration for the shop, but if you're interested, God knows the locals certainly aren't.' They followed the young man to a section on the right where there was an array of birdbaths and little wall fountains. 'Sorry,' he began again, 'it's been one of those days. My name is Robert,' so they duly introduced themselves.

'No, I actually want a large one.'

'Well, come this way,' and in a small opening, with flowering plants in pots, stood centrally a very large cast iron fountain with three dishes to catch the water and let it spill yet again to the lower dishes. 'I've had it for ages. It's sort of become a shop fixture and it's now a bit rusty and needs a good clean and paint. Now have a look over here.' They followed him down a narrow path, crowded either side with pots of roses. They rounded the end of a shed and gazed in surprise.

'It's enormous,' exclaimed Carmel.

'Yes, it's been the bane of my life. A client ordered it and when it arrived she refused to take it, claiming I had deceived her about the size, the bitch, so there it sits. Oh, don't worry, there is another piece to fit on top again. It stands almost four metres high. I told the bitch that she should measure carefully first. So stupid! And now I am stuck with it. What am I saying? You can see the weeds around the bottom. It's been here for well over four years.'

The recast stone fountain Robert was showing was the type that one sees in public gardens with swirls and putti in all directions, though from what Hazel could see it had a good line to it. But the bottom basin which stood, or leaned, against the back of the shed had an enormous diameter, much larger than he needed and so they returned to the other cast iron one that also stood almost three metres high and the jet of water, which was not working, would obviously operatically make it even taller. As there was only one other client looking about, Robert worked out quickly that a smart lady with a large hat, a black BMW and a smart queen generally equalled good business. He showed them the trees Hazel was interested in and they discussed the plants that would do well, he thought, in the garden room.

'Do you have cross beams in the room?' asked Robert.

'Yes, in between every window.'

'Great! I have two dozen really big hanging baskets filled with cascade petunias or even five-leafed ivy. It will look wonderful and I also have some good teak furniture. Doesn't sell well here—the locals want canvas or cast iron. You just can't win.'

They continued looking about at the vast array of plants and pots. 'Listen,' said Hazel, if I buy a lot of things will you give me a good price?'

'Absolutely,' came the response, and Robert disappeared, returning with an order book. With the ground plan and dimensions of the garden room Hazel had drawn Robert was able to see easily what was needed. Carmel wandered off, leaving the two men discussing the merits of orange against lemon trees, and how much terracotta pots cost. When she returned, they were just doing the final adding up. Hazel was very surprised at how much this was all going to cost and as he had been doing the accounts on the computer he wondered if this purchase was rather extravagant. Clearly, Robert sensed this, 'I'll tell you what, Hazel. Let's round the figure off and I will toss in the big cement fountain as well.

'What on earth would I do with it if I've just purchased the cast iron one?'

'Hazel,' suggested Carmel, 'Why not take it and fit it into the centre of the square in front of the house? I think it would look great.'

'I think' he replied,' it might also look very new and very pretentious.'

'It won't look new after four years lying behind the shed here. It's picked up a good patina. Go back and have another look before you say no.'

So whilst Robert and Carmel were discussing a pair of lemon trees in big terracotta pots, Hazel wandered back to behind the shed to have another look at this fountain. He glanced at the base on its side and the tall central section and then in the grass found the piece for the very top, a strange putto with his head turned upwards with a trumpet in copper in his mouth, which obviously the water spurted out from. He stood staring at the pieces and then slowly returned to the others.

'Well?' prompted Carmel.

'I'll take it. Sebastian will love it.'

'Seeing you have been such great clients, let me take you to lunch,' Robert offered. 'There's a little restaurant, one of the very few about here, that is quite close. I'm sure you'll like it.'

When they were seated in the restaurant, Robert said, 'I can't tell you what the clients prefer around here,' as the drinks were served and the orders taken. 'But how come you are here at the end of the world,' he laughed, looking at Hazel.

'Oh, it's a long story, but I've only been here a bit over three months.'

'Wow, and buying fountains already!'

'Yes, it seems so.' Hazel's voice was weak as he wondered how he was going to justify this extraordinary bill and whether the two fountains were really necessary. 'Oh well,' he thought, 'the big one was almost free,' but in the back of his mind he was still a little uneasy at the cost of it all.

They chattered on, and all decided they must meet again. Robert said he couldn't deliver the goods until the following Tuesday. This was all agreed and they stood up to leave.

'Oh, just a minute,' Hazel exclaimed. 'I must have the measurement of the base of the cast iron fountain, as the bricklayers start on the floor tomorrow morning,' so they returned to the nursery and the diameter was obtained.

'Don't worry: all the reticulation equipment is included in the price, and if you want the cast iron fountain I can send David with it tomorrow, but not all the other stuff. He will show you how to fit in the pump.'

'That would be fantastic,' replied a joyful Hazel, 'that way there can't be a mistake.'

'OK, a cast iron fountain tomorrow.' They left the directions to Killkenny and set off.

'Thank goodness I remembered the measurements, and how kind to deliver it tomorrow.'

'Yes, a really nice guy. They are rare around here,' agreed Carmel, laughing.

* * * * *

As they had made good time on the return, Hazel phoned Matthew to say they would collect Sebastian and gave him instructions on the things to take out of the freezer.

'In this climate, thawing is no problem at all. I hope you like Thai food?'

'I adore it.'

'Great. Sebastian and Matthew are mad for it, too.'

Carmel was more relaxed on the way back as well as being delighted with her deal on a pair of lemon trees in Italian terracotta pots. 'Oh, Hazel,' she said, while adjusting her sunglasses, 'do you believe in coincidence?'

'Good heavens, Carmel, what a question! No, I don't think so.'

'So you believe everything is ordained.'

'More or less. Why do you ask?'

'Well, I believe the same, so it couldn't possibly be a coincidence, seeing as we don't believe in them, that Ashley is often at this nursery in Robert's company.' She glanced at Hazel and the pair of them began to laugh. 'And to think I thought he was creating an Italian garden! How stupid am I? Even Doris said he doesn't know one plant from another. Matthew doesn't have any contact with Ashley, does he?'

'I think not. It was through Bob we have had all the problems. He is a shit, Ashley. I once said to Matthew that I thought I would talk to Mr Lester and see if we could legally sue him but Matthew said that it would be very difficult for him, as instantly his father would be implicated in this extortion affair, so I just left it, but, let me tell you, your cousin or not, if I have the slightest problem in the future I will, through Mr. Lester, have a law suit on him at once,' replied a very determined Hazel.

'Good for you. I have never understood why people have handled Ashley with kid gloves, as if he is, oh so special. He's not. He is a con and that's the depth of him—shallow, I believe, is the word we are looking for, but very dangerous.'

'Well,' Hazel went on in a lighter mood, 'he had better watch out after all. I am a man with two fountains.' Carmel was screaming with laughter. It was the first time for ages she had been with someone that she was really enjoying without any complications.

*   *   *   *   *

As they approached Killkenny, through the heat haze they could see a shape that was obviously the school bus, and Carmel put her foot down. The car responded perfectly. As the bus deposited Sebastian, they pulled over to the side of the road to let it pass.

'Darling, grab the post,' and Sebastian raced to the letter box to withdraw two letters and a card.

'Hazel, Hazel, guess what!' then he finished the sentence before Hazel had an opportunity to respond. 'I'm going to be an altar boy. Father Keven is going to start training three of us next Monday. Look I brought my top home. It has a hole in it for you to fix. Oh, Hazel, Matthew will be so happy.'

'I'm sure he will,'

'Congratulations, Sebastian,' said Carmel. He said thankyou and handed Hazel the mail.

'Oh, just a minute,' as Carmel began to enter the gates. 'Sebastian, have a look in your house. There should be two parcels,' at which the boy bounded out of the car and swung open the door to 'his house' as it was called, and returned with the two large parcels, one at a time.

'Here, let me help you,' offered Hazel and they were deposited on the back seat, with Sebastian describing a day's adventure at St. Mary's.

As Carmel pulled up close to the cottage, Sebastian was out in a flash. 'Matthew, Matthew,' he cried, but couldn't find him. Only a minute later he saw him come around the corner of the homestead. Sebastian flew toward him. Carmel was amazed—she had seen them in one another's arms that morning but it seemed they hadn't seen one another for a month. Matthew swung him around, with the boy's arms around his neck.

'I am going to be an altar boy, Matthew. Father Keven said I could. Isn't it good?'

'It's fantastic. I am so proud of you,' and they kissed and hugged one another.

'Hi,' said Matthew, as they returned, to Carmel and Hazel. 'Would you both like to see something interesting?'

'Why not?' smiled Carmel, as they walked around the main house to a site behind and not far from the garden room. It had originally been a deposit for excess but mainly discarded fencing wire. An enormous mound of it rose, all rusty, with old crooked metal poles. It had been a junk heap for years of everything that fencing-wise had had its day, but with the new works over the last two months, the heap had grown like Mount Everest, a tangle of rusty wire. Matthew had decided as it was so close to the house it had to be taken away, so that morning the truck had arrived and with an excessive use of expletives one man after the other found the rusty wire curl up like a snake and then spin out scratching them painfully. It was the second load that was being heaped on with a mechanical shovel that at some stage became caught in the base of something and Matthew was called to sort the situation out. The mechanical arm under all the soil and rubbish had hooked onto a metal bar and become caught. The men, with Matthew's help, finally extracted it, only to find that underneath all this rubbish was a series of old railway lines with cement laid in between. Once they lifted or broke through one section it turned out to be an enormous cistern, approximately four metres by eight metres. Matthew had the damaged top section removed, seeing the men had the equipment to do so, so that when Hazel, Carmel and Sebastian arrived at the back of the house there is was, at one metre fifty deep, the prospective swimming pool already in place.

'Well, you boys don't do things by halves, do you? A swimming pool already,' Carmel quipped.

'I don't believe it,' was Hazel's amazed reaction, moving over to the very edge. 'It's just perfect for a swimming pool, but why do you think they just forgot about it? The cistern, I mean. It's completely dry inside.'

'Perhaps over the years the water pipes from the windmill just burst, or broke, and as no one has lived here for such a long time the water went somewhere else and the cistern just dried up.'

'Hm, I suppose so,' said Hazel. 'I've been looking at a site on the internet for pool liners and filtration systems. This may not cost such a fortune after all.' He was silently justifying this to himself against the day's expenditure. Sebastian was beside Matthew and then moved behind him. He put his arms around him and poked his head through his arm. 'Matthew, will you teach me to swim?'

'Certainly. You will end up being the best swimmer in Australia.'

'Wow! I must go and tell Jan that I am going to be an altar boy.'

'Sebastian,' Hazel interrupted, 'take the cottar over to Jan and see if she can repair it.'

'OK,' and off he ran, leaving his school bag on the ground, only to return and grasp it and then dash to Jan for his homework and the news he had to give her.

'He is so enthusiastic,' said Carmel.

'Yes, he's wonderful,' replied Matthew, with a pride that was obvious to all. They moved back to the cottage, chatting and laughing about the joys of renovating.

'The shearers' quarters are finished,' Matthew announced, as he opened the door for Carmel. 'The last of the painting was finished today, more than a day early, thank goodness, as we will be using them at the end of this month.'

'Why?' asked Hazel.

'Because we start shearing at the end of February.'

'Oh, do we?' grinned Hazel. 'Silly me! I thought they just zipped the fleece off these days.'

'Oh, if only!' exclaimed Carmel. 'My bills for the shearers would be considerably less,' and she burst into laughter at the thought of a zip fitted from one end to the other of a sheep. They then began to tell Matthew of their purchase during the day.

'Why two fountains?'

'Well, I thought Killkenny needed sharpening up. Anyway, I'll leave you to two to chat—I have some serious work to do in the kitchen. Matthew, why don't you get Carmel a drink and then take her for a proper tour of the house. She only rushed through this morning.'

Matthew duly poured Carmel a drink in their dining room, which had two etched glass balls suspended from the ends of the curtain rod, Sebastian's gifts for Christmas. It was, to say the least, a modest room, but Carmel felt completely relaxed and comfortable. She and Matthew renewed their acquaintance after not having seen one another for a long time, then they moved across to the house for a full tour.

'It's strange. I never remember the interior of this house,' Carmel remarked. 'It had been closed up many years before I came to look at it with my father, but I am surprised that the house is so large and so out of keeping with all the other houses around here. It's just so grand.'

'It will be, when Hazel is finished,' he laughed. 'I think he's out to make it one of the most important homesteads in the district.'

'I have no doubt he'll make it.' She smiled and walked through the reception room on the right as one entered, to find it was ready now for painting. On the side near the window was the grand piano under a sheet of canvas. She lifted the canvas and then the lid before playing a few chords. 'Ouch!' she exclaimed, wincing. 'I think the piano tuner is needed.

'He certainly is, but he says he won't come until the piano is in its final position and that's not going to be for a few weeks, I think, as the floors have to be sealed and the walls painted or papered. I really don't know what Hazel has in mind, but come and have a look here.' They moved back through the hall and the room behind the reception room, to the dining rom. The two big French doors were swung open and the vast space that was to be the garden room opened up in front of them.

'I think this is going to be great,' said Matthew,' although honestly I haven't a clue as to how it will finish up. Sebastian's very excited about this space.'

'I agree with you,' she said, 'the space here is wonderful and with a fountain splashing and trees and plants everywhere you will have your own little garden of Eden.'

'Yes, I suppose we shall,' he agreed.

They headed back to the cottage but not before Carmel had handed to Matthew the two large parcels from the back of the car that Sebastian had collected from the post. She sat down in the dining room to a table already laid and another drink was poured, with wonderful aromas wafting in from the kitchen.

'I think if I lived here,' she said,' I should be sorry to leave this cottage. It has a real feeling of being lived in—not like mine, room after room but no people. Yours here is the exact opposite and I am quite envious.'

'Don't be,' he replied. 'Sometimes it's very crowded.'

The screen door banged shut and a voice said, 'Hazel, Jan says she can fix the hole in the frill around the bottom and she says it needs a bleach and a wash but it will be ready for Friday.' Sebastian came back into the dining room and sat on Matthew's knee, surprising Carmel with their intimacy.

Hazel swept around the corner. 'Sebastian, what happened to the candles?'

'Oh, I forgot!' He rushed into the kitchen to remedy the situation.

'Hazel,' asked Matthew,' what's in the large packages? And by the way, I put them on your bed. You see, Carmel, sometimes a cottage like this is a bit cramped.'

'I don't think so at all,' she replied, in a serious way. Hazel took a sip from his glass and went out, only to return with one of the packages which he tore open, kneeling on the floor with Sebastian almost standing on top of him. He withdrew a large sample book of silk viscose samples to be used as curtains and upholstery for the house.

'Get me the other one, please, Sebastian,' and after a squeeze past Hazel and the side table he ran out and returned with the other. This one contained a large wallpaper sample book. Carmel knelt down and flicked through the fabric swatches.

'These are just beautiful,' she said. 'If I have you over to my place could you also order me some of these?'

'Of course,' answered Hazel. 'It's not a problem at all.'

'What is all the material for?' asked Sebastian.

'It's for the curtains and bedspreads in the house,' Hazel replied.

'Oh, what colour do I have?'

'Whatever you like,' came the reply.

'Matthew, what colour shall we have?' the boy asked, flicking over the samples of fabric on the floor. 'I like this one, Matthew, don't you?'

'Don't you think that deep red might be too hot a colour for here?'

'Oh no. I think it will be very nice,' and he continued turning the samples but always returning to the red ones.

'OK, clear them away. Dinner is almost ready,' announced Hazel. Even though it was quite light outside, Sebastian lit the candles on the table as he did every night, and they all took their places. Hazel brought the food in on a large tray and served everyone. Carmel reached for her napkin, only to witness nobody making a move and instinctively did likewise. 'Benedictus benedicat per Christum Dominum nostrum. Amen,' intoned Sebastian, smiling as he turned to Carmel. 'I don't need my card now—I can remember all of it.'

'I think you've done very very well,' she replied. He thanked her in a very formal manner and they began a wonderful Thai meal that Hazel excelled in cooking.

After dinner, conversation continued as did the wine. Sebastian excused himself and went to his room to watch television. Matthew and Carmel reminisced about people they knew but both were extremely careful not to leave Hazel out of the conversation.

'Oh, no one knows,' laughed Hazel. 'It's Pat's secret. He refuses to let anyone see his creation, not even Sebastian. It's all locked up in the room over the coach house. Every spare moment he is there, banging and carrying on. I have no idea what it's going to look like but it's his masterpiece and good for him. He seems to be easing out from under Bob's thumb and that can only be good for him.'

'Yes, it's about time, but I don't know why it has to be a secret,' commented Matthew.

'Simple,' said Carmel. 'It's because it's totally his. If no one else sees it, then it is exclusively his surprise to everyone, but in his own time.'

Hazel agreed. 'You're absolutely right. But I must confess I am curious.'

*   *   *   *   *

As Carmel drove home, she had a warm feeling that the evening had been shared. They had all played their separate roles but as a group together they worked, and this gave her a great deal of satisfaction. She had many acquaintances but until now Gerald had been her closest, if not only, friend. Now, with Hazel and Matthew, her social horizons were becoming a little wider. She had never made friends easily, basically because she never trusted people completely and was always ready for a backlash on relationships, but this one, this evening, did not produce this wariness that she had with most people. She had known Matthew for years and Hazel for almost three months but to have dinner with them in the cottage with Sebastian was to be received as a special friend and this she liked. She still rolled around in her mind the?????? of the 'two Spaniards' and was still surprised at the public affection for one another, the hugging and kissing. She couldn't remember any eleven year old like that and then something jogged her memory. Timothy Osbourne and Doris, 'same age, 'same love' she said aloud as she turned the corner for the last twenty minute drive to home. Yes,' she thought,' it's the same. Timothy was only eleven like Sebastian,' she thought, running the situation through her mind, but the relationships are different, or are they, she mused.

*   *   *   *   *

Next day, as Hazel drove Sebastian to the bus, he passed a truck with pieces of cast iron painted dark green tied down with rope coming up the drive and pulled over to let it pass.

'Be there in twenty minutes,' he shouted out, and continued to the gate.

'Is that the fountain?' asked a curious Sebastian.

'Yes, and I hope the base section will be in place by tonight.' Hazel waited until the bus came toward them, having collected Sarah Wallace.

'I don't like her,' was Sebastian's reply to Hazel's question. 'She thinks she is very clever, but I think she is pretty dumb.' Hazel gave him a kiss and he slid out, opened the gate and waited for the bus. Hazel turned the car and headed back up the drive.

If Robert Patterson from the nursery had been handsome, David, his assistant, was not. He was charming and helpful but even if he had lost twenty kilos he still would never have been called vaguely attractive. The builders, bricklayers, Hazel and him, after a short discussion about drainage, moved the cast iron base into the garden room. After further discussion a site was finally arrived at. The rest of the pieces were off-loaded: David said when he had time he would transport the others but would need the other truck with a mechanical arm, as the reconstituted stone was so heavy. When the garden room was finished they were to give him a call and he would be happy to bring out all the trees and plants. So a happy, whistling man called David headed off down the drive in a cloud of red dust.

The painters were now working in part of the house, and on Thursday Otto was to arrive with some of the glazing requisites to begin work, so the day passed with Hazel moving between one work force and another. As he walked back to the cottage at lunch time he noted on Jan's temporary clothesline a very white cottar drying in the sun, and smiled to himself as he went indoors.

*　　*　　*　　*　　*

Every week for Hazel pivoted around Thursday, Bradbury day, a hectic day that had to be very well organised: a large note pad in the kitchen determined everything that was required for the following week. On Thursday mornings Sebastian didn't take the bus, but went with Hazel, for a very chatty drive. With him this morning, as well as his school bag, was a plastic sack with his repaired, washed and starched cottar, of which for some reason he was very proud. Jan had done a fine job of recrocheting the tear in the decorative border around the bottom and so the damaged section was now invisible.

Hazel dropped him off at school, then set about the shopping. It all seemed so easy, moving from one shop to another, when one had the items and not the other, and then the ever time-consuming supermarket, where all the perishables were left with the name 'Killkenny' on them for either Hazel or Jan to collect, depending on their arrangement, and before he knew it it was one o'clock and off he went to the Railway for lunch.

'Hi!' greeted Gerald. 'I believe you've made the acquaintance of Robert Patterson,' before Hazel could respond to his short greeting.

'Yes, he's a very pleasant guy.'

'Sure is. Ashley's hot for him. I think they are having something together. Unfortunately, Robert isn't so good at passing on the news,' Gerald laughed.

Hazel asked him where Carmel was. 'No idea. She is generally the first here,' at which he stood up and went to the bar for a bottle of wine, but he could not help noticing that Hazel had changed since he had first met him. He wasn't so skinny now; he was tanned, which was not difficult in this climate, but when he had arrived his skin had been very white and so he had a weak look, it appeared to Gerald, but now, with the exposure to the sun he was much changed, bronzed and his reddish-blond hair had become almost as blond as Gerald's. 'Hm, he was thinking, Hazel is going to be worth a try', smiling to himself. However, he wasn't the only person who had noticed a physical change in Hazel. Carmel, Jan and Doris had also noticed it: he was more relaxed now, not so fraught as when he had arrived three months or so ago. But someone else had noticed the change as he sat opposite him every evening and most lunchtimes, and was very pleased with the metamorphosis.

Gerald began the 'move in', but Hazel was instantly aware of the game and steered the conversation in another direction, which only made Gerald the more determined to direct it back. Suddenly, the side bar door slammed shut and Carmel entered, dressed as usual in black, but today her face matched the outfit.

'What's wrong?' ask Gerald.

'What's wrong!!' she shouted, so that everyone at the end of the bar where they were sitting stopped and turned their heads. 'That fucking David Osbourne—give me a drink!' A glass was handed to her at once.

'Money troubles,' offered Hazel.

'Exactly! I'm sorry. How are you boys?'

'Oh, we're OK,' Gerald replied, looking into Hazel's green eyes.

'Well, give us the bad news,' said Hazel.

'The bad news is that somehow David Osbourne has managed to embezzle me out of A\$365,000. Can you believe it, the rat? Mr Lester and I have been over everything. There are still some documents I have to get from the bank, but that shit—'

'Hello all!' came a cry and Doris swung into the bar. 'Hello, Trick,' she called, as she saw him at the end of the bar, drinking with friends. He waved back.

'Well, what's been happening,' she started, cheerfully. 'Oh dear, Carmel, you don't look too good. What's up?'

'What's up?' I'll tell you what's up. That fucking David Osbourne has somehow stolen three hundred and sixty five thousand dollars from my investments, that's what.'

Doris sat down slowly and narrowed her eyes as Gerald at once made for the bar for another bottle and glass. 'I am missing approximately five hundred and fifty, or five hundred and fifty two, thousand.

I was with Mr. Lester all last week trying to sort the problem out. The moment we have everything organised, or should I say all the documents in order, I shall take legal action at once and sue.'

'I have told Mr Lester to do the same. I can't believe we were so stupid as not to check more carefully the investment portfolios. Leaving everything in David Osbourne's hands we must have been insane. I could kill him!' Carmel spoke cynically.

'I wonder how many other people he has swindled,' queried Gerald.

'I imagine all of his wealthier clients, to be sure,' Doris replied, looking at Hazel. 'And we thought old Anthony O'Malley was a fool to put his money in the hands of someone who drank at the Commercial and here you are with sound investments and a cheque for 2.3 million to be deposited in your account at the end of this month, in fact next Friday, and we have been well ripped off.'

Hazel was surprised that his whole banking and administration of Killkenny were so public. He dreaded to think what they would all say when they found out how much he had spent on two fountains and, it seemed, half the nursery.

Gerald and Hazel sat opposite one another, which had Doris at one end near the wall and Carmel with her back to the bar. Perhaps it was her angry entrance or the conversation that had tempers flaring and the conversation louder than usual that attracted two men's attention halfway down the bar in jeans and tee shirts, who had given up trying to hold in their overweight stomachs. The taller of the two ambled down to where they sat. 'What's the problem, cutie?' He was obviously drunk and out for some fun.

'Fuck off!' spat Carmel, still in a rage over the embezzlement. The man put his hand on her shoulder. She immediately spun around and knocked it off. 'I told you to fuck off. Are you stupid? Don't you understand a simple instruction?' and turned back to the others.

'What are you looking at?' he said to Hazel, who was closest to him and pushed his shoulder upsetting his drink. Hazel spun into action but this time he saw himself defending Carmel and so his self-control was not as it should have been. The man was silly enough to take a swing at Hazel, who dodged it and didn't wait for another. The crowded bar suddenly opened back, leaving them space. Hazel just attacked furiously with his fists and then his legs. His foot flew in all directions and the man went down in a heap, only to have his friend come to his rescue to deal with this poof. Hazel was fired up, breathing deeply and regularly and swung his foot around, even before the second man had a chance to lift his fists. He kept striking, bouncing back and forth on the balls of his feet.

It took Trick and two of his friends to settle Hazel down. One of them, from the other side of Hazel, slipped and fell into Doris's lap. Hazel began to relax his breathing, and slowly stood still as the barman and the bouncer dragged the two drunks out of the bar. Carmel stood up and put her arms around Hazel and kissed him. 'Thanks,' she said. 'I think we all need a drink.'

'Coming up,' responded Gerald.

'Well, Doris,' commented a chirpy Trick, 'it's been a while since you've had a man between your legs,' and everyone laughed, except Trick's friend, who turned bright red.

'I'm so sorry, Mrs. Wallace. I sort of tripped.'

'Ah, that's your story,' laughed Trick. 'Come on, after an experience with Doris you need a drink.'

'Impertinent, that Trick,' said Doris. 'I don't know why that type of person is allowed in here. Why don't they go to the Crown and get drunk.'

All around them the tables and chairs were stood up again, put into their original places and the bar returned to its normal rhythm. The waitress arrived and orders were taken, with her making a snide joke at Gerald's expense about the good-looking barman, which everyone chose to ignore.

A handsome woman pushed through the luncheon crowd and made for their table. 'Oh, Carmel, Mrs. Wallace, I'm so sorry. We were out at the back checking the beer deliveries. Oh, I don't know what to say.'

'Oh, it's all right, Violet,' replied Carmel, 'but it's a bit of a bore when our friend here has to defend me in your hotel.'

'It's outrageous,' put in Doris in a haughty manner, as Gerald stared into Hazel's eyes. 'I bring my family here and we find we have to defend ourselves against your feral clients.'

'They're not our clients,' Violet snapped sharply. 'The manager from the Commercial called us this morning saying these two were looking for trouble—'

'—and it's trouble they got thanks to Mr. Hazel, who risked life and limb to defend my niece.'

'Oh, I am so sorry, Mrs. Wallace. I will have a couple of bottles sent over to your table on the house.'

'Thank you, Violet,' added Carmel. 'Hazel is the interior decorator I was telling you about.'

'Oh no!' Violet said, shaking her head. 'And this is not the first time you have had trouble here. I don't know what to say.'

'That's all right. These things happen,' Hazel replied.

'But not to my family. I won't have it,' exclaimed Doris.

'OK, Auntie, let it go. It's been a difficult day for everyone with the exception of Gerald, it seems, who, by the look of him with that smile, has fallen in love again.'

'Do you think perhaps next week you could give me a moment or two to talk about a facelift for the Railway?'

'Certainly. It will be a pleasure,' Hazel smiled.

Violet thanked him and disappeared, only to return with a wine cooler with a bottle of champagne in it.

Conversation settled back to embezzlement, gardening and decorating homesteads, especially Killkenny. 'I do hope,' said Doris,' I shall have an invitation to see this garden room. It sounds just so nice.'

'Let's hope so,' was Hazel's response. 'It's now lined, the flooring is going down and Otto will come and change the glass but only when the flooring is finished.' They all laughed, knowing Otto only too well. 'He was out a few days ago and re-glazed the big window on the staircase. It looks wonderful. No more red and yellow panes of glass.'

*   *   *   *   *

Driving home with all the supplies, Hazel felt extremely exhausted. The heat, the drama at the hotel—is it all worth it, he thought, and then thought again, yes, it was all worth it, especially a man with electric blue eyes and thick black bushy hair. Yes, it—or he—was worth it. He waited at the gate for Sebastian, for even though he could have collected him from school he knew the joy Sebastian received from being able to put his hand in his pocket and pay for an ice cream, the same as the others, and a twenty minute wait was not the end of the world.

'Hazel,' said Matthew, excitedly,' what the hell happened? Carmel rang and told me that you had single-handedly defended her against two drunken louts.'

'She's exaggerating,' was the reply. 'Now, give me a hand with the parcels.'

'Sure.' Matthew shook his head, smiling. At this point, Sebastian, after embracing Matthew, walked over to Jan's to see about his homework. Matthew dumped a supermarket sack down on the bench as Hazel walked into the kitchen.

'Oh, there's a message from Carmel—well, it's more like an instruction to me.'

'What are you talking about?'

'Carmel told me I was to give you a kiss from her.'

'Did she, indeed?' Matthew walked over, took the sack from Hazel's hand, placed it on the bench then took him in his strong muscular arms and held him for a moment before kissing him.

'I must get Carmel to call you with instructions more often,' Hazel murmured.

'I don't think I need a second set of instructions,' Matthew whispered and kissed him again before releasing him. Hazel leant back against the bench.

'Well, Matthew, where do we go from here?'

'Forward, but slowly, if you don't mind.'

'I don't mind at all,' Hazel agreed. 'Oh, the supermarket has finally got coconut milk in, so I have something special for you tonight.' He halted the conversation for a moment, 'and Sebastian.'

Matthew just smiled. 'I'll get the last bags from the car and then I will get you a drink.' He disappeared to do as he offered. Hazel began unpacking, only to be interrupted by a telephone call.

'Hi, Hazel, it's Tony. How are you? Did you get the sample books we sent you?'

'Oh yes. I'm sorry, I should have called you to say thanks.'

'Not a problem. Oh, Hazel,' Tony began again in a very calculating voice that Hazel knew only too well, 'do you have the books in front of you?'

'No, but if you hang on for a moment I'll get them.' He returned to the dining room and placed both the large sample books on the table. 'OK, what's the deal?' he asked.

'Turn the wallpaper book to???? and the fabric book to the name 'Orlando'.'

This Hazel did. 'Well, what am I supposed to do now?' he asked.

'Do you like them?' was the response.

'Sure. A bit safe but fine. Why?'

'Because I am fucking well stuck with them, 65 rolls of the paper and 70 metres of the fabric. Interested in a deal?'

'Give me the whole story first,' demanded Hazel.

'We'll, Mrs Rule—you remember her, a fabulous client—we did the big house in Albany Road Toorack and the beach house at Portsea. Well, she wanted an overhaul of the house in Albany Road and chose this stock. I didn't ask her for a deposit as she has been such a divine client, and now—'

'Now what?' interrupted Hazel.

'She's caught the sky bus.'

'What are you talking about?' Hazel was confused.

'Dead. She's dead. She had a heart attack on Wednesday night and died, and did sweetie, leaving me with all this stock. The daughter won't consider taking it and I have laid out all the cash. I just thought that if you were interested you could have it for what I paid, on the condition you take it all. I can't clear all this stuff in the shop and I think you could do something with it. What do you say?'

Hazel wrote down on a scrap of paper the prices. 'I'll call you back in an hour. I will have to see what Matthew thinks.'

'Oh, Hazel, dear, I see we haven't been letting the grass grow under our feet.'

'No, Tony, dear, we haven't. Shall we say an hour? Fine,' at which he hung up, took a deep breath and glanced at the two books. It was here Matthew found him. 'What's wrong?' he enquired.

'Come here. Do you like this wallpaper?

Matthew glanced at a beige, cream and pink huge damask pattern highlighted in gold. 'Do you think it's a bit safe?' he asked Matthew.

'What do you mean, 'safe'?'

'Well the sort of paper you would find in a matron's home in a smart suburb.'

'No, I like it. The pattern is much bigger, but it's similar to what was on the walls before.'

'Yes, it is a bit, but beige. I was thinking greens or blues—a bit of life in the house.'

'I think once the garden room is done that will be enough green for us all, don't you think?

'Hm, I suppose so,' so he told Matthew of the deal Tony was offering on the paper and co-ordinated silk and viscose fabric.

Matthew picked up both books and headed for the door. 'Come on, Hazel, let's see what it looks like in the house.' They walked across in the late afternoon sun and into the shadows of the house.

'It's not so bad, I suppose,' said Hazel. 'There's miles of paper and fabric. I suppose we could do the hall and the two reception rooms with it. OK we will take it. It saves us a fortune. Now, I must get back, I think. I left something on the stove,' and he raced back to the cottage, leaving Matthew to wander slowly about in the silence of this big old house, something he had never done before. He crossed the hall diagonally, glancing at the new staircase window, by courtesy of Otto, and walked into the dining room. Theatrically—which was most unlike him—he flung wide the French windows that opened directly into the garden room, now under construction. He couldn't imagine it finished, but he knew it would be marvellous. The windows that faced west Otto had begun to replace with glass of a grey cast that cut out forty per cent of the raw light, making the two windows on the side seem softer, yes, 'softer' was the adjective he was seeking for the whole house. Having grown up in Jan's house by the gate, this house now was slowly becoming for him a dream come true. He had been a visitor in most of the big homesteads round the district when he was younger: he had always been in great demand; but this house was different. It was prouder, perhaps, a little arrogant in defying the elements, a gigantic mansion in tin with a tower and now a garden room. He moved to one of the broken windows and looked out to a flat, unbroken landscape in which he hoped this next month to begin planting rows of trees. Then he looked down to the old cistern that he knew, when Hazel was finished, would look wonderful: a swim after a hot day's work—wow! wow! That was living!

'Matthew, Matthew!'

'I'm here, Sebastian.' The boy rushed through the dining room, down some temporary steps and threw his arms around Matthew. 'Matthew, this room is going to have trees in it and look,' he said, moving toward the fountain base which was a third closer to the dining room.

'Careful, Sebastian. 'The cement isn't dry yet.' He returned to Matthew's arms. 'Come on, handsome, Hazel will have dinner for us, I think. We might just be having something special tonight.'

'I like Hazel,' Sebastian stated seriously. 'He is always nice to me. He likes you too.'

'Yes, we both like Hazel. Come on.' He led him back through the house, collected the books and made for the cottage in the knowledge that it was going to be their favourite Thai food for dinner.

* * * * *

Hazel returned from dropping Sebastian at the bus, hearing again that he and Mrs Carstairs were very good friends, that he could play just a little and was surprised it was so hard to play the piano but was doing as Freda Carstairs directed.

'Hazel, Hazel!' Jan cried out as he alighted from his car. 'Can I have a minute?'

'Sure—providing it doesn't cost me money!' he quipped.

'Well, I'm afraid it's going to if you agree to it.'

'Try me. Oh, by the way, where are Matthew, Pat and Bob? Matthew didn't say anything to me this morning.'

'Oh, they are over at the shearing shed, getting everything ready for the shearers. They are due in next Friday, so the sheep will be brought up in the next few days. It's hard work for them, even though the contract shearers do all the work. There is still a lot of organising to do.'

Hazel was surprised that Matthew had not told him of his new work schedule. 'Anyway, sorry, Jan, what did you want?'

'Well, it's this,' and she unwrapped a plate from what seemed to Hazel to be two metres of bubble wrap. The plate was a Sevres porcelain plate with swags of flowers and putti with ribbons set in loose ovals; these shapes were in turn filled in behind with the traditional Sevres blue. 'It's eighteenth century. My sister has two of them but she says that this one will give you the clearest idea.'

'Idea for what?' Hazel was not sure where the conversation was going.

'For the church decoration.'

'Oh, well it looks fine to me, but what does your sister plan to do?'

'She would paint the church just like the plate,' replied Jan in a flat tone, 'and you would only have to pay for the materials.'

'Very well, have the carpenters taken down the panels yet?'

'Oh yes, but one broke, so they cut a new one.'

Here Hazel sighed. 'OK, whatever you want Jan,' and kissed her, knowing full well that the moment she went back into the house she would be joyously organising the decorations of the inside.

The painters had a week ago finished the painting of the shearing shed and the shearers' quarters. The smell of fresh paint could be smelled and now they were beginning on the exterior of the homestead with scaffolding everywhere. Everyone was praying that there would be no wind, as a freshly painted house with a coating of red dust due to the wind would mean they would have to start all over again. Otto arrived exactly on time in his little white van and donned a perfectly clean white dustcoat that was stretched to the limit. He wore on his head a white baseball hat. Hazel thought that with the enormous stomach and huge buttocks he looked even more like a goose than ever. He went straight to work with his assistant after a very formal good morning.

Everything seemed to be fitting into place, slowly, slowly, oh how slowly, thought Hazel and started back to the cottage, only to hear a yell.

'Hazel, come over here!' He walked over to the garden room to resolve yet another little problem. While there, deciding on the width of the stairs, a truck horn was heard and he looked through the window to see David from the nursery with the other fountain and the water pumps to recycle the water. He came over and had a look at the cast iron fountain base. 'Hey, you guys have got it right first time.' He got a sarcastic 'thanks' in reply, then he and Hazel with the foreman went to oversee the offloading of the second fountain. The mechanical arm lowered the base and the other sections in a heap near the church. He gave a wave and drove off.

'Smart arse!' commented the foreman. 'Because they deliver goods they think they are all bloody experts.' Then he went back to the laying of the brick flooring in the garden room, while Hazel disappeared into the cottage to check his emails and to see if he could contact someone local to fit a lining to the cisterns and a filtration system.

*   *   *   *   *

Doris had called Mr. Lester and wanted to know when they should begin to sue David Osbourne. Lester cautioned her and told her to wait.

'Wait? What for?' was the brusque reply.

'If, Mrs Wallace, you give me a week, I plan to contact Mr. Osbourne on your and your niece's behalf and attempt to apply pressure on him to return the money. If we take legal action immediately you may not gain all the funds that you are missing.'

'Thank you, Mr. Lester,' said Doris, in a haughty voice, 'one week only,' and hung up.

The telephone rang in David Osbourne's office, which was situated in a very smart complex, and his secretary, Bev, switched him through.

'I think, Mr. Osbourne, we had better sort out a certain problem in the investments of Mrs. Doris Wallace and Miss Carmel Wallace.' There was dead silence. 'Well?'

'I don't have any idea what you are talking about,' replied David Osbourne quickly.

'Oh yes you do, Mr. Osbourne and I can and will email you all the irregularities in these women's investments. My suggestion is this. You will, after looking at the email, transfer—and I shall leave you the bank account numbers of Mrs and Miss Wallace—the said sum in less than one week.'

'And if I don't,' Osbourne replied arrogantly.'

'Simple, Mr. Osbourne,' and here he played his trump card, 'I shall follow what Mrs. Doris Wallace wants to do and sue you for embezzlement. As you know, Mr. Osbourne, Mrs. Wallace has no great love for you.'

'I'll let you know.'

'Don't bother. The banks have been alerted and will contact my clients the moment the money is placed in their accounts. Good morning,

Mr. Osbourne, and don't forget Mrs. Wallace stipulated 'in less than a week'.' He hung up.

David Osbourne was now very worried. He would have to float a loan to pay back the amounts, as he hadn't time to liquidate cash from investments. He was furious: to personally throttle Doris would have given him the greatest of pleasure, but he was also worried that there were a few other clients whose money he had misused and if every one hammered him he would be in very hot water indeed financially, as well as with the law. He also knew that Doris was just waiting to strike back in the hardest possible way as a result of Timothy's death, that she blamed him for.

It was here that Doris began to plan her revenge on him. She sat down and penned a list of all her relatives and friends she knew had David Osbourne as their accountant and solicitor. She copied from the telephone book all the numbers, ready to strike the moment the bank notified her that the money had been placed in her account. She telephoned Carmel and explained what Lester was doing but withheld the plan she had in mind to bankrupt Osbourne, which she was sure would be inevitable, as she was certain her's and Carmel's funds were not the only clients' money he had used. She was absolutely correct, but she wanted more. She wanted the full hand of the law on David Osbourne's neck and a jail sentence was what she was focussing all her energy on.

*   *   *   *   *

This week saw the preparation for shearing at Killkenny and Thursday, as Hazel made for Bradbury with Sebastian on board, he saw trucks and cars moving in around the shearing quarters. Bob, Matthew and Pat had brought up to the paddock closest to the shearing shed the huge flock of sheep, ready for shearing, perhaps that afternoon, but definitely the following morning. Hazel was as interested as Sebastian. As they slowed down to have a look at the action, 'I didn't think we had so many sheep,' commented Sebastian in a very business-like way.

'Nor did I,' confessed Hazel, and placed his foot on the accelerator as they headed for Bradbury.

'Father Keven is very strict, you know,' said the boy. 'There are six altar boys and we are three on one side and three on the other. We have to do exactly what he says. You know you are not allowed to look at the rest of the school kids. We just look straight across at one another.' He went on to tell Hazel yet again the whole process he went through every Friday morning at the regular Mass held at the church next door to the school.

Hazel parked and went in to see the Principal. 'Bye, Sebastian, see you at the gate tonight.' With a quick 'OK' the boy disappeared in a side gate and was swallowed up in a throng of young students.

'Do come in, Hazel,' she smiled at him.

'I won't take up more than a couple of minutes.'

'That's all right. It's fifteen minutes before assembly.'

'How is Sebastian doing?' he asked.

'Do sit down. Fine—I've been keeping an eye on him and he is grasping all his subjects very well. I am very pleased with him and you.'

'Me?' he said, surprised.

'Yes, the fact that you and Matthew allowed me to keep him back one year. It really is proving worthwhile. I wish more parents would listen to me. I have a young girl here that would also have benefited from repeating the year as she was so immature, but her parents refused to accept the staff's recommendation and this year she has real problems. Oh, by the way, Freda Carstairs is totally intoxicated with Sebastian. She thinks he is the finest, most beautiful lad in the world. He has done wonders for her.' She laughed.

'Our piano still hasn't been tuned, but I hope in ten days' time, when the papering is done and the floors are sealed, the piano can be placed in a permanent position. I'm afraid the piano tuner refuses to come unless the piano is in position.'

'I don't think ten days will worry our little Mozart.'

'Do you mean he is good on the piano?' asked a surprised Hazel.

'Apparently yes. In this short time he has taken to it like a duck to water. I will tell you something but you must promise to keep it a secret.' Hazel promised and leaned forward. 'He is learning to play a very simple piece of ballet music just for Matthew. Isn't that sweet?'

'Yes, it really is very sweet. Could you tell me when it's Freda Carstairs's birthday. I think a gift from Sebastian would be appropriate.'

'Oh, that's easy,' laughed the Principal. 'Freda and I celebrate our birthdays together and can you believe, on the first of April. I know, April Fools Day,' and broke out again into a hearty laugh.

'Thanks so much for your time and telling me about Sebastian,' Hazel said.

'We are very happy with him at St. Mary's'

'Thank you,' he said, quietly.

* * * * *

Hazel walked down the path to his car and was aware of a feeling in his chest. Yes, he was proud of Sebastian and if someone had told him six months ago he would be looking after an eleven year old boy and really gaining satisfaction from it, he would have told them they needed to be certified.

He walked into the Railway Hotel as usual right on one o'clock, most of his shopping done, and noticed Doris, Carmel and Gerald at their usual table. They all stood up and kissed one another, this time including Gerald, who held his arm for just a split second longer than was necessary and it did not go unnoticed by either of the women. Hazel noticed an odd calm, and Doris had a smile like the cat who had just consumed a litre of cream. 'Just a moment.' She stood up and moved towards a crowd of people.

'What about another, Gerald?' asked Carmel. He got up, not before putting a hand on Hazel's shoulder as he passed. Carmel lent down and picked up her handbag, opened it and withdrew a small package.

'Thanks, Hazel,' and she lent over to kiss him.

'What's this for?' he asked, in surprise.

'Well, last Thursday you came to my rescue. This Thursday it's my turn to say thank you.'

'Oh, Carmel, you have made a mistake.'

'Really?' she smiled.

'The direction you gave Matthew was most gratefully received.'

She burst into a very broad smile. 'Well, I told you, but this is exclusively from me.'

He opened the little parcel, to find a pair of the most exquisite cufflinks he had ever seen in his life. 'They are just you,' she assured him, smiling, 'and I can't think of a single person who could wear them better.' Hazel gazed at a pair of quartz, cut like diamonds but surrounded by diamonds on a high gold mount with a gold chain and bar.

'You won't believe it, but all the gold is Australian. An old uncle of mine passed on and left everything to me, so I think it's time now to hand them on.' Before Hazel could say a word, she lent down and opened an invisible pocket on her Hermes handbag and withdrew the invisible pack of cards. She shuffled them and then laid out only one. She looked at Hazel and then immediately returned her gaze to the single card, turning it, with a smile from ear to ear and a mist covering her eyes. She collected the cards and returned them to the invisible pocket.

'I am as happy as you are,' she said, and held Hazel's hand. 'Give him time and you are going to be the happiest couple on God's earth.'

'Over here!' came a cry, as Gerald returned from the bar, having chatted up the barman yet again but to no avail. 'Up with the glasses;' a white damask cloth was suddenly flung across the small table, and a waitress laid out the cutlery.

'I have ordered for everyone today,' said Doris, in a very superior way. 'The champagne's on the way.'

'I went to the bank this morning,' said Gerald, 'anticipation high, funds low,' at which everyone laughed. Gerald was such a spendthrift. He lived only for the moment: good-looking, everything in his grasp—but once he had it, he didn't want it anymore, the challenge was over.

'Hazel,' he said, 'what are you doing next month? My parents have, with a bit of pushing, agreed to pay for a holiday in Bali. Will you come with me?'

Hazel was a step ahead. 'Oh, if only, but duty calls,' and smiled sweetly.

The entrance of a dozen oysters each heralded the unspoken information that David Osbourne had paid into both Doris's and Carmel's accounts the amount he had embezzled.

With champagne and oysters, and lots of hysterical laughter, the three of them waited to see what Doris had organised for the main course.

'Auntie,' asked Gerald, 'what on earth were you doing this morning sitting in your car for hours?'

'Just telephoning a few friends, you know how it is when you forget old faces and then something prompts you to say hello.'

Carmel looked at Doris and turned her head a little to the side. 'Doris, are you sure it was just social?'

'Oh, of course.' Doris feigned surprise. 'Oh, here's Trick. Well, how are we, Trick?'

'Oh, we're fine, Doris,' he replied, being one of the few younger generation that was not obliged to address Doris as Mrs Wallace. 'Back here again this week for a man between your legs?'

Although he laughed, Doris missed the joke. 'Be very careful, Trick,' she warned. 'I may just start remembering some of your other little party tricks, so to speak.'

'Enough said.' He leaned down to give her a kiss. 'Look out for men, Doris.'

'Oh Tick, isn't that funny. I was just going to say that to you—' He laughed and very quickly absented himself from the group in case Doris became just a little too vocal.

The lobster was judged by all as delicious, and Doris was well pleased.

'OK, Auntie,' said Carmel. 'Spill the beans.'

'Oh, Carmel, I feel if we are being not politically correct you are asking me to tell you why I feel so light-headed.'

'Have it your way, but what's up? I know you only too well. We are not here to celebrate your bank account as well as mine being in a healthy state. What exactly are we celebrating?'

'Oh, Carmel,' Doris narrowed her eyes and tightened her lips, 'how is he going to pay?'

'Who?' asked Gerald, innocently.

'Mr. David Osbourne.'

'Auntie, what have you done?'

'Who me?' Doris looked up at the ceiling fan and drained her glass. 'Gerald, ask them for another bottle.' Her smile was more of a smirk, her eyes narrowing ever more. 'He is now going to pay and pay dearly, for you see,' she said, directing her words to both Hazel and Carmel, 'I have telephoned everyone I know and told them that

David Osbourne is a swindler and they have probably lost all their investments.'

Carmel took a deep drink. 'I thought of doing it, but didn't have the courage.'

'Oh, but you should have. It would have reinforced what I told everyone. You do realise he is now going to jail, and I couldn't be happier.' She spoke in a joyous and spontaneous way. 'Yes, to jail. It's where he belongs. But I must say your cousin took it very badly.'

'Which cousin?' asked Carmel.

'Ashley. You see it turns out our ever-smart, elegant Ashley has private investments with David Osbourne. You know, Carmel,' and now Doris was speaking in a very serious manner, 'there is such a thing as divine justice and this is it.' She finished with a determined fist hitting the table. A shiver ran down Hazel's spine. Here was an older woman out for blood: then he stopped for a moment and tried to put the equation in another form. What if a person, not necessarily David Osbourne had been the cause of Sebastian dying from negligence and indifference. Would he really feel any different to Doris? He knew in his heart he most definitely would not; he would also go for the jugular vein.

After lunch, he also made for the bank and was elated to know the supermarket chain had paid the 2.3 million into the account. 'Thank the saints,' was his excited response to the information. 'I can now start to pay some bills.' He collected the last things he needed and then headed home with two extreme viewpoints rushing in and out of his mind, love and revenge. Love he accepted readily—Matthew was the most wonderful but the most secretive man in the world. And revenge. Doris had stepped over that fine line between love and hate and as the emotions for both are the same, from a little boy she truly loved, to his father, she was determined to destroy.

CHAPTER SEVEN

A Funeral and Two To Come

CHAPTER SEVEN

A Funeral and Two To Come

The work was gathering momentum at Killkenny. The shearers had finished and they recorded a record clip, much to Matthew's delight. He now settled back into a period without the stress of the organisation required to shear this vast number of sheep, just short of twenty thousand. The show sheep that were to be bladeshorn were to be done in the middle of August but the rest looked decidedly happier without their woolly fleece in this terribly hot weather. Matthew was now consulting an expert on the re-sowing of vast pastures with a different type of grass, one that was much more adaptable to the climate, and he was preparing to plant out five thousand hectares as an experiment. Pat was having a great time with the rented mechanical digger, opening up the soil for at least a thousand small eucalypts to be planted in the following month. Bob did what was required, but little else, but for the moment all was calm, so Hazel didn't make waves. On Saturday nights, Bob and Pat regularly went to Bradbury for a drink at the Railway with their respective acquaintances but Matthew never left the property: once a month, perhaps, for the hairdresser, but that was it. He now had no desire to be anywhere but

Killkenny with Sebastian, and Hazel was filling a part of his life that he found challenging.

The house was nearing completion, the wallpaper had been hung, the floors sealed and the furniture re-located in the rooms, the large Victorian paintings looked surprisingly well on the heavy wallpapers and it was Matthew who said to Hazel he didn't think the effect was at all 'matronly'. Hazel had to agree, but the word 'pompous' did come to the back of his mind as the antique furniture was placed in position. Sebastian had been adamant that his bedroom be in a red damask and needless to say had his way, but he never used it. He still slept with Matthew in his room, but kept his clothes in his red room. Hazel let this situation be. He was sure it would be better for an eleven year old boy to sleep in his own room but as Matthew had no complaint Hazel remained silent. The piano was finally re-tuned and every night for half an hour Sebastian could be heard practising.

But the garden room was the gem of the house. It had a fountain that splashed gently, the walls were painted a soft celadon green, between the windows rose to the ceiling trellis pilasters with large terracotta pots at the bottom with jasmine beginning to make the climb to the top. The section nearest the door was designed to be seen whilst eating, giving a restful atmosphere. The two thirds behind the fountain were supplied with comfortable settees in teak with generous cushions in a tiny pattern of two tones of green, but the impact came from the trees in huge pots, oranges and lemons, huge tubs of bamboo and twelve very generous hanging baskets in front of the windows, where petunias spilled over the edge. All around were broad but shallow terracotta pots filled with white bedding begonias, so the whole effect was one of green and white. Hazel had studied this very carefully. At the very end, between the two French doors, stood an empty plinth surrounded by a variety of different shaped pots of all different dimensions, again massed with white bedding begonias. The empty plinth was the result of Hazel not being able to locate something satisfactory to place on it; he was torn between a piece of sculpture or an enormous urn but for the present it remained vacant.

This room now became the centre of the house. They took drinks here before dinner and occasionally the table and chairs near the divan were used for lunch and even dinner, depending on how much had to be moved between the kitchen and the table. The lighting was very discreet; when lit in the evenings it seemed like a faraway place, all green, with white reflected plants, a great contrast to the harsh conditions just beyond the walls.

The pool, after many ups and downs with the filtration system, was now working and Hazel had had a two metre pavement in brick made to surround it. Much further out, a tall wooden paling fence with a hedge plant that Carmel had suggested was planted all the way around it, so hopefully, in a year or so, the whole fence would be invisible. A dripper system supported this positive decorative idea. If Matthew was beautiful clothed, in a swim brief he almost made Hazel faint. A great deal of time was spent by the three of them at the pool.

When all of this was more or less finished, they invited Carmel to dinner. 'Hi, am I late?' came a cry as she opened the screen door to the house.

'Coming!' and Hazel swept up the corridor from the kitchen. 'Carmel, you look divine!' As usual, she was in black but this evening she had obviously opened the safe and was wearing a most splendid diamond necklace and earrings.

'I only wear them so no one notices the nose,' she laughed.

'Come through,' said Hazel.

'It looks fabulous, Hazel.'

'You haven't seen the best yet.' He smiled and took her, after a look at the two large reception rooms, through to the dining room, which had the French doors closed. He flung them open to a vista that completely stunned her.

'Oh!' was all she could muster at first. 'Hazel, it's just fabulous.'

'Come and say hello to the boys,' and from the end doors Hazel and Carmel turned and walked to the swimming pool, where Matthew and Sebastian were yelling and playing in the water.

'Our guest is here,' shouted Hazel.

'Hi, Carmel!' Matthew extracted himself from the pool, leaning over to help Sebastian out. This was necessary as it had one depth only.

Carmel felt suddenly in need of a drink or to sit down, she wasn't quite sure which. Matthew came forward and, careful not to drip water on her, gave her a kiss. 'Glad you could make it.' She tried to reply only to find her voice was an octave higher than usual. O God, he is magnificent, she thought, that olive skin and black hair, broad hairy chest. Oh, I really do need a drink. Hazel was not unaware of Matthew's impact; it happened to him every day, but he came to Carmel's rescue and they returned to the garden room for drinks which had been prepared. When they were alone she looked at Hazel and shook her head. 'He's unbelievable.'

'A drink, darling?' he smiled.

'A bottle is more in order, I think,' she replied, then gaining her equilibrium she began to praise the decoration of the house. 'It's such a change from only a few weeks ago. I can't believe it.'

Matthew and Sebastian entered and went through to change. Carmel this time sighed, sending Hazel into fits of laughter.

'I know. It happens to me every day.'

'Half your luck!' came her reply, and with the fountain splashing merrily away and waiting for the others, they chatted about the garden room, Carmel admiring everything.

'You know, I thought the minute the reception rooms were finished—and they are not completely finished—we should enjoy using them, but somehow we have gravitated to the garden room, and Sebastian is the only one who uses one of them when he practises the piano.'

'Oh, how's he getting on at school?' she asked.

'Well, the Principal seems very pleased with his progress and apparently Mrs Carstairs is overjoyed to have him as a pupil, so everything seems fine. We held him back a year on the Principal's advice and it seems that what she suggested has suited Sebastian perfectly.'

'He's a beautiful boy—no wonder Freda is pleased to have him as her exclusive student. Doris told me about the arrangement. I must see if I can arrange it for you and Matthew to come and see Doris's home. The living room is vast. It holds, as you come in the door, a pair of ornate Victorian wardrobes. She had the mirrored sections in the doors removed and glass fitted, and a mirrored back fitted to each one and clear glass shelves, all courtesy of Otto and there are hundreds of tiny decorated boxes that she and Timothy designed and made, some of them are just exquisite.' She reached for her glass. 'As they became more skilled they used books on eighteenth century snuff boxes and Fabergé boxes. They were real professionals and they used every type of material to produce these little gems. It's definitely worth a visit just to see these two large wardrobes filled with their masterpieces.'

'Doris must have felt very proud, directing this young man,' replied Hazel.

'Oh no, it was the reverse. Timothy was the master. Quite often he would destroy the decoration and they would start again. Some of them are covered in the most sumptuous papers Doris ordered from a store in Melbourne onto which they glued tiny pearls or fake diamonds or rubies. You really have to see them. Doris is immensely proud of them.'

'I suppose his parents have some of them as well,' suggested Hazel.

'No, not one. The whole collected remained in Doris's hands.' Laughter and lively conversation announced Matthew's and Sebastian's return. 'The house is superb,' she went on.'

'Well, the choice of wallpaper and fabric in the reception rooms is Matthew's. I thought they might look a bit matronly,' Hazel suggested.

'Hardly. It looks perfect. Were the paintings here or did you buy them?'

'We haven't bought any furniture or decorations, only the things in the garden room here that I bought with you. Everything else was stored and we just dropped them into place.'

Sebastian moved over to Matthew and lent against his chair. 'I can almost play the piano,' he said in a shy way to Carmel. 'Mrs Carstairs is teaching me.'

'That's fantastic. You will soon be able to play a duet with me.'

Sebastian looked at her and then Matthew, not at all sure what a duet was. Hazel laughed and explained it to him. Sebastian thought it very interesting that two people could play the piano at the same time and thought that next Thursday afternoon he would have Mrs Carstairs clarify the situation.

'Do you play, Carmel?' asked Matthew.

'I used to, but I haven't opened the lid of the piano at home for ages.'

'Well, if that's the case, we shall expect a little entertainment from you this evening, shan't we, Sebastian?'

'Oh yes,' he replied, not quite sure if the entertainment meant playing the piano.

After a delicious Thai meal they moved to the reception room and took their seats. Carmel raised the lid and sat down at the piano. She ran her long fingers up and down the notes and then began to play. She hadn't felt so relaxed for years and then wondered if it was 'relaxed' she felt or 'safe'. She came to the conclusion it was a combination of both. They all applauded.

'That was great,' said Hazel. 'You're fantastic.'

'Once upon a time!' She laughed, turning to face them. 'You see, when I was young, I was the only child and I had no friends so the piano for me was a world into which I escaped. Come over here, Sebastian.' He went up to share the piano bench with her. She showed him how to play 'Chopsticks', the simplest of duets and after the third attempt they seemed to get it almost right. At least, Sebastian managed to get it almost right.

As tomorrow was a school day, Sebastian said good night to all and went upstairs.

'He's a great little man, isn't he?' smiled Carmel.

'Oh yes, he is,' Matthew agreed and they moved back to the now enchanting garden room, with all the lighting turned on.

'It's amazing,' Carmel commented, as she stood on the steps leading into the room. 'It really is magic. I love it.

'Matthew,' said Hazel, 'will you get Carmel a drink and entertain her while I just tidy up here.'

As she sat down, she looked at Matthew's handsome face and concentrated for a split second on the electric blue eyes. 'Now I understand why you so rarely come to Bradbury. Why on earth should you? You have both constructed a beautiful safe haven and a wonderful family. I am completely envious.' She continued to look at him. 'Yes, a perfect family in a perfect place.'

'Well, Hazel has worked almost day and night to put all this together for us. It's mostly all his expertise—I couldn't have done it. Sebastian adores it, as I do. You know, the funny thing is I have in a short period of time forgotten, well almost forgotten, the chaos that we lived in at the front gate. When I was there with the shearers I walked around a completely empty field. There wasn't one trace of a place that I had lived in for twenty years. It's funny how you forget so quickly.'

'I think it's easier to forget the immediate. It's the past that occasionally creeps back into one's thoughts.' As she reached over to place her glass on the side table, her telephone rang. 'Oh, I'm so sorry, Matthew. I was sure it was turned off.'

'It's not a problem,' he insisted. 'Go ahead and answer it if you want.'

She extracted her phone. 'Yes, yes. Oh, Doris, may I call you first thing in the morning. I am at dinner with friends.' She hung up, just as Hazel returned. 'Mary has died,' she said, slowly.

'Who is Mary?' he asked.

'David Osbourne's wife, Timothy's mother. She has been so very, very ill and for such a long time, she didn't even know Timothy had died. It's all so very sad, this story, and that fucking David Osbourne is the result of all this sadness.' Hazel sat down beside her. 'I'm glad she has gone,' Carmel went on. 'No one should suffer that pain.'

'Did you know her?' Hazel asked Matthew.

'When we were younger, but I don't think I had seen her for ten or fifteen years.'

'Oh, this is going to be a drama, this funeral,' sighed Carmel. 'Can you imagine Doris having to be in the same place as David Osbourne. I do hope there won't be a scene. I just couldn't bear it.'

'What do you think about this new grass seed?' asked Matthew, changing the subject. 'We are planning this autumn to plant out five thousand hectares of it.'

'Are you really?' she sounded surprised. 'My manager says it's a waste of good money.'

'I don't agree,' replied Matthew. 'The property is only producing half of what it's capable of. We get approximately 20 inches of rain a year and that's a normal year. Some years much more and yet the same turf has been on this paddock for a hundred years or more with no super-phosphate or trace elements ever applied to it. I am certain I can lift the level here.' He spoke determinedly, reaching for his glass, which was nearly empty. He rose to fill the others' glasses as well as his own, then sat down again.

'What do you think, Hazel?' she asked.

'I haven't a clue. Matthew is the expert.'

'I believe it's certainly worth a try,' argued Matthew. 'In fact when all these trees are planted to make barriers, the top soil we lose as a result of erosion should be halved, with the combination of trees and this new grass strain. We are going to try the worst part of the property first and if it's a success then we shall reseed the whole lower part.'

'Well, you two are out to change the world,' smiled Carmel, 'and, you know, I believe you will do it. Matthew, harping back to the funeral next week, are you going to come?'

'I guess so. Hazel can look after Sebastian, as my parents will also be going. My mother actually knew Mary when she was well. She often had lunch on Thursdays with her and my aunt.' He sighed.

'I imagine Doris will have a reception back at her place—without David Osbourne, of course,' said Carmel in a flat tone. 'Oh, I just know this is going to be very difficult.'

On her way home, two different thoughts flashed back and forth in Carmel's mind, the funeral for Mary and the great changes and the happiness that she witnessed at Killkenny. She liked being with Hazel and Matthew and felt she could speak openly on any subject, which she did, although she always steered clear of any conversation that might be directed toward Ashley. She recalled what Hazel had said some time ago, about not taking out a law suit out against Ashley for his dishonesty and fraud, that it would implicate Bob and indirectly Matthew, and this he was not prepared to do. She wondered if she was in the same situation. Would she have sued Ashley or not?

* * * * *

The funeral was set for Monday afternoon at 3, and Doris had telephoned her relatives and friends letting them know there would be drinks and light refreshments back at her home, about which Jan and Matthew had been separately notified. It was a mercilessly hot Monday afternoon, without a breath of air, as the mourners filed into the church. Mary having been a Wallace, all the Wallaces were present and this formed a large band, as well as friends. David Osbourne sat in the front row and two pews back on the other side sat Doris, stony—faced, dressed completely in black. Foolishly, David Osbourne's clothes seemed anything but a mourning outfit: blue trousers, no coat, blue shirt and a red tie. This only angered Doris all the more. Before the funeral rites began, Doris stood up and went to the coffin. On it she placed a little white box, beautifully decorated by Timothy, then returned to her seat, chosing not to see David Osbourne at all.

Carmel had kept a seat free for Matthew and when he moved down the aisle to join her, two pairs of eyes fixed on him, those of Gerald and Ashley, and both of them had the identical thought. His tall, solid figure in black trousers and crisp white shirt and black tie, his black hair and those powerful blue eyes made both Ashley and Gerald think that the reception back at Auntie Doris's was not going to be so grim after all. Carmel had telephoned Father Keven and explained the details of the situation and that Doris might just be waiting to make a scene in church or out of it, so to be very careful how he worded the eulogy. For Doris, it was like burying Timothy all over again and Carmel held her hand, but the tears flowed abundantly.

After the Mass, everyone followed the hearse to the cemetery and Matthew was surprised at the number of headstones that bore the name 'Wallace'. Mary was interred beside Timothy; 'united in Paradise' were Father Keven's last words, which had Doris in a flood of tears. David Osbourne, for once, was intelligent. When he noted Doris herself, he made a rapid exit, knowing full well that when this last part of the funeral was over Doris would be out for blood and he was right, but she was to go unsatisfied if she had planned a fight, as her fighting foe disappeared so quickly.

The mourners headed back to their cars and those invited snaked their way back to Doris's house. Matthew went with Carmel, who said she was so relieved that everything had gone smoothly. 'I really was so afraid that Doris would just explode,' she said, 'but don't worry, there will be plenty of poisonous conversation over drinks at Doris's.'

'I hadn't seen Ashley for years,' he said. 'He looks harder than I remembered.'

'Yes,' replied Carmel, 'and just a little more vicious, and what did Cherly look like, dressed for a garden party, I thought.

Matthew laughed. 'Don't be bitter,' he said.

'Who? Me?' but she smiled.

It had been many years since Matthew had been to Doris's home and the impact was the same, this enormous single-storey dwelling with a tower, that seemed to spread out in all directions. It was heavily planted with trees, which softened it off a little, but it was a very impressive Italianate mansion.

Carmel knew everybody there but if she really thought about it, probably only Gerald and Matthew could be classified as friends. She had warmed to Hazel at once and was delighted to be invited to their home for dinner and was planning the minute this funeral reception was well over to invite Hazel, Matthew and Sebastian for dinner at her home. She instinctively set herself as Matthew's guardian, knowing her two cousins only too well.

'Well, Matthew, how are you?' asked Ashley, as he deliberately strode over to speak to him.

'I'm fine,' replied Matthew, very formally.

'A good wool clip this year?' Ashley's tone was superior.

'This year, yes,' was the curt reply, at which Ashley immediately changed the subject, understanding at once the innuendo. 'You must come over for a drink one night,' he went on. 'We have so much to catch up with. I can't remember when I saw you last.' He was looking at Matthew with a slight smile.

'I'm afraid his social calendar is filled, Ashley,' interrupted Carmel who had joined them.

'I am sure he could make an exception for me this time,' urged Ashley, smiling broadly.

'Sorry, Ashley, but it's just impossible. Carmel, you promised to show me the boxes.'

'Certainly, Matthew. This way.' They turned and went toward the display wardrobes. To say Ashley's nose was out of joint was an understatement. The one thing Ashley took very personally was rejection and it annoyed him immensely, as it so rarely happened—but he had to admit Matthew was a stunner. It was Gerald who was the one to gain from this rejection. He moved over to Ashley and gently made a play for him, and in the state Ashley was in he accepted the game and the two of them moved to a corner of this vast living room to compare notes and to make an arrangement for a quiet drink together very soon. So although Ashley's pride had taken a blow, he managed with Gerald to pick up face.

Doris swept from person to person, chatting lightly and then on to another. She spotted Carmel and Matthew admiring the little boxes on display.

'What do you think of them?' she asked.

Matthew spun around. 'I've never seen anything like them,' he replied. 'They are magnificent and each one different from the next.'

'Oh yes. We never did the same design twice. Isn't this one beautiful?' She pointed to a little box covered in metallic blue paper and borders in two shades of gold. In the centre, on the lid, was a little portrait of an eighteenth century man and around it was a similar gold border, this time in tiny glass diamonds.

'It's just wonderful, Mrs. Wallace,' he said, 'but they are all wonderful.'

'Yes, they are,' she agreed, looking into the case. 'Oh, is that the time? I just wish to say something to everyone before they start to leave.'

Out of the corner of his eye, Matthew saw the strangest person: he was short and incredibly thin, with a haunted face. He didn't walk but seemed to skate about the room, changing plates and filling glasses.

'Carmel, who is that strange person?' he asked, pointing to the waiter.

'Oh, Matthew, that's Simon, Doris's youngest son. He must be thirty five or something now.'

'He looks so odd.'

'So would you if you had lived with Doris all your life.' She laughed.

'May I have your attention?' Doris had to repeat the cry again. 'May I have your attention! I am so glad you could all come back here after the very sad funeral but I have one or two things to say to you all.'

'Here we go,' whispered Carmel to Matthew.

'It concerns a certain David Osbourne. If any of you here still have your business or investments with him, you are insane,' she shouted. There was dead silence; not a glass was heard on a table. 'David Osbourne,' she continued, 'managed to steal from me 565,000 and roughly the same from Carmel.' All heads turned in the direction of a tall woman, dressed as usual in black. 'We have transferred all our business and investments into the hands of Mr Lester, and if you don't do the same thing at once, unlike us, you will not get your money back.' They all began to look at one another, slightly nervously. 'It appears that only the O'Malleys were the clever ones, and Matthew here has reaped the benefits, while we haven't made a cent on our own investments. I don't think the interest covers banking charges.' Then, not being so tall, she stopped and forced her way through the crowded drawing room. 'Oh, here you are, Ashley—'

'This will be good,' Carmel whispered again to Matthew.

'Well, Ashley, what have you got to say about all this?'

'Nothing, Auntie,' he said quickly.

'Come on, Ashley, you can do better than that. Haven't you invested with David Osbourne a great deal of your mother's money?'

He moved from one foot to the other. 'That's my business, not yours,' he snapped.

'No, Ashley, the truth is it's not your money at all and in fact when I spoke to Angela, she had no idea you had made this unsound investment with Osbourne.' Now, she cut out the Christian name. 'I am not happy about this at all. Just because Angela is bed-ridden, I see no reason why you should take advantage of her.' Here she was interrupted from the other side of the room.

'I think it would be wiser, Doris, if we kept this conversation private,' suggested Cherly.

'Oh, do you?' Doris spat out. 'How apt of you to pass such a bland, dreary comment!' Doris was winding herself up. 'The reason I have brought this up, dearest Cherly,' she went on sarcastically, 'is because most people here are going to lose a great deal of money and they happen to be my relatives and friends. I happen to know my nephew a damn sight better than you. Oh, by the way, in future, Cherly, just in case it slipped your empty head, the colour for a funeral is black, like the rest of us are wearing, out of respect for Mary. If you think dressing like a parrot has endeared you to the family you have made an alarming error.'

Cherly had the feeling that a shot-gun blast in Doris's direction would be an excellent idea.

'You see,' continued Doris, turning to the assembled guests, 'the reason I am explaining this is that Osbourne and Ashley have lost money on their deals and you can bet your socks that they will recoup it with your money, leaving you without a cent. Isn't the scenario something like that, Ashley?' Ashley was black with rage: first, to be turned down by Matthew, and then Doris, his own aunt, attacking him in front of everyone.

'One last thing.'

'Thank God for that,' snapped Ashley, sarcastically.

'Oh, Ashley, don't be upset. You know you haven't changed since you were a little boy,' Doris smiled at him in the most patronising manner. 'Always a bad loser! You see, Ashley, if it hadn't been for Mr. Hazel, Carmel and I might have lost our money, but Mr. Lester saved the day and the money we had returned to us is probably a large part of your shaky investment with Osbourne.' She turned to her guests. 'Go to Mr. Lester at once, or you will lose everything.' Then she walked across the room to thank Father Keven for attending. He was feeling very awkward to be in on a family feud, but thought that if there was ever to be another Inquisition, he had Doris's telephone number.

'Well,' remarked Carmel to Matthew, 'that should cut the Christmas card list for next year!' She linked her arm through his, smiling, and they walked to a large table simply laden down with food and drink. They helped themselves as Ashley glared cross the room at Doris talking to Father Keven. To make a sudden exit, he knew was fatal, but to remain here was hell. He saw Carmel and Matthew at the table and watched another little scenario of Gerald, who had waited his time and now moved in, but Gerald had not counted on Carmel. He realised too late that to get to Matthew he had to go through Carmel, who had set herself up as Matthew's minder.

'Matthew, I haven't seen you for years. You look great,' he said, smiling.

'Yes, doesn't he?' replied Carmel. Although she was his closest cousin, he sensed at once she was not going to be of any help at all in attempting a conquest of Matthew, so the conversation remained socially bland. Gerald excused himself after a while and returned to Ashley. They had made an arrangement for a drink at a later date, and they both acknowledged that Matthew was even better than either of them remembered.

Jan moved over to Matthew and said Bob was keen to go, so as this was Matthew's mode of transport he said goodbye to Carmel, who said she would call tomorrow. He then sought out Doris. 'Thank you, Mrs. Wallace, for your hospitality and thank you for showing me the magnificent collection of little boxes.'

'It's a great pleasure, Matthew. I should like to invite both you and Mr. Hazel here for dinner one night, with Carmel. I'll see if I can get it organised and speak to Mr. Hazel on Thursday at the Railway.' With that, they left, as did some of the other guests.

Carmel swept over to Ashley. 'How are we, Ashley?' she enquired in a chirpy voice.

'Just fine,' was the sarcastic answer. 'If I didn't think I would get life in jail I would cheerfully shoot Doris.'

'Oh, come on, Ashley, she could have been worse.'

'How?'

'Simple. She could have announced exactly what your investments were, or are, with David Osbourne. Imagine how that would have helped your popularity, and by the way my suggestion is, dear cousin, to get yourself a very good lawyer, as you are going to need one.'

'What are you talking about?'

'Ashley, Doris is going to sue Osbourne for embezzling funds, and if you are implicated you may well do a 'stretch', I believe it's called, in jail.'

'Doris got all her money back. What's she bitching about?'

'Oh, Ashley, I though you would have known. Doris has refused to take five thousand back, so she now legally has a right to sue for embezzlement.'

Ashley went white. He had thought that if Doris had received everything she had lost then this issue would die a natural death. It had never crossed his mind that she had orchestrated the situation so she could make sure that David Osbourne could, and would, be prosecuted to the full. Ashley felt a sudden wave of nausea and he had a sinking feeling that he was in a very difficult legal situation.

'Thanks, Carmel. I'll make an appointment to see someone I know in Mortlake tomorrow.'

'Ashley,' she said, 'for once in your life, smarten up and not a word of this to Osbourne, because I can assure you when he is prosecuted— and he will be, Doris will see to that—he will take you with him and I don't think your property is going to stand a second mortgage, do you?'

'How the hell did you know about that?' he said in a harsh whisper.

'Ashley, word gets about, so be very, very careful. You can't afford even the tiniest mistake, and listen, Doris is prepared to put up with you—'

'Oh, how grand of her,' he interrupted, sarcastically.

'Strangely, I think she likes you, although I can't imagine why. But Cherly she loathes, so my suggestion is this: keep Cherly as far away from Doris as possible and if things get really rough, you may find Doris will go in to bat for you, but I can assure you she will not do anything if she thinks Cherly is to gain by it. The attempted slap in the supermarket was not a clever move on Cherly's part and she is damn lucky Hazel saved the day.'

'OK, I'm going now. Thanks for the advice,' and off he went dutifully to Doris and thanked her for the afternoon, remembering every single word Carmel had said.

'You could have been a bit more help,' said Gerald, in a snaky manner, as they were among the few remaining guests.

'Why, darling, I noticed you and Ashley making plans. Surely you wouldn't want Matthew as well?'

'Hm, you know what I mean. He is so handsome and—' Here Carmel interrupted him 'and,' she said, continuing the conversation, 'just happens to be living with a dear friend of ours, Hazel.'

'Lucky bitch,' was the sharp reply.

'Well, when you are seeing Ashley is it just for a drink?' She turned her head and lifted an eyebrow.

'Ha, ha, ha,' returned Gerald, moving away to speak to an aunt he hadn't seen for ages.

'How is the garden room?' Carmel turned around to see a smiling Doris.

'Oh, it's magic, yes, magic is the right adjective, I'm sure. The boys would be delighted to show you if you wanted to see it,' knowing full well that Doris was pea green with envy that she, Carmel, was the only person they had invited to Killkenny. 'I'll have a word with Matthew and Hazel this week. Perhaps I could collect you and we could go for a drink.' Doris smiled. 'That would be lovely, Carmel, dear.'

*   *   *   *   *

Matthew related to Hazel every detail of the afternoon when he returned to the garden room after a swim.

'Well, it seems that you've had an action-packed time,' laughed Hazel.

'You know, Hazel, I had no idea that Doris Wallace could be so dramatic and gosh, when she becomes angry!'

'Yes, I have seen her once like that with David Osbourne. She is not a girl to cross and think you'll get away with anything. Still, I quite like her. I suppose it's because I have lunch with her every Thursday, well, most Thursdays, at the Railway.'

'Oh,' said Matthew with a smile, 'and Ashley asked me for a drink.'

'Really?'

'It's all right,' Matthew reassured him, noticing a change of tone in Hazel's voice. 'Carmel saved the day and we told him I had a full social calendar.'

Hazel glanced across at Matthew and smiled, but inwardly he was beginning to find that the more he heard of Ashley the more he was beginning to dislike him, even if he had never met him: a move in on Matthew changed the dynamics, so now he felt quite comfortable loathing him.

'What do you think of the glasses?' he asked.

'Where did you get them from?' Matthew replied.

'The other cottage, this afternoon. I was sorting out the last of all those cartons—and, gosh, there were hundreds of them—and these beautiful crystal glasses and four matching decanters were in a tea chest behind the cartons. I think there must be sixty or eighty glasses of all sizes.'

'I think they're very elegant.' Matthew held his up to the light and turned it around.

'But I also found bits and pieces of silver and they are engraved with a very decorative 'K' on all the bits, but nothing is complete. It seems as if there was perhaps a lot of it in boxes and they have become separated. But I just don't seem to be able to find the other pieces. Perhaps the O'Malleys sold it off some time ago.'

'I don't know.' Matthew shook his head. 'I didn't even know there was silver in the boxes. As you have probably noticed, none of the boxes or cartons are labelled.'

'Oh, don't I know it!' came the exasperated reply.

A banging of the screen door announced Sebastian's arrival. He at once climbed all over Matthew.

'Careful,' he warned, and moved his glass out of harm's way.

'I'll leave you two to it,' said Hazel. 'It's time to play chef.'

'Hazel, can we have the same as last night, please,' begged Sebastian. 'It was really good.'

'You'll have to wait and see,' at which he disappeared up the steps into the dining room and through to the kitchen.

Hazel had indeed had a busy afternoon, sorting out crockery, glassware, whatever silver there was, table linen—all these things had remained unpacked for what seemed well over fifty years, and he was somewhat exhausted working in the heat, taking one carton at a time to the house, unpacking, washing and stacking it all away. There still remained ten or eleven boxes to unpack properly, but he had opened them and gone through them only to find that most of them contained glass and china, an enormous quantity of dinnerware in white with a royal burgundy band trimming the edges, fine gold lines and again the letter 'K' in gold in a decorative gold surround. There must have been at least three hundred pieces, thought Hazel, enough to open a restaurant, from plates to tureens, huge platters all in perfect condition, except for fifty years of grime and red dust. The letter 'K', I suppose, he thought, stands for Killkenny, but how odd: one would have assumed that the O'Malleys would have used their own initial.

Later, while dining off the re-found china, Hazel spoke to Matthew about the initial 'K' which was also on the few bits of silver that remained at the bottom of a box, but he could shed no light on the mystery, as he thought the same as Hazel, that it was very strange not to use your own initials.

'Perhaps,' Matthew suggested, 'this huge dinner service was simply purchased by old Mr. O'Malley and the initial came with it.'

'Perhaps,' was the reply.

'Hazel, this is nicer than last night's,' commented Sebastian, giving himself another helping.

*   *   *   *   *

After dinner, Sebastian practised on the piano a piece of music that Matthew thought was vaguely familiar and then he went upstairs to watch television. In the evenings, Hazel and Matthew now generally sat in the garden room with a drink, chatting about the day's work and the projected workload for the forthcoming days. This evening, they were discussing the church. Otto had called to say that the windows would all be in place next week, due to the simple design that was sandblasted into the pale blue glass that was flashed with a soft mauve colour.

'I am dying to see the panels your aunt is painting,' said Hazel.

'Oh, I knew I had to tell you something,' he said, standing to refill their glasses from a table underneath a large potted orange tree. 'Mum wants to know if my aunt could use the cottage for a while. Mum is more than happy to have her stay in their house but Aunt is not keen on Dad at all, so the cottage would be ideal, as we are not using it now.'

'It's fine with me,' replied Hazel. 'I'll give it a tidy-up tomorrow and as there are quite a few bits and pieces of extra furniture, it will be a little more comfortable.'

Matthew looked at him for a moment, saying nothing, then, 'You know, Hazel, whether it was the cottage where we were all on top of one another, or now, in this enormous house, you have the capacity to make whatever space there is comfortable. I hated living with my parents and at an early age Mum bought me a television for my room, so I ate with them and Pat, but as soon as the meal was finished I went to my room and closed the door. This is the first time I have been in what I would consider a real family, where we all share.'

'And I'm glad I have been part of all this,' said Hazel, softly. 'I thought when I first came here that I wouldn't be able to stick it out, so to speak, but now I can't imagine living anywhere else in the world, even if the landscape is a trifle inhospitable.'

'But you've created your own landscape here in this garden room. Oh, and Carmel told me at the funeral reception that all of Bradbury are dying to see this room but she has been telling everyone it's good manners to wait until you are asked.' He laughed loudly. 'Do you know, Hazel, only four months ago no one would have ever thought of coming to Killkenny and now everyone is waiting for an invitation.'

'I think we'll let them wait for a while,' replied Hazel, grandly. 'Oh, changing the subject, Matthew, the big stone fountain will be erected on Friday. I think the foundations for it are enormous. I am sure they have made a mistake.

'It's very large and it's reconstituted stone, so it is bound to be heavy. By the way, how are we going to lift the pieces up on top of each another?' he asked. 'I asked the bricklayers and they say with a block and tackle, whatever that is. I personally thought it might be easier to hire a crane to do it, but they know best.'

'I think I'll have a top-up,' said Hazel, settling back. 'I am so tired tonight, those blasted cartons and boxes go on for ever—as does this heat.'

* * * * *

The cottage was made ready for Jan's sister, with Jan insisting she help Hazel prepare it. 'It will be so good to have Rhonda here for a little while—I am so looking forward to it. She has finished two panels already for the ceiling but said she may as well paint the walls in situ.'

'That's fine with me,' agreed Hazel. 'She can stay as long as she likes. Oh, Jan, what about all this crockery with the letter 'K' on it?

'I haven't a clue,' she answered. 'I didn't even know that there was crockery in the boxes.'

'And the rest?' Hazel went on. 'I noticed that you are sorting out all the religious things in the first room.'

'Yes, but so much is in really bad repair. Rhonda will give me a hand to repair the two saints. Those bloody vandals threw something at one and it has bleached out the colour on St. Anthony's robe and the Christ child needs some work as well. I've started to make all new altar cloths—the old ones are in shreds and they are only in cotton. The vandals used them to clean their shoes by the look of it.

I managed to do a deal in the sale at Cromies a few weeks ago and bought a whole bolt of linen, the very fine narrow stuff they used to use for guest towels. They had had it for years, so I got a really good buy.'

'I'll re-imburse you for any expenditure. Just write it all down and give it to me,' he said.

'Don't be silly, Hazel. If you're paying for the whole church I think that I can afford a bit of linen,' she replied forcefully.

Hazel gave in, suddenly aware that this was Jan's way of contributing to something that was very important to her.

*   *   *   *   *

The only work left to the carpenters was the church, a bit of repair to the large cottage that doubled as a store-room, the coach house and the yards for the ram sales, so when they couldn't work on one project they moved to another site. The bricklayers had the steps for the church, the big fountain and the floor in the coach house left and then that would complete their programme. Hazel had got to know them all as four months of intense work and intense arguing had bound them together in this enormous project. Killkenny was looking thoroughly resurrected. The old abandoned elephant was now on its feet and in a short time would be ready to trumpet completion.

Thursday morning, just as Hazel called Sebastian for the second time, his telephone rang and a most apologetic Otto announced that, due to difficulties beyond his control, the windows for the church could not be fitted until the Friday of the following week. 'Oh damn!' exclaimed Hazel, as he hung up. 'Oh well, the painters can start anywhere on the outside.'

Just then Sebastian raced out. 'Sorry, Hazel, I forgot my money,' and they headed off together to Bradbury, leaving Matthew and Pat and a very disgruntled Bob beginning, now that March was here, preparing the five thousands hectares for re-sowing, beginning to organise the planting of the hundreds of small eucalypts as wind breaks, and replacing the dead trees on the drive. Bob thought the whole exercise was stupid and out of Hazel's earshot was quite vocal about it, but was obliged to do as Matthew diplomatically directed.

Hazel scuttled about Bradbury with a shopping list in one hand and parcels from previous shopping in the other, including dark green paint and a large tin of undercoat for the copper. Each time he went to Bradbury, the previous day Pat would hand him a list of things he required for his umbrella, which still no one had seen. Hazel would return with what he required and Pat, with the packages under his arm, would secretively head off to the room in the coach house and behind a locked door throw himself into his creation.

Hazel met Jan at the supermarket as arranged and he carried out to her four wheel drive several cartons of white wine which he and Matthew were quite able to consume without any problems at all. It had been one of those days, hot, and with a strong wind, so he was more than happy to join Carmel and Doris in the air-conditioned Railway Hotel.

'Where's Gerald?' he asked.

'Working, for once!' replied Doris with a smile, as they all exchanged greetings, then settled down to serious gossip.

'Oh, Doris, you're just the person to help me,' he exclaimed.

'If I can,' she replied, sitting a little more upright, so Hazel told the story of the huge dinner service in burgundy and gold with the initial 'K' on each piece. 'Whose initial is it?' he asked.

Doris smiled. 'Well, that's a story. You see, the whole dinner service was imported from England in the last part of the nineteenth century by old Anthony O'Malley's mother, so it's been on the property for well over a hundred years. You see, she was from Killkenny in Ireland and missed it very badly. My mother and old Mrs. O'Malley were friends, although she was much older than my mother. I don't remember her at all. The property was obviously named after her birthplace and she ordered that enormous dinner service with the

'K' for Killkenny. I remember my mother said it gave her the greatest pleasure to see that very decorative 'K' in gold on every piece of the set.'

'But there are also a few pieces of silver with the same decorative initial.'

Here, Doris looked at Carmel and then into her almost empty glass, which Hazel filled. Not another secret, he thought, noticing that Doris had become very quiet and that was most unlike her.

'How did you know about the silver?' asked Carmel, and Hazel suddenly realised that this conversation was taking a very strange turn. Why was Carmel asking? 'I found it in the bottom of some cartons with the dinner service, some knives and forks. There was also a sauce boat and some other small pieces but all with the initial 'K' on them. Did the O'Malleys at some time sell it all off?'

Doris looked at Carmel. 'You tell him, Auntie,' she insisted.

'Well,' Doris began,' it wasn't sold.' Here she stopped. Hazel was now more than curious but the subject was interrupted by the waitress. They ordered and Hazel steered the conversation back to the silver. 'Well, if it hasn't been sold and we don't have it, who does?' he demanded.

'Ashley,' the two women chorused together. Hazel looked at the two of them, both looking a little sheepish. 'I can only draw the conclusion that if Ashley has the silver, he stole it with the help of Bob. Am I right?

'Yes,' answered Carmel, 'you are exactly correct.'

'Does he have all of it?' and here Hazel played very cunning.

'What do you mean, 'all of it'?' asked Doris in a surprised way.

'Well, 'lied Hazel,' I have the inventory sheets that were packed in the bottom of one of the cartons.'

'I think that you will find the sideboard in Ashley's dining room is filled with it, except if I remember the initial 'K' is turned to the wall, so it all appears to have no monogram at all,' said Doris. 'I'm sorry to tell you this. You will probably think that we Wallaces are a ghastly lot.'

'Not at all,' said Hazel, 'in fact Matthew and I would like to invite you both to dinner when it's convenient for you.'

'Oh, Mr Hazel,' beamed Doris, 'that would be just so wonderful. I am more than curious to see your and Matthew's restoration of Killkenny, which brings me to another point.' (Oh, thought Hazel, not more theft?) 'I believe Matthew is re-seeding five thousand hectares this autumn. Carmel told me. Do you think it will be a success? It's very expensive to do that, isn't it?'

'Matthew believes it will be a great success, as he thinks that Killkenny is only producing half of what it could.'

'Really?' said a most surprised Doris. 'Half. Well, well. I must sit down and talk to him. My half-wits at home haven't a clue about pasture improvement.'

'Nor does my manager,' agreed Carmel. 'I told Hazel he thinks it's a waste of money.'

'Well, I am with Matthew,' said Hazel. 'We shall experiment with five thousand hectares and if it shows results then bit by bit we shall re-seed the whole property.

'Hm,' murmured Doris, 'and you're also planting trees this autumn as well.

'Yes, hundreds of hem. They are in crates at Killkenny now. Pat waters them each evening. I am surprised how quickly they are growing in such small pots.

'Well, it seems that Killkenny has the lead on all of us,' commented Doris. 'First Mr Lester and now pasture improvement and tree planting. And I am told you had a record wool clip. Not bad, Mr. Hazel, for only four months' work.'

'Oh, it's Matthew who's done it all. You see, it was Mr. Lester who told me to make Matthew the manager and keep Bob in the background.'

'He's a bright man, Mr. Lester,' commented Carmel, joining in the conversation. 'He has completely re-organised my investments. I have sold off just about everything on the stock exchange and he has converted it into apartments in Melbourne. The return will be quite a different affair from what Osbourne was doing. I can't believe I was just so complacent and let him do what he wanted with my money.'

'Yes, Mr. Lester has also re-organised my investments.' Doris took care to leave David Osbourne's name out of the conversation. 'But I am most interested in speaking to Matthew about this pasture enriching. My property is not producing as it should but part of that has to do with three uninterested sons.'

*   *   *   *   *

Hazel, driving home, was furious. So Ashley had all the Killkenny silver. Well, it wouldn't be for long, he thought, and he began to hatch a plan to blackmail Ashley to return every single piece, right down to the tiniest salt spoon. He decided not to tell Matthew anything about it for now, as he was working with Bob, and it might make for a difficult situation. Besides, Matthew probably wouldn't approve of the scheme that he was still formulating in his mind.

He collected Sebastian and in a cloud of dust headed up the drive, with Sebastian telling him all about his music lesson with Freda Carstairs and how he liked her so much. When they drove between the two palm trees which heralded the entrance to the homestead complex, in the large square that housed a church surrounded by trees, stood the base level of the enormous fountain. Hazel felt a little embarrassed, and the word 'pretentious' filtered into his mind.

'I think it's going to be fabulous,' said Sebastian. 'Will it shoot the water up very high?'

'I don't really know,' Hazel replied, in a weak voice, wondering what everyone would think of it complete.

After dinner he told Matthew that he had invited Doris and Carmel to dinner and did he have any preference for a day. 'No, any day is fine for me,' he smiled, pouring Hazel a drink. This was now almost a fixed ritual that after dinner they sat for an hour or so in the garden room and just chattered to one another about the day's events.

'Oh, Matthew, I am really worried about this other fountain.'

'Why? It isn't finished yet.'

'Exactly! Look at the size of it now, and not even half of it is in position. Don't you think it's just a bit showy?'

'Look, you thought the same thing here in the garden room when it was under construction and now we just take it for granted. Once the other fountain is up and functioning it will be the same.'

'I hope so.'

*   *   *   *   *

The next day, Hazel sat down in the dining room alone with a sheet of paper and roughly worked out how much silver must have been required to support this huge dinner service. The service was for twelve and the large table and twelve chairs were obviously meant to complement it. So he began with the pieces he had and worked out what exactly was missing. Then he suddenly remembered Doris's comment that the sideboard in Ashley's dining room was covered in it, so there had to be a great deal more than just flatware, and how was he to get a look at it before he tackled Ashley about its return? And what exactly was it all?

Doris and Carmel were bidden for Tuesday evening at 7.00 and to the minute Carmel's black BMW arrived through the sentinel palm trees.

If Doris was surprised, so was Carmel. The fountain was in place and working! The bricklayers had finished it only two hours before their arrival.

Doris looked about in wonder. She had a vague memory of Killkenny but the house she never remembered being so large or so grand, and like all the surrounding structures neatly painted and in good repair. 'I don't remember a big fountain,' she said.

'Oh, don't you?' Carmel smiled. 'Well, just wait till you get inside.'

Doris's eyes missed nothing: the church without its windows, the cast iron trim on all the verandas. 'I see our Mr. Hazel has been repairing and decorating,' she said approvingly as she alighted from the car.

Sebastian bounded out to meet them: Doris hadn't seen him for years and was genuinely shocked at his appearance and his likeness to Matthew, who had followed him out.

'Well, young man, how are you?'

'My name is Sebastian.'

'And mine is Doris.' She put an arm on his shoulder and kissed Matthew.

A great many adults disliked Doris for her autocratic ways, her lack of patience and her ready temper, but for some odd reason children adored her and Sebastian followed suit.

'What happened to your church windows?' she asked the boy.

'Some vandals broke them all and now Mr. Otto is going to make them new.'

'Let's get in out of the heat,' urged Matthew and they moved into the air-conditioned house.

'Well, Doris, I'm glad you could make it.'

'So am I,' she smiled, and Hazel took her for a tour while Matthew, Sebastian and Carmel made for the garden room, Matthew having relieved Carmel of the two bottles of champagne she had brought.

'Sebastian, will you put these in the refridgerator, please.' He disappeared with a bottle in each hand. 'It's a bit smarter than I remember it,' she said, as Hazel showed her the reception rooms. 'I remember the paintings. There should be ten of them. They were bought at auction in Melbourne en bloc.' She trailed around after Hazel, re-discovering a past that had been regenerated into a future. Sebastian joined them.

'Well, Sebastian, I hear from Freda Carstairs that you are a little genius on the piano.' He nodded his head. 'Well, let's have some music.' He sat down, turned his sheet music to the correct page and began to play a very simple tune. Doris looked at this domestic scene and knew instantly that without Hazel all this couldn't have been possible. A round of applause at the completion gave Sebastian a great sense of satisfaction. He came over to Doris and whispered, 'I am learning a piece of ballet music for Matthew for his birthday but it's a secret.'

'I won't tell a soul,' she whispered in return and he took her hand to go to the other reception room.

'Was all the furniture here?' she asked.

'Yes, it must have been a very over-furnished house, because we still have some left.'

'Yes, I remember it being very busy.'

As they moved to the hallway she looked at the big window on the stairwell with a very ornate curtain arrangement drawn back, showing the pale blue glass border, sandblasted with tiny leaves and flowers.

'I don't remember that at all,' she said.

'It's new,' Hazel replied. 'The red and yellow border panes were just too much.'

312

When they passed into the dining room, 'The furniture is the same but it's so much smarter,' she said, noticing the Killkenny dinner setting.

Sebastian opened the French doors and Doris was as flabbergasted as Carmel the first time she saw the garden room. 'Oh my!' was all she could manage as she glanced about the enchanted space with background music and the fountain gently splashing. She moved through the room, glancing at every pot, every tree. She was fascinated with the filtered sun streaming in through the windows, with forty per cent of the sun blocked out, a much softer light. Then through the window she noticed the swimming pool. 'Well, well,' she finally managed, as she sat down. 'You boys have certainly done yourselves proud. It is all wonderful.' As Carmel said later, for Doris to pass a comment like that meant she really was impressed.

'Champagne, Mrs. Wallace?' Matthew offered.

'Oh, Matthew, you must stop calling me Mrs. Wallace now. It's Doris.' She settled into a comfortable chair near him and was astonished at the similarity between him and Sebastian. 'Now, Matthew, I want to know everything about this new grass you are planning to plant and the type of eucalypt you think will survive best here,' and for half an hour she went over his ideas thoroughly. 'I don't suppose you want a job at my property, do you?'

'Thanks, but no thanks. This is my home now and I'm very happy here.'

'I can see that,' she replied, narrowing her eyes slightly. Then she turned and glanced around her, while the others were discussing something else. 'Whoever would have thought to fill a big room like this with trees and a fountain, she thought, and way out here.

Hazel left the group and in ten minutes returned to announce dinner was ready. The evening continued to be a great success, eating off the Killkenny china and using the beautiful glasses, but, Hazel thought, missing the Killkenny silver. It was a subject that was not touched on this evening, nor was the subject of Ashley.

It was after dinner that coffee and drinks were offered in the garden room. Here, Doris saw it at its most dramatic, all carefully lit, and she thought it was like being in a film, only this was real. But of everything Doris remembered of this special evening it was a little boy who stood up and said grace in Latin, and it reminded her of another little boy who now was not with her any more.

*   *   *   *   *

When Sebastian was dropped off from the bus each afternoon, he always collected the post and this afternoon there was a letter for Matthew which was rare. Sebastian placed it with the rest of the post on the table as usual in the garden room, then raced upstairs to change into a swimming costume before going down to join Matthew, already in the pool.

'There's a letter for you,' he said, splashing water on Matthew, who returned the same. 'I'll have a look in a minute,' he replied, and swam to the end and back. Sebastian was making real progress with his swimming. Matthew was a very good and patient instructor.

In fact, Sebastian was making progress in all directions, the interaction with other children at school, learning to play the piano, learning to swim. His whole world was now very open, whereas before it had been a very closed existence with a governess and Matthew for an hour before dinner every evening. He never missed his parents at all as no one spoke of them and he had never really known them, so he suffered no loss. For him, this was the first time he had been really happy: to his mind he had absolutely everything he had ever wanted in his whole life—Matthew and now Hazel, without whom he knew he would have trouble, and as Hazel had right from the start put Sebastian on a diet, the results after four months were showing. He was beginning to grow taller but the overweight problem was almost unnoticeable, even in a swimming costume, so he no doubt felt better in himself. The other thing he loved was Hazel's cooking, as both he and Matthew loved Thai food.

Hazel also in this period was feeling good and secure. Matthew was closer to him than ever, although neither of them had had the courage to take the last step in case it alienated the other, so on an emotional level even though they were totally dependent on one another they were in a strange way treading water, each waiting for the other to make a move and each afraid of making it.

'Matthew, would you like a drink?' Hazel called out.

'Coming!' Lots of yells and laughter from the pool announced another ten minutes would pass before drinks. Hazel made himself comfortable and was feeling very pleased with himself. He had all the accounts up to date and was following to the letter what Mr. Lester had asked in keeping them in order at Killkenny.

Sebastian came through first and said he had to go to Jan for his homework. He went upstairs, changed, grabbed his school bag and dashed across to Jan's. As Matthew came through the door in his briefs and with a towel around his neck, Hazel handed him the letter addressed to him. He opened it gingerly and took a large sigh.

'Everything OK?' asked Hazel.

'Yes, thanks, at last.' He left the room and returned in a white tee shirt and khaki shorts Hazel had bought for him. In fact, Hazel had completely re-organised Matthew's wardrobe. He had purchased everything new and dumped all that he had owned at the opportunity shop. Matthew was a passive spirit when Hazel was around and readily accepted his advice.

They were talking about the invitation that Doris had extended to them for the following week when Hazel's telephone rang. He stood up and collected it from a side table. 'Killkenny,' he answered. 'Oh, good evening, Mr. Lester. What? Are you sure?' Hazel's voice quavered. 'What shall we do?' He stood in silence as Mr. Lester passed on the information to him. 'Will you contact the other solicitor for me and find out everything about Sebastian?' Here Matthew spun around and moved over to Hazel, whom he noted had become very pale. 'Fine, yes, as long as Sebastian is all right. I will wait for your call. Thank you, Mr. Lester.' He put a hand on Matthew's shoulder.

'Matthew,' he whispered, 'Keven is dead.' He walked back and flopped down in a chair.

'What happened?' Matthew asked, though he was much more interested in where legally this left Sebastian.

'It was a car accident in Indonesia. It was apparently raining and the car left the road and fell into ravine or something. They were both killed outright, Mr. Lester said.'

'Where does that leave Sebastian?' asked a very worried Matthew.

'He's fine. I still remain his guardian, so nothing changes but who has Keven left his half of Killkenny to? That's going to be a problem, a real problem for us all.'

'Are you sure everything is legally guaranteed for Sebastian?' asked a very upset Matthew.

'Pour me a drink. I'll be back in a moment.'

Matthew looked around him. His world had finally turned from the happiness of the past and suddenly in the time it took to answer the telephone everything had changed. The security of the future suddenly seemed anything but that.

'Come here,' said Hazel, returning with his laptop. He opened all the legal documents Mr Lester had sent him concerning Sebastian and then he looked into Matthew's worried eyes. 'Carmel,' he said. 'The cards: you see I have all this information because Carmel somehow or other saw the future and it was she who sent me to Mr. Lester for all the information about custody of Sebastian and he in turn sent me all the legal documents.'

'Carmel? But how could she possibly have known?'

Hazel was very upset. He had loved Keven very much. They had been friends for years but strangely enough this preoccupation of Matthew for Sebastian's future tended to eclipse his loss.

'Here it is,' and they read through the document.

'There,' Matthew said, pointing, '*in the case of one guardian pre-deceasing the other, the one remaining will take full custody of Sebastian Peter O'Malley until he turns twenty one years of age and will be responsible for all legal and financial affairs for him.*' Matthew sighed deeply and lifted Hazel to his feet, almost sending the laptop to the floor. He held him in his arms without saying anything and Hazel felt warm tears of relief run down onto his neck. They stood like this, which seemed for Hazel an enchanted moment, until Matthew slowly drew away.

'I'm sorry,' he said.' I was so worried.'

'Never be sorry because you love someone, Matthew. It's the most wonderful thing in the world and it's the only thing really worth fighting for.'

Hazel resumed his seat, as did Matthew, and Hazel was aware of finishing his glass rather suddenly and having the odd sensation he was floating. He looked into Matthew's blue eyes and wondered desperately if he felt anything like the same.

*   *   *   *   *

Two Australians coming back to Australia is one thing, but the bureaucracy involved in sorting out two dead Australians is something else. In Keven's will, his Melbourne solicitor said he had wished to be cremated and so legal documents fluttered back and forth through the Australian Embassy in Jakarta and the solicitor in Melbourne. Keven's body was cremated in Jakarta but there were problems in returning the ashes to Australia. This bureaucratic pingpong continued for weeks and all the time at Killkenny it was an anxious Hazel, Matthew and staff who waited to see who was going to share the property with them as whoever inherited Keven's share plus his properties in Melbourne would have an equal say in the running of it and half of the profits. A nasty thought ran through Hazel's mind: what if he had left his half to Ashley? After all, they had been lovers at school, their properties touched one another, their parents knew one another.

Oh God, if that happens we are in a real mess, as it would mean that Ashley had a half say in the running of Killkenny and would insist on re-opening the boundaries and Killkenny would become as before, a satellite for Ashley's property. 'Goodbye, Silver,' was Hazel's parting thought.

The Wallaces, that is Doris and Carmel, immediately rallied, but there was really little to be said or done. It was now mid-March and the sowing and tree planting had begun, so as Hazel said, they went ahead as normal until they found out what was in the will.

Hazel also had another scenario on the will, that Keven had left everything to his new boyfriend with whom he was totally besotted. Hazel had heard via Mary that they were planning to buy a house in Indonesia in the north as they loved the tropical climate, so perhaps he had changed his will prior to their departure to seek out this house. If this were the case it would perhaps be the boyfriend's inheritance that would take a slice of Killkenny. The only satisfaction that he had was that Mr Lester had stated it was impossible for the inheritor of Keven's estate to force the sale of Killkenny unless Sebastian agreed and under the act drawn up by Keven and his solicitor this was impossible until Sebastian was twenty one years old and only then when he took complete legal control of his half.

*   *   *   *   *

The postponed dinner party at Doris's finally happened, and on the arranged date, a Friday night, Matthew, Hazel and Sebastian were suitably dressed to be received by the matriarchal Doris as they rang the front door bell. Hazel was most impressed with the house: Matthew had not been exaggerating when he said it was large—it was in fact enormous. When built, this homestead carried a staff of ten indoors. Doris herself answered the door. 'Do come in, please,' she smiled and as she was about to shut it, Carmel's car pulled up behind Hazel's. 'Come along,' shouted Doris and they all moved through an enormously broad hallway, floored in Victorian tiles, with walls well covered with paintings and prints, forming a decorative covering over them.

'Come through,' and after everyone had greeted one another they followed Doris through to the large drawing room which Matthew recalled filled with people only three or four weeks ago.

'Well,' Doris asked, when seated with the others, 'what's happening with Killkenny? Who is the new half?'

'We don't have a clue,' replied Matthew, taking over. 'We'll only find out after the funeral when the will has been read and probate granted, so we just have to wait and pray.'

'Both seem to be essential,' said Doris. Sebastian had stood up and moved beside Matthew, with one arm around his shoulder, and was looking toward the door at the two large lit wardrobes that held all Timothy and Doris's little boxes.

'Shall we have a look?' suggested Doris. Matthew and Sebastian followed her across this vast room, lit by two enormous chandeliers. Matthew noted that, without the large number of people he had seen before, the space was larger and grander. Carmel remained with Hazel for a moment and reached down to her handbag. From the invisible pocket she drew out her cards, shuffling them and placing them in front of Hazel. He cut the imaginary pack and she re-shuffled them, then turned over the top card. She smiled, collected the cards and returned them to her invisible pocket.

'There is justice in this world,' she said. 'Now, come and have a look at the boxes.' Hazel couldn't believe the tiny boxes, all decorated like eighteenth century snuff boxes; the colours and workmanship were sublime. 'They are very professional,' confessed Hazel. 'You worked as a perfect team.'

'Yes, we did,' Doris replied softly.

'Come on, Sebastian,' Carmel interrupted, 'let's see if Doris's piano is in working order.' She led him across the drawing room to the bay window where a grand piano stood silently waiting for a 'maestro'. He played his little piece and was warmly applauded and then sitting beside Carmel he watched her long white fingers skim across the keyboard as she played a piece of Chopin.

'Very good, Carmel,' Doris congratulated her. 'I'm surprised you still play so well.'

'Thanks, Doris,' Carmel narrowed her eyes in reply, and then for the second time began the duet 'Chopsticks' with Sebastian.

While listening to the music, Hazel was more than curious to ask Carmel exactly what she saw in her invisible cards, but his sixth sense told him just to wait and not ask.

They moved to the table and everyone had a little card with their name on it in front of where they were sitting. These took the form of silver animals with slits in their paws into which the card was inserted. Sebastian was most impressed: he had a bear, but beside his was another little card written in Doris's careful hand, 'Benedictus Benedicat per Christum Dominum Nostrum' and he smiled. They all sat except Sebastian, who very professionally said grace in Latin and was delighted to hear everyone respond together with 'Amen'. It was moments like this when it was easy to see the pride on Matthew's face.

'Well, how's the seeding going?' asked Doris.

'Finally finished,' Matthew replied, 'and the last of the trees go in this coming week.'

'Well, you have been working at top speed. Reverend Mother always said to waste time was a sin and she was so right.'

The odd thing about the meal was, first, this huge dining room that could easily have seated twenty but with the table closed up and only the five chairs around; the distance across the table made it impossible to hand anything directly to someone else. The room, Hazel thought, was rarely used; it had a tired, museum look about it, but very grand it was. A huge Persian rug covered the floor, with a vast sideboard on one side, laden with semi-cleaned silver. Then something happened that gave Hazel the feeling that he had slipped back a century. Doris rang a table bell and her son Simon glided in to serve the meal he had prepared, but he didn't eat with them. In silence he changed plates, filled glasses and, in his own way, slid around the dining room. 'I'm sorry,' Doris said.' There's none of your wonderful Thai cooking here, I'm afraid, but Simon is a whizz with fish.' It was pronounced by all to be excellent. Simon blushed and disappeared to prepare the next dish.

'Where will the funeral be?' asked Doris.

'I think it should be at Killkenny if we can get the church in some sort of order. You see, Jan's sister is now staying with us,' Hazel answered.

'Really?' Doris said.

'Well, in a manner of speaking,' interrupted Matthew. 'She is staying in the cottage as she is not fond of my father at all, but it's great company for Mum while she paints in the church. Mum sits with her, crocheting borders for altar cloths and things, happy as can be.'

'Yes, it's been a lonely life for your mother,' said Doris.

'If there's a Mass at Killkenny and Father Keven says Mass you will have to serve for him,' Carmel said, looking directly at Sebastian.

'I think I can do it now, if he helps me a bit. I sometimes forget the water at the end.' Everyone laughed.

After the meal they returned to the drawing room and an easy relaxed evening followed, with Sebastian leaning against Matthew on the big Victorian settee.

'He's a good boy,' commented Doris, 'so well educated socially. Mine were disasters, running about, especially Ted.

'He hasn't changed even now,' Carmel added sarcastically, as she disliked Ted immensely. 'Feral' was the word she always used to describe him.

'Oh, I forgot to tell you,' Doris began, 'I went with a friend of mine past Killkenny yesterday to visit Angela—oh, she is in a poor way, enormous!' This quiet chatter continued among the adults.

As for Sebastian, he had had a day at school, a swim in the pool, a race about to see his new one-month-old puppy for the first time—Hazel had allowed him to keep one of the new pups for himself, so his time had been spent between school, Matthew, Jan, Hazel and this puppy called Red, named for his ginger coat. All of these together added up to a very tired young lad who silently put his head against Matthew's chest and with Matthew's arm securely around him, drifted off to sleep.

'I couldn't believe Angela,' went on Doris. 'She is bedridden, but I couldn't even recognise her. She is so swollen! Oh, a real mess! And the room has the most disgusting smell of body odour and disinfectant. I know they have a home nurse in three times a week but obviously that Cherly is of no use or help at all, and the room is simply gloomy with an enormous television perched up on a chest of drawers. I told her it was her own fault—no exercise and too much food.'

'You must have made her day,' quipped Carmel.

'She's not long for this world, I fear. You can always sense death, can't you?' Doris asked generally.

'I've never thought of it,' Hazel replied. 'My experience is that death generally comes when you least expect it. Look at Keven. Who would have thought that seeking a romantic hideaway in Indonesia would end up in a tragedy like this.'

Doris helped herself to port. 'Indeed, indeed,' she agreed. 'But I tell you Angela is not long for this world.' If any of the three adults with Doris this evening had had any idea why she went to see Angela, they would have been truly horrified.

Goodbyes were said and a sleepy Sebastian kissed Doris and Carmel goodnight, then Matthew picked him up in his strong arms and carried him to the car. Carmel turned to say goodnight to Doris and was surprised to see a grin from ear to ear.

CHAPTER EIGHT

Ashley

CHAPTER EIGHT

Ashley

No matter which way Hazel turned the equation he could not find a foolproof method of blackmailing Ashley into returning the stolen silver without implicating Bob and indirectly Matthew. Rhonda, Jan's sister, was almost invisible: Hazel rarely saw her. Whereas Jan was very overweight, despite now being on a diet and time would tell, Hazel thought, Rhonda was as thin as a rake, tall, with closely cropped grey hair and dressed, as most of the women in this district were, virtually in men's clothing. She had dull eyes and thin, sunken cheeks and a pronounced nose but when you were close to her you could feel an intense energy that always made Hazel feel uncomfortable.

The windows had been installed into the church and the last ceiling panel fitted up. The effect was of an airy space where only cherubs and roses, held together by pink and burgundy ribbons, floated effortlessly across the upper part. Rhonda was now working on the panels surrounding the lower part of the walls, about one metre forty in height. These were taking the form of faux marble panels, with rosettes in each corner. The altars, having finally been finished, were in place and the marble panels worked very well with the faux marble walls. Hazel left all of the church interior to Rhonda and Jan. He had the feeling that every time he entered the church and they were there he was intruding, so he decided to leave them to it and if they needed him for something they would seek him out.

After quite some time, Keven's ashes had still not arrived. They had been delivered to the Australian Embassy, which refused to have anything to do with them, insisting that the family take responsibility, but any correspondence to the Australian Embassy inIndonesia, Keven's solicitor in Melbourne, Mr. Lester in Bradbury, Hazel at Killkenny and all the way back again led nowhere. Just when they thought all was well, the box or metal container went missing, so this process now had dragged on for almost a month with no one at this stage even sure where the ashes were.

Hazel woke one Saturday morning very early, when he heard a very strange noise, not close, but in the distance, and couldn't quite understand what it was. He rose and looked out of the window only to see, to his great surprise, a grey sky. By eight in the morning a very fine rain had begun to fall.

'I don't believe it,' he said, aloud, 'rain!'

It was still warmish but it was raining. He opened the balcony doors upstairs under the tower and stepped out, watching and smelling the rain.

'What are you doing?' asked Matthew, on his return from the bathroom.

'Look, it's raining! Can you believe it, rain at last!'

'Perfect timing,' replied Matthew, with a smile on his face. 'This is exactly what we need for the new seed and the trees.' He stood beside Hazel and put an arm around his shoulder. 'If we can get this will sorted out so we know what's happening, everything will be just perfect.'

'Yes,' agreed Hazel, 'just perfect.'

'Red, Red, go back to your mother. You are not allowed to get wet,' cried Sebastian, carrying his pup back to the mother in drizzling rain, with Matthew and Hazel laughing on the upper balcony.

'He is so sweet,' Hazel said. 'He's becoming a really nice young man. You know, Doris is mad about him. She has only seen him twice, but Carmel said she speaks very highly of him.

'He's great,' Matthew agreed, tightening his grasp on Hazel's shoulder. 'He's not the only one.' Hazel smiled.

*   *   *   *   *

Ashley's trip to Mortlake had occurred on the day when Doris made the trip with her friend to see Angela. Cherly went to see a friend and Ashley spent more than an hour with a solicitor trying to work out a legal way to extricate himself from the investment scandal with David Osbourne as well as keep his own money. In his suave way, he managed to put on a brave and sophisticated face but after an hour of sharp interrogation by the solicitor, Ashley felt anything but suave and sophisticated: he wanted to sue Osbourne immediately for the return of funds but the solicitor pointed out the fact that if he sued for the funds it would probably keep him out of jail but he was highly unlikely to get much of the money back. Ashley was disappointed and angry. How could he have been such a fool as to believe David Osbourne? Doris had been right, David Osbourne was a swindler and he had lost a lot of money or, to put it in a more correct form, a lot of his mother's money. He was now in a very awkward situation moneywise and it was going to have to be Cherly's cash that would have to keep them afloat financially. To sell the property with a mortgage on it would gain him little, so it was probably better to stay where he was. If only that damn Hazel person hadn't arrived, he would have had all the pasture at the back he needed as well as a handsome cut of the wool clip. Now that this financial avenue was cut off he had to rely on what money Cherly had and whatever Angela had in her many bank accounts.

But he wasn't the only person suing David Osbourne. Doris had signed the papers in Mr. Lester's office three weeks before as he had quite a few others when they realised they had nothing in their investment portfolios: all the information they had received annually had been false. David Osbourne had been arraigned before a magistrate and he was now facing charges of embezzlement of private funds for his own use. This theft, if proven—and that was not going to be difficult to do—would lead to a three to five year jail sentence.

This news gladdened Doris's heart as she told Carmel, Hazel and Gerald at the Railway on Thursday. When she left to speak to Trick about some transport she wanted, Carmel looked at Gerald. 'Well,' she said. 'What?' came the reply and he placed a hand on Hazel's arm.

'How did the drinks go with Ashley, Gerald?' He withdrew his hand from Hazel and reached for a drink.

'Oh, that? He's all talk,' looking down into his drink.

'I take it nothing happened?' Carmel asked, baiting him.

'Well, hardly.'

'What do you mean, 'hardly'?'

'You know, the same old thing. He's a bit of a waste in bed and really that scar isn't attractive,' Gerald stated grandly.

'A scar?' Hazel joined the conversation.

'Oh yes,' said Carmel. 'Men have them—war wounds.' She laughed.

'Where was the scar?' Hazel enquired in a slow and very deliberate way.

'High up on the inside leg, left—oh no, right leg. Why?'

'Is the scar diagonal?' Hazel asked.

Carmel was becoming interested as she immediately picked up that there was more to this gentle to and fro questioning.

'Yes, I believe you're right.' Gerald answered. 'Anyway, how the hell do you know anything about Ashley? You said you have never met him.'

'Not here,' Hazel said through gritted teeth, narrowing his eyes. 'I can't believe it. I knew an Ashley Wallace, as I told you both, but I had no idea it was the same person. I knew him, oh, fifteen or sixteen years ago. The scar was the result of a fall on a metal stake.'

'That's right.' Gerald sounded surprised. 'Don't tell me we have both been to bed with the same guy!' He began laughing but Carmel noticed that Hazel had not seen the funny side of it.

'We know Ashley is a rat,' she said, 'so why don't we leave it there for the moment.' She could see that Hazel was becoming very angry.

'Listen,' said Gerald,' I have to rush. I have a damn appointment with the dentist. What a bore!' At which he rose and disappeared into the busy lunch crowd.

Hazel's face turned to stone. Carmel saw it and said, 'You will do exactly what I tell you. Are you listening?'

'Yes,' was the sharp reply.

'The moment you arrive home and have a moment with Matthew—and I mean the first moment, don't delay—tell him everything. Do you hear me?'

'Yes,' replied a dejected Hazel. 'I always worried that the Ashley I knew and the Ashley next door might have been the same, but after a time it just seemed impossible. Oh, how fucking incestuous this all is!'

'What are you talking about,' Carmel asked.

'Well, look at it this way, Ashley slept with me and before me Keven and well afterwards Gerald. What a happy little story!' he ended, sarcastically.

'Forget about the others. Concentrate only on Matthew. He's the most important man in your life.'

'Oh, Matthew,' sighed Hazel. 'He hates Ashley because of the swindling of money from Killkenny. Imagine how overjoyed he is going to be when he hears that I once lived with him.'

'Did you?'

'Well, sort of. He had his apartment in Domain Road and I had a mousehole. I was at teacher-training and he was at the University. Eight months of happiness and he just disappeared.'

'My dearest Hazel, Ashley was never at the University. I know this story very well. He got in with a smart crowd, so to speak, and ran Angela up a real set of debts. The apartment was Angela's. He was involved in a very shady deal and got into trouble with the police. Enter Cherly, who thought him wonderful, and her father, who bailed him out of trouble financially. He married her—I went to the wedding in Toorak with Doris. From the first moment Doris saw Cherly she hated her and the feeling was reciprocated. Doris always said that there was a man behind this marriage but we would never have guessed it was you. Ashley has always slept around ever since he was forced to come and live here.'

'What do you mean, 'forced'?'

'Simple. Both Cherly's father and Angela together threatened to cut him off without a cent so he had no option, but he is alarmingly deceitful, as you well know.'

'I'm afraid I do,' said Hazel. 'I've never told anyone, but the night before he disappeared it was the summer holidays and I had my whole summer savings in my top drawer—I know, silly me! No Ashley. No cash. If I remember, I had to work all summer as a waiter.'

'I'm sorry, Hazel. He's such a shit.'

'Ashley I don't care about, and that's the truth, but I am most concerned about what Matthew will think.'

'Tell him at once. These things, via Gerald's general broadcasting, inevitably get back. You must get in first. Believe me, Hazel, everything will be fine.'

'I'm glad I caught you both,' said Doris, sitting down. 'I have just been speaking to Heather. I told her Angela is not long for this world but what I would like to know is how on earth they will get her out of the door. She is immense now. Her face is so bloated. Such a shocking state she's in. But still,' and she smiled, 'she will die knowing she did the right thing.' With that she stood up. 'Well, I must be going. And thank you for your little 'Thank You' card. Sebastian draws so nicely. Bye!'

'I must dash, too,' Hazel said. 'At the bank last week I had to wait almost half an hour. Bye, Carmel, and thanks, I will do exactly what you said.' He stood and gave her a kiss, then left.

The moment he was gone, Camel drew from her bag her imaginary cards, shuffled them and turned the top one over. She collected them and returned them to her invisible pocket. 'Waitress!'

'Yes, Miss. Wallace.'

'I'll have a glass of champagne,' as she smiled a very knowing smile.

*   *   *   *   *

To Hazel's surprise the bank was really empty and the transactions were completed in a flash, so he now had time to spare. He walked to the end of Main Street, to the little antique shop. He wandered around, looking at this and that and his eyes settled on a polished wooden box inlaid with brass trim, about twenty five by eighteen centimetres and thirteen deep. He unlocked the box and opened the lid.

'It's nice, and it's in good condition,' commented the owner of the shop. 'It's a good price.'

'How much?' Hazel asked. He remembered the last time he had bought something here the lady had driven a hard bargain.

'Forty dollars, and as you see the lock works perfectly.'

'I'll give you thirty,' Hazel replied, pulling the money out of his pocket.

She looked at him and the fact that he was carrying other parcels. 'Put the box in that supermarket bag and remember you haven't bought anything from me today.' As she spoke she took the thirty dollars and stuffed it in her pocket. Hazel noted that the cash register remained silent.

* * * * *

But, driving home, Hazel's usual sparkling courage began to fail. He loved Matthew with all his heart: he had never had a real relationship, a growing one, like this, where they shared everything and they trusted one another. To chance a confession that might jeopardise this made him feel anything but secure. Their relationship had never been stronger: Matthew now had no hesitation in giving Hazel a hug or the other way around, but beyond that they had not developed any further, partly out of respect for one another and a situation that just never came along. Hazel pulled into the gateway just as the bus was seen coming, this time not out of a heat haze but out of a background of drizzly rain.

'Hop in!' cried Hazel. 'How was your piano lesson?'

'Oh, good. I can now understand which note is the same on the sheet and the keyboard. It's very complicated, you know.'

'I'm sure it is, far too complicated for me,' and he smiled.

'Do you think Red got wet today?' Sebastian then asked.

'Probably.'

'I bought the dish. Look.' He withdrew from his school bag a shiny dish that couldn't tip over. 'I went with Mrs. Carstairs—the pet shop is near the school. It's nice, isn't it?'

'It's very smart,' agreed Hazel. This purchase was necessary as Red had now become Sebastian's foremost companion and after a lot of discussion he was allowed to come into the garden room but absolutely no further. As a result, Sebastian now had breakfast in the garden room with Red licking his lips as Sebastian ate. But every time a plate was put down, Red managed to upset the entire contents all over the floor, much to Hazel's annoyance. So he had sent a letter to school to ask if Sebastian could have permission to purchase a suitable food container for the dog. Hazel could have purchased it easily but he thought that as Sebastian now had his dog he must learn responsibility. The principal had had a word with Freda, who was only too willing to accompany him to the pet shop.

When they arrived at the homestead, Red was waiting near the big fountain as usual and recognising the car raced forward to greet Sebastian. This was now the pattern but in the drizzling rain Hazel shuddered at a wet dog stalking about the garden room.

'Hazel!' came a cry as he began unloading the car of his purchases. 'Hi!' and Jan came forward. 'A delivery van arrived with some big parcels for you. I took the liberty and had them put in the hallway of the house. They said the freight had been paid for in Melbourne.

'Thanks, Jan.'

She watched a rather dejected Hazel move back and forth between the car and the house, offloading the goods. Then Sebastian went to do his homework with her, with a wet Red in hot pursuit.

After everything was put away, Hazel opened up one of the two large parcels and in the first was a letter. 'Dearest Hazel, I knew you would want them over the top, so here they are and you will note at half price. All my love, Tony. Kisses from Mark'. So Hazel unpacked the curtains and swags for the two reception rooms without much enthusiasm. He went to get the ironing board and pressed the creases out, leaving them lying on the floor, then he crossed the hall and proceeded to repeat the exercise. He was halfway finished when he heard Matthew enter.

'Hi,' Matthew shouted, 'I'm going to have a shower. I'm all wet and dirty. I'll see you in a minute.'

The minute to Hazel felt like two hours and he began to feel very nauseous. He folded up the ironing board and returned it with the iron to the service room, only to meet Matthew coming down the stairs.

'Will you help me for a moment?' asked Hazel dully.

'What's wrong?' Matthew asked, sensing this was a Hazel he didn't know: he only knew a Hazel with the energy for ten people. 'Oh,' he went on, as he glanced at the curtains stretched out all over the floor. 'These certainly are glamorous. OK, Hazel, out with it. I have never seen you so quiet.'

'Sit down, Matthew. I have something to tell you.'

'I'll stand, if you don't mind,' so Hazel began to explain what Gerald had said about Ashley and he fitted into the picture, his relationship with Ashley all those years ago. He had one hand on the stepladder and looked directly into a pair of electric blue eyes. There was dead silence. 'I'm worried that you'll think less of me,' Hazel almost whispered.

'Hazel, don't you have any faith in our relationship?' asked Matthew.

'You are the most wonderful man in the world and you know how much you mean to me.'

'Then tell me,' Matthew insisted.

'I love you, and have from the first moment I saw you.'

Matthew stepped forward and took Hazel in his arms. 'You know, for a bright guy, sometimes you are a bit slow. I have come to love you in stages, and each stage is different from another. I have never had a love affair—it just didn't seem right for me.' Hazel's heart sank. 'Until now. Hazel, I can't imagine ever living with anyone else. In fact, I don't want to. I only want to be with you and if that's part of being in love, then I am in love with you. We can develop all the rest. For me, it will be another stage, and one,' he went on, smiling, 'that I am looking forward to.'

He didn't have an opportunity to say anymore, as Hazel kissed him and they held one another in their arms in a silence that sounded like a symphony.

'Isn't it funny,' Matthew said, 'that this shit Ashley seems to have indirectly done us a favour?'

'Yes, so it seems,' Hazel replied, feeling as if he were floating between the carpet on the floor and the ceiling. 'No matter what happens, Hazel, we shall always be together. Now I have something to ask you.'

'Anything.'

'You won't go back to Melbourne, will you?'

Hazel smiled. 'I will never go anywhere without you, whether you like it or not.'

'I like it,' he said and kissed him again. 'Come on, beautiful, let's get these curtains up,' and they spent the next twenty minutes hanging the curtains and the huge, extravagant swags, complete with braids and fringe. When the first room was hung, they stood back, arm in arm, just looking at them.

'I like them,' decided Matthew. 'There is just so much of them.'

'Hm, you're right. Would you describe them as theatrical?'

'A little bit, but they look a bit better than Mum's orange terylene numbers you made her throw away.' They both began laughing and had to hold on to one another again.

The second room was hung in half the time and an elated Hazel handed Matthew a bottle of champagne with two glasses, saying that they should have a drink to celebrate 'just everything', then disappeared.

Carmel's phone rang. 'Hello.'

'Carmel, it's Hazel, you are so fabulous. Thanks so much.'

'Darling, that's what friends are for. By the way, are you all free for Friday evening?'

'We shall be there, and thanks again.' He hung up and walked into the now much grander reception room, to find that Matthew had opened the bottle and two glasses were ready to be consumed.

'To us.' 'To us.' They smiled and began the first real evening of the rest of their lives.

* * * * *

'That telephone! Who is ringing at this hour—drinks time—sacred! Yes, Killkenny—Oh, Mr. Lester. What? I don't believe it. When? Oh, well, there is not much we can do about it. Yes, that would be kind. Do I have to go to Melbourne? OK. Thank you so much. Good night.' He hung up. 'Are you ready for this?'

'Tell me' replied Matthew, rather worried.

'Someone has made a mistake at the post and sent Keven's remains back to the Australian Embassy in Jakharta.'

'I don't believe it!' he exclaimed in astonishment.

'Another ten days, they think, then Keven's solicitors will notify Mr. Lester and I will have to go to Melbourne to pick up the ashes. They will then call in the people concerned with the will and it will be read. Can you believe the mess?'

'No, I can't. I have never heard of anything like it.'

'Matthew, where are you?' came Sebastian's voice.

'I'm in the front room,' he shouted, as the boy bounded in.

'I bought Red a bowl that doesn't tip over. He's going to be very happy.' At which he kissed Matthew.

'And where is Red now?' asked Hazel.

'With his mother. I don't think she likes him biting her.'

'I'm sure she doesn't,' laughed Hazel.

Sebastian looked at the curtains: 'Gosh, they're very big, aren't they?'

'Do you like them?'

'I think so.' He was completely overwhelmed by the sheer amount of fabric that now surrounded the windows. He turned his head. 'Oh, they are in the other room too,' and he went in. Because of the amount of fabric, the sound was different, softer, and the echo that was heard before in these two grand rooms had disappeared.

'Sebastian, if you go upstairs to your room, you will find a little surprise,' said Hazel. The boy rushed up the stairs to his room, to find that the cardboard shoe box was gone and in its place was a beautiful box containing his money, and with a key. He returned. 'Thank you, Hazel,' and gave him a kiss. 'I like the key very much.' Then he went into the other room to practise his piano piece and even this sound seemed softer, due to the acoustic effect the curtains had.

*   *   *   *   *

Friday evening arrived and in soft, misty rain they headed off to Carmel's. They had decided on Friday as Sebastian did not have school the next day.

'Carmel, we have got great big curtains,' he cried,' in the two front rooms. They are very nice.'

'I'm sure they are,' she laughed. 'Come in.'

They followed her into a large sitting room. When they had come up the drive through the rain they saw an extremely large red brick Victorian house, set amongst trees with a veranda that encircled it, trimmed with decorative cast iron. From the exterior it was a very grand house, not as large as Doris's, but then in this whole district there was not a house as large as Doris's: not very many of the local houses could boast a full-sized ballroom such as Doris had not used for twenty years. The living room was not like Doris's, either; it screamed 'chic'. When Carmel had inherited the property and had plenty of money, one of Gerald's boyfriends for a time was an interior designer he had simply picked up in Sydney and she used this talented young man to overhaul a very second-rate interior into very smart international look, where she seemed perfectly at home, a mixture of oriental objects and furniture with English antiques and some modern pieces as well. The look was judged by Hazel to be a great success.

'Thanks,' said Carmel. 'My only stipulation was that what the designer did would not date and this was done about twenty years ago, so it's been worth the investment.' She gave them a tour of the house and before dinner while they had a drink, seated comfortably, she played on a black lacquered grand piano.

'You know, Sebastian, you are a great influence on me.'

'Oh yes,' he replied, not quite sure what he was agreeing to.

'I haven't practised for years and it's now become a rediscovered skill.' She played for a short while and then insisted Sebastian try something but as he didn't have any music he found it a little difficult to remember but he made a valiant attempt and was well applauded for his effort.

They ate in a small dining room which had a large lacquered Japanese screen with birds and flowers inlaid in soap stone. Sebastian was fascinated. A maid served an excellent meal, the main course being fish, which Sebastian, not to mention the others, loved. This evening everyone was in fine form and the jokes and one-liners had everyone in hysterics, especially Hazel's contribution. Doris had been invited but as Angela had taken a turn for the worse, she went to see her.

'I think Doris is up to something,' said Carmel.

'Why?' Matthew asked.

'Well, she seems to be extremely keen on Angela dying, which is not at all nice. I think Angela is in some pain but she is on medication, so she must be reasonably tranquil, but to have Doris fluttering about the bed can't be too restful for her.'

'Or for Cherly,' laughed Hazel, and so the conversation continued, with Ashley's name not mentioned once.

The evening finished on a slightly more serious note, the subject of re-seeding. 'You have been very lucky,' said Carmel to Matthew. 'You have planted at just the right time and the rains have been just perfect for grass and trees.'

'We have a section on the lower part, two thousand acres. I think that next year, providing our new partner doesn't object—'

'Your new partner?' interrupted Carmel.

'He means whoever Keven has left his half of Killkenny to.'

'Oh, I see,' she said quietly and smiled.

'I should like to see if I could crop it.'

'What, with wheat?'

'Yes, what do you think?'

'We tried it here one year and had a drought. You can imagine the harvest—zero. There was hardly enough for a hundred bales of straw—a disaster. I have never tried it again but if you're going to try next year I might give it a go as well.'

'Well,' commented Hazel, 'we might just end up being more than just good friends. I mean business partners as well.'

'I think that's a fine idea, Hazel. What do you think?' she asked, turning to Matthew.

'I don't see why not. We can certainly cut costs if these two big properties share expenses. We will have to sit down and work it all out, but I am for it, providing we don't have trouble with your staff.'

'My staff could be prosecuted for taking money under false pretences!' she laughed. 'No one here lifts a finger unless it's necessary. I spoke to Trick last Thursday and it seems he knows someone who's looking for a job. I'll have to see about it. If I need a hand to interview him, will you help me out, Matthew?'

'Of course. Just give me a ring.'

As she said thanks they noticed a sleepy Sebastian snuggling up against Matthew, so they called it a night.

'Oh, by the way, Hazel, I am dying to see your curtain extravaganza.'

'Any time you're free, just drop in. You're always welcome.

'Thanks for coming,' she said, as she waved them off in the drizzling rain.

*   *   *   *   *

Hazel knew very little of the relationship between Bob, Pat, Jan and Rhonda. They had lived their own lives and were quite apart from his. Matthew controlled Bob and Pat, while Jan and Rhonda just seemed to have re-discovered one another and remained in each other's company. But Hazel could see a light in the window of the cottage that was now being used as Rhonda's living room when he went to bed most evenings. Jan had, bit by bit, and with Pat drafted in to help where brute strength was required, moved all the pieces that belonged to the church into position. The room in the second cottage where this had all been stored was now almost empty. The statues of St. Anthony and the Holy Mother had been cleaned and where necessary Rhonda had repaired them. The damaged pews had been returned and altogether the interior was taking on an ecclesiastical finish. Hazel was alarmed at how much the joiner had charged for the restoration of the pews and telephoned and complained bitterly. The result of his sharp call had achieved a 20% reduction in the bill, but, as Hazel said, it was still far too high.

The greater part of the work was now finished. The carpenters had only the saleyards behind the coach house and the second cottage that was now completely empty to finish, as Jan had emptied out the church things and Hazel had taken away the enormous number of cartons with china, glass and all the domestic bits and pieces that had once been a part of the main house.

Doris was now going to see Angela twice a week, much to Cherly's annoyance and when Doris arrived Cherly was conspicuous by her absence. Angel was completely lucid and she and Doris spoke for hours about the past, relatives and general gossip but each time Doris saw her she seemed a little more ashen in colour. Occasionally her burgundy Mercedes would whip up the drive to Killkenny where she was always invited to stay for dinner which she liked immensely.

'They are just what I want,' she said, looking at the new curtains, 'exactly what I want but in gold. The curtains in the ballroom at home have just had it. Simon somehow managed to bring one set down, rods and all. Do you think you could manage it for me?'

'Well, I have to go to Melbourne to sort out Keven's ashes and if I slip over and take all the measurements and we decide on a colour. Oh, I still have the sample book here—it has to go back. Take it with you tonight and see if there is something you like,' said Hazel. He noted that Doris went back to look at the extravagant curtains four times before she left after dinner, but during dinner she managed to put this trip to Melbourne in another light.

'Mr Hazel, if the person or persons who inherit Keven's half share of Killkenny decide they require another manager, never fear, I have a place for you at my home.'

'Thank you,' was Hazel's half-hearted reply.

It was later, talking to Matthew, that he realised he was not paid directly from the Killkenny accounts. He had been paid by Keven himself and he thought that meant the flat he offered him was gone as well. It now placed him in a very awkward situation. It was, he thought, highly unlikely that the new half-owner of Killkenny would automatically put him on the pay role. He might be Sebastian's legal guardian but that did not necessarily mean that the new people had to pay his wage. It was now starting to wear him down. It was the uncertainty of everything; it was also a very worried Matthew, as he knew, with Hazel in control, Sebastian was safe but it didn't follow that the new half-owners were going to be quite so concerned about a little eleven year old boy.

*   *   *   *   *

In the week that followed, Hazel was invited to lunch at Doris's to measure the curtains for her ballroom. He was, to say the least, surprised at this vast space with four floor to ceiling windows on one side that were matched opposite by mirrors. It was just the dimensions of this room as well as the emptiness of it that gave it its impact. He duly took all the measurements and from the swatch book of sample fabric that he had chosen from so too did Doris, but gold was the colour she preferred as that had been the colour of the original curtains, now in shreds. Due to time and light, they had rotted away. Doris had remarked that she and Carmel were going the next day to see Angela,

'Well, organise yourself and come to dinner. I shall expect you when I see you.' He kissed her and sped off home, knowing he had to collect Sebastian at four.

*   *   *   *   *

The following day, Carmel, under extreme sufferance, went with Doris to see Angela. Although Angela was also her aunt, she had never had much time for her. 'Too grand' and 'going nowhere' was Carmel's description of Angela. Still, she went. The burgundy Mercedes drove around the circular drive and parked in front of the main door. Doris alighted, as always with her perfectly lacquered hair not moving unless her whole head moved with it. The maid answered the door and they entered only to be confronted by Ashley. 'Well, Ashley, it's years since I have been here,' remarked Carmel.

'I'll leave you two to it. I'll be with Angela,' said Doris, and disappeared down an extremely dark, long corridor.

'Well, aren't you going to show me around?' asked Carmel, and begrudgingly Ashley did as asked. Carmel was surprised how suburban this big house was, and wasn't sure if it was Cherly's taste or Angela's but assumed Angela's. Large, pale green walls with tiny watercolours or etchings. Bitty, yes, thought Carmel, it's all very bitty and it looks as if it has been furnished with left-overs, which was strange. Angela did not lack funds, just obviously taste. It was the dining room that was Carmel's principal interest and there it was, an abundance of large pieces in silver, crammed onto an enormous 1930s sideboard. It was like the whole house, looking as if at some time someone had just emptied it all out and then was forced to refill it on the cheap. All the walls were the same pale green in every room, and in every room were venetian blinds in cream metal. It was cold, this big house, almost as if no one really cared for it, antiseptic in a certain way. It could not be called minimalist, because that required a certain skill: these interiors simply showed no taste whatsoever.

'Well, Ashley, how did you get on in Mortlake with the solicitor?' Carmel asked outright.

'I think everything should be all right but he doesn't think I will get much back. You and Doris, it seems, were the lucky ones.'

Carmel smiled. 'If you, dearest cousin, had not been so greedy or a little more careful with your spending, you would not have ended up in this mess.' Ashley was about to say something sarcastic but bit his tongue. 'My other advice is this. Sleep with Gerald but be careful what you say to him. He has a habit of broadcasting private information that you may find damaging.'

'How the hell did your find out about Gerald?' he demanded, blushing somewhat.

'Simple, darling. Gerald is a wealth of information, like the scar so high up on your—is it right or left leg?' she teased.

Ashley was furious. 'I'll kill him!'

'Oh I don't think so. You are in enough trouble now, without a sex murder playing to a full house.'

'Ha, ha, ha,' he said between gritted teeth.

'Oh, Ashley, do show me your Italian garden. I was speaking to Robert Patterson the other day. He sends his regards.' She delivered this in a most knowing way.

'Careful, Carmel, you may well go before Gerald.'

'Darling, don't be silly. I am simply passing a kind thought from obviously yet another—' here she stopped and turned to face him '—male admirer. Now, which way into the garden?' as she smiled sweetly.

Ashley showed her down the long dark corridor to a side passage and out to the garden where an avenue of dead box bushes terminated in a small empty birdbath.

'You had better get some hints from Killkenny,' she murmured, smiling patronisingly. 'Now you must take me to see Aunt Angela.'

They went indoors and he left her with his mother and Doris, contemplating strangling Carmel and Gerald together.

'Carmel, how nice of you to come,' said Angela, and Doris, as usual, kept the conversation going. Carmel was shocked at Angela's condition. She was indeed bloated, the mountain under the bedclothes was all Angela and her face was like a balloon, but she chatted on and laughed as if she were just about to get up and go for a walk, something she had not done for almost eighteen months.

Driving back from Ashley's to Killkenny, Carmel remarked that she thought that at this stage Angela should be in hospital.

'Why?' asked Doris. 'She is dying and she knows it. She is not afraid and she feels comfortable in her own home. She has a nurse who calls three times a week, so there's no problem. The maid sees to anything she wants and the morphine is there when it is required.'

'I suppose so,' replied Carmel in a lost way.

'It's the way I should like to go,' went on Doris. 'Reverend Mother always said that, with faith, the saints were always there and therefore there was nothing to fear.'

'I spoke to Ashley,' Carmel sighed. 'He seems a little nervous. You know the situation with Gerald.'

'Heard a whisper,' was Doris's reply. 'I'll never understand why Gerald just doesn't find the right man and settle down. This tomcat performance is just so silly and in this day and age damn dangerous.'

'I couldn't agree more,' Carmel said. 'He's handsome, popular, with a million friends, but with lovers he is a total disaster every time and taking on Ashley is basically suicide.'

Doris just had time to agree before they stopped at the gateway to Killkenny. Carmel got out and opened the big wooden gates.

'Look at all the stakes!' Doris cried. 'There must be hundreds of new little trees.' They scanned each side of the drive, seeing new small trees filling in the gaps all the way up to the house.

'Just in time for a drink,' laughed Hazel, as they entered the house and the rain began again. 'I complained that the hot weather would never end and now I am complaining that the rain won't stop. We are never happy!'

Carmel nodded agreement, while Hazel linked arms with her to go through to the garden room, only to be stopped by Doris.

'Look,' she said, pointing to the new curtains. 'Aren't they just marvellous?'

'Good heavens!' exclaimed a surprised Carmel. 'They seem to fill the room. Very dramatic!'

'Where's Sebastian?' asked Doris.

'He's with Jan, doing his homework.'

'Really?' She had not been aware of this. 'Well, Jan was the cleverest of her year at school. I must give her that.' She spoke a little patronisingly as they moved on through the dining room to the garden room, where Matthew welcomed them.

'My God, he's beautiful!' thought Carmel. 'Half Hazel's luck!'

* * * * *

The following day began grey, with the clouds moving swiftly across the sky heralding rain for the late morning. Hazel took Sebastian and Red, as was now the habit, to the front gate, then returned. A bowl of food was required to train Red to remain at the homestead and not wander off in search of Sebastian.

The phone rang and Hazel answered. Mr. Lester explained that Keven's ashes had been returned much quicker than expected and he was needed in Melbourne on Sebastian's behalf on Monday morning. He gave Hazel the address, which he already knew, having had to go there to receive his legal guardianship papers for the boy. As this was Tuesday, he began to make a list of things he had to take and phoned Mary, who was overjoyed that he was coming to stay with her for a week.

'Divine, darling. The champagne is on ice.'

The rest of the day, apart from a pleasant lunch with Matthew, was spent as usual, cleaning and tidying, washing so both Matthew and Sebastian had clean clothes and in the general housework that a large house required. At 3.30 he went to collect Sebastian, but as it was now raining steadily, he turned back into the house to collect Matthew's large oilskin raincoat as he had left his car down by the church. Matthew was in the bottom paddock with Pat as there was some problem that, despite all this rain, a windmill was not working properly. He donned the coat and made for the door. As he opened it, he saw the rain pouring down, and as he went to pull the door shut his telephone rang.

'Hazel,' came Sebastian's voice, 'the bus has tipped over. We are in a big hole and I am afraid it's going to fall to the bottom.' He began to cry. Hazel ran as never before to the church.

'Jan,' he screamed, 'there has been an accident. Get the four-wheel drive and some rope quickly.'

Jan, who was talking to Rhonda, dropped everything and fled across the square in pouring rain.

'Keep talking to me, Sebastian. Can you hear me?'

'Yes,' came a sobbing voice. 'Hazel, the bus is moving. It's going to fall.'

'Don't move. Where are you, in the front or the back?'

'In the back,' came the plaintive response.

'Don't move!'

He leapt into the passenger seat as a wet Jan slammed her foot on the accelerator and they tore off down the drive.

'Sebastian, where exactly are you?'

'We slipped on the road near the corner where the church used to be.'

'Don't worry, darling, we are on our way. Jan, it must be that ravine just down from the church, around from the crossroads.'

'Goodness, it's half full of water,' she replied, worriedly. 'When I get to the gate, get ready to get out and open it, then get back in quick smart.'

After what seemed an eternity, through the rain, the gates loomed up. Hazel bolted out of the car in the huge raincoat, now flapping around his legs, opened the gate and sprang back into the four-wheel as she again placed her foot down on the accelerator.

'Can't we go any faster?' begged Hazel.

347

'Hazel, I'm going as fast as this machine will go. Give me a break.'

'Sorry!' at which everything flashed in front of him in the most horrid of scenarios. What if something terrible happened to Sebastian and what of Matthew? He would be inconsolable. At one point the telephone conversation between Sebastian and Hazel cut off. Hazel was terrified that something had happened but his phone rang again and he heard Sebastian's voice. 'I dropped it. The bus is on its side. Hazel, all the seats are upside down,' and he began crying again.

'Who is on the bus with you?'

'Hazel, it's just me. The driver and Sarah are out, but when I move the bus goes up and down.

'Don't move, no matter what happens. Stay still. I'll be there in a moment.'

But the moment seemed never to come. Then, finally, through the rain, they saw two lone figures on the side of the road. The fencing that blocked off the ravine from the road was smashed and as they pulled up an hysterical bus driver call Dan began shouting at them. 'It's the brakes!' he yelled.

'Shut up!' shouted Jan and they peered over the edge. The bus had skidded and slid over on its side and fallen onto a projection with a steep drop beyond. Four metres below was what seemed a brown muddy lake.

'Sebastian, can you hear me?' said Hazel, tying the rope around his waist.

'Not like that, you fool!' exclaimed Jan. She re-tied it. 'You'll bloody strangle yourself.'

'Tie the other end to the four-wheel. If you can't get me up, drive the jeep. OK?'

'Yes,' was the nervous reply.

'Sebastian,' Hazel began, with Jan holding the rope as he climbed down the red mud slope to the bus. The door was open and facing up. 'Sebastian,' he called, 'can you hear me?'

'Yes, Hazel. Get me out. I'm scared.'

'Don't move until I tell you.'

Hazel lowered himself to the doorway. 'Hold me there, Jan,' he shouted and he looked inside. 'OK, climb over the first seat and walk little by little on the windows.' This he did. 'Stop!' screamed Hazel, as he had made only a metre's worth of progress: the bus was moving a little. The soil from underneath it was slowly beginning to fall away. Another car could be heard racing up the road towards the scene of the accident. It turned out to be Cherly, as Ashley was not at home. Sarah had called her the moment she had clambered out, as she always sat in the front seat whereas Sebastian had always travelled in the back section.

Cherly began the full emotional extravaganza. 'Shut up, or I'll pitch you over the side!' snapped Jan, realising that any extra drama wasn't helping matters. The bus driver, Dan, and Jan held the rope.

'OK, try one step,' which Sebastian did and little by little he followed every single direction Hazel gave. 'Give me some more rope!' he yelled, and Jan let out a little. 'More!' he screamed and again the rope was let out. He was now half in and half out of the bus door and could see Sebastian. Every move he made was complicated by the enormous raincoat which seemed in the way. 'Another step. OK, another.' Hazel reach in and grasped Sebastian's hand. 'Put your hands around my neck quickly.' Sebastian did so, only for both of them to hear a sound that meant quite clearly that the soil underneath the side of the bus with all the rain was giving out. Hazel yelled, 'Pull us up! Sebastian, put your feet together!' As they both began to rise, the bus began to sink. One man on a rope is heavy, but Sebastian and Hazel together was an enormous strain.

'Cherly!' yelled Jan. 'Get in the jeep and more it forward until the rope is taut. Now!' Cherly did as she was told, as Hazel and Sebastian hung against a wall of red mud. Hazel's upper waist area was hurting with the strain. When the rope was taut Jan let go and raced to the jeep, pulled Cherly somewhat unceremoniously out of the driver's side and jumped in. She slowly began to move the jeep forward. Hazel and Sebastian, now being free of the bus, dangled on the end of the rope, then there was a sudden squelching sound as the bus slid smoothly down splashing in the brown, muddy water below, leaving Hazel with Sebastian in his arms, suspended over the ravine in mid-air. By now, Jan had drawn them up to the edge. Sebastian held on to Hazel for dear life: he was terrified, yet assured at the same time that everything would be all right because Hazel was there.

'They're at the top,' yelled Dan, and Jan put on the handbrake, leapt out of the jeep and raced over.

'Give me a hand,' she demanded of Dan, and between them they pulled an exhausted and very sore Hazel, with Sebastian, over the edge, first Sebastian, taking an arm each, then repeating the exercise with Hazel, who just lay for a moment gasping for air. The rope had cut into him but not badly, due to the heavy raincoat he had cursed earlier.

'Well,' remarked Jan, 'I've seen you looking better!'

'Thanks, sweetie,' said a red mud-covered Hazel.

They now heard cars from both directions, as before they had arrived, Dan had called the police and Rhonda had rushed out to find Matthew to tell him of the accident.

Sebastian's phone rang. 'I'm safe now, Matthew, but Hazel is all covered in mud.'

Jan had untied the rope and threw it into the back of the jeep. 'Sorry I was so rough with you,' said Jan to Cherly.

'It's OK. You were wonderful. I wouldn't have been able to do it.'

Matthew's car arrived a few minutes before the police. He leapt out and ran in the pouring rain across to Sebastian and folded him into his arms, crying.

'I'm all right now. Hazel pulled me out of the bus.' Matthew walked over to Hazel, who had just stood up, covered in mud and still in Matthew's heavy raincoat. He looked at Hazel and then embraced him. Whilst his head was on Hazel's muddy shoulder, 'I love you,' he said and kissed him, and against grasped and kissed Sebastian. But his heart missed a beat as he glanced at the bottom of the ravine to see the bus on its side, half flooded with brown muddy water.

'I think,' said Hazel, 'Jan deserves half the praise. It couldn't have been done without her,' at which Matthew walked across and kissed her.

'Thanks mum,' he said, with tears rolling down his cheeks. It was, she thought, the first time he had kissed her in twenty odd years.

The police arrived and after they had made statements about what had happened everyone headed off home, soaking wet and exhausted. Sebastian went with Matthew and Jan drove Hazel back, needless to say at a slightly slower pace than the initial dash. 'You know, Hazel, I didn't think you would last here. I thought you were, how do you say it, all bobbles and fringe, but you're not. You're all right, Hazel.'

'Thanks,' was his reply, as he rubbed his ribs. 'You're pretty sharp yourself. If you hadn't thought how to pull us up, Sebastian might have finished at the bottom, perhaps drowned.'

She said nothing, and they arrived home just behind Matthew and Sebastian, with Red barking excitedly. As Hazel walked toward the house something stopped him. He took off the muddy coat, walked toward the church, entered, knelt down and prayed. As he stood up, he noticed Jan just behind him, also praying—two very different people but offering the same prayer of thanks.

Matthew carried a muddy Sebastian in from the rain, with Red under some illusion this was a new game. The boy showered and dressed, and as it was nearly six o'clock, sat with Matthew in the garden room, with Matthew's arm around him, explaining again and again the accident. Hazel collected the raincoat and entered through the back door, dropping the coat on the veranda and showering in the downstairs bathroom so as not to leave mud stains right through the house. He later went upstairs, dressed and made his way to the garden room to hear his phone ringing in the bathroom where he had left it.

'No, he's OK, just frightened,' said Hazel to the Principal, who was extremely worried about the accident. They chattered on for a moment and she said she would call back about another bus being available in the morning.

Then Carmel called, having heard the news via Cherly and then it was Doris, but the most upset of all and in tears was Freda Carstairs, whom the Principal had called to reassure that all was well. 'Oh, I can't tell you how relieved I am,' Freda said, sniffling. 'How absolutely terrible! I shall make sure that there is a real inquiry into this, I can assure you.' She sounded very determined. 'His guiding saint has truly been with him today,' and with an exchange about music progress she said good night.

Hazel suddenly realised he was very tired and flopped down with Matthew and Sebastian. 'Here, I think you could do with this.' Matthew handed him a glass of wine.

'How do you feel now?' Hazel asked Sebastian.

'Oh, I'm good now, but I was very frightened before you came and got me,' and he stood up and went to Hazel, threw his arms around him and kissed him. 'Thanks, Hazel. I knew you would save me.' Hazel kissed him and the boy said he might just go and see Red, as the rain had stopped.

'Sebastian, I think you should go and say thank you to Jan.'

'Oh, yes,' he replied, nodding his head.'

'And then straight back for an early dinner.' He said OK and off he went.

'He's a real surviver,' smiled Hazel.

'Come over here,' Matthew said. Hazel moved to the divan beside him. Matthew put his arm around Hazel's shoulders and kissed him. 'You are just fantastic,' he said. 'When Aunt Rhonda gave me the news I can't tell you how scared I was. The thought of something happening to Sebastian and to you, it seemed like my whole world was about to collapse. I have had this feeling in my life once before. It is the helplessness that is killing. Thank goodness, Hazel, you were there.'

'Any time!' and Hazel leant over to kiss him.

They had reached, in Matthew's mind, yet another sage and there were only one or two to go before this relationship was fully developed, but Matthew as well as Hazel was both fully aware that the last two hurdles were the easy ones.

* * * * *

If the day had been harrowing for Cherly, there was more to come. She had tried to phone Ashley but his phone was switched off. He was at the solicitor yet again in Mortlake. She drove up to the front door with a trembling, slightly hysterical daughter, who had had no problem climbing out of the bus but seemed more concerned that her school uniform was smeared with red mud.

'Mrs. Wallace, Mrs. Wallace!' came a hysterical scream as she alighted from the car.

'What's wrong, Betty?' asked the exhausted Cherly.

'Old Mrs Wallace is dead. She's dead. She has stopped breathing.'

'Take Sarah in and clean her up,' she demanded, and made her way to Angela's bedroom. She was indeed dead but before Cherly pulled the sheet over her face she noted a joyous smile on her face, as if she had received some very good news. She tried again to contact Ashley and finally the phone rang 'engaged'. She continued until he finally answered ten minutes later.

'Ashely, where the hell are you?'

'With the solicitor. Why?'

'Well, first your daughter has been in an accident in the school bus, but thank God she is all right.'

'Oh, yes, thank goodness,' was the bland reply which annoyed Cherly no end.

'And, if you're interested,' she spat, 'your mother is dead, so I suggest you get yourself home immediately and sort out the arrangements.' She hung up.

She would have been even more angry had she known exactly where he was. 'I'll have to go. A drama at home.'

'Must you?' asked Robert Patterson. 'Can't you stay here in bed a little longer?'

'No, I can't,' Ashley said, playfully, then rose, dressed and began the long drive home. His mind now was working like a threshing machine, every little point due to his mother's death he was fitting into place. The money, the property, everything at last was his, his to use as he wished and to manipulate as he desired. Now he had complete control of everything. He just had to extricate himself from the disastrous investment mess with David Osbourne and then he was free. All those long years trapped on this property with his mother and his wife!

A thought passed through his mind: sell it, get rid of the property, go back to Melbourne, his old lifestyle, but this time with a great deal of money. The big apartment in Domain Road was still there but let, not a problem, and then he thought through the equation again. Keep the property, let it to someone and return to live in Melbourne, but no matter which way he looked at it there was a hitch: Cherly. Oh well, he didn't need a cover if he was living in the apartment in Domain Road. If she wanted a divorce, all the better—her parents were very wealthy, there wasn't a problem. At last, freedom, no more sheep, no more worries about paying staff! This was all in the past. In Ashley's fantasy he had forgotten one thing, the mortgage on the property. This would count no matter how much money Angela had left and this he didn't know, as she was very secretive about the total amount of her money, which quite often angered him, as he never knew financially where he stood, and quite often he had to depend on Cherly for cash rather than his mother.

He entered the house and Cherly immediately told him who to call about funeral arrangements. After this was done, with the funeral director saying they would call for the body that evening, the police were already on their way. 'Hm,' he thought, 'everything is working out at last.' But then, all of a sudden, he had a nasty thought: David Osbourne held his mother's will. He had seen a copy, but he would have to telephone David Osbourne to have the will read and he had a week ago sued him. Now what was he to do?

*   *   *   *   *

The funeral was arranged for Thursday afternoon and the Railway was packed for lunch, with the locals in much better clothes than usual, and rather than cope with Doris's bitter remarks they had anticipated this and phoned Violet the day before to reserve their table. Both Doris and Angela were seen as the matriarchal controllers of the Wallace families and Angela could be as ruthless as Doris but socially was much more staid and formal. Despite their great difference in personality, they had remained oddly close friends all their lives. They were first cousins and above all Wallaces. They had been to school together and they had shared secrets and jokes all their lives, childish as they were, according to Carmel. But strangely, Doris didn't seem to be as upset as most would have thought. She arrived as if for the usual Thursday lunch but this time dressed in black and had to virtually push her way through the very crowded bar area as it appeared the entire Catholic community from the surrounding districts was present to pay their last respects to Angela Wallace.

'I think you're mad,' said Carmel to Hazel, who today was sitting with Matthew for the first time at the Railway. 'Why drive for virtually a whole day to Melbourne when you can take a light aircraft from Mortlake? You are there in one and a half hours.'

'Really? I had no idea there was a flight service from here.'

'We're not living in the back of beyond here,' Doris said, in a superior way. 'You can book it on the internet. There are flights Saturday and Wednesday at 10.30. You can leave Saturday, Monday is the solicitor's appointment and you can pick up the ashes and come home Wednesday or Saturday.'

'Come home' was what Hazel heard and for the first time in his life he understood the word 'home', not an apartment somewhere, but a place where there was someone you loved, who loved you, and everything that went with it. He smiled at Carmel. 'Yes, I'll get on the internet as soon as I get home.'

'Good to see you're dressed well,' said Doris, smiling at Matthew. The fact that she had been invited to Killkenny and had reciprocated meant to Doris that they were her extended family and her personal possessions. The latter, for some people, was difficult to cope with, but for Hazel and Matthew this was fine. The conversation was very much about the bus accident, with Matthew championing Hazel's bravery.

Trick, dressed in black jeans, white shirt and black tie which seemed to be the uniform for the men here today, came over. 'Hi Doris! Hi folks!' he beamed. 'Wow, how's the hero?' he carried on, looking at Hazel.

'Thanks,' replied Hazel, feeling embarrassed.

'Nice going, Hazel.' Then he leant across and to Hazel's, not to mention everybody else's surprise, kissed Hazel on the cheek and smiled. Then he looked into the crowd. 'Oh, gotta go. The Missis is here.' Hazel glanced across the bar near the door as a glamorous model-like woman of about twenty eight to thirty, all in black, with long blonde hair, searched the bar for Trick. Hazel looked at Carmel. 'Don't say a word, and I told you she is crazy for him. Oh well!' as she drained her glass.

'Where the hell do you think you're going?' cried Doris, as Gerald made a late appearance in white jeans and a pale blue polo shirt. He stood still and looked at her, as did a section of the bar, as she had raised her voice.

'What are you on about?' Gerald replied defensively, glancing sideways at Matthew.

'Am I to take it that you are under some bizarre illusion that you hope to attend Angela's funeral?' she asked, now standing.

Gerald had the funny feeling he was in serious trouble. 'Well, I am sure Angela wouldn't mind, at least I am attending.'

'Not in that party outfit you're not.' She raised her voice further. 'How dare you hold Angela's memory in such low esteem! Get the hell out of here and return dressed as you should. Now!!' she shouted. Gerald instantly admitted defeat and left. 'I can't think what has come over him. How dare he—and my nephew!'

'Have a drink, Auntie,' said Carmel, and the bar settled back to normal with a din of chattering and speculation about what would be the outlook for Angela's property now.

The arrangements were that after the funeral Mass the reception was to be held at Ashley's, so Matthew would go with Carmel and she would bring him back and stay for dinner. Hazel would go early to collect Sebastian as he was not going to the funeral, never having met Angela—and he certainly did not want a confrontation with Ashley.

Everything went according to plan, except that Ashley decided to jump the gun. Taking his courage in both hands he phoned David Osbourne to make an appointment for Friday morning for the reading of the will. Only to his horror Bev sharply informed him that Mr. Osbourne did not hold the latest will or any of his mother's investments.

'What?' he cried in disbelief, assuming that David Osbourne was out to give him a hard time. 'Where are all these legal papers?'

'I suggest you try Mr. Lester,' Bev answered, sarcastically and hung up on him.

He stood completely still, as if he had been instantly frozen. He felt a wave of nausea and smelt a rat, a very nasty rat whose name began with D. He searched and found Mr. Lester's number and the secretary connected him.

'Yes, Mr. Wallace, I have all your late mother's documents in my office. They were sent over by Mr. Osbourne when your mother made her new will.' Now Ashley felt that his plans for his freedom and his future were starting to slip away. 'I shall contact the other beneficiaries and shall we say 11.00 Friday morning?'

'What other beneficiaries?' cried Ashley, raising his voice.

'Eleven o'clock Friday morning. Good morning, Mr. Wallace,' and he hung up.

What the hell was happening? Who was also getting a share of the property? Doris? Hardly, he thought: she has enough money to throw away. Then who?

* * * * *

'Oh, what a dreary turn,' said Carmel, as she sat down with a drink in the garden room with Hazel and Matthew. 'I can't think why Ashley and Cherly never get it right—awful food and practically no alcohol, tea or coffee. How them!

'The church was packed,' Matthew said. 'There were so many people outside unable to get in. I can't remember anything like it, only perhaps Father Ryan's funeral.'

'I'm sure that Angela was more than happy at the turn out today. Thank goodness it didn't rain.'

A car horn sounded outside and Matthew went to see who it was.

'I thought I should find you here,' said Doris, as she looked at Carmel. 'Well, what a dreary reception. Angela would have been furious. I am sure no one these days has that sort of food and by the way, Carmel, did you get a drink?'

'One,' was the brusque reply.

'Me, too. Very stingy is our Cherly but at least she was dressed in black this time.'

'I say, Auntie, didn't you think Ashley looked very nervous. I hadn't realised he was so attached to Angela.'

'He wasn't. They barely spoke to one another for years. No conversation.'

Hazel's telephone went, so he excused himself.

'So many of those people I haven't seen for years,' added Matthew.

'Lucky you,' came the comment from Carmel.

'Oh, that's better,' Doris said as she drank a glass of champagne.

'I must say, though,' Matthew went on, 'that Trick hasn't changed at all. He looks exactly the same as when we were at school together.'

'An ageless leprechaun,' stated Doris, 'and the wife looked very smart. I liked her hat. Oh, Carmel, where did you get your hat?' Doris had a glint in her eye as she spoke.

'Why, do you like it?'

'Well. I must tell you the truth. It looked like an exhausted fruit bat that had collapsed on your head!'

'Thanks, Auntie. How very kind you are,' came the sarcastic reply.

Hazel returned, looking quite perplexed.

'What's wrong?' asked Matthew.

'Well, that was Mr. Lester's secretary and I am required at his office at 11 o'clock tomorrow morning, but what on earth for? I have everything I need to go to Melbourne on Saturday. Oh, by the way, Carmel, thanks, I have booked a seat to fly to Melbourne and made arrangements to be collected, but what does Mr. Lester want?' He dashed off to add another setting on the table, passing Sebastian on his way in.

'Can I bring Red in to show Doris?' he asked.

'Yes, but not through the house. Through the doors at the end of the garden room and no further, and that means that before we have dinner you must take him back to the others, otherwise he is going to want to come into the dining room.'

'Oh, great! I'll go and get him,' at which he raced out through the front door, allowing it to slam behind him.

The conversation over dinner was basically post-funeral, but everyone noticed a particularly contented Doris, which was most unusual and, as Carmel thought, dangerous. There was also a great deal of conversation about the bus accident, with Doris declaring after hearing Matthew's version that Hazel was definitely the hero of the day, but this he denied, saying that without Jan it would have been impossible, so all agreed that her fast thinking also saved the day. As they left, Doris smiled at Hazel. 'I shall be seeing you shortly,' she said. Hazel was a little confused but let it go.

*   *   *   *   *

Friday morning Hazel dropped Sebastian at the bus, or rather a new bus, as there was now an enquiry as to what was the problem with the accident, human failure or mechanical failure. He drove off ahead and raced about the supermarket buying the extra bits and pieces that Matthew and Sebastian would need for the week whilst he was in Melbourne. This should have taken no time at all, but when he looked at his watch he was amazed it was a quarter to eleven and he rushed through the checkout and straight up to Mr. Lester's office in Main Street. As he parked and hurried across, he was surprised to see

Doris's burgundy Mercedes parked close by, but thought nothing of it. He opened the glass door and hurried in.

'I'm sorry,' he said, 'I have an appointment with Mr. Lester.'

'That's fine,' the secretary replied. 'The others have just arrived.'

'Others?'

'Yes. Go through.' He opened the door into Mr. Lester's office only to see seated in front of him Doris and Ashley. Ashley's eyes opened like saucers. 'God!'

'Not quite,' responded Hazel sharply. 'It's been some time since I've seen you.'

'Er, yes,' was the only reply.

'Oh,' Doris joined in, 'Carmel did say that the two of you many years ago were close friends,' and she smiled. Hazel was surprised how composed he was. Ashley looked older but still had a certain charm and then his mind went into another phase: Ashley thief, Ashley embezzler, and above all, Ashley unfaithful. He sat down with Doris between them. Ashley felt quite startled at Hazel's change of appearance, tanned, blonde hair, much more handsome than he remembered, but he felt a pressure on him like a huge wet blanket and he was beginning to gasp for air.

'Shall we start?' asked Mr. Lester.

'Certainly,' smiled Doris.

Ashley still had not worked out what either of these two people were doing here and in a burst of arrogance demanded to know the answer to this situation.

'Simple, Mr. Wallace. Mrs. Wallace is a beneficiary, as is, indirectly, Mr. O'Hara.'

'Hazel did not even know my mother,' he spat.

'Shall we start?' asked Mr. Lester, yet again.

Ashley settled back into his chair. 'This is a farce,' he said.

'Not quite, Mr. Wallace. You see, your mother called me to see her and I went to her. With her signature I claimed all the documents and investments held by Mr. Osbourne.

Now, Ashley was starting to feel very clammy.

'After going through them all with her, she decided to write a new will to protect the property.'

'Really?' interrupted Ashley in his arrogant way.

'Settle down, Ashley. Be a good boy.' Doris said, patronisingly.

Ashley was now becoming angry. He saw all of this as a plot and he knew instinctively that Doris was in it up to the hilt, but what the hell was Hazel here for, he wondered.

'Your mother had three bank accounts. The larger of these, moneywise, will be used to pay off the mortgage on the property.'

Ashley suddenly began to see his chance for escape narrowing.

'The second account will be held over for investments of which I have been put in trust until your daughter turns eighteen years old and then she, with you, is free to alter or sell the investments. Until then they remain with me.

'I will contest this,' cried Ashley in a loud voice.

'I wouldn't, Ashley, even think about that,' Doris purred. 'There is still an enquiry into Osbourne's shady investments and your name appears on the documents.'

Ashley immediately moved uncomfortably in his chair and waited for the rest of this disastrous will reading.

'I leave to my dearest cousin Doris Wallace two of my diamond broaches of her choice. The other jewellery is to go to my niece.'

Ashley began to grind his teeth. He could feel everything slipping away from him and in the middle of this, literally, was Doris.

After all the other details had been gone through, it left Ashley virtually as he was now financially, with no real gain, as the property had been left to him and his daughter and no sale could be made until she turned eighteen, which meant seven long years away.

'I now come to the last point,' announced Mr. Lester, adjusting his glasses. 'There is one small account here at Bradbury. This is to be used to pay for the entire education of Sebastian Peter O'Malley.'

'What!!' screamed Ashley.

'Please let me finish,' Mr Lester insisted, with no one more surprised than Hazel. 'The apartment in Domain Road, South Yarra, is to be held as a guarantee that if the money in the account is insufficient, the rent from this apartment (which shall be administered by Mr. Lester) shall be used to offset schooling fees, beginning at once. This I have done in recompense for the illegal use of the O'Malley property for many years without my knowledge.' Ashley glared at Doris. His mother only knew this via her. 'The silver held in my home that was taken illegally from the O'Malley residence, Killkenny, is to be returned, every single piece, or I give Mr. Lester permission to draw up a legal document and submit it to the police.'

Asley was white with rage. Never before had he been stripped of everything in one go and he knew that as soon as Doris had a drink at the Railway Hotel the entire community would be aware of all of it. He stood up. 'Is that all?' he asked, sarcastically.

'No, not all,' said Hazel. 'I shall send Pat for the silver this afternoon. Oh, Ashley,' he continued, in a rather theatrical way. 'I have the inventory sheets for the silver. Shall I send a copy with Pat?'

'It's not necessary,' Ashley replied, sharply, as Hazel also rose to his feet. He was genuinely surprised how changed Hazel was. 'Oh, Ashley, dear,' and here Hazel was beginning to have some fun. 'I'll take a cheque from you now, in front of Mr. Lester and Doris for A$2,000.'

'What the hell for?' he spat out.

'Oh, Ashley, don't you remember leaving my bed and helping yourself to my holiday wages?' Ashley went bright red. 'Oh Ashley, how could you?' said Doris in a haughty tone. He gave a deep sigh, gritted his teeth together but remained motionless. 'I'm sure Mr. Lester has a pen.' A pen was handed to him from Doris. 'Ashley, dear, do use mine,' Doris smiled falsely. He withdrew his cheque book from his pocket and wrote the cheque.

'Who do I make it payable to?' he asked sarcastically.

'Leave it blank, Ashley dear. I'll fill it in myself.'

Ashley threw the cheque on Mr. Lester's desk and began to stride to the door.

'One moment, Mr. Wallace,' Mr Lester interrupted him. 'I believe you are using a solicitor at Mortlake. My advice is this. Don't! The solicitor is a personal friend of Mr. Osbourne and I have a nasty feeling that perhaps he doesn't have your better interests at heart.'

'Sit down, Ashley,' ordered Doris. 'It's time you and I, with Mr. Lester's help, resolved this damned mess.'

Hazel excused himself and left the office, walking on air. Sebastian's schooling safeguarded, fantastic; even if the new partner in Killkenny kicked up about other expenses, at least his schooling expenses were guaranteed. He cashed the cheque at the bank and happily thrust A$2000 in his pocket. Well, this is a bonus for Melbourne, he thought. Carmel again had proved right

Doris did go in to bat for Ashley. With all his mother's investments and legal documents in front of Mr. Lester, Ashley confessed to every stupid investment he had made with David Osbourne. With Doris's sharp brain and Mr. Lester's they arrived at a solution which solved the problems. Mr. Lester began the process of suing David Osbourne for the money Ashley had foolishly invested and was sure with the help of a little verbal blackmail and the threat of legal action he might be fortunate and receive at least half of it back. Ashley breathed a sigh of relief, especially as Mr. Lester explained that the only person that would get a jail sentence would be David Osbourne, not him.

* * * * *

Hazel headed back to Killkenny with the joyful news to tell Matthew and at three thirty dispatched Pat with half a dozen of the cartons from the big cottage to retrieve the silver. For Ashley this was a disastrous day, but somehow he, with Doris's insistence, had managed to retrieve a certain equilibrium. She insisted, after Mr. Lester's office, that they have an early lunch together and a call to Gerald assured Ashley that he would not be isolated for lunch. He was surprised that the moment this legal debacle was over Doris never mentioned it again and carried on at lunch as if it was just the thing to have lunch with her two good-looking nephews. Gerald couldn't have been happier and Ashley couldn't have been more nervous or ill at ease.

After lunch, Doris noticed Gerald and Ashley deep in conversation. Men, she thought, they are all the same. We save them and all they think of is one another.

* * * * *

When Pat arrived at three thirty, the silver was packed into the cartons without much conversation at all, Pat feeling as awkward as Cherly. Although it all needed a good clean, Hazel arranged the majority of the large pieces on the sideboard but this time with the engraved monogram 'K' facing outward.

The next morning, early, Matthew and Sebastian drove Hazel to the Mortlake airport.

'Come back soon, won't you,' smiled Matthew.

'Promise,' was the reply and he kissed them both. 'I will call after I have all the information from the solicitor. And, Sebastian, don't forget the two presents for the first of April, one for the Principal and one for Mrs Carstairs. They are wrapped and labelled.'

'I won't, Hazel, I won't.'

He waved as he headed across the tarmac to the light plane waiting to leave for Melbourne, with two large packages under his arms.

CHAPTER NINE

Dearest Hazel

CHAPTER NINE

Dearest Hazel

'Darling, you look divine!' came a cry as Hazel came through the barrier with a small bag and two large parcels. The two of them ended up in one another's arms. Their conversation was non-stop all the way back to Mary's. 'Don't worry, darling, a delicious diet lunch!' and they began laughing.

'Mary, the house looks stunning.'

'It should—you designed it,' and Hazel toured Mary's totally re-vamped house, with everything co-ordinated as opposed to before, when it was a mishmash of styles and tastes.

'Champagne!' cried Mary, after showing Hazel to his room. They moved through to the living room with Antonio Banderas's smiling at them from his ornate gilded frame.

'Oh, Hazel, it's so divine to have you back. Do you really have to return to the outback?' she asked.

'The answer is simple: yes,' he smiled,' and I will show you why.' Whilst sipping champagne and eating delicious nibbles, as Mary called them, Hazel showed her, on his digital camera, virtually a five month period of his life.

'Darling, who is that?' asked Mary.

'That, my sweet, is Matthew. He is divine.'

'Isn't that Sebastian?'

'Yes, it's when we were by the pool,' and the conversation continued being illuminated by the photographs for some time. While having lunch, Mary asked for the camera and quickly flicked through the photos.

'Aha, exactly! We have an appointment directly after lunch, Hazel. Eat up.'

'What's the mystery?'

'You'll see,' she replied, as he went on to explain to an astonished Mary that the Ashley Wallace at Bradbury was the Ashley Wallace he had known and loved many years before in Melbourne. He told her all about the dramas and the theft, but in his recounting of his five month period she noted the name of Matthew was used extensively.

'Hazel, are you in love with Matthew?' she asked, bluntly.

'Yes, I am. And can you believe it, for the moment no sex.'

'Fantastic,' she said, emptying her glass and thrusting it in Hazel's direction. 'You see, darling, you're growing up. I am very proud of you,' and she laughed.

'Thanks,' said Hazel, not quite sure how to take the comment.

After lunch, she took his camera and downloaded several photos of Matthew stripped to the waist at the pool, and Sebastian. She pointed them out.

'What's all this for,' he enquired.

'Darling, you are so slow. With the long-lost cash from Ashley, who sounds a right shit, you sweeties are going to have two paintings done by our lady with the very washed out Indian clothing.'

Hazel raised his head. 'What a fabulous idea,' he responded.

'And not only that, but we are going to stop at Mrs. Bennet's Antique Shop on the way, because I saw on Thursday a marvellous pair of gilt frames similar to Antonio's in the living room. And they are not expensive, so, sweetie, throw down the last drop and off we go.'

Having purchased the frames they then, having telephoned earlier, returned to the artist and her ginger cat. She greeted them quite formally.

'I see,' she said, looking at the photos. 'Do I have a free hand?'

Hazel, looked at the photos of Matthew and Sebastian again. 'Yes. The work you did for Mary was fabulous.' He handed her the deposit as she insisted on cash. She took the measurements of the frames and said they should take them away as they didn't serve any use for her and she would call Mary when the pictures were done. The rest of the payment was to be in cash. Having agreed to that, they left the crowded studio, with the fat orange cat still on a cushion on the mezzanine, glancing at them with half-open eyes.

'Is there anything you want to see or do?' asked Mary.

'No, let's go back to your place.'

They returned just in time to begin drinking again and reminiscing, but most of all laughing. Hazel was very aware that this type of conversation and use of adjectives varied between the country and the city, and it surprised him. Mary had taken the week off so she was going to enjoy every last minute of Hazel.

'I can't believe Keven's dead,' she said, 'not that I saw much of him after you left. Twice a month, perhaps, and then he fell in love with this young guy who came to work in his office. I have never seen him so happy. He was so alive and he doted on the boy—well, boy, he was twenty four, I think, but he had a very young face and they went to Indonesia twice, I think. I only met the boy twice. He was nice, a very quiet lad and to think it has ended like this. Oh, it's so depressing:

when you finally find love you can lose it, oh so quickly! Don't make a mistake this time, Hazel.'

'I shan't, not this time. I really know what I have this time, not a treacherous Ashley.'

'But you told me ages ago he was married.'

'Yes, he is, to a woman called Cherly, but it hasn't stopped his affairs with men. It seems at present he is having an affair with his cousin, who, believe it or not, looks exactly like a young Troy Donahue—a blond bombshell!'

'And Matthew?

'I know what you're going to say, and you're right. He does look Spanish, because his great-grandmother, I think, was a Spaniard, so he has been blessed with Antonio Banderas's good looks.'

You can say that again,' Mary nodded and laughed. 'Those photos by the pool—he is divine, so handsome.'

'Mary, you must come and stay with us. You will love it. It's not even a two hour flight.'

'Darling, I should probably have to pay excess baggage with my weight.' He joined in her laughter.

'I take it the diet isn't working.'

'No, sweetie. I have just given up. I don't go out much now. I watch our boy on DVD, eat, drink, sleep and go to the clinic. And that's about it.'

'No man on the horizon?' Hazel asked.

'Not a man on the earth, I think,' and they clinked glasses, laughing.

At that precise moment Hazel's telephone rang. 'Yes,' he answered. 'Oh, really? Oh well, I don't have much choice, do I? Very well. Goodbye.'

'What's wrong,' asked Mary, noticing Hazel's face.

'They have changed the day from Monday to Wednesday. What a bore!'

'You mean Keven's solicitor?

'Yes. I was so hoping to get this over as soon as possible. It's been such a weight on my mind. You see I don't really know where I stand. I may well be Sebastian's legal guardian but at present I am being paid directly by Keven or his estate. But if the new person or persons don't think that's a good idea where does that leave me?' He reached for his glass, and went on. 'In the middle of the outback, without a job or income, although I must say this is the first time in my life my bank account has been in a good condition. I bank my salary and all my expenses are covered by the estate so I spend very little.'

'I don't believe it, Hazel. At last, at your age, a bank account with money in it!' she commented, laughing.

'Yes, I suppose it is funny after all these years of abject poverty,' he declaimed, dramatically.

'I would have put it down to not holding down a steady job,' was her opinion.

'You know, Mary, I am really happy at Killkenny. I didn't think I would be able to cope with it but little by little it grows on you.'

'You mean you have fallen in love with Matthew.'

'Well, yes. He's great and now we get along really well.' Here he related the story of the bus accident.

'Good heavens, Hazel, you didn't tell me about that!' she exclaimed.

'Well, it was only last week and I thought I would save the story for now.'

'So we are playing Indiana Jones as well, are we?'

'This is the first and I can assure you the last time. My ribs are still a bit tender. Thank the saints I had that big raincoat on, as it cushioned me a bit.'

'Was Sebastian all right?'

'Yes. He was obviously a bit shaken but in a couple of days he was fine. I noticed that he was closer to Matthew than ever in those two days and to Red.'

'Who on earth is Red?'

'Well, I don't think by any stretch of the imagination he could be called 'pedigree' but he is a dog and the first dog Sebastian has been able to call his very own, so he is very special to him. He now rides to the front gate every morning and some evenings as well, depending where he is, but if he can't be found to go to the gates he is waiting patiently by the big fountain for Sebastian's return.'

'Hazel,' said Mary, suddenly, 'I have an idea.'

'Really?' he muttered in an offhand manner.

'Talking of Red has just jogged my memories of animals of the past. What say we go to Mass in the morning. I will ring the priest and offer Mass for Keven and then spend a day at the zoo. They have a good restaurant.'

'Why not?' he smiled. 'You know, I haven't been to the zoo for a million years.'

'It's great. It's been constantly updated and it's so pleasant now. No animals in tiny cages—it's fantastic.' She stood up and went searching for her telephone directory to call the local priest for the following morning.

Hazel cooked dinner, refusing to go out to a restaurant. 'You know,' he said, preparing behind the big bench as in the old days, 'both Matthew and Sebastian are mad for Thai food.'

He continued recounting hundreds of intimate details of living at Killkenny, the problems initially with the garden room, the swimming pool, the fountains.

Mary listened intently to everything Hazel had to say. This was a different Hazel, this was someone who had finally found his niche in life. He was positive, whereas before his general attitude was viciously negative. He had changed, Mary thought, for the better and she hoped desperately that the new partners of Killkenny would see his worth and continue to employ him. If not, she saw her old and dearest friend heading toward a depressing period in his life as he had said his whole world revolved around the place and Matthew and Sebastian.

*   *   *   *   *

The next day went off exactly as planned: after Mass they both felt Keven's absence and a certain heaviness fell on both of them. First it had been Jeffery and now Keven; neither of them had many real friends and to lose two was a real loss.

They bought their tickets and walked through the turnstile into the zoo. Hazel couldn't believe the change. It was marvellous, with all the noise from the trumpeting of elephants to the high pitched screeching of monkeys. One entered a world where you were being viewed, not the other way around.

'Oh, Sebastian would love this,' said Hazel.

'Well, there you are. Why don't you bring Matthew and Sebastian down here for a week. I have three spare bedrooms. You can use them any way you wish,' she ended, with a smile.

'Naughty,' was Hazel's response.

'I hope,' she said, as they headed for the restaurant, 'that you noticed the colour of my outfit.

He looked very puzzled. Mary was wearing a long, dark blue pleated skirt and white shirt with a dark blue jumper around her shoulders, as the day had heated up.

'I don't understand,' said a confused Hazel.

'This morning I thought of wearing grey but at the last moment thought it unwise as I didn't want the zoo keeper herding me into the elephant compound!' They both broke into hysterical laughter with their arms around one another. 'I miss you terribly, Hazel. You have no idea.'

'I know. I miss you, but things seem to have changed in my life.'

'And it's a change for the good,' she confirmed, with genuine charity as they went into the restaurant arm in arm.

* * * * *

On their return home, Hazel excused himself and moved to the living room where he phoned Matthew, with Antonio Banderas smiling at him, while Mary clattered about in the kitchen. Just to hear his voice convinced Hazel more than ever that he just couldn't live without him and they chatted on. He also spoke to Sebastian who said quite bluntly, 'Matthew can't cook.' Hazel assured him he would be back next Saturday afternoon and did the Principal and Mrs. Carstairs like their birthday presents. The reply was in the affirmative and so Hazel was quite pleased.

'Come home soon, Hazel. We miss you,' said an intense Sebastian. 'Red misses you, too.'

After speaking again to Matthew, explaining he now couldn't see the solicitor until Wednesday, he said he missed him very much and this sentiment was repeated by Matthew.

Hazel moved back into the kitchen and found that Mary had filled two glasses.

'Cheers!' he said, and glanced at a newspaper that lay on a chair.

'Look, Mary, there's a light fixture sale in Burwood Road. Do you think we could go tomorrow?'

'Why not? What are you looking for?'

'Those glass things—I don't know what you call them—that catch the wax from candles. I have been afraid to light them in case the wax drips over everything.'

'Hazel, you do have electricity at Killkenny, don't you?' she asked.

'Of course, but this chandelier was in one of the reception rooms. I was going to have it electrified but Matthew liked it with candles so we moved it to the dining room. When the rooms were being repaired they transferred the pulley system with it.'

'What on earth would you need a pulley system for?'

'Well, it's more a ratchet system. You don't think that you get up a ladder each time to change the candles, do you?'

'I have never really thought about it. How does it work?'

'Well, there is a little handle in the wall with a porcelain knob. You just turn it and the chandelier lowers. You change the candles and turn the handle in the opposite direction and the chandelier returns to its original position.'

'Really? So that's how it's done. I would never have guessed.'

'I think you'd better let me in there,' Hazel said, pushing her to the other side of the bench and taking over.

'There are fresh tuna slices. Oh, you have a look, darling! You're the expert.' They laughed and joked the whole evening.

'Just imagine if we had Ray Kemp here in his blue and white striped swim briefs. Oh!' The laughter continued as they reminisced about the past, their school days and the swimming star that they were both passionately in love with.

'You know,' said Mary, 'he is probably fat, married and bald.'

'Can't be,' replied Hazel, turning the tuna. 'He will always be the god of the swimming pool.

'Hazel, you're impossible. But I would give anything to see him now, wouldn't you?'

'No,' he said, slowly. 'If I close my eyes, I can see him in that wonderfully small bathing costume, that stunning body, the black wavy hair, the strong jawline. If I saw him now, and he was different—and I guess he must be, since we were at school with him twenty years ago—it would destroy the marvellous image that has remained fresh in my mind for all this time. I would hate to destroy it.'

'I suppose you're right,' she agreed, refilling the glasses. 'Yes, you are right. It's that image from the past you rarely use but when you do it satisfies that particular moment and it's always positive. Yes, Hazel, you're right, but ideally,' and she said it with a smile, 'we could have him right here as we remember him twenty years ago.'

'That, sweetie, is another equation, impossible, but what a delicious thought.'

*   *   *   *   *

The next day, over breakfast, Hazel said to Mary, 'Darling, I need an enormous favour.'

'Oh yes? What is it?'

'Could you bear, this week, to have lunch with two screaming queens?'

'Hazel, that is like asking me if I drink. Of course, darling, who?'

'Tony and Mark. I have to return these two sample books to them and they gave me a good discount so I should at least take them to lunch.'

'It's fine. I love Mark, but Tony can die with his secret, but yes, whenever you want.'

Hazel telephoned Tony to organise this, with the return of the sample books and the order for Doris's ballroom curtains, which Tony was very enthusiastic about.

'What number Burwood Road is it?' asked Mary as they drove in drizzling rain. 'Thank goodness we went to the zoo yesterday. What a miserable day!' Hazel gave her the number. 'Oh, it's much further out.'

They chatted on until, 'There it is,' cried Hazel, as an enormous sign announced a closing down sale. Mary parked and they walked back to the shop under a large umbrella.

They went in and looked about. It was a huge floor space with every type of light fixture possible to imagine, from the smart, expensive to the ordinary, economical type. They separated and wandered about and then Hazel saw it, a beautiful chandelier, a copy of an antique one. He reached up and flipped over the sale ticket. God, I can't believe it's so expensive, he thought, and began to look at other chandeliers, but inevitably ended back at the same one.

Mary was looking for a smart table lamp and couldn't find one. She passed a large display table, covered in the most awful lamps in pink or blue, obviously for children's rooms. No wonder children grow up with problems, she thought, and out of interest bent over and flipped the price tag so she could see the price. To her horror she felt a hand lightly slap her buttocks. She immediately stood up, swung around and saw a skinny youth of perhaps twenty four or twenty five, with thin lips, dull grey eyes and dark hair that was slicked back with gel. The total effect was ghastly.

'I like big girls,' he smirked and went to place a hand on Mary's breast.

'You put one hand on me and I will flatten you,' she warned in a steady but sharp voice.

'Come on! I could open your legs. We could have a great time.'

'Live your fantasy with someone else, birdbrain.'

At that he moved towards her. 'I have something between my legs you are dying for.'

'Forget it. I haven't brought my tweezers.' Then he lurched forward. Mary's instant reaction was attack. She thrust one closed fist in the direction of his face, catching him on the upper cheek. Her ring cut into his skin, which began to bleed.

'You fucking bitch!' he screamed loudly, attracting everyone's attention. Hazel heard the scream and swung around only to see Mary push this young fool backwards with her considerable weight and force. He stood upright for a split second then crashed onto the table with the pink and blue lamps. Down they all came with a deafening crash onto the tiled flooring.

'What's happening?' shouted a grey-haired man with glasses rushing up the aisle at the same time as Hazel reached Mary. The youth was completely dazed and remained amongst the broken china with a 'special sale' sign on his chest.

'Roland, what happened?'

'I'll tell you what happened,' snapped Mary. In a strong, determined voice she recounted the incident.

'Oh, I don't believe it. My son is a very good boy.'

'Oh, he is, is he?' she said. 'Come here.' She grabbed the boy's greasy hair and pulled his head back hard.

'Leave me alone, you bitch!' he screamed and attempted to raise himself.

'Look at the pupils,' she said to the owner father. 'Do you see they are incredibly dilated? Do you understand?' He looked at his son and then at Mary, completely confused. 'The word starts with D and ends in S and, just in case you are a sheltered parent, the middle letters are

R U G. Have you got it?' Her voice was louder now and much more authoritarian.

He helped his son up and they disappeared.

'Are you OK?' asked a worried Hazel.

'Yes, darling. All in a day's work, but perhaps it might be wise to stay with me in case this guy has two or three more sons addicted to something.'

The owner with the grey hair and glasses returned to Mary. 'I'm so sorry,' he began. 'I never thought that my son would ever be interested in drugs. He has never wanted for anything in his whole life. This information will be a real blow to my wife.'

'My advice is this,' returned Mary. 'I am a child psychiatrist. Your son is too old for me to treat but get him some professional help at once and cut the easy finance line now.'

'Oh, I shall,' he replied, obviously distressed. 'I am so sorry. If there is anything you want here I am more than willing to give you and your friend a very special price.'

'We'll have a look around. Don't worry, I won't press charges,' she said, and the man returned to his office.

'Are you all right,' Hazel asked again.

'Fine. It's such a pity that that degenerate thought he could have an easy game with me as opposed to someone gorgeous,' at which she laughed, though Hazel could see that she did not consider it a pleasant experience.

'Seen anything you like?' she asked.

'Yes, but even on sale it's very expensive.'

'Let's have a look.' Hazel threaded his way between the tables to the zone where he had seen the chandelier he liked.

'Yes, it is expensive,' she agreed, turning over the price tag. 'Let me have a word with the owner.' She disappeared and came back with a little difficulty, as the spaces between the tables was very limited.

'Hazel, I think this place, for a girl my size, is really like having a bull in a china shop. I am terrified I am going to knock something over. Oh, look over there. What do you think?' There was yet another table with a sign which read 'Must Go Last Days'. They walked over and found exactly the table lamp Mary was seeking, at a reasonable price. 'I must have it. What do you think?'

'I think it is perfect for your living room. Antonio is going to adore it,' he said. 'And by the way, what's the best offer on the chandelier?'

'Darling, it's not one but a pair. The price is for the pair. He says he will discount it even more. He doesn't want any problems. I feel sorry for him. He obviously loves the kid but just chose not to see anything he didn't wish to, and now his world is falling around him. I really feel for him.'

'I want the pair,' insisted Hazel. 'We have two reception rooms with the electric cord and a bulb on the end. Very post-modern!' He laughed. 'These would be fabulous.'

'Hazel, darling, you don't think that they are a tinsy bit too big do you?' she asked, looking at the enormous light fixture dangling from the ceiling.

'No, not at all. They will just finish the rooms off. Oh, thank the saints I have brought the cheque book. I may as well spend it, as I know that from Wednesday this may all come to an end. Well, at least Matthew and Sebastian will have a beautiful house.'

'Darling, everything will be all right. Don't worry,' she tried to reassure him.

*　*　*　*　*

Tuesday lunch with Tony and Mark wasn't as bad as Hazel had feared, and Mary was in fine form. 'Imagine, boys,' she laughed, 'the only time a guy has slapped my arse and he is a drug addict.'

'Them's the breaks, sweetie,' said Tony, laughing, 'but seriously, one does have to be careful these days. Some of the clients we have are proving to be a real handful.'

'We had a client,' Mark added, 'no names, but she ordered an enormous amount of stuff and was super-positive, just divine, champagne, the works. Darlings, a week later—thank God, we hadn't started the work—she came into the shop like a lost soul and announced she didn't want any of it and never wanted to see us again. The problem is that if you order at once you're caught with all your finances in bolts of fabric no one wants.'

'By the way, what did you think of your curtains and pelmets?' asked Tony.

'They are great,' Hazel answered. 'Hence the order from Doris Wallace.'

'Thanks for that,' said Mark. 'We can do with the work,' and luncheon continued in a lighter vein with plenty of laughs and a matching quantity of wine.

*   *   *   *   *

That evening, Hazel phoned Matthew to say that a delivery van would bring to Killkenny in two or three days two large chandeliers and a box of candle drip-plates in glass. I bought a few extra,' said Hazel.

'What? Chandeliers?' asked Matthew.

'No, no! The drip plates for the one in the dining room. They will arrive in big open crates, so you will have to telephone the electricians to fit them up. There are also the large dimmers. They will know how to do it.'

'We hope!' was Matthew's reply. 'I think we'll wait until you're home, so you can organise the length of them.' Here he stopped.

'Are you there?' asked Hazel.

'Oh, Hazel, I am missing you like crazy. I can't believe you have only been gone since Saturday. It seems an eternity until next Saturday afternoon.'

'Don't worry. I'll be back quicker than you think. Wish me luck for tomorrow.'

'I love you, Hazel. It doesn't matter what happens tomorrow. We both need you.'

'Thank you,' Hazel replied, softly. 'I will call you immediately I have finished with the solicitor. I love you. Goodnight.

* * * * *

Wednesday morning, Hazel rose early and was visibly very nervous.

'Darling, how long do you think it's going to take?

'I don't know. Maximum half an hour. Oh, Mary, what if it is left to a real cretin who wants to sell? What on earth would I do?'

'But, Hazel, you told me that as you have power of attorney for Sebastian they can't force a sale without your signature.'

'Yes, I know. I just feel so vulnerable. I suppose if they won't keep me on at Killkenny I could get a job at the Railway Hotel. I am sure Doris and Carmel would put a good word in for me.'

'Hazel, relax. You are making this worse than it is. By the way, what are you going to do with Keven's ashes?'

'I haven't a clue. I suppose the directions will be in the will. Oh, I don't think I can really go through with it. The thought of being separated from Matthew and Sebastian and even Jan is just too terrible.'

'Hazel, do you want me to come with you?

'No, no. I guess I can do it.'

'Well, here's what we will do. You go to the solicitor for your appointment at eleven. I will meet you at 11.30. We shall have a drink and then a good lunch. I know a divine place in the city and we will celebrate.

'We hope,' he muttered as he adjusted his tie.

'Come on, let's get going,' Marry urged. 'The traffic gets a bit heavy, so we don't want you to be late. Here, take this with you.'

'What on earth for?' he asked, surveying a black fabric carrybag.

'Darling, what do you think you are going to do with the ashes?'

'Silly me!' he grinned.

'That's the spirit, sweetie. Have you got your identification?'

'Yes, and all the copies of the documents from Mr. Lester.'

'OK. We're off. I'll leave you in front of the office and find a car park and be back here in half an hour.'

Hazel leapt out of the car, and Mary drove off. He crossed the narrow foyer and took the lift to the third floor where he entered the office of Keven's solicitor. He introduced himself to the secretary and sat down to wait. The door opened and a youth of perhaps twenty five or twenty six stepped in, very good looking, with brown hair, pale blue eyes, very tanned and obviously someone with no problem about self-esteem. He sat down after announcing to the secretary that he had an appointment with the same solicitor. Hazel took a deep breath. This was the worst scenario he could have imagined, a young person expensively dressed, not seemingly interested in anything. How on earth was he going to be able to convince him to keep him employed, rather than use the money for another designer suit or something?

Hazel attempted to begin a conversation with 'Good morning'. He spoke in a quiet tone: the young man turned to look at him but failed to reply. Oh great, thought Hazel. All is definitely lost. This is one of the young guys Keven picked up, had a wild affair with and in the heat of passion changed his will to include him. Well, I must say at least Keven had good taste in men.

The wait seemed eternal and Hazel came to the conclusion that the magazines on the table in front were the dreariest he had ever looked at. At last the solicitor opened his door, came out with a client, shook hands and turned to the two of them sitting down.

'I am afraid there has been a mistake,' he announced. 'I am so sorry.'

This is not my day, thought Hazel.

'Mr Anderson, we tried to call you this morning but your home number did not respond and you did not leave us your mobile number. If you would like to go and have a drink and come back in half an hour I can see you then, but not as we had planned at eleven.' The good-looking young man stood up and without a word went out of the waiting room.

'Come with me, please,' said the solicitor and they went into his office, where he closed the door. Hazel was now completely confused. If that boy wasn't the new half owner of Killkenny, where was he or she?

'First, the box on the side table is Mr. O'Malley's ashes. I will be more than pleased to see them go.' He laughed. Hazel was absolutely rigid, as if he were extremely cold.

'Are you all right?' asked the solicitor.

'Yes, just nervous,' replied Hazel, smiling weakly. There was a knock on his door and Hazel swung his head round to see who he was going to have to deal with, but it was the secretary, who placed documents that had obviously been asked for earlier on the solicitor's desk.

'There is no point in going over everything again. I believe Mr. Lester has informed you of your position as guardian of Sebastian O'Malley. This does not change.' Here he handed Hazel a letter. 'You can read it while I just sort the will out. Hazel opened the unsealed envelope and drew out a sheet of paper, which began,

Dearest Hazel,

I have not altered my will from when I remade it at the time you agreed to share guardianship of Sebastian with me. I should have kept in contact with you but I just have not. I am off to Indonesia with Paul tomorrow and I had the urge to telephone you but my courage failed me. I am leaving this letter with my secretary and she will, I hope, send it on to you.

I can't tell you how happy I am. I can't believe I have found someone who just makes everything I do worthwhile; to share with him in absolutely everything is the most exciting thing that has ever happened to me and indirectly this is due to you. You have always been there when I needed you, even the first time, I remember, when you literally did battle for me and always have been someone who would listen to my endless problems. The fact that you unselfishly took on the responsibility of Sebastian and Killkenny only because I asked you leaves me in your debt eternally, for, you see, it has been in this period, while you have been slogging it out in the outback, that I have had the opportunity to meet Paul. If I had been at Killkenny this wonderful experience could never have happened, so thank you so very much.

When I come back from Indonesia I will rewrite this will but you will always be taken care of, no matter what. I should like to leave Paul all my property in the city as well as my office and my practice, but I shall call you when we return and we shall sit down and work it all out. I wish you, Hazel, a love like mine.

All my love
Keven

Hazel felt the tears rising behind his eyes and blinked.

'The letter should have been sent to you before Mr. O'Malley left to go to Indonesia but it ended up here with the other legal documents so I just kept it for you.'

'Thank you very much,' was all Hazel could say.

'Well, the last time I saw you we made you guardian of Sebastian with power of attorney for the running of Killkenny. Half the property,' here Hazel held his breath, 'is Mr. Sebastian O'Malley's and the other half Mr. Keven O'Malley left to you on several conditions.'

Hazel sank back in his chair completely amazed.

'Me?' he said. 'But the other beneficiary?'

'There are none,' came the reply. 'You are to continue administering Killkenny but you cannot under any circumstances sell your half unless Mr. Sebastian O'Malley agrees when he turns twenty one.' At this stage Hazel's stomach was turning somersaults and he was shaking somewhat. 'All the properties in Melbourne are yours. You can dispose of them as you wish, including the architectural practice. There are the two terraced houses, one from where Keven O'Malley worked and his residence, three flats in Grey Street, East Melbourne and his deceased parents' residence in Malvern and that includes the contents, of course. The flats and the house in Malvern are at present tenanted. His personal bank account will be paid into your account on the probate of the will and until that time your salary that was determined by Mr. O'Malley will continue.' He then went on to explain the legal proceedings for land transfer and so on, but Hazel was not listening. 'Matthew' that was all he could think of, 'Matthew'. He could go home to Matthew and it was half his now, Kilkenny. He couldn't believe it.

'Is that all right, Mr. O'Hara?' the solicitor asked. 'Do you have any questions?'

'One question and one request.'

'Go on.'

'Is there anything in the will about the ashes?' The solicitor said there was not, only that he was to be cremated. Having power of attorney, it was for him to decide what would be proper. 'What is the request?'

'Would you please send a copy of all this to Mr. Lester.'

'Certainly. That is not a problem.'

Hazel went to stand up but felt very, very weak. He went over and put the box of ashes in the black bag that Mary had lent him, said his goodbyes and headed for the lift. When he reached the foyer, the first thing he saw was Mary. He walked slowly over to her, put his arms around her and began to cry. It was the result of the pent-up emotions over a long time, the not-knowing and the threat of somehow or other being separated from Matthew.

'Oh, Hazel, we'll work it out. You will come and live with me. There's not a problem with money either. I am doing very well now, enough for both of us.'

'Mary,' he said, stepping back, with tears rolling down his cheeks. 'Keven has left me everything, including the half share in Killkenny,' he said, quietly.

'What!' she screamed. 'Hazel, oh, Hazel!' and grabbed him in her arms. 'I knew it would all work out, darling. Come on, we both need a drink.' Arm in arm they made their way to a bar and ordered champagne, then went to a restaurant for lunch. After sitting down, Hazel handed Mary the letter Keven had written before he left for Indonesia.

'I'm glad he found real happiness,' she said. 'It took him all his life to finally find the right man but he made it and that's fantastic. You must think positively about it, Hazel. He had slept with a lot of guys and he was very handsome but there you go, he finally made it.' She reached over to put her hand on his. 'And so have you, Hazel, after a long time, so don't fuck it up!'

Hazel gazed at her. 'I won't. I promise.

'Good. Now, where the hell is the drinks waiter?' As usual, they both broke into laughter.

Back at Mary's, Hazel phoned Matthew, now feeling much calmer.

'What's wrong? Why didn't you call me?' asked Matthew, sounding worried.

'Because I have had lunch and now I feel I can talk without shaking.'

'Oh, Hazel, what happened?'

'Keven has left it all to us.'

'Us?' Matthew said, in disbelief.

'It's all in my name, but that means us. He wrote a letter in which he wished me a love like his. It's a pity, I could have told him I already had that love but you can read the letter when I get home.'

There was a silence on the end of the phone. 'Are you still there?' queried Hazel.

'Yes, I'm here. I can't believe it, Hazel. We are all safe.'

'Yes, darling, everything is fine.'

'Come home, Hazel,' he said, softly. 'I miss you like hell.'

'Pick me up from the airport at Mortlake as planned. I'll give you a call before, but I will see you in two and a half days. Don't say anything to anyone until I talk to you first.' They said their goodbyes and hung up.

Hazel walked into the kitchen, walked up to Mary and embraced her. 'Thanks so much,' he said.

'Darling, what for?'

'For when you thought I had lost everything and you offered to look after me and house me. You are the most wonderful woman in the world.' Mary didn't reply, but the firm grip in which they held one another said it all.

* * * * *

The next two days were frenetic. Hazel wanted clothes for both Matthew and Sebastian and then there was a dash to *Media World* for CDs for Matthew. It was there that Mary pointed out a CD and asked Hazel if he knew it.

'No,' he confessed, he didn't.

'Oh, Hazel, this is your life,' she screamed, laughing. 'Really, the main theme for this marvellous ballet music to '*Spartacus*' is you, it's your life. It takes a long time to get there and then the uplifting swell as it finally takes the theme to the top—it's you!'

'Oh. Who wrote the music?'

'Khachaturian,' she answered. 'You must know the music. Listen, promise me that you will play it with Matthew alone.'

'I promise,' he said and with a great many other ballet CDs they left the shop laughing and joking, but at the same time both of them beginning to feel the tension of parting. During the two final days they spent every minute just enjoying the luxury of one another's company.

When they arrived home, laden after a visit to an outlet shop for men's and boys' clothing on Friday night, they dumped everything and dashed to the fishmonger Mary knew. Four dozen oysters began the list and they just kept going. 'Diet food, darling!' They ended up hysterically laughing together, much to the fishmonger's amazement.

When they arrived back at Mary's, Hazel began in the kitchen. Mary excused herself and said she had to check her emails. 'Yes' was heard, not just in her house but probably across the entire width of the suburb of Hawthorn. Hazel dropped everything and rushed into the small room at the end of the corridor Mary used as a computer room.

'Mary, what's wrong?' he asked, genuinely concerned.

'Hazel, not a word! Back to the kitchen and open the bottle in the fridge door marked 'Moet'.'

Hazel was most confused but this whole week the only thing that had made sense was the monkeys screeching from the trees at the zoo.

'Are you sitting down?' Mary asked.

'Hardly, darling. Who has a chair in front of the stove?'

'Is the bottle open?'

'Mary, the bottle is not only open but two glasses are full. What is the mystery? What the hell is going on?'

'Well, Hazel, it's been a long story.'

'Mary, why didn't you tell me you had a lover?' he replied, sharply.

'Oh, Hazel, it's not quite like that. I worked on a case that was just so sad. The father was an Australian and a drug addict as was the Italian girlfriend. There was a child that no one wanted. The child was beaten and the pair of them were before the courts. The child was sent to me because he refused to cooperate in the foster care situation. He was a real problem but we made it.' She smiled. 'Strangely a big tart like me and this little boy after only five or six sessions had something going. I made applications to the courts and on my email they have granted me custody of this little boy.'

'Mary, you are divine,' said Hazel, 'to collect someone that no one else loves and make it work.'

'Well, the future will see if it works, but I am sure I can do it and he is so sweet, so determined.'

'Aren't all men?' laughed Hazel. 'What's his name?'

'Give you one guess.'

Hazel lifted his glass and met hers. 'Antonio' they chorused together.'

'But, Mary, how old is he?'

'Ten,' she replied.

'Well, then, I think that's even more of an excuse to come to Killkenny with your new Antonio. Sebastian's more or less the same age. Oh, Mary, it's all working out so well.'

'You know, Hazel, if someone had told me some time ago that a drag queen called Hazel was going to end up in the outback with the custody of a young boy he loves and a beautiful Spanish lover, I would have told them to walk into a brick wall.'

'How times change.' Hazel downed his glass.

'But they don't, you know.' She spoke thoughtfully. 'Look at us. We are the same as when we were at school, both of us would have killed for Ray Kemp in his tiny blue and white briefs. We haven't changed, it's the situations around us that have. In a funny way, Hazel, we have remained stationary while the events of the world spin out of control. Gosh, just think, less than a year ago we had two real friends, Jeffery and Keven and now, in that void, someone else has slotted in, in their own way. It's strange, isn't it?'

'Yes. I suppose it is,' agreed Hazel, 'and it's also very sad. Keven was so happy with his young friend and now?'

'Now, Hazel, you have, thanks to his love and respect for you, an opportunity to do just as he did—love.'

'Mary, just changing the subject, I took the liberty early this morning of contacting a delivery service.'

'Really? What for?'

'Well, I have noticed that on the other wall in your living room the few prints on the wall are, if I may say so, a little bit weak.'

'You may not say so,' replied Mary, beginning to take the defensive tack.

'So, sweetie, the big eighteenth century landscape I have stored is to be delivered next week and it will fit in beautifully here.'

'Oh, Hazel, I can't take that. It's been the one thing you have adored all your life.'

'It was the only thing, but now I have someone else and the painting belongs here. I do hope the young Antonio likes it.'

She smiled, though the tears were visible. 'He will, Hazel, he will.'

*   *   *   *   *

Late Saturday morning for both of them was a moment of great sadness but great joy. They had both found in the most unlikely situations someone to fill their emotional lives, but their bond was stronger than ever.

'Now,' started Hazel, having made a sarcastic comment about excess baggage, 'you must promise to come to Killkenny.'

'Only if you promise to come with Sebastian and Matthew to Melbourne for a week.'

'I promise,' they chorused together, and held one another tightly.

'I'll miss you, Mary.'

'Me, too,' she said, with tears streaming down her face. 'Call me the minute you get back and I'll telephone you when the paintings are ready.' They parted and Hazel walked through the barriers toward the little plane on the tarmac. 'It's only two hours away,' he thought, getting into the plane, wondering if the picture frames had been stored correctly. As the plane flew higher and higher in the direction of Mortlake the sadness of being parted from his closest friend began to dissipate and the expectation of seeing Matthew again began to grow.

*   *   *   *   *

Once on the ground and with a large trolley carrying his loot from the city, Hazel went through the barriers into Matthew's welcoming arms. They held one another just long enough for the onlookers to realise they were not brothers.

Sebastian was ecstatic. 'Hazel, you have been away too long! You must stay with us,' he said, determinedly. 'You know, Red misses you too.'

Hazel smiled. Home, he thought, this is it.

On the drive back, it was Sebastian who did most of the talking, recounting school, what Red had done, the fact that the church was finished and Auntie Rhonda, as he now called her, was going to stay forever.

'Oh, really?' said Hazel.

Sebastian was in the back seat and asking what was in the parcels. 'Oh, we have to wait until you get home and then you can have a look.' He felt Matthew's hand gently rest on his knee and if Hazel had been a Christmas tree all the lights would have shone with a glorious knowing, that Christmas, or no Christmas happiness depends on the right person who responds like an electric switch to another.

At home, Red barked and jumped over all of them, excited to be in his secure family. The baggage was taken indoors but not before Hazel had taken Mary's black carrybag into the church and deposited the casket with Keven's ashes on the high altar. He then returned and joined both Matthew and Sebastian, taking the parcels indoors.

It was a strange sensation for Hazel. It was the first time he had spent away from Killkenny since he had arrived there six months before and to come back only after a week's absence made him feel he belonged there more than ever. Suddenly the emptiness of the landscape wasn't quite as daunting. There were new trees and with the rain the opportunity of new pastoral growth. He felt for the first time in his life he belonged and as he gazed around at the buildings, now all in pristine condition, this tiny microcosm of the world seemed right and ready for a positive future but only on the condition it could be driven by love.

Before he had even unpacked, his telephone rang. 'Congratulations,' said Carmel.

'Thanks,' he replied, wondering how on earth she knew but then remembering the cards. He asked her what she was doing for dinner and when she answered 'Nothing' he suggested she should get herself over as it would be a Thai night. 'The boys tell me they are starving'. He laughed as he walked into the dining room finding to his surprise that all the silver was gleaming. 'Wow!' he exclaimed, looking at Matthew.

'We all got down to it, Mum and Auntie Rhonda and me.'

'I cleaned some spoons!' claimed Sebastian.

'You've all done a great job,' Hazel said, and unwrapped the bubble plastic from the two empty frames, watched by the other two.

'Hazel,' said the confused boy, 'they haven't got anything inside them.'

'Not yet. You'll have to wait and see what goes inside.' He decided the perfect place was on a blank wall in the dining room on the opposite wall from the big sideboard, now groaning under the weight of the newly-cleaned silver. He went out and returned with a hammer and hooks. Soon, the two elaborate empty gilded frames stared out at the sideboard.

He then unwrapped the gifts for Sebastian first, but the thing he was most excited about was a collar in metal and on the tag engraved 'RED', with, under it, the telephone number of the homestead. Off he rushed to see if it fitted and to find Pat to make any necessary alterations to the length.

'The clothes are great, Hazel,' said Matthew, 'but you didn't have to spend your money on me.

'I can't think of anyone I would rather spend it on,' he replied. They moved, arm in arm, to the garden room for a drink and to wait for Carmel. 'Read this.' Hazel handed Keven's letter to him, which he duly read and returned.

'So it seems from his letter he had always intended to leave you his share of Killkenny.'

'So it appears. It's just a pity he hadn't told me. It would have saved a lot of heartache and worry.'

'Well, everything has worked out satisfactorily,' commented Matthew, 'but I feel so sorry for Keven to have found exactly the man he wanted and to finish like that.'

'If they both loved one another, perhaps it hasn't finished but is only starting in another world,' Hazel said in a quiet voice. They spoke about the houses and what to do with them. Matthew suggested that if might be wise to see Mr. Lester first and see what he said.

'Yes, I think the same. If Sebastian decides in seven years time he wants to go to university, he has accommodation.'

'Let's not think so far ahead,' urged Matthew. 'Oh, by the way, what amount is left in Keven's accounts?'

'I haven't a clue. Mr. Lester will have to find that out through Keven's solicitor. Whatever the account is, I shall divide it into three, a third each for you, Sebastian and me, but this depends how much is there. There may be very little, as they did a lot of travelling in Asia. We shall have to wait and see.'

Matthew leant over to kiss him. 'Why don't you put my third into Sebastian's bank account?' he suggested.

'I wasn't aware he had one,' Hazel replied.

'He does,' and he was about to continue when the doorbell rang.

'I didn't hear the car,' said Hazel, jumping to his feet. 'My God, is it that time? I haven't even started preparing,' and he fled to the door. 'Carmel, you will have to keep Matthew company for a while. I have some magic to do in the kitchen.' He disappeared.

'A drink?' Matthew offered.

'Thanks,' was the reply.

'You are not going to recognise me in the future.'

'Oh? Why?'

'Because Hazel has virtually bought me a new wardrobe in Melbourne.'

'I think that's great,' Carmel said. 'I'm sure that now Killkenny is in good hands you will both be entertaining a bit more.'

'Perhaps,' he said.

'You've been very fortunate with the rain. Your new pasture has a real chance of survival.'

'Yes, I'm pleased. If we have a break now and some more rain in a couple of weeks' time it will be perfect.'

'What have you decided about the funeral?'

'Hazel wants a small funeral here and then he wants to scatter the ashes.'

'Good idea, but be careful who you invite or you will have half of curious Bradbury here.'

'That's exactly what we don't want,' Hazel said, coming back in. 'It will be just us, the priest, you and Doris. If we can have it late, I think a sit down dinner later is nicer.'

'Great idea,' agreed Carmel. 'Do you want me to organise Father Keven? I know him quite well. What evening do you want?'

'It doesn't worry us, but any weekday. Ask Father if he would like to stay for dinner.'

'Done,' she declared, and the conversation moved on to other subjects, including Doris's ballroom curtains.

'If I really cast my mind back,' said Carmel, 'Doris hasn't used the ballroom for ten or fifteen years. I wonder if, with these new curtains, she plans to go into an entertaining period in her life.' They laughed together. 'Oh, I was forgetting, Hazel. Do you want me to invite Ashley to the funeral?'

There was dead silence. Everyone knew that Ashley at school had been Keven's lover. Hazel's reply was immediate, as he stood up. 'Ask Matthew,' and he headed for the dining room to make last minute preparations.

'Well. I don't know,' Matthew said. 'I can well do without him, but give him the option to say no.'

Carmel smiled. Our Matthew is not only beautiful, she thought, but very astute as well.

A bang on the garden room door announced Sebastian and Red. 'Look, Carmel!' He pointed out Red's newly fitted collar. 'It's very smart. Red likes it a lot.' He came up and gave her a hug.

'I think it looks great,' she said. 'He is a very fine dog.'

'Yes, he is a fine dog, aren't you, Red?' The dog assumed this was the signal to jump all over Sebastian.

'Take him outside and back to the others. It's time for dinner,' at which they both disappeared.

'He loves this dog,' said Matthew.

'He's a lucky boy, now,' agreed Carmel. 'He is surrounded by love and that is the most productive form of energy that exists.'

* * * * *

The funeral was for six o'clock on Wednesday evening. Father Keven officiated in the newly decorated church, with a nervous Sebastian assisting. The funeral was as planned, just the Killkenny staff, Carmel, Doris and Rhonda, but as they all entered the church, a car drove into the forecourt in front of the church and Ashley alighted. He said hello briefly to everyone and took his place. He couldn't believe that this painted interior with putti ribbons and flowers was the same little wrecked church he had passed every time he went to Bradbury. His eyes wandered all over the interior and to the back of man with thick black hair sitting beside Hazel.

The funeral Mass was brief but very touching, with nothing exaggerated and the readings were about love, as was the eulogy. After the Mass, Rhonda departed to her cottage, while Bob and Pat headed home to watch the late news with a beer in hand but Jan joined them for dinner. She had lost fifteen kilos and looked better for it, but there were still a lot more to go. Doris, with her usual lacquered hair, took over and Ashley was in two minds whether to stay or go. Matthew sensed this and spoke to Hazel and then went over to him.

'You are welcome to stay for dinner. Hazel has prepared a place for you.'

'Thank you very much,' he replied and followed the others to the garden room. He thought that on this unsure ground it was probably wise to stay as close to Doris as possible, even though he would have much preferred Matthew.

Drinks were served and a very pleasant evening ensued, with Father Keven stating that he thought the restructuring of the church was splendid, even if he did have to say Mass with his back to the congregation.

'As it should be!' cried Doris. 'None of this silly modern nonsense!'

He laughed and said he quite liked saying Mass like that, but the Bishop had other ideas. And he would always be happy to say a Mass at the little church dedicated to St.Antony.

The conversation moved on and after dinner they all took drinks and coffee in the reception room, with Carmel entertaining them on the piano. Ashley's eyes were everywhere, the paintings, the deluxe curtains, the rugs, the furniture. At dinner he had been seated by Hazel so he looked straight across to the sideboard and the silver, this time with the 'K' to the front. He was genuinely surprised at the opulence of the house as opposed to his own, but the electricity cords from the ceiling obviously signalled that there was even more to go to finish these large rooms. While Sebastian moved across to play with Carmel, Ashley asked Matthew as he was sitting next to him, 'What about the light fixtures?'

'The chandeliers will be installed next week,. There has been a hold-up in the delivery.'

'Of course,' he replied, weakly. Ashley knew that Killkenny had come into some money but was overwhelmed at what he thought must have been the bill for all this work and he gritted his teeth to think that, sitting in this luxurious setting, he was by law expected to pay for all Sebastian's schooling.

The evening ended well, with everyone keeping up with one another, except Ashley, whose conversation was brief. He considered the evening similar to walking on thin ice.

* * * * *

The next day, while Hazel was preparing lunch for Matthew, there was a cry at the back door and he swept out expecting Matthew, but to his surprise it was Jan.

'Come in,' he said, and she walked into the large modern kitchen. She had never seen it before and was quite impressed.

'You could open a restaurant with a kitchen like this,' she commented, smiling.

'Really?' Hazel responded without much enthusiasm.

'I have come to talk about Rhonda.'

'Sit down, Jan,' and he motioned her to a chair. 'What's wrong?'

'Well, it's what's right that's the problem. You see, Rhonda really likes being here. She has laid a canvas down on one of the bedroom floors and is using it as a little studio. She has always hated Bradbury and I was wondering if you would consider letting her stay. I mean, the cottage isn't occupied and I am sure we can come to some arrangement for the rent. Besides it's great company for me.'

Hazel moved around, Jan stood up and he gave her a hug. 'She can stay on one condition: that you lose another eight kilos before Christmas,' which set them both laughing.

'Thanks, Hazel. You don't know how much this means to me.

'I couldn't let my fellow rescue team down,' he commented. 'We'll work the rent out later but it won't be much.' A very relieved Jan disappeared to pass on the good news to her sister, whom Hazel saw later in the afternoon, prior to collecting Sebastian.

'Thanks, Hazel,' she said. 'It's very kind of you.' She spoke in her usual deep voice and with short sentences.

'I would like you to do me a favour,' he went on. 'In the panels you have painted around the church, is it possible to paint an inscription in the one near the front?' When she said it was, he added,' I would like you to paint it like the lettering on a grave stone, and it must have the name 'Keven O'Malley', his date of birth, when he died and a quotation. I've thought about this a great deal, and decided at last *'Always face the sun and your shadows will fall behind you.'* It's from Hellen Keller.'

'It's nice,' she replied. 'Bring it to me, written out exactly as you want it and I'll do it. And how much do you want for the rent?

'You work it out with Matthew, but it will be very reasonable, I promise.' He left her, to drive down to collect Sebastian.

* * * * *

The next Thursday saw Hazel with a briefcase full of documents and ready for an exhausting morning with Mr. Lester, and he was correct. Mr. Lester took control of the situation without any problem and they decided, or rather he decided and Hazel agreed, that the letting of the three apartments in East Melbourne, the house in Malvern and the two terraced houses in South Yarra had to come under one letting agent. He said he had contacted the two architects that remained in Keven's office studio, offering them the opportunity to rent it with all the equipment in situ and said he was waiting for a reply. If they didn't accept what he thought was a reasonable rent then he would, through the letting agent, advertise it for another architect at what Hazel thought was a very high rent, but said nothing. Once all Keven's affairs were organised, Mr. Lester adjusted his glasses. 'Oh, two more things. Keven O'Malley's bank account stands at A\$900,000 but there is a lot of money owing for work done. We will press immediately for it all to be paid into the account. The second matter, Mr O'Hara, concerns you. You must now, as half-owner of Killkenny and now with a very healthy bank account, write a will in order to protect Sebastian O'Malley and bring it to me in a rough draft next Thursday.'

'Oh,' replied Hazel

'Don't worry. Give me just an idea of what you want and I'll put it into legal jargon.'

'Thank you so much,' Hazel said and left, as another client stood up to enter.

'Oh, please, just a moment. 'Hazel stepped back into the room and out again. 'Sorry. I needed the answer to a little legal problem.'

'Hm,' commented the elderly woman and went in, shutting the door quite firmly. Perhaps she thought Hazel would reappear.

*   *   *   *   *

Then there was the usual dash to the supermarket, the greengrocer and the hardware store, every Thursday it was the same, and finally a flop into the Railway. When he entered there was only Carmel at their usual table.

'Hi!' she greeted. 'Busy morning?'

'I'll say,' Hazel replied. 'One hour with Mr, Lester. He tells me I have to write a will by next Thursday.' Carmel did not say a word but bent over and from her Hermes bag unzipped the invisible pocket and withdrew her invisible pack of cards. She dealt them out, after shuffling them in the form of a fan, and turned them over. She looked very carefully at them, then collected them and returned them to the invisible pocket. She poured Hazel a glass of wine and then one for herself. She smiled at him saying, 'Yes, Hazel, write it exactly as you are thinking now, but it won't be used for many, many years,' and went on to say that she was angry she hadn't followed Matthew's example and planted out new pasture. 'Now it's too late but next year I will take Matthew's advice. Oh, and I am getting rid of my manager. Trick has found me a young man and his wife, who trained at an agricultural college, so let's hope for the best. The rest of the staff are on hot bricks I'll get rid of them, too, and they are not wrong unless they get off their backsides and do some work.'

'Who has to get off their backsides?' asked Doris, joining them. 'And where is Gerald today?'

'Not sure,' Carmel told her, 'but a little bird told me he had a luncheon appointment with Ashley at the Crown today.'

'Traitor!' responded Doris, in a haughty manner. 'You save their scrawny necks and they break ranks. Really, anyway, the food is lousy, Heather told me, all re-heated stuff. That's why their salads have so much vinegar on them, so what they don't use at lunchtime they use again in the evening. You wouldn't catch me eating at the Crown. Oh, just a minute, you order. I have just seen Heather come in.' Doris pushed through the crowd in the direction of Heather.

Carmel waved her hand: the waitress took their order and for another bottle and glass. 'Doris is sure to come back for a drink. I was very entertained the other night at Killkenny for dinner. I thought Ashley's eyes were going to drop out. He's isn't used to such luxury.'

'Well. He would be even more overwhelmed if he saw the two reception rooms now. The chandeliers are hung and working. They do give the rooms the finishing touch.'

'I cannot wait to see them.'

'Well, come for dinner on Friday night. It's fish alla Thai.'

'It's a date,' she laughed.

'But Carmel,' Hazel began, 'what do you mean about Ashley being unused to grand interiors? After yours and Doris's homes, isn't his the next biggest?'

'Yes, but Angela lived a really Spartan existence. Oh, I forgot: you haven't seen the house. Well, it is big. It has an enormous reception ballroom at the side, but no furnishing and all painted this hideous pale green, so I think he expected, despite the local rumours, to find Killkenny the same. Remember, the last time he saw Killkenny before the other evening was when everyone was living at the gate.'

'Do you think they will do anything with the house now that Angela's dead?'

'It will depend on Cherly. Ashley, as you heard when Angela's will was read, is fairly strapped for cash. Perhaps Cherly's parents might help her out. Who knows?'

Doris returned, buzzing. 'Heather tells me,' she said, leaning over in Carmel's direction, 'that—and we must be politically correct here—that she thinks her daughter is a homosexual woman.' She sighed with a certain amount of satisfaction about passing on the latest piece of gossip.

'Well, good for her,' Carmel commented. 'I'm surprised there are not a great many more, especially if you look at the quality of men around Bradbury.' Hazel laughed.

'It's not a laughing matter,' Doris said, sharply. 'Poor Heather is quite upset. Still, I told her to think on the positive side. Her daughter will save a fortune on school fees.'

'I'm sure that went down well, Auntie,' was Carmel's dry comment.

'Well, I don't think she grasped it, really. Some people never see the trees for the forest.' She stood up and went to speak or pass on this latest gossip to another friend of hers, leaving Carmel and Hazel gazing at one another, trying to work out what the misquoted proverb Doris had used had to do with Heather's daughter.

*   *   *   *

Every time Hazel summoned up the courage to speak to Matthew about the will, something came up. On Thursday evening, Sebastian took over with his music; both Matthew and Hazel were very surprised at how, in just five months or so, he had grasped how to play the piano. Matthew was so proud of him.

Friday evening, Carmel came to dinner and on Saturday night Matthew went to bed early, having worked all day with Pat and Bob, but doing most of the physical work, extending a pass from the lower pastures and that part of the property to the higher part. At the front they had had great problems at shearing time moving the flock up this small pass, so they were widening it to twelve metres as opposed to its present three.

Saturday evening, as usual, Bob and Pat went to the Railway for a drink, and to pass the evening Jan and Rhonda had dinner at Jan's as Bob was not present. Rhonda still hated to be in Bob's company. It was not until about 9am Sunday that something happened that changed the balance of Killkenny. Hazel was up and sitting in the kitchen, having a cup of coffee. Sebastian had been up long before and was out playing with Red.

'I've overslept,' said Matthew, coming into the kitchen, where he gave Hazel and kiss before sitting down to breakfast.

All of a sudden there was a banging on the front door. 'Matthew, Hazel, quick!' shouted Pat and the two of them, fearing an accident to Sebastian, rushed to the door, where a white-faced Pat stood there.

'Come quick. Dad's dead, I think.' The three of them raced across the square and into Jan's house. Hazel quickly went into Bob's bedroom and checked his pulse. Nothing, nothing at all. He pulled the sheet over his head and announced that Bob really was dead.

The police and the priest were sent for and later in the morning the hearse arrived to remove the body. Jan showed no sign of grief at all and continued as she had every day; whether the shock came later or she didn't suffer no one knew. Pat seemed completely confused. He didn't know what to do. Matthew, who had had a very poor relationship with Bob all his life, felt for Jan at this moment but felt no loss at all for Bob, especially as he had always declared that Matthew was no son of his. Rhonda's only callous comment was 'At last!'

The funeral was held at Bradbury the following Friday. The autopsy result was that a massive heart attack, not helped by a large alcohol content in the bloodstream, had killed him. The funeral was very well attended. Bob had been born in Bradbury and was a regular at the Railway, so everyone knew him. After the funeral Jan had organised a reception at the Railway, as for everyone to travel back to Killkenny was not feasible. Hazel and Matthew left early on the pretext they had to collect Sebastian, but this was not true, as Rhonda was now taking turns with this exercise.

When home, Hazel said to Matthew, 'I've decided to cast Keven's ashes on the new pasture.'

'Why?' asked Matthew, helping himself to a drink.

'Well, I think it's right, to put the ashes where there is the hope of regeneration—it is very valid. I am sure Keven would agree.' Matthew just grunted. 'I now have to speak to you on another important issue but you must promise not to interrupt me until I have finished.'

'Very well. Off you go.'

'I spoke to Mr. Lester the Thursday before last and yesterday I took to him as requested a rough draft of my will. It will be ready for signing next Thursday. You see, I have left everything to you and Sebastian. You will take exactly what I have, the half share in Killkenny and when Sebastian is twenty one you can both sit down and work out the next stage in your lives.'

'Hazel,' Matthew began.

'Just a moment,' interrupted Hazel, raising one arm. 'There is just one more thing. You will be required to come with me next Thursday as I have asked Mr. Lester to make you co-guardian with a power of attorney for Sebastian, so if anything happens to me you will automatically become his guardian until he is twenty one years old.' Matthew said nothing. He just looked into his almost empty glass. 'Oh, another thing. You said to me the other day Sebastian has a bank account but in my file I have no record of it.'

Matthew sighed, stood up then moved to stare out of the window into a grey sky. 'I opened the account for him when he was born,' he said slowly, but didn't turn around for a moment. When he did tears were rolling down his cheeks. 'I have never told anyone,' he went on, wiping his eyes with the back of his hand. 'Blackmail is a filthy word and it makes everything and everyone it touches dirty.' He returned to the big divan and sat beside Hazel.

'You don't have to tell me anything, if you don't want to,' Hazel said.

'You have a right to know now. You have been so good to Sebastian. Without you, we might have been separated.' He looked down at his feet. 'When Peter O'Malley met Sandra Jane, she was desperate to get hold of him for the money but she couldn't become pregnant by him. He apparently was virile but had no sperm count or something. She knew quite a bit about Killkenny, although she hated it and somehow she found out about Dad and Ashley's illegal dealings and she sought me out and threatened that if I was not the sperm donor she would turn my father over to the police. You see, I was dark, as were Peter and Keven, so Sandra Jane thought nobody would know the difference and would remain silent.' Here he stopped and looked at Hazel. 'What would you have done?'

'The same as you,' and Hazel held his hand. 'so that is why Sebastian and you are identical, so that's the mystery.'

'That's not all,' he said. 'You asked me about his bank account. I opened it for him when he was born and I have been putting money in it for all his life. I didn't know what the future held for him and in those days there was talk that Peter O'Malley wanted to sell Killkenny. Sandra Jane and Peter, once Sebastian was born, abandoned him. For her, the deed was done and she had married Peter, as she had wanted to, so Sebastian and I grew up together and everything should have been just like that except that they came to Bradbury three days before they were killed in the accident and Sandra Jane told me in private that they were sending Sebastian away to the same boarding school where his father and Keven had been as a full boarder. I just don't know what happened to me. I knew this girl and the same day as Sandra Jane told me that they were going to take Sebastian away I married her. Don't ask me the logic of it, because there just isn't any. I never slept with her. I think I just cried for three days. The divorce came through without any problem, thanks to Mr. Lester, and, if you remember, a couple of months ago I received a letter. It was the decree of nullity from the church. But after the accident, everything with you started to go right for Sebastian.'

'Does he know?' asked Hazel, quietly.

'That I am his father? No, and I don't want him to. Can you imagine the legal wrangle over his inheritance?'

'Yes, you're right,' admitted Hazel. 'I think we'll let sleeping dogs lie.'

Matthew brushed his tears away and held Hazel in his arms. 'I think it's time for me to move to an important part of our relationship. Sebastian won't be home for an hour or so. He's with Carmel. You know I always had the oddest feeling that Carmel knew all about this.'

'She is a very clever and intuitive person,' Hazel agreed. They stood up and hand in hand went to Matthew's room where he shut the door, and, first or last, is not important, but a stage was begun that was to carry them through the rest of their lives in happiness.

* * * * *

The following Thursday, two major events occurred. A very nervous Matthew entered Mr. Lester's office at 11.30am with Hazel. It was one of the rare occasions when he had left Killkenny. They sat down in front of the lawyer, who directed his conversation today mainly at Matthew.

'Do you realise what this document means?' he asked. 'You will be required to share with Mr. O'Hara all responsibility for Sebastian O'Malley until he is twenty one years of age.'

'Yes,' said Matthew. 'I am well aware of the responsibility,' and with a shaky hand he signed the document that was witnessed by the lawyer and his secretary.

'He is now your legal responsibility,' Mr. Lester said quietly and was surprised to see tears begin to roll down Matthew's cheeks. He brushed them away, then they shook hands and stood up to leave the office.

'Oh, just a moment.' Matthew's heart fell. 'Mr. O'Hara, perhaps when you have time, I think that it's foolish to let this money that has now been placed in your account lie idle. There is a shop here coming up for sale in an excellent position, large and rented very well. Think about it and drop in and we will have a chat next Thursday, and at the same time I will go over the rough draught of your will and see what we can do. I will email my legal version of it to you, so go over it carefully so that next Thursday we can have it ready and signed. By the way, Mr. Saunders, you will also need a will by the quick look I have had at Mr. O'Hara's. You had better send me in a rough draught with Mr. O'Hara next Thursday.'

As they went out into the drizzling grey late morning, Matthew just held Hazel's arm and looked at him. 'No one can ever take him away from me now,' he said in a whisper.

'No,' smiled Hazel, 'never. Come on, I have a surprise for you.' They walked up to the Railway, under the shop verandas with Hazel glancing at the merchandise but Matthew seeing nothing. A great fear had finally been removed from his life, that of being separated from Sebastian.

'Hi, what an honour!' laughed Carmel, and gave them both a kiss. 'I think this is the first time you have joined us for our Thursday lunch.' She attracted the waitress's attention. 'Champagne, and every time a bottle is finished, bring us another. It's a very special day.'

'I can't believe it,' Matthew said, and then became very careful of what he was saying. Carmel sensed this at once. 'Not another word.' she smiled.

'Wow, Christmas!' exclaimed Gerald, as he squeezed Matthew's shoulder in passing, to sit in his usual seat. 'What brings you to town?'

'A bit of legal business.'

'Oh, how boring! If I hear one more thing about Osbourne, I am going to scream. Everyone is up in arms. Doris tells me he is to be sentenced next week. She is hoping for life, but I think he'll probably get three to four years—the number of people who lost money is incredible.'

'Yes, some of them are in financial difficulties, I know,' agreed Carmel. 'Oh, there's Doris.' She was speaking to Trick, both of them very absorbed with one another. Doris had crossed arms, with her handbag suspended from one elbow.

'This is not good news,' Carmel suggested, and then in an instant, she turned her head and looked at Matthew. 'Be very charitable, Matthew.

He will pay you back tenfold. Gerald, make yourself useful. I notice there are some empty glasses.'

'Oh, Carmel,' he began, as Matthew, not being used to Carmel, went to ask her what she meant, but a shake of Hazel's head silenced him.

'Carmel,' began Gerald, 'just guess who Ashley is having an affair with?'

'Robert Patterson,' she said, turning her head with a smile.

'How the hell did you know?' he asked.

'Hazel and I worked it out months ago when we went to his nursery. I see you don't look too broken-hearted.'

'Not at all,' he said in a grand manner. 'Men are a dime a dozen. Besides, Doris tells me he is strapped for cash, so I can't really expect a holiday in Paris, can I?'

'Well, not with him, but you never know.'

Doris and Trick came over to the table but it was a very serious Doris who sat down in the vacant chair beside Carmel and looked directly across at Hazel and Matthew. Trick pulled up a chair and sat down.

'I have something to ask you two. It's a good thing you are here today, Matthew. We can get it all done now.'

Hazel and Matthew looked at one another in total bewilderment. Trick began, as Doris helped herself to a drink, 'You know this Osbourne thing,' he said, addressing himself to Hazel and Matthew. 'Well, on one of the properties they are laying off workers. It seems the only way to survive for the moment. They have done it in a fair way—last to be employed is first to go—but in this particular case it's not so fair. You see, it's a young couple. He's about your age,' he said, looking at Matthew, 'and they have had a really rough time. They have a kid and he has been very sick. I forget the name of what he had but the bills for hospital and so forth—this guy's father died and left him nothing but debts so he is really strapped. Nowhere to go and one month's notice, and he hasn't been there long enough to even get much holiday pay.'

Here Doris interrupted. 'You need a new hand, especially as Bob is now departed and you can financially support this little family. He is as honest as the day is long.'

Hazel looked at Matthew and knew in his heart that Doris had decided everything anyway. 'You'll have to ask Matthew,' he said. 'He is the manager at Killkenny.'

Doris swung all her attention to Matthew and played her trump cards. 'The little boy is the same age as Sebastian, so it will be company as he grows up and,' she went on, looking at her totally empty glass, 'and he drinks at the Railway.'

It was Carmel's earlier sentence that echoed in his ears, 'be charitable, Matthew, he will pay you back tenfold'. Matthew looked at Doris and then Trick and Carmel, to whom he winked. 'He can start the minute he is finished at the Wallaces. Tell him to contact me,' and he looked at Hazel. 'I'm sorry, but your skills are going to be needed again to get the big cottage ready for him.'

'I think we'll manage,' Hazel replied, wondering how.

Gerald summoned the waitress. 'I'm starving,' he said to the group, noticing that Doris seemed very content. She motioned him to refill her glass after ordering.

'I shall drop in and see the Principal of St. Mary's this afternoon' she announced, as Trick was about to leave.

'Not going back to school, are we, Doris?'

'You never know,' she smiled as he left.

'What are you going to see the Principal for?' Gerald asked curiously.

'The school holds a charity foundation of which I am on the committee and we raise money and donate it,' she spoke pointedly, looking at Hazel and Carmel,' to cover school fees for the genuinely needy. This family—and by the way the name is O'Farrell—are in a difficult situation and they are going to take the little boy out of St. Marys and place him in the state system.' Here, everyone knew she was drawing a parallel with Timothy Osbourne. 'It shall not be done and if we have a shortfall of fees for extras, and the like, I think the four of us should pick up that shortfall.' She glanced at Carmel, Matthew and Hazel.

'It's fine with me,' said Hazel. 'And with me,' chorused Carmel and Matthew together.

'Fine,' Doris said. 'Reverend Mother would have been very happy,' and tucked into her steak.

* * * * *

The O'Farrell family settled into a barely completed cottage at the end of the month. Carmel had been right: Daniel O'Farrell was a good and honest worker and Matthew was very pleased with him. It took Sebastian and Peter O'Farrell a few days before they decided they were good friends, and that was due to Red introducing them to one another.

Jan suddenly found she had another young boy for homework each evening and loved it. She had changed: her rough approach had softened noticeably. This, Hazel thought, was the result of her sister Rhonda living close to her and also no Bob any longer. She was losing weight, as Pat was also, due to a sensible diet and the swapping of ideas with Enid O'Farrell also helped. Enid was a tiny woman but with plenty of energy. Her young son now was at last making progress healthwise and the following summer would see him and Sebastian yelling and playing in the swimming pool while Red slept on the side in the shade.

* * * * *

At the beginning of July, Mary came up for four days, bringing with her the long awaited portraits which, when framed, looked 'fabulous', as Hazel exclaimed. They were painted in the same style as Mary's painting of Antonio Banderas, with two pairs of blue eyes staring out and two enigmatic smiles. Hazel was elated with them. Matthew preferred at dinner to sit with his back to them. He said it was like looking into a smart mirror.

'Hazel, it's all so fabulous,' said Mary, getting the grand tour. 'The house is enormous and to think you lived in a mousehole before.' She laughed.

She adored Matthew on sight and the feeling was reciprocated. They spent the first night reminiscing. Mary spoke to Sebastian several times before he warmed to her and she noticed that if he was ever not sure, he always went to sit next to Matthew or simply put his arms around him. She said to Hazel the next day, 'I don't think that Sebastian is ever going to need my professional services,' and smiled. She slipped her hand into his. 'Well, Hazel, you have finally made it and I am so proud of you. Matthew and Sebastian are great. I am sorry for myself, but as you say we are only a couple of hours away and as I have proved that a light aircraft can support me there's no problem.' They walked back into the garden room for a drink before dinner.

Mary did come again and the second time she brought her young charge, who enjoyed playing in the pool with Sebastian and Peter. Life continued at this pace, with everything fitting together. The re-seeding of the five thousand acres had been a real success and they lost only fifty or so trees out of 2000. A new planting was envisaged for the next autumn.

Doris's ballroom curtains had arrived and, unbeknown to all, these were for a huge party to celebrate her sixty-fifth birthday, which was a success, with Doris, as expected, 'belle of the ball'. It was a very proud Freda Carstairs who watched Sebastian play his first little concert in front of all Doris's friends.

August brought the ram sales, which was financially a great success, and this was Pat's triumph. The umbrella he had remade was finally brought out from under lock and key and placed above the podium where the auctioneer sat. 'I feel like an Indian prince,' he joked with Pat, who was as proud as can be.

Life followed an easy pattern now. Sebastian had decided he wanted his own red bedroom, so that removed a slight hurdle to a romantic affair. They saw Carmel often, but, no matter how much Hazel tried, Matthew refused to contemplate a holiday. He only wanted to stay at Killkenny, and as Hazel wasn't moving without him and living with him was a holiday anyway, he agreed and just enjoyed himself.

Every now and again, he remembered what Carmel had seen in her cards about Sebastian many months before, he and Gerald's reply to the relationship between Matthew and Sebastian. Hers was that they were lovers, Gerald's father and son, and his chums. They were all correct, he mused, and ran his hand through Matthew's thick black hair as he turned over and went to sleep.

THE END